A FINE DISGUISE

"If you don't think I am privy to military secrets," Eden said, glaring at her masked captor, "then why am I here, enduring your loathsome presence?"

Sebastian stared into her blue eyes. He couldn't resist reaching out to touch this proud, defiant beauty.

When his gloved hand cupped her chin, Eden slapped it away. "And don't think you can seduce information from me, either. Having recently discovered what love is, I would never settle for your tawdry imitations of supposed affection." She strained against her bonds. "Kindly untie me."

"Do I have your word that you won't attempt escape?"

"Would you give your word if the situation was reversed?"

"Yes. Then I would set about to plan my escape."

"Why should I lie when we both know I would escape the first chance I have?"

"Then why ask if I will untie you?"

When his gloved hand skimmed her cheekbone and his lips touched hers, she nearly fainted in shock. It couldn't be, she tried to tell herself . . . it's a coincidence, that's all . . .

It's no coincidence, came the quiet voice of reason. The man she loved and her disguised captor were one and the same!

BOOK YOUR PLACE ON OUR WEBSITE AND MAKE THE READING CONNECTION!

We've created a customized website just for our very special readers, where you can get the inside scoop on everything that's going on with Zebra, Pinnacle and Kensington books.

When you come online, you'll have the exciting opportunity to:

- View covers of upcoming books
- Read sample chapters
- Learn about our future publishing schedule (listed by publication month *and author*)
- Find out when your favorite authors will be visiting a city near you
- Search for and order backlist books from our online catalog
- Check out author bios and background information
- Send e-mail to your favorite authors
- Meet the Kensington staff online
- Join us in weekly chats with authors, readers and other guests
- Get writing guidelines
- AND MUCH MORE!

**Visit our website at
http://www.zebrabooks.com**

MINE
FOREVER

Carol Finch

Zebra Books
Kensington Publishing Corp
http://www.zebrabooks.com

This book is dedicated to my husband Ed
and our children—Kurt, Jill, Christie, Jon and Jeff—
with much love. And to our granddaughter, Brooklynn.

ZEBRA BOOKS are published by

Kensington Publishing Corp.
850 Third Avenue
New York, NY 10022

Zebra and the Z logo Reg. U.S. Pat. & TM Off.

First Printing: February, 1999
10 9 8 7 6 5 4 3 2 1

Printed in the United States of America

One

Virginia, 1781

In Eden Pembrook's opinion, the good Lord made an oversight when He put so few hours in a day. There simply wasn't enough time for a woman to do all the things that needed to be done.

"Rodney, please deliver this basket of food and supplies to the Traherns," Eden instructed the servant. "Barnaby is still recovering from his battle wounds, and the family is struggling to make ends meet."

"Yes, Miss Eden." His arms overloaded, Rodney Emerson scuttled out the front door of the spacious plantation.

"Eden, can we leave now?" Elizabeth Pembrook grumbled from the corner of the foyer, where she was ensconced in a Windsor chair.

"Just give me a few more minutes," Eden said as she wheeled toward the troop of servants who awaited her instructions.

Elizabeth's gaze glittered with mounting irritation. "Your 'few minutes' are likely to span an hour," she muttered.

Ignoring her younger sister, Eden glanced at the housekeeper. "Maggie, I haven't had time to visit our patients this morning and—"

"Don't worry, Miss Eden." Maggie's smile lit up her face. "I'll tend them for you."

"Make certain you give special attention to James,"

Eden said. "He seemed a mite sad last night, even after I spent an hour trying to cheer him up."

Eden scooped up the basket of eggs and pastries that arrived from the kitchen. "Please deliver this to Sam and Betsy Hillman. They lost their son in battle—"

"Eden, can we go now?" Elizabeth interrupted.

"In a minute," Eden said. "Now then, the grooms need to deliver these supplies—"

The sound of thundering hooves drew Eden's attention. She pivoted to see a shabbily-dressed rebel soldier galloping across the front lawn. Hurriedly, Eden doled out the baskets of food. "Take these to the Ramseys, Scotts, and Quinns."

When Eden scurried down the steps to greet the new arrival, Elizabeth slumped deeper in the chair. She was beginning to think she would never reach Stevens Tavern to enjoy the activities at the semi-annual country fair. The highlight of the social season was already in progress, and Elizabeth was anxious to mix and mingle. There was a certain someone waiting to become her escort—someone who might turn his attention elsewhere if she didn't show up soon. Elizabeth was sure to die of a broken heart if he did!

"Miss Bet, I have heard enough of your whining and nagging," Maggie scolded. "Your sister has scores of last-minute details to tend, and here you sit like a pampered princess, scowling at delays. I swear, Eden has spoiled you rotten. You should be volunteering to help her instead of fussing every other minute."

Elizabeth glared resentfully at the black maid. Maggie always defended "Saint" Eden. The other servants were no better, Elizabeth mused bitterly. They bowed and scraped over Eden, while Elizabeth was shuffled out of the way, given the worst chores—and ignored! Living in the shadow of everybody's guardian angel was a difficult cross to bear.

Elizabeth longed for the day when she could spread her wings and take control of her own life. This blasted war had spoiled just about everything!

Eden appeared in the doorway, smiling impishly at Elizabeth's puckered expression. "Well, Bet, do you intend to sit here all day? Have you decided not to attend the fair?"

With a huff and a glower, Elizabeth vaulted to her feet, shook the wrinkles from her gown, and flounced outside.

Eden pivoted toward Maggie who lingered at the head of the staircase. "Bet is young and impatient for life," Eden said in her sister's defense. "Don't fault her for what comes naturally."

Maggie bristled at that. "You have coddled that girl and you know it. Bet is impatient and ungrateful. If she wasn't so self-absorbed, she could be of tremendous help around here."

Eden grinned at Maggie's comments. Because Eden insisted on teaching all Pembrook servants and staff to read and write, Maggie expressed herself well—and frequently. Eden believed it was important for slaves and servants to be educated.

She had never forgotten that tragic day seventeen years ago when disaster struck. She had sent a note home, begging for assistance, but the servants couldn't decipher the message. It had been two hellish hours before the rescue party arrived.

Two hours too late . . .

Nowadays, messages—like the one she had just received from Daniel Johnston, the rebel soldier—arrived to update her on the war's progress. Eden refused to let the network of communication break down because servants couldn't read. Furthermore, books were a source of knowledge, inspiration, and pleasure that no one should be denied, Eden reminded herself. She was a scholar who advocated the necessity of books and acquisition of knowledge.

"I have tried to be both sister and parent to Elizabeth,"

Eden murmured, casting her musings aside. "It seems I have been ineffective."

Maggie flashed Eden a meaningful glance. "You have done more for Miss Bet than your mama did for you and we both know it."

Eden winced at the unpleasant memories that flashed through her mind.

"I'm sorry, Miss Eden, I should not have said that. Now you best be on your way before your sister has a conniption. Patience, as we both know, is not one of Bet's virtues."

"Eden! Hurry up! I'm wilting out here in the sun!" Elizabeth called.

Eden took one last look around the foyer to ensure all her tasks were complete. Satisfied, she breezed outside to join her disgruntled sister in the carriage.

"Just because you have decided to become a spinster doesn't mean I am not actively seeking a husband," Elizabeth grumbled. "You know perfectly well that the country fair is my opportunity to remind Peter Dalton that I am still alive, since you rarely let me escape from this prison of a plantation."

Eden cast Bet a withering glance. "You do have a flair for the melodramatic, don't you? And you know perfectly well that your striking beauty draws dozens of admirers, Peter included. It's your sour disposition that might repel Peter."

"My disposition will improve considerably when we arrive at that damned fair before it closes down for the night!"

Eden cocked a brow as Elizabeth flounced into a more comfortable position on the tufted seat. Bet's face turned beet red when she realized what she had said. When Eden dissolved into laughter, Elizabeth's anger melted instantly.

"Blast it, Eden, how do you do that?"

"Do what?"

"How do you smile and make the world seem a rosier place?" Elizabeth scrutinized her sister with a newfound sense of understanding. "That's why men find you so intriguing, isn't it?"

"What are you babbling about? Men don't find me fascinating. Haven't I had several fiancés who have come and gone the past few years?"

While Jacob Courtney drove the carriage toward Stevens Tavern, Elizabeth reclined against the seat. Suddenly, she was seeing Eden in an entirely different light. "Now that I think on it, I find it odd that all your fiancés begged off—or so you claim. You persuaded them to retract those proposals, didn't you?"

Eden stared across the rolling hills, wondering how long the serenity of Virginia would last. According to the news she had received from Daniel Johnston, this peaceful pathway, flanked by thickets of bayberry, catbrier, and holly might soon be trampled by British soldiers. The forests of pines, black cedars, and cypress trees might be used as firewood. The sandy knolls might soon be stained with the blood of battle.

"It was the other way around, wasn't it?" Bet persisted. "None of those men really suited you, or perhaps—"

Bet gasped when another revelation struck her like a bolt from the blue. "Or perhaps the truth is that you discarded your chance at happiness because of *me!*"

Eden grimaced at the horrified look on Bet's face. "Maggie is right. You have become too self-absorbed." She reached over to pat Bet's hand. "Of course, now that you have had time to reconsider the comment, you realize it was an absurd thing to say, don't you?"

Elizabeth pinned her sister with a probing stare. "You *have* sacrificed your happiness for me, because Papa hasn't been here to care for me, haven't you, Eden?"

Before Eden could deny it, Elizabeth hurried on. "Good gracious, you *are* a self-sacrificing saint and martyr! Well,

I will have no more of it, do you hear me, Eden? I am eighteen years old and I can take care of myself. You needn't reject another marriage proposal because you feel obligated to me. And I will also be assuming more of the duties you have heaped on yourself."

"I would appreciate that," Eden said.

"And you can devote more time to finding a husband who suits you."

"I don't need a husband. At my age, I am too set in my ways to be married."

"Horsefeathers! Twenty-four isn't so old."

"Thank goodness your language is improving," Eden teased.

"Don't try to sidetrack me, Edeline Renee Pembrook. I have heard you curse several times when you thought no one was listening. Even saints lose their tempers occasionally."

"Now, for example? When dealing with precocious sisters?" Before Bet launched herself into another eye-opening revelation, Eden gestured southward. "Ah, here we are, Bet. Enjoy the festivities."

Elizabeth was poised on the edge of her seat, intent on pursuing a topic Eden didn't want to discuss. Smiling, Eden hopped down to greet the friends and neighbors who had congregated around the carriage.

"May I help you down, Miss Bet?" the coachman asked.

Elizabeth tilted a proud chin. "That won't be necessary, Jacob. I plan to follow my sister-the-saint's example and *float* down from my perch. I also intend to be less of a burden henceforth and forevermore."

Jacob Courtney nodded approvingly. "And may I say I am impressed by how quickly you have grown up, Miss Bet."

Having aged years during the jaunt to the fair, Elizabeth hurried off to find Peter Dalton, hoping a flock of eligible females weren't beating her time.

***

Sebastian Saber sat atop his muscular black stallion, surveying the boisterous activities near Stevens Tavern. The atmosphere surrounding the country fair was far removed from the death and destruction of battlefields in the northern and southern colonies. Canvas tents were filled with hand-crafted trinkets and succulent pastries, not soldiers preparing for attack.

Farmers congregated to barter and trade livestock. Children's laughter erupted near the puppet show stage and the greased pig contests. Arenas for cudgeling bouts were being roped off, and musicians were tuning up for fiddling contests. Jugglers in colorful costumes enthralled spectators and acrobats tumbled around the grassy courtyard. Bowls of punch—spiced with brandy, cinnamon, and nutmeg—were set on tables teeming with heaping trays of food.

Here a man could forget his weariness and the atrocity of war that roiled around him. After long, grueling hours in the saddle, Sebastian was anxious for diversion.

"Enjoying yourself, Sebastian?" Micah Bancroft strode over to uplift a glass of punch. "You have struck such an impressive pose on that prized steed of yours that a number of eligible ladies are requesting introduction to my dashing cousin." He took another sip of his punch, then frowned. "Now, how was it you said we were related?"

"I'm your uncle's second wife's nephew," Sebastian replied. "I'm your cousin-in-law."

"A cousin is a cousin." Micah waved his bejeweled hand, dismissing the technicality. "Now climb down so I can introduce you to all the females who are eager to meet you."

Sebastian glanced at Micah, who was three years his junior. Micah was the fashion plate of Virginia gentry in his navy-blue waistcoat, jacket, and matching breeches. His periwig was slightly askew, after bumping shoulders with the congested crowd and tipping his glass to drink more than his share of spiked punch.

Sebastian gracefully dismounted and tethered his horse. "My only interest in the fair is entering my stallion in the races." At least that was what he wanted the country gentry to think.

Micah chuckled, sipped more punch, then nodded a greeting to Daphne Cunningham, the voluptuous redhead who was staring at Sebastian with blatant interest. "Too bad you aren't in the market for a wife. Considering all the interest you are attracting, you could take your pick. Except for one charming, unattainable beauty, of course."

"Who? The redhead?" Sebastian cast a disinterested glance in the woman's general direction.

"No, I suspect you will know who she is when you see her."

Sebastian smirked at the ridiculous comment. He had been cured of romantic notions eleven years ago, when a blond temptress taught him that wealth and titles were more important to women than loyalty and affection. It wasn't a lesson he had allowed himself to forget.

Sebastian's sweeping gaze landed on a female in bright yellow velvet. She stood out like sunlight spearing through gray clouds. Distracted, he sipped his drink and apprised the woman with the eye-catching smile. Sebastian didn't consider the woman a ravishing beauty, because she didn't possess porcelain skin and the tall, classical physique the British highly praised. She was too petite, her features too elflike, her skin the color of honey.

Stunning and striking better described this woman, Sebastian decided. She radiated an intense spirit, her flaming chestnut hair glowing like a halo around her face.

"Sebastian?" Micah nudged Sebastian, then grinned smugly when he realized who had captured the man's attention. "Told you that you would know her when you saw her."

Sebastian dragged his attention to Micah, but his gaze darted sideways when he heard the woman's soft, bubbling laughter.

Micah burst into a snicker. "So much for merely racing horses, eh, Cousin?"

"Who is she?" Sebastian questioned. Their eyes met momentarily, then the woman turned her disarming smile on the soldier who approached her.

"That is our beloved angel-turned-spinster." Micah uplifted his glass in respectful salute. "In five years she has turned down seven fiancés. I am proud to say I was one of them."

"Seven?" Sebastian did a double take. "You speak highly of a woman who discarded you?"

"Discarded me? Of course not," Micah contradicted. "I simply realized that it wouldn't be to our mutual benefit to marry. Furthermore, only a resentful fool would speak unkindly of Saint Eden. Her generosity and benevolence are widely known in these parts."

Saint Eden? In Sebastian's opinion, the words *saint* and *woman* were contradictions in terms. "What's wrong with the chit?" he asked bluntly.

"Wrong? Why nothing, nothing atall," Micah insisted.

"Fickle, flighty, devious, temperamental?"

"Certainly not!"

"Then she must be a tease who makes promises never delivered," Sebastian concluded cynically.

Micah's bloodshot eyes narrowed and he took offense on Eden's behalf. "Never!"

"Then why has she discarded seven fiancés in five years?"

"Because Edeline Pembrook, daughter of General Leland Pembrook of the Virginia Militia—"

Sebastian frowned at the all-too familiar name. Part of his clandestine assignment was to familiarize himself with the area around Pembrook Plantation—for reasons not yet disclosed by the British command.

"Edeline simply outgrows her need for her suitors once she acquires all the knowledge they possess," Micah explained. "A woman of superior intelligence intimidates most men. A submissive wife is more dependent and uncomplicated. When those facts are brought to a man's attention, he has the good sense to retract his proposal."

Sebastian's silver-gray gaze narrowed as he watched Micah drain his glass—again. "*Outgrows* men? Women don't outgrow men," he said with absolute certainty.

Micah threw back his bewigged head and laughed heartily. "Perhaps you would like to wager on that, Cuz. I'm curious to see how you fare against a woman whose astute intelligence and remarkable capabilities put her in a class by herself."

Propping himself against the tavern wall, Sebastian nursed his punch and reassessed Edeline Pembrook. "Then, by all means, tell me about this legendary paragon."

Ignoring Sebastian's sarcasm, Micah elaborated. "Eden was left to manage the family plantation when her father took command of the militia. Leland obviously passed his keen wit and knack for disciplined organization to his older daughter, because the tobacco plantation is prosperous and self-sufficient. Eden is exceptionally well read and hungry for knowledge. She has patterned herself after Eliza Pinckney who tried agricultural experimentation with indigo."

Sebastian was aware of Eliza Pinckney's experiments with indigo, ginger, alfalfa, cotton, and Guinea corn. The industrious young woman from Charles Town had made a fortune selling indigo for dye to England.

"Eden has planted various crops," Micah went on to say. "Her revolutionary ideas have begun to catch on, because she's a successful businesswoman. Pembrook fields boast corn and maize, and the gardens teem with vegetables and flowers. Her plantation has become a showcase for new ideas."

Sebastian snorted at the glowing accolades heaped on Spinster Pembrook.

"Don't scoff, or I shall turn her loose on you," Micah threatened. "Even a cynic like you would succumb to her charms, I'll wager."

"I think," Sebastian said with ill-disguised skepticism, "that you are excessively fond of exaggeration."

"You're game then?" Micah's white teeth gleamed. "Allow me to introduce you, Cousin."

Sebastian found himself towed through the crowd, but he stood firm in his conviction that Saint Eden was an illusion of fanciful men and fools. He had yet to meet a woman worthy of the high praise Micah showered on Eden Pembrook and he seriously doubted that an introduction to this particular woman was going to change his low opinion of the fairer sex.

"Eden Pembrook, there is someone I want you to meet."

Eden pivoted at the sound of Micah's voice. She appraised his powerfully built companion, who appeared to be in his early thirties. The man, dressed in expensive, tailored black velvet, looked very distinguished. Yet, Eden sensed an earthy quality and dynamic presence that defied his civilized veneer.

This, Eden decided, was the man Daphne Cunningham had been raving about for the past hour. Daphne claimed to have experienced love at first sight. Now Eden knew why Daphne was so enthralled. If outward appearance was a woman's top priority in judging a man, then she could easily be intrigued by those silver-gray eyes, surrounded by long, thick lashes, and wavy hair glistening like black flames.

As for Eden, she had five years' maturity on her friend—and a good deal more sense than to gush and fawn over a man. Even so, the man still drew the attention of an academic mind, which Eden prided herself on possessing.

Eden smiled cordially at Sebastian. "I'm glad you have joined in the festivities, sir. A friend of Micah's is a friend of mine."

"Cousin, actually," Micah put in.

Sebastian felt the instantaneous warmth of Eden's smile. He stared into eyes as clear and blue as morning sunrise, marveling at the pull of awareness she aroused in him. But he would be damned if he knuckled under to that engaging smile, especially after Micah challenged him to this ridiculous wager.

What did Micah expect him to do? Drop onto bended knee and propose marriage at first meeting? Not bloody damn likely. Sebastian, in his misguided youth, had made a similar mistake. He sure as hell wasn't going to play the fool again!

Once betrayed, forever cured, that was Sebastian's motto.

"Eden, this is Sebastian Saber."

Sebastian said nothing when Eden grasped his hand and stared him squarely in the eye, as a man would do. Highly unusual behavior for a woman!

"Miss Pembrook," he said then, inclining his head ever so slightly.

Eden met Sebastian's unblinking stare head-on, then dropped her hand away. "You have the most intriguing eyes I have ever seen. I can understand why the young ladies have been swooning over you." She graced him with an impish grin. "Come to break a few hearts, have you? One of my friends is anxious to meet you. May I introduce you to her?"

Sebastian was stunned by Eden's question. He couldn't believe she was pointing him in another woman's direction. It left him feeling that he didn't measure up to her high standards. Was this some kind of reverse strategy?

"Sebastian is racing his stallion this afternoon." Micah grinned as he purposely baited his trap. "He's Arabian."

"Which is Arabian? You or your horse?" she teased.

"The horse," Sebastian murmured, lifting her hand to brush his lips over her fingertips.

Eden arched her brow, as if amused by his feeble attempt to charm her. Sebastian felt the absurd urge to exert more effort to win her over. Damn, this encounter wasn't going as he anticipated.

Her smile intact, Eden withdrew her hand once more. "I am interested in integrating Arabian blood into my livestock," she said. "I am impressed with the strength and endurance of the breed. Is your stallion available for breeding purposes? Could I see him?"

Sebastian had never been dismissed in favor of introduction to a horse. He was shocked by the disappointment he felt.

"Perhaps you could explain your practices of grooming and caring for horses," she suggested as she strode toward the stallion tethered in the distance.

"And in return, you can explain how you managed to cast aside seven fiancés in the amount of time it takes to break a horse to ride." Sebastian wondered why he'd blurted that out. It must have been smarting male pride, he decided.

Eden stopped short. "I assume Micah was gossiping. Apparently he told you that I didn't meet his expectations and that he grew tired of me, as did all the others."

"Did they?" Sebastian seriously doubted it. This was not an ordinary woman.

"They did, all seven of them," she confirmed.

Sebastian smiled. "If you say so."

"And don't think for a moment that you have to feel an obligation because Micah introduced us. I know that I am not the kind of woman who invites a man's prolonged attention."

Sebastian seriously doubted that.

"I'm sure you realize that pretending even a polite interest in me is a waste of your valuable time."

His lips twitched, amused by her leading comments. "How perceptive I am."

Eden studied him studiously. "Extremely perceptive. It's in your eyes. They speak of intelligence and insight."

Sebastian was beginning to understand why seven beaux, who had supposedly ditched Eden for more interesting pursuits, still held her in high esteem. She had the uncanny knack of planting thoughts in a man's mind, then nurturing them until he believed he had conceived the notion himself.

Micah Bancroft and his predecessors had been jilted, Sebastian was sure of it. Yet, all Eden's fiancés came away thinking they had broken the engagements—for the best interest of both parties, of course. Eden graciously accepted the blame—and none of the credit—for rejecting proposals. Why?

"Now then, tell me about this magnificent stallion," Eden requested. "The Arabian has been well stabled. That, in turn, tells me about you. You take pride in this animal. Have you used supplementary rations to keep him in top physical condition?"

Before Sebastian realized it, he was explaining, in precise detail, the ratio of grain formula he'd designed. It dawned on him that Eden used flattery to distract a man by filling him with self-importance, then posed casual-sounding questions that led the conversation in the direction she wanted it to go. This woman was definitely subtle, astute, and shrewd, he noted. She could draw a man in with her leading questions before he realized what had happened.

Eden circled the spirited steed, cooing at him, then

pausing to run her hand across the width of his shoulders. "I knew there had to be a special combination of nutrients," she said thoughtfully. "This stallion couldn't cover mares and run races without proper rations."

"Continuation of exercise is precisely the point," Sebastian maintained. "Most studs merely graze between servicing mares, or stand idly in stalls."

He couldn't believe he was having this conversation with a woman. Yet, here he was, letting this unusual female pick his brain . . .

Sebastian jerked up his head abruptly, startling the stallion. The Arabian pranced sideways, but Eden didn't back away. She called softly, soothing the steed with the gentle stroke of her hand.

Sebastian wondered how it would feel to have those gentle caresses gliding over his flesh—and then cursed his male body's reaction. Damn it, the woman had him fantasizing. She wasn't paying the slightest attention to him. He should be insulted, not aroused.

"This truly is a remarkable animal," Eden was saying when Sebastian got around to listening. "I would love to have him cover my mares."

When she smiled at Sebastian, he stood there like a tongue-tied idiot, wondering when, and how, he had lost control of this encounter. Nothing was going as expected in the stupid wager he had made with Micah. He hadn't charmed or intrigued Eden in the least. His horse had her undivided attention!

"Perhaps I should use your theory of exercise with my bulls," she said pensively. "With more exercise and proper ration, I could prolong bull productivity with cow herds."

Sebastian found himself rattling off the measurements of corn, barley, and sorghum content to maintain livestock—and Eden soaked up his advice like a sponge.

He cast Eden a discreet glance, once again reminded that she had skillful techniques of gathering information.

Yet, he could think of no reason why he shouldn't share his expertise with her.

Eden pivoted to smile at him. "You obviously raise cattle as well as horses," she presumed. "You are exceptionally well informed. I believe it is vital that we all learn to be self-reliant if we are to be successful. We have been too dependent on England for years, and the Crown would like to keep us under thumb. When we win this war, we must remain independent-minded and innovative.

"Now that we have outgrown the Crown, and its long-distance decrees, we will become a nation to be reckoned with, don't you agree?"

Sebastian remained perfectly still, refusing to react to the leading question. That was one topic he could not—and would not—discuss with anyone. He drew the line at how much information this cunning female could pick from his brain.

"I'm in need of a glass of punch. Will you join me?" he asked.

Eden stared at him for a moment, seeing that certain something that had disturbed her at first meeting. There was much more to this handsome rake than met the eye. She couldn't pinpoint what it was about Sebastian that affected her so strongly, but she vowed to remain immune, indifferent. She had promised herself long ago that she would avoid serious involvement with men. She knew what kind of heartache and turmoil could spill over into other lives because of it. She refused to let history repeat itself, and vowed to devote her time and energy to improving the plantation, helping instead the less fortunate, and providing for her sister until she married.

And there would not be a contracted marriage for Elizabeth, she reminded herself. If Bet wished to wed, then it would be by her own choice. Too many women were forced into loveless marriages. And too many women had forsaken their own families to turn to other men when they couldn't find satisfaction in the marriage bed. And that's when disaster struck—

Eden involuntarily stepped back a pace when the tormenting thought sneaked through her protective defenses.

Sebastian stared at her astutely. "Is something wrong?"

Shadows clouded her enchanting face and dimmed the sparkle in her eyes. And then Eden smiled brightly, masking the troubled thought. Sebastian had the unshakable feeling this lovely paragon harbored forbidden secrets. There was a hint of misery behind her sunny smile. What thought tormented her, draining the color from her face? he wondered.

"I believe I'm ready for that drink now," she said.

Mulling over their unusual conversation, Sebastian escorted Eden to the refreshment tables. This complex woman puzzled him, challenged him, intrigued him. She was an enigma, with secrets in her eyes.

Ah, secrets, thought Sebastian. He was well versed on the subject of secrets himself.

TWO

Sebastian stood apart from the crowd, glancing back and forth between the cockfights to the left of him and the cudgeling bout to the right. Customary wrestling maneuvers had been discarded in favor of biting, kicking and eye-gouging.

His gaze circled the area, noting the continuous attention Eden received. The woman was starting to irritate him—greatly. Although she had treated him courteously and respectfully, he couldn't make himself be satisfied with that. None of the men presently vying for her attention seemed able to scale that invisible wall that kept her unattainable. Although she greeted everyone with a cheery smile and gracious charm, Sebastian wasn't content to be one of the enamored masses.

It was unsettling to realize that the woman who had captured his interest, on an elemental and intellectual level, had been content—or he should say *eager*—to foist him off on other females the first chance she got.

First, Eden had introduced him to Daphne Cunningham who dropped about twenty curtsies and fawned incessantly. Then Eden appeared every half hour, accompanied by another female offering. Sebastian had met enough giggling chatterboxes to last him a lifetime.

As Micah Bancroft predicted, Sebastian felt himself

magnetically drawn to the woman who intrigued him most by showing no particular interest in him.

"Now what do you think of the Rebels' Angel?" Micah slurred as he propped himself against the wall beside Sebastian.

Sebastian grimaced. "I think you're drunk. You would singe the angel's wings if you breathed on her."

Micah grinned, undaunted. "I'm celebrating."

"Celebrating what, for God's sake?"

"The fact that you've fallen beneath Eden's charms. Knew you would, Cuz. I've been watching you watch her."

The muster call of the bugle, signaling the first horse race of the afternoon, saved Sebastian from Micah's taunts. In hurried strides, Sebastian headed toward his horse, mounted, then glanced sideways to see Eden uprighting Micah who was stumbling all over himself.

The man was a lush, thought Sebastian, but he would sober up soon enough. The British were bringing battle to the gentry's doorstep. Soon, Virginians would experience the turmoil other colonies had endured these past years.

With an experienced hand, Sebastian reined the Arabian into position. The pint-size jockey, who was mounted on Micah's Turkish mare, surged toward Sebastian, shooting Sebastian an arrogant grin. Sebastian ignored him. The lad would soon learn his lesson in humility. The Turk and his cocky jockey were going to eat dust.

A pistol blast sent the line of eight horses lunging onto the stretch of road that had been marked off for racing. Eden felt excitement spurting through her as the powerful steeds thundered away from the starting line. Unfortunately, it didn't turn out to be much of a contest. The black Arabian stallion made the other horses look as if they were standing still.

Eden's admiring gaze focused on the stallion that gleamed blue-black in the sunlight. Not only could the Arabian run like nothing she'd ever seen, but Sebastian's equestrian skills were exceptional. She envied a man's opportunity to race, while a woman was left standing aside to watch.

If the Arabian sired colts in the Pembrook herd, she promised to enjoy her own private races in an obscure meadow. She would delight in straddling a horse that could run like that midnight-colored stallion.

A cheer went up around Eden when the Arabian crossed the finish line two lengths ahead of Bancroft's Turkish mare. Within seconds, a group of men swarmed around Sebastian, offering to purchase the amazing horse, or—at the very least—pay whatever stud fee Sebastian named.

"I'm sorry, gentlemen," Sebastian drawled as he dismounted. "I've already accepted an offer for the Arabian's services."

"I'll double the offer," someone on the outer edge of the circle spoke up.

"I'll triple it" came another generous offer.

"I gave my word," Sebastian declared. "Miss Pembrook and I made an agreement hours before the race began."

Dozens of bewigged heads turned toward Eden in synchronized rhythm. Smiling, Eden nodded confirmation.

Sebastian ambled toward her when the disappointed crowd strode off to watch the second heat of races. "There's one stipulation I forgot to mention," he said, flashing her a suggestive smile.

"And what might that be?" Eden asked.

Sebastian thought this perceptive female knew exactly

what he implied, but he stated the stipulation in plain English for her. "I come with the horse."

Her sanguine smile remained intact; the innuendo had failed to ruffle her feathers.

"I would never have thought otherwise," she said smoothly. "I wouldn't allow this magnificent animal out of my sight, either. But I assure you that the stallion will receive the best of care."

When Eden tried to artfully dodge the meaning of his comment, Sebastian became more persistent, determined to rattle her impeccable self-control. "I prefer to discuss my accommodations, not the horse's."

"You're welcome to stay at our plantation, or to come and go as you please," she said generously.

Sebastian gnashed his teeth. Was there no way to fluster this female? In his opinion, Eden was too generous, too self-contained, too damned perfect. His inability to draw any kind of reaction—other than that cheery smile—was maddening. A devilish urge to provoke any emotion besides polite indifference rose within him.

Sebastian took a step closer, erasing the respectable distance she kept between herself and all men. "I'm sure the arrangements for the Arabian will be more than adequate. It's the fee I wish to discuss."

"You are a reasonable man," she said very deliberately, taking a retreating step.

One black brow lifted in amusement. "Am I?"

"Of course you are. Otherwise, I wouldn't be negotiating with you." Eden graced him with the kind of smile Sebastian was beginning to detest. "You declined several generous offers after the race. You aren't a man who goes back on his word, you said so yourself. You're fair-minded and respectable." Her lips pursed, then she added, "I can see that clearly in your eyes."

Now she was trying to tease him into living up to the

expectations she'd established for him. Maybe the rest of her male admirers were too dense to recognize mental subterfuge when they encountered it, but Sebastian sure as hell wasn't. Eden was not going to outsmart him, damn it!

"Do you always look for the good in all mankind, Saint Eden?" he asked flippantly.

"Why would I want to seek the worst?"

"Because, sometimes, the worst is all you can find."

"In you? Nonsense. You're an honorable gentleman."

"So you keep telling me, and of course I'm supposed to believe it," he flung back.

"Of course you should believe it," she insisted.

When she smiled up at him—for the hundredth time—Sebastian swore under his breath. By God, he was going to get a reaction from this female if it was the last thing he did!

"Think again, Eden." He leaned down, his face a scant few inches from hers. When she tried to retreat into her own space, Sebastian pinned her between him and the stallion. "The fee I demand for the Arabian's services is you."

Eden didn't bat an eyelash. She smiled that infuriatingly sweet smile—again.

"I'm hardly worth the price. You would be sadly disappointed."

"I'd like to be the judge of that."

Eden laughed lightly. "You are teasing me again. You delight in being mischievous."

"Do I?"

"Of course you do," she said without hesitation.

When he leaned closer, Eden's upper body arched back to ensure they didn't actually touch. That aggravated Sebastian beyond belief. The way she avoided him, you'd think he was poison.

"You are gravely mistaken, sweetheart," he drawled. "I want you in exchange for the use of my stallion. And another thing, I think you're hiding something. I can see that in *your* eyes."

When she simply stood there staring at him with that annoying, self-controlled expression, Sebastian cursed in exasperation, then turned on his heels and strode off.

The voice of conscience should have been snarling at him, because he had been purposely—and persistently—rude. But damn it, he was losing Micah's ridiculous challenge—and miserably! He appeared to have no effect whatsoever on this woman. He couldn't even ignite her indignation.

Seething in frustration, Eden glared at Sebastian's departing back. "Obnoxious cur," she hissed under her breath. "Insufferable lout!"

It had taken every smidgen of control to refrain from doubling her fist and socking him in the jaw after he propositioned her. How dare he insist that she was the price demanded in exchange for the Arabian's stud fee!

Eden stamped back and forth across the lawn, spewing muffled curses. That devilish rascal seemed intent on annoying her, and she had done absolutely nothing to invite his hostility.

His rude badgering had spoiled her mood—and her evening. While her friends and neighbors were whirling in rhythm with the music, Eden was wearing a path on the grass, simmering in irritation. She would never forgive that man for straining her well-disciplined control. She had spent her life mastering her emotions. And now that rapscallion had come along.

Wheeling around, Eden went in search of her groom, Jacob Courtney. She was not going to risk another unnerving encounter with that man. There was no telling how long she could keep her temper from rising like a high tide.

Torchlights blazed down on the circle of coachmen who had gathered to play cards while their employers danced the night away. Eden lingered in the shadows, listening to the men's carefree laughter. The light slanted across Jacob's beaming smile as he raked in his winnings.

Eden's shoulders slumped. She didn't have the heart to drag her groom away when he was enjoying himself so.

Lurching around, she strode off to locate her sister. Elizabeth was dancing with Peter Dalton, gazing up at the young man with stars in her eyes. Eden couldn't bring herself to spoil Elizabeth's grand mood.

Determinedly, she pasted on a smile and approached her sister. "I'm going to check on our patients," Eden said. "Jacob will be waiting to drive you home."

Elizabeth frowned. "How do *you* intend to get home?"

"I've found another mode of transportation," she said brightly. "Enjoy yourself, Bet."

"I am, Eden. Oh, I am!"

Well, at least one member of the family was happy, Eden thought as she threaded through the crowd. She scurried through the deepening shadows to reach the footpath leading to Pembrook Plantation. A brisk walk would give her time to get her temper in hand.

Taking the shortcut home, Eden mentally listed the tasks that lay ahead of her the following day. With the threat of war at hand, she needed to stockpile food and find a safe place to hide the livestock, in case marauding British patrols swarmed the plantation . . .

Muted voices and nickering horses suddenly caught Eden's attention. She slowed her pace and pricked her ears to the threat of danger. Moving silently between the

black cedars and cypress trees, she noticed a cluster of
men in the distance. Were British spies relaying information? she wondered. Or was this a pack of thieves preparing to pounce on unsuspecting fair-goers?

Eden had heard that robberies were on the increase
in the area. Sweet mercy, if she wasn't careful, she might
be accosted by highwaymen!

She backed away, deciding to cut across the meadow
to the main road. The route would be longer, but it might
be safer. And confound it, if it wasn't for that pesky Sebastian Saber, she wouldn't be out here alone. If she ran
into danger, it would be his fault.

Would it truly? she asked herself. The man hadn't ordered her to venture off alone at night, had he? To blame
him would suggest that he exerted some sort of control
over her actions—which he most certainly did not! If
Eden met with calamity it was her own foolish fault. She
was not going to give Sebastian Saber credit for it!

Twenty minutes later, the thunder of approaching
hooves overrode the sounds of cicadas and frogs. Eden
glanced over her shoulder to see the silhouette of man
and horse racing toward her. She sent a prayer winging
heavenward, asking for divine assistance. *Dear God, if I'm
about to be accosted by a thief, please give me the strength not
to show fear.*

"I should have known" came a mocking voice from
the darkness. "The angel goeth where mortal man fears
to tread. You must consider yourself indestructible."

Eden inhaled a fortifying breath and kept walking. She
was not, repeat *not*, going to allow Sebastian Saber to in-
furiate her again. She could handle this rascal as easily
as she dealt with other wool-brained men. She would simply have to use her wits to outsmart him.

"You have decided to leave the festivities early, too, I

see." She tossed him a smile as he reined the stallion beside her.

He frowned. The man seemed to grow even more irascible when she tried to be nice to him. Maybe she would simply kill him with kindness and be done with him.

"I came looking for you, but you weren't to be found." Sebastian dismounted and fell into step beside her. "Where the hell is your groom, woman?"

"Jacob was involved in a card game, and he's waiting to drive my sister home," she explained, though she didn't consider it any of his business.

"And so here you are, alone at night, with only your saintly reputation to protect you," he scolded. "For a supposedly intelligent woman, you aren't showing much sense."

Her fist coiled. The man didn't know how close he was to being clobbered. Resolutely, Eden kept walking.

"I want to talk to you," he demanded when she set a swifter pace.

"Fine, come by the plantation at a decent hour in the morning."

"I don't keep decent hours."

Eden gritted her teeth, but didn't break stride. "Very well, then, what do you want to discuss with me?"

"Our arrangement."

Eden vowed to hold her temper. "I assured you that I would provide the best possible care for the Arabian. You can instruct the stable boys yourself and see to the supplemental rations."

"Your generosity is overwhelming, but that is not what I'm referring to and you know it."

"I don't have the faintest idea what you mean."

Totally exasperated, Sebastian grabbed her arm and swung her around to face him. When she smiled that unflappable smile, Sebastian growled, "I've had enough of your polite indifference, woman."

"That is all you will ever receive from me," she flung back, then tried to loose herself from his grasp.

Sebastian stepped forward to detain her—and accidentally trounced on the trailing hem of her skirt. When he collided with Eden, he snaked out an arm to steady them both, but Eden reared back.

Thrown off balance, Sebastian tripped, his legs entangled in Eden's skirts. He yelped when he toppled like a felled tree, but he had the presence of mind to brace himself before the ground flew up and hit him.

Sebastian landed atop Eden, causing the air to gush from her lungs. He hadn't intended to sprawl on her, but now that he was here, he found himself in no hurry to get up.

He had inadvertently accomplished his purpose of getting a rise out of the estimable Miss Pembrook. She definitely wasn't staring up at him with that cheery smile that irritated the hell out of him. She had lost her charm at long last. In fact, the paragon was spitting mad. Her eyes spewed blue flames and she was hissing at him like a cornered cat.

Finally, a breakthrough, he thought.

"You bastard!"

Sebastian was so amused to learn that Saint Eden had a temper that he laughed out loud.

"Get off me!" she railed at him.

Sebastian grinned. His victory at the race track didn't compare to the gratification of getting under this particular woman's skin.

"Now, about our bargain—"

"Damn the bargain and damn you, while I'm at it." Eden swung her arm, thumping the male shoulder that was shaking with amusement. "Get off me this very second!"

Sebastian didn't budge. He was having more fun than he had had in weeks. His male body was soaking up the feel of soft feminine flesh gyrating beneath him.

When Eden realized she had allowed Sebastian to shatter her composure, she stopped struggling and lay absolutely still. Although she was vividly aware of every well-sculpted inch of his masculine body, she ignored the unfamiliar sensations coursing through her.

She would not allow this rapscallion to upset her, she promised herself. She had learned to cope with every adversity she encountered. She could handle this man. She would simply humiliate him into crawling off her.

Eden stared up into the grin that reeked of triumph and male arrogance. He was enjoying this—for now. But he wouldn't for long, she assured herself.

"Who was she, Sebastian?"

"Who the hell was who?"

"The woman who turned you into such a cynic. Your behavior indicates you have lost respect for women. You are trying to humiliate me to compensate for being humiliated. You truly think this will ease your pain? It won't, you know. I pity you, and I do sympathize with your frustration. It must be difficult to realize that you are unloved and unwanted."

"I'm not falling for your forgiving paragon routine, Eden." Sebastian propped on his elbows and stared pointedly at her lush lips. "For a kiss, and nothing less, I'll let you up."

Eden met his challenging smile. "I would rather kiss your horse."

Sebastian flinched when slapped with the insult. If ever a woman needed to be kissed senseless, left to react without thinking first, it was Eden Pembrook.

"This particular kiss is nonnegotiable," he whispered as he cupped his hands gently around her face.

Eden froze, but Sebastian kissed her so tenderly that tremors swept through her. She was shocked to realize that she was responding to his unexpected gentleness. Sweet mercy! What was there about this ornery rascal that made her react so quickly, so thoroughly?

Gentle hands glided along the pulsating column of her throat and trailed over the exposed flesh of her breasts. A strange, unfamiliar heat coiled inside her when his index finger tunneled beneath her bodice to brush her nipples. Her betraying body arched toward his questing fingertip, and Eden gasped at the flood of pleasure that washed over her.

She made a feeble attempt to resist, but his moist lips whispered over her cheek, then reclaimed her lips. Fire coursed through her like a river of leaping flames.

This wasn't supposed to be happening! She should be outraged, repulsed. She should shove him away—but she didn't. She was savoring the unique sensations that crippled her mind and made her feminine body ache for something she couldn't name and didn't understand.

When Eden melted in his arms, Sebastian groaned. The taste and texture of her silky skin beneath his hands and lips left him aching with need. He felt himself sinking into a dimension of time and space where he had no control over his body. He simply responded to the taste of the sweetest innocence he'd ever known.

He moved, letting Eden feel his desire for her, teaching her the vivid difference between his body and hers. His hand brushed over one throbbing peak, and then the other, feeling her tremble in response to his bold caress. His hand ventured lower, gliding beneath the high-riding hem of her gown to make intimate contact with her thigh.

She tensed, but he languidly stroked her and heard her breath catch.

He watched her eyes widen and her lips part on a shattered breath when he traced a caress over her inner thigh. He had awakened Eden's desire and realized that she could become a wildly passionate woman when she shed her inhibitions. Her responses triggered something wild and reckless in him.

God, he wanted her. He wanted her here and now . . .

The realization of where *here* was shot through Sebastian like a bullet. They were beside the main road, sprawled in the grass for any passerby to see. Lord, had he lost his mind? If someone saw the resident angel being seduced, Sebastian would be strung up to the nearest tree and burned in effigy!

Clamping down on his raging desires, Sebastian rolled away. In one swift, effortless motion, he drew Eden up beside him. When her knees wobbled, she clutched at his arm for support. He watched embarrassment flood her cheeks. He wondered if she intended to smile her way out of this predicament. To his surprise, she lurched away from him and burst into tears.

Sebastian felt like a complete ass. He had spent the entire day trying to break through Eden's cool resolve. Now that he had, he wasn't very proud of himself.

"Eden, I—"

When he tried to curl his hand around her elbow, she jerked loose and wobbled down the road. "Don't touch me, damn you. Aren't you satisfied?"

Tears streamed down her face, reminding Sebastian of diamonds sparkling in moonlight. Sobbing, she tugged her drooping gown into decency.

"Don't ever come near me again, curse your black soul!" she hissed through her tears.

"Eden—"

"There is no bargain between us. Take another offer."

"We still have a bargain. I gave my word. The Arabian is at your service."

"I don't want him and I don't want you, either!" she railed at him.

"You will get the Arabian nonetheless," he decreed.

Sebastian cursed himself soundly. He had risen to Micah's drunken challenge. For some ridiculous reason, he had been determined to draw a reaction from Eden, to rattle her, irritate her. He had been too cynical to consider her the saintly paragon everyone thought she was. He had set out to prove everybody wrong, because he had no faith in women.

All he had accomplished was earning Eden's hatred, while his interest in her multiplied. She presented a difficult challenge. He wanted to know why he had seen that hint of misery behind her smile. He wondered why she was so determined to remain an unattainable martyr.

And why did she make excuses for friends and accept blame that wasn't hers? What was she hiding?

When Eden trotted down the road, sobbing in great gulps, Sebastian mentally kicked himself all the way back to his horse, mounted up, and reined up beside her.

"I well and truly hate you," she spat at him, refusing to glance at him.

"At least you feel something," he contended.

"And that pleases you?" She stared straight ahead, swiping at the stream of tears. "Your colossal male arrogance objects to my indifference, doesn't it? You wanted me to react to you as I have to no other man, is that it? Well, I have, and I assure you that I'll hate you till I die!"

"Truly? You have a strange way of showing a man how much you despise him," he heard himself say—and wished he hadn't. He had antagonized her too much already.

Eden lost her temper, breaking the solemn vow she had made seventeen years ago to never again to let fear or anger rule her emotions. Sebastian's taunts had pushed her past her limits.

She whirled around, her bright-colored skirts billowing, glowing in the moonlight. Her abrupt movement startled the high-strung Arabian.

When the horse bolted, Sebastian was too distracted to recover from the sudden leap. The horse plunged off, catapulting Sebastian through the air. He landed with a thud and a groan.

Head held high, Eden strode off to retrieve the horse that had stopped to graze. Without the slightest concern for Sebastian's condition, Eden piled onto the saddle and headed toward home. She raced away, letting the rush of wind dry her tears.

Sebastian could crawl back to Micah's plantation—or not. She spitefully hoped the thieves she had seen in the thicket would swoop down on that scoundrel. That's what he deserved for tormenting her!

Sebastian scraped himself off the ground as Eden cantered off on his horse. He hadn't walked a dozen paces before he heard a rider thrashing through the underbrush behind him. When Tully Randolph appeared, Sebastian shifted uneasily.

"Having trouble with yer stallion, yer lordship?" The man's deep-chested chuckle hovered in the damp night air. "Or was it the *laidy* who got the better of you?"

Sebastian scowled as he accepted the meaty hand Tully extended to haul him onto the back of the steed.

"I don't hold with toying with proper ladies," Tully said. "That isn't why we are here, unless our orders changed and you neglected to tell me."

Sebastian settled behind the bulky man who out-weighed him by forty pounds. He should have known Tully would be somewhere in the near distance—keeping vigil.

"Did you fetch my bags from Bancroft's plantation?" Sebastian questioned, purposely avoiding the subject of Eden Pembrook.

"All taken care of, yer lordship."

"Don't call me that."

"Old habit," Tully said with a shrug. "I only keep up pretense when I have to. But you seem to enjoy breaking new ground, don't you? Never knew harassing respectable laidies was up your street."

Sebastian swallowed a curse. Tully had obviously seen—and heard—Eden shouting her fury, and guessed what had ignited her temper.

"The lady is none of your concern." Sebastian hoped that would be the end of the discussion; it wasn't.

"She shouldn't have been yer concern, either," Tully flung back. "I should think a man who is leading a double life would be reluctant to complicate the situation. What the devil got into you?"

"We are not having this conversation," Sebastian insisted obstinately.

"No? Sounds like we are to me." His broad chest shook with amusement. "And I suppose we didn't have that little chat in the thicket with British reconnaissance, either."

"Tully . . ." Sebastian said warningly.

"Aye, yer lordship?" he asked in mock innocence.

Sebastian let out a long breath, then turned his attention to the initial purpose of his stay in the area. "Did you make final contact and send off the dispatches?"

"Done."

"Then our business here is concluded for the time being."

"Mine, maybe." Tully glanced over his shoulder to stare pointedly at his longtime employer and closest friend. "I would say that you have some fancy talking to do to restore yourself to the lady's good graces. And we aren't discussing a strumpet, you know. If you were in need of a bit of fluff, you should have said so. I could have made the arrangements for that, too."

"I promise to make amends with Eden Pembrook when time permits," Sebastian promised.

"That was Eden Pembrook? The one they call the Rebels' Angel?" Tully hooted. "Lord A-mighty, what the hell has gotten into you?"

Sebastian clamped his mouth shut when Tully reined the steed toward the obscure cabin nestled by the swamp. Until today, Sebastian Saber had devoted himself totally to his clandestine assignments, playing a dangerous game of intrigue without getting sidetracked.

And then along came that infuriating female with secrets in her eyes, and suddenly, Sebastian found himself behaving like an ass.

For five years he had practiced the art of delving deeper than outward appearance to accomplish his missions. He knew all the nuances of proper protocol, but he hadn't behaved like a gentleman in Eden's presence. Fact was, Sebastian had been raised and groomed to be at ease in places colonial aristocracy only dreamed about. But this wasn't the British court, and one false move in this perilous game he played could end in disaster. He had better not let himself forget that.

Willfully, Sebastian set aside his regrettable dealings with Eden. Though he owed her an apology for his disrespectful behavior, he had to delay making amends. He had pressing matters to attend and this was not the time for the kind of distraction Eden Pembrook caused. This entire day had been a frustrating disaster. And tonight he had . . .

Sebastian refused to replay the incident on the road, because it was an embarrassing reminder that he had disregarded the good sense he had spent thirty-two years cultivating!

If Eden Pembrook did indeed hate him till her dying day—as she swore she would—Sebastian wasn't sure he could blame her. He had disgraced himself, all in the name of bruised male pride.

Three

Eden regained her composure by the time she reached the plantation stables, but she wasn't ready to forgive Sebastian—ever. He had awakened sensations, taught her things about herself that she hadn't wanted to know. Passion, she'd found out, meant losing control, being swayed by yearnings of the body rather than restrained by common sense. Finding herself at the mercy of her feminine desires was unsettling, frightening.

She wished she had never laid eyes on Sebastian Saber. He was a disconcerting, perceptive man who saw past her cheery smiles, demanding more than she was prepared to give.

And what, Eden wondered, made him so determined to poke and probe until he provoked an upheaval of emotion? Why had he made her some kind of crusade? How did he know she had something to hide? How had she given herself away, when she had concealed her awful secret from the rest of the world for years, seventeen years to be exact.

Eden unsaddled the stallion and left him munching hay in a sturdy stall. Resolutely, she drew herself up to dignified stature, then strode toward the house. If she could slip past Maggie's observant gaze, she could take refuge in her improvised bedroom without being questioned about her puffy eyes and tear-stained cheeks.

Fortunately, Maggie had retired for the night, and Eden hurried upstairs to undress.

The niche that was now her bedroom was a converted storeroom, one which boasted a wide window. Eden had made certain of that. Narrow confines, which blocked her view of the outside world, made her uneasy. Her apprehension of closed spaces was the one fear she had difficulty dealing with.

Eden had vacated her spacious quarters to accommodate the wounded soldiers in her keeping. Since the public hospital in Williamsburg couldn't care for the rising number of injured rebel soldiers, Eden had turned her home into an infirmary. Dr. Curtis had taught her the basics of caring for his convalescent patients, and in turn, she had passed along the physician's instructions to Elizabeth and Maggie, who helped to tend the wounded.

Snuggling beneath the quilt, Eden pondered how many more lives would be disrupted by this endless war. How many more wounded soldiers would come and go from the plantation before the rebels enjoyed victory?

Whatever the number, her fellow patriots would be treated with kindness, generosity, and consideration. Each man would know that his efforts were appreciated, that he was a hero in his own right. And when the wounded men were strong enough to venture home, Eden would send them on their way with an encouraging smile.

Yes, with a smile, she told herself. And what business was it of Sebastian Saber's that she smiled to conceal tears and frustration?

Damn that unpatriotic lout, she silently fumed. Why hadn't he enlisted in the Virginia Militia to repel the British from the colonies? He probably didn't want to dirty his hands with war, not when he could strut around the countryside, reaping profits from his magnificent stallion and flinging rude propositions at women.

Sebastian Saber was nothing but a footloose dandy

whose primary concern was his own lusty pleasures. He had no honor, no integrity, no allegiance to the colonies. He had most likely sponged off Micah Bancroft before flitting off to persuade some other gracious southern planter to take him in.

Well, Sebastian Saber wasn't going to dawdle around Pembrook Plantation. He could retrieve his stallion and leave. Eden would simply locate another Arabian stud to improve the livestock's bloodline. Perhaps she couldn't find that black Arabian's equal, but she wasn't about to pay the price Sebastian suggested!

Eventually, she fell asleep, but her dreams betrayed her. She saw Sebastian's silver-gray eyes glistening down at her, felt his gentle caresses that made her burn with indescribable need. She felt her body catching flame as his hands and lips fluttered over her flesh and unlocked even more startling secrets . . .

Eden came awake with a start. Her body throbbed with remembered sensations, and she cursed the man who tormented her. Sebastian had penetrated her defenses. He was the most dangerous man ever to draw breath. There and then, Eden made a pact with herself to avoid future encounters with him.

Through the midnight shadows, three riders approached Thaddeus Saber's cottage which was nestled in the pines. Thaddeus shuffled over to set a pot of coffee on the stove. While his late-night guests washed off the layers of dust from their long journey, Thaddeus placed a tray of bread and cheese on the table.

"What news do you have from our armies to the south?" he inquired of the leader.

Gerard Lockwood grabbed a slice of buttered bread, then glanced over at the heavyset man who looked to be pushing hard at seventy. "The northward march has be-

gun. The Carolinas have been seized by the British and
left to the army of occupation. Most of the rebel resistance
has been thwarted, except for attacks from that pesky
Swamp Fox and his guerrilla band."

Thaddeus nodded. "We're fortunate the Swamp Fox's
strike force isn't large enough to wage a full-scale war
against King George's regiments. Not even our man Tarleton, and his Tory brigade, are a match for that shrewd
rebel soldier."

Gerard reached for a chunk of cheese and munched
upon it. "Swamp Fox is the least of our worries. Your report that General Lafayette is marching south leads us to
believe the Continental Army has guessed our plans to
take control of Virginia. But the rebels will be at a great
disadvantage when Lord Cornwallis arrives to make Virginia his stronghold. He'll take control of the colony and
cripple American economy."

Thaddeus set a steaming cup of coffee on the table and
resumed his seat. "Washington will be helpless to stop the
siege of Virginia while he is left to contain Sir Clinton in
the north."

"Exactly." Easing back in his chair, Gerard Lockwood
sipped the strong brew. "By the end of the year, the revolt
will end and I will be promoted from customs officer to a
powerful dignitary who lords over my foolish colonial
neighbors."

Gerard glanced curiously at the stoop-shouldered old
man. "Have you received the new dispatches I'm supposed
to deliver to Cornwallis?"

Thaddeus levered himself from his chair and hobbled
toward the cabinet. After retrieving the leather pouch, he
took his seat. "I received word from two intelligence agents
that Lafayette's forces are minimal. With Lord Cornwallis's
vast manpower, he should have no trouble squelching the
Marquis de Lafayette and sending the young dandy limp-
ing back to France where he belongs."

Gerard grinned at the satisfying thought. "Cornwallis would like nothing better than to squish Lafayette like the little red-haired bug he is. Defeating the Frenchman would break the rebels' morale. They consider General Washington's French prodigy some kind of hero who has come to save them from the British hordes. But nothing is going to prevent the Crown from crushing this rebellion and bringing the colonists under thumb."

Thaddeus withdrew a dispatch from the pouch and deciphered the message. "Our agents captured a rebel courier headed south to Richmond. He was bearing messages from the Patriot commander-in-chief himself. The Patriots have discovered several Tory spies working in the area around New York and caution everyone to tighten security. The British intelligence is receiving information about Patriot activities."

Thaddeus smiled faintly as he glanced up from the message. "General Washington has even expressed concern that British troops might burn his home at Mount Vernon. He sent a warning to his plantation to prepare for the possibility. The general also sent a request to his dentist, asking for pliers to repair his rotting wooden teeth."

The three Tory soldiers guffawed at that last bit of news.

"When this war is over, Washington may not have anything left except his ill-fitting dentures," Gerard sniggered. "I, however, will be handsomely rewarded for my loyalty to the Crown."

"And I will be receiving a pension for deciphering and relaying messages between the Royal Army and Tory troops," Thaddeus said. "For now, times are hard, and I have to depend on my grandnephew to bring supplies." He gestured toward the tin cups. "You have my grandnephew to thank for this steaming brew. My meager income doesn't stretch that far."

"Sebastian Saber will have far more important duties to tend before long," Gerard insisted. "I submitted a plan to

Tarleton and Cornwallis, one that was inspired by Benedict Arnold's deceptive maneuver."

Thaddeus frowned at the announcement. "Arnold barely escaped execution after passing information from Patriot headquarters to our British officers. If you recall, his emissary wasn't that fortunate. The Patriots strung up Major Andre for treason. Benedict Arnold would have been on the gallows, too, if he hadn't fled to the British frigate without a minute to spare."

Gerard waved off the old man's concern. "The strategy worked once, and it will work again. Just as Arnold pinpointed the weakness in the Patriot defenses at West Point, so the British could take the stronghold, I plan to ensure the same thing happens in Virginia."

"Just how is this scheme supposed to work?" Thaddeus questioned.

Gerard smiled craftily. "You'll find out in due time. The dispatches from Cornwallis should be arriving tomorrow. Our spies are reconnoitering this area to gather information. Soon, Williamsburg will be a hotbed of activity. If my plan unfolds as expected, the rebels will be laying down their arms and forced to surrender, betrayed by one of their own highly esteemed officers."

Gerard dropped a pouch of coins on the table for the old man's trouble, then motioned for his two aides to follow him outside.

Thaddeus shook out the money, frowning when he noticed the American currency mixed with the British coins. Unless Thaddeus missed his guess, Gerard Lockwood had not only been surveying the area, but he had also been dabbling in robbery. Lockwood was taking advantage of his position as leader of the Tory band that aided the British. The man was a part-time officer and a full-time thief.

Thaddeus picked up the empty cups, then tucked the worn leather pouch in the cabinet drawer. He predicted there would be frequents visits to his remote cottage in the weeks to come. The shack was already becoming a rendezvous point for Tory and English soldiers who shuttled dispatches through the outspread forces.

Now that the battlefront was shifting to Virginia, the cottage would be a central relay station. Thaddeus made a mental note to request more supplies and food for his expected guests. He was certain he was going to be doing a great deal of entertaining during the midnight hours.

After Eden made her rounds to check on the wounded soldiers, and returned the breakfast trays to the kitchen, she strode off to check on the Arabian stallion who now enjoyed free run of the meadow. When Eden was bombarded with questions the morning after the magnificent stallion appeared at the plantation, she had explained that she had made arrangements to breed the mares—and hadn't she paid dearly for that privilege! Since Sebastian hadn't arrived to collect his valuable property, Eden had taken advantage of the stallion's presence. For more than a week, the Arabian had been running with Pembrook mares.

The stallion appeared to have no complaints. Indeed, Eden suspected him of enjoying his duties thoroughly. The Arabian had been prancing around, practicing mating rituals, circling the herd with his head held high and his tail in the air.

Eden chortled in amusement as she propped her arms on the fence rail. The magnificent stallion was showing off for any mare that cared to watch him prance and strut. Here, she reminded herself, was a demonstration of the fundamental purpose of the male from every species: flaunting masculine prowess.

The Arabian nipped at the roan mare he had singled out as his newest conquest. The mare kicked and whinnied in protest. Eden decided it must be the natural instinct for the female to put up resistance, or at least pretend to reject male advances at the onset of the ritual.

In shameful fascination, Eden watched the stallion bolt up on his back legs to cover the mare. Eden had never actually watched the mating procedure which was reported to be offensive to feminine sensibility. She did admit that it was rather unsettling . . .

"I see the Arabian is keeping his part of our bargain."

Eden started at the sound of the baritone voice that came from so close behind her. She had been too distracted to realize an unwanted visitor had arrived. Her face flamed as the stallion took possession, nearly bringing the mare to her knees, but Eden couldn't bring herself to glance back at the man who stood behind her.

"Take the stallion and leave," she said stiffly. "The Arabian has serviced several mares this week. I've had my compensation for what you did—"

Eden clamped her mouth shut so fast she nearly clipped off her tongue. She was appalled at how quickly she lost her composure when Sebastian Saber was around. The man had become the lighted fuse attached to her temper. She was reacting and speaking without thinking first—an unpardonable sin in her book!

"No sugar-coated pretense for my benefit?" Sebastian edged up beside her to lean his elbows on the railing. "Good. I can do without your polite indifference, Eden."

When his shoulder brushed hers, she sidestepped to keep a respectable distance between them.

"I have come to apologize." Sebastian shot her a sidelong glance, noting the blotches of pink that stained her cheeks. "Your secrets are safe with me," he murmured. "What happened last week will not happen again."

"There never was a question as to that." Eden tilted her chin to a determined angle, still refusing to do Sebastian the courtesy of glancing at him while she spoke. "I will not allow it to happen."

Eden was forced to watch while the stallion performed his duty with great enthusiasm. It was either that or face Sebastian. She chose to stare straight ahead, though she blushed profusely while the stallion rode the mare.

"Sometimes things happen that even strong will is helpless to prevent," he contended.

When Sebastian curled his forefinger beneath her chin, he saw her blue eyes flash fire. He heartily approved of the transformation, even if Eden herself resented the slightest display of emotion in his presence.

"Things such as this . . ." he added as he drew her resisting body to his.

"Let me go!" she hissed at him.

"Not until you accept my apology for what happened last week."

"Never," she said stubbornly. "I enjoy hating you too much."

He smiled wryly. "Hating me for making you aware that you're a woman with a woman's needs?"

"No, for strong-arming me like a boorish brute. I have no respect for men who rely on superior strength because they cannot battle with their wits."

Sebastian winced when the remark scored a direct hit, but he didn't release her. Damn, why couldn't he be immune to this complicated female? Why couldn't he be satisfied to leave well enough alone?

Sebastian found his head moving instinctively toward hers. He wanted to retest his fierce reaction to her, to tame her, to understand her. He couldn't be content until he dismantled those defensive barriers to find Eden soft and responsive in his arms—just as she had been that night a week ago.

He had discovered the real Eden Pembrook that night. She was a woman teeming with inner spirit and fiery passion. Only when she had been in his arms did he sense that she had truly come to life, that she had forgotten whatever it was that she seemed hell-bent on hiding from him and the rest of the world.

Eden wasn't sure who she hated most at the moment—this seductive devil or herself. She felt the explosive reaction between them the instant their bodies touched, the moment his sensuous lips slanted over hers, summoning a response she was helpless to restrain.

Dangerous sensations bombarded her, as if it had been minutes instead of days since Sebastian had kissed her. He was shattering her self-control again, making her want what she vowed never to have. He was absorbing her willpower, turning her into a shameless hypocrite.

Common sense whirled off in the wind when Eden felt herself racing toward the unknown, risking the danger she sensed in this mysterious man. She knew absolutely nothing about him, except that he had the most amazing knack of making her burn alive, making her hunger for his masterful kisses and caresses.

When he nudged her lips apart with his questing tongue, her resistance slipped another notch. She could feel hard, demanding desire clench his body, then ricochet through hers. She could taste him, breathe him, and the coil of wanting intensified until she was trembling with the vivid knowledge that this man, alone, aroused her.

Eden was shocked to find her fingers raking through his thick raven hair. Suddenly, she was kissing him back with a hunger all her own, feeding the fire that burned in the very core of her being.

When her body arched involuntarily into his, she heard him groan, felt his powerful arms contract, felt the whipcord muscles of his thighs mesh closely to hers.

Sweet mercy, she was surrendering to the very man she had vowed to hate for a dozen justifiable reasons. She . . . *liked* the taste of him, the feel of him. She . . . *wanted* him.

Startled by the intensity of that forbidden realization, Eden launched herself backward. Her trembling hands clenched on the fence rail, and her knees knocked together while her toes curled up in her shoes. She staggered to orient herself while the hazy world around her wobbled on its axis. His effect on her was shocking, frightening!

Sebastian steadied himself when riveting desire pelted him like a barrage of gunfire. He, who had rehearsed every last word of his apology, found his tongue stuck to the roof of his mouth. Damn it, not only had he not apologized, but he had broken his promise to keep his distance from Eden. She was a complication—a distraction—he didn't need.

Hell's teeth, he had spent a week trying to cool his heels—or whatever part of his anatomy needed cooling off after that regrettable fiasco on the road. But he hadn't cooled down a damned bit, and he wondered if he ever would.

Sebastian and Eden stared at each other in confusion for a full minute, dragging in snatches of breath, attempting to come to grips with their volatile reaction to each other.

"You and I have a definite problem," Sebastian said, stating the obvious.

Eden half collapsed against the fence. Definite problem was right! Nothing had ever hit her this hard and left such lingering aftershocks. It was glaringly apparent that she couldn't trust herself alone with this man.

"What the devil is wrong with us?" she wheezed, clinging to the fence as if it were her salvation. "We don't even like each other."

Sebastian barked a laugh. It relieved the tension vibrating through him. He could function better now that temptation was four feet away from him.

"It must be some kind of curse," he said.

Eden blew a recalcitrant strand of chestnut hair from her flushed face, then inhaled a deep breath. "Never seeing each other again should break the curse," she diagnosed.

Sebastian leaned leisurely against the fence, choosing not to watch the Arabian enjoying the kind of satisfaction he was doing without. "I'm not sure separation will be one hundred percent effective."

"Eden!"

Sebastian pivoted to see a lovely young woman scampering around the corner of the barn, her mahogany curls bouncing with each step, her vivid green eyes sparkling with excitement.

Elizabeth stumbled to a halt when she noticed the man standing beside her sister. "Oh, I'm sorry, Eden, I didn't know you had a guest."

Eden gestured toward her companion. "I don't believe you were introduced to Sebastian Saber while we were at the fair. Sebastian, this is my sister, Elizabeth."

"You own the Arabian," Elizabeth acknowledged. "He is truly a magnificent creature . . ." Her voice evaporated when she caught the movement in the pasture and saw the stallion proving his virility. "Oh, dear . . ."

"Did you want something, Bet?" Eden prompted when she saw her sister's face flamed with embarrassment.

"Um . . . er . . . yes," Elizabeth stammered. "I came looking for you. James has been asking for you. He has decided to give your suggestion a try."

"Has he?" Eden perked up immediately. "He has fought me on this for over a week."

Curious, Sebastian trailed along behind the Pembrook sisters, mulling over the differences he noticed between the two women. Their eyes and hair color were not the same, and there was something—

"Won't you come inside, Mr. Saber," Elizabeth invited. "I didn't mean to be rude. It's just that . . ." Her voice trailed off and she smiled lamely, unsure what to say when Eden didn't eagerly second the invitation.

"Thank you, Elizabeth. I could use a drink." Sebastian was also anxious to learn who this James character was, and why he had been fighting with the resident angel. Was it possible that there was another man in the area who didn't buckle beneath Eden's disarming smiles and grovel at her feet?

Now here was a man Sebastian had to meet!

When Sebastian strode inside the plantation house he gained immediate insight into Eden's private life. The home had a spacious, elegant quality about it. The rooms boasted expensive furnishings which were spaced widely apart. The windows stood wide open, allowing shafts of sunlight to stream into every room.

He noticed some titles of the reading material on the parlor table: *Animal Husbandry, Rights of the Colonists Asserted and Proved,* by James Otis, *Inquiry into the Human Mind,* by Thomas Reid, *Anatomical Treatise on the Structures of the Viscera,* by Marcello Malphigh—Those seemed only a few of the books Eden kept as reference.

Sebastian also noted the newspaper articles written by such highly acclaimed Patriots as Samuel Adams and Patrick Henry.

Eden was definitely well read, a credit to her cause of liberty.

With a glass of sangaree in hand, Sebastian followed Eden upstairs. He had no idea what to expect when he reached the bedroom. What he saw was a roomful of wounded soldiers lounging on rows of cots in what he assumed was once someone's bedroom suite—and he could guess whose!

Sebastian watched a sunny smile claim Eden's enchanting features. She swept across the room with celestial grace, pausing to speak privately with every soldier, before she halted at the foot of the cot that was farthest from the door. Sebastian's astute gaze flicked over the sandy-haired man who looked to be in his midtwenties. The sheet covered his lower extremities, but the partial loss of a leg was unmistakable.

Memories came flooding back in a rush. Sebastian could almost hear the screams of agony and smell the coppery scent of blood. Resolutely, he jerked himself back to the present.

Eden blinked in surprise when she realized Sebastian had followed her upstairs. He moved as silently as a shadow. Now here he was, leaning against the doorjamb, smiling politely at her patients.

"This is Sebastian Saber," she felt obliged to say. "He owns the handsome Arabian that won the race, hands down, at the fair."

After a round of how-do-you-dos, James Pike levered himself onto the edge of the cot, modestly holding the sheet around his waist. "I've been thinking about what you said, Eden." A resolute expression settled over his face. "I'm ready to try."

Sebastian pushed away from the doorjamb and strode forward. Clearly, the young soldier had waged his private war with bitterness and resentment before making the decision to strap on the artificial stump that lay at the foot of his bed.

"Perhaps I could be of some help," Sebastian volunteered. "Eden, why don't you wait for James and me in the hall."

When James smiled gratefully, Eden realized the soldier preferred a man's assistance in this matter. Flashing James an accommodating smile, she stepped into the hall and closed the door.

For more than a week she had tried to coax James into strapping on the peg leg Dr. Curtis had left for him. James had adamantly refused. He simply lay there, staring up at the ceiling, claiming that a stump of a leg would never make him whole again.

For days on end Eden had assured James that his wife

was not repulsed by his injury and that she longed for his return home. Eden had reminded James of the one visit his wife had been able to make to the plantation. She urged James to live for the day he could be reunited with his wife and infant child.

Yet, James had slumped into depression, and Eden feared he intended to harm himself. She had dedicated time and effort to bolstering his spirits and self-esteem. And at long last, James had begun to cope with the loss of his leg . . .

A steady thump echoed on the wooden floor behind the bedroom door, followed by Sebastian's commanding voice. "Again, James. Don't favor your left side. That's it. Now lengthen your stride. Good. Try it again, at a faster pace this time."

More silence behind the door, then the thumps resounded.

The door hinge creaked open and James appeared, dressed in breeches for the first time in weeks. Although Eden had never been prone to overt displays of affection, she hugged the stuffing out of James. The soldier teetered backward, forcing Sebastian to prop him up.

When Eden stepped away, the sparkle of sheer happiness in her eyes nearly brought Sebastian to his knees. Eden could flash smiles easier than anyone he knew, but this particular smile was exceptionally radiant. The shadowed secrets in her eyes were momentarily forgotten.

Ah, that Sebastian could be the recipient of such a glowing smile! As for James, he was blinded, humbled. Even Sebastian, who never considered himself the sentimental sort, felt a lump clogging his throat.

"Oh, James, you look positively wonderful," Eden enthused. "Wait until Bet and Maggie see you. They will be delighted!"

James clutched Eden's arm before she could summon her sister and the housekeeper. "Thank you, Eden. If not for you and your tireless persistence, I would've given up on myself." He gestured his ruffled blond head toward the bedroom. "And so would the others. If ever there is anything I can do for you, anything at all—"

"Just go home to your family and have a good life, James," Eden requested, her dazzling smile intact. "It's all I ask. Your wife is so anxious to have you home. She loves you, needs you."

"I realize that now. I just needed you to convince me I hadn't lost my worth." He leaned down to skim his lips over her forehead. "You're an absolute angel, Eden."

Eden slid Sebastian a discreet glance, wondering if he would scoff at the comment. When he didn't, she turned her attention back to James. "I only reminded you of how important you are to your family, friends, and country, until you remembered it for yourself."

Sebastian was sure Eden had used her knack of asking leading questions and providing strong comments to bring the tormented soldier around to her way of thinking.

"James! Is that you?" Maggie and Elizabeth chorused from halfway up the steps.

While Maggie and Elizabeth fussed over James, Sebastian drew Eden aside. "How long have you been doing this?"

"Doing what?" she questioned.

"Opening your home to the wounded."

Sebastian felt like a king-size imbecile. Berating this angel of mercy, of all things! He had been too judgmental, too cynical. A new kind of respect dawned in his eyes when he stared into Eden's pixie-like features. She might well be hiding secret misery, but her generosity and kindness were overwhelming.

"The hospital is overflowing with patients," Eden explained with a shrug. "We had room to spare."

His lips quirked as he lifted a dark brow in contradiction.

"We have room to provide much-needed care," Eden

amended. "It is the least I can do for the wounded Patriots who have defended our country and endured this brutal war. I remind myself daily that any of these men could be my father."

A clanking noise in another room sent Eden scurrying away. To Sebastian's amazement, he found six more young soldiers lying on a row of cots.

How many wounded soldiers was Eden housing, feeding, and smiling encouragingly upon?

Sebastian strode off to answer the question for himself. By the time he introduced himself, and chatted with the men in the four upstairs rooms, he had counted twenty-two men in various stages of rehabilitation.

Sebastian felt like a royal ass. Now he understood the reason for the knowing smiles and sweeping praise Micah Bancroft heaped on Eden. She was indeed the rebel's guardian angel.

By the time Sebastian made the rounds to visit Eden's patients, he found himself at the head of the steps, peering down at another unexpected scene. Eden was in the midst of what looked to be organized pandemonium. She was issuing orders and stuffing heaping baskets of food into the waiting arms of her servants. The charity brigade was on its way to the homes of neighbors-in-need. Another of the angel of mercy's daily good deeds, no doubt.

When the crowd dispersed, Sebastian ambled down the steps, humbled and impressed by all he had observed. He clasped Eden's hand and dropped a pouch of coins in her palm.

She peered questioningly at the leather poke, then at him. "What's this?"

"A contribution. I regret every unkind word I have said to you," he murmured before he walked out the door without looking back.

"Well, if he isn't the most befuddling man I have ever met, then I don't know who is," Eden said.

"Who is?" Maggie questioned as she appeared at the parlor door.

"Sebastian Saber."

Maggie waddled into the vestibule with dust cloth in hand. "Where did he come from? I looked up and there he was. He took immediate interest in our patients, asking them all sorts of questions about their regiments and the locations of the battles where they'd fought."

Eden shrugged. "I don't know all that much about the man."

"What does he want?"

Eden frowned pensively. "I'm not sure."

Maggie chuckled and shook her head. "Why should any of us be surprised to find another stranger wandering around this house? The second floor is crawling alive with them, after all."

Eden glanced up to see Elizabeth sweeping gracefully down the steps in her best green silk gown. "Where are you going, Bet?"

"Since I have finished my chores I thought I would go for a ride in the buggy."

"Oh? A new pastime?" Eden inquired. "This is the fifth ride you have taken this week, as I recall."

When Eden stared suspiciously at her, Elizabeth waved off all concern. "Don't look at me like that. Saints aren't allowed to frown."

"I am not a saint."

"No? Try telling that to the men upstairs," Bet said before she breezed out the front door to call for a carriage.

"What has gotten into that girl?" Maggie questioned, staring after Bet. "You would think every day was a holiday around here."

"She's young and vibrant," Eden excused her sister. "Bet needs diversions for as long as they will last."

"It wouldn't hurt you to have a diversion or two," Maggie suggested.

With a shrug, Eden ambled to the barn, surprised to see the Arabian was still in the pasture with the mares. She had expected Sebastian to take his stallion with him when he left.

Purposely casting thoughts of Sebastian aside, Eden sought out the stable boys to order an increase in rations for the cattle. If the cows could produce milk for seven months rather than five months out of the year—on Sebastian's ration program—it would help Eden feed her "family." Sebastian certainly seemed to know what he was talking about when he discussed breeding and caring for livestock . . .

And just where had he acquired all that information? she wondered. Where had he come from?

Eden made a mental note to ask him when he returned, or at the least, question Micah about his enigmatic cousin. Now that she and Sebastian seemed to be operating under some kind of unspoken truce, she was going to delve into his background. The man was too mysterious by half!

Four

Tully Randolph stopped in his tracks when he saw Sebastian whittling on a hollow stump that had been stripped of bark. A variety of tools sat beside him on the porch outside the secluded cabin by the swamp.

"What the hell are you doing, yer lordship?"

"I'm fashioning a wooden leg," Sebastian said without looking up.

"For whom?"

"A Patriot soldier."

"A Patriot?" Tully parroted. "You better watch who ye'er seen with, lest certain folks start asking questions you don't want to answer."

"I know what I'm doing." Sebastian assured his friend.

"You sure as hell didn't last week," Tully grunted. "Did you retrieve the Arabian and make amends?"

"I'm working on it."

Tully glanced around. "Where's the stallion?"

"Still having the time of his life at Pembrook Plantation."

Tully grinned. "Free stud services to compensate for that disgraceful fiasco, yer lordship?"

"Something like that."

"The lady still hate you?"

There was a noticeable pause.

"Yer lordship?" Tully prompted.

Sebastian glanced up from sanding the wooden leg he'd spent the afternoon designing. "Yes?"

Tully appraised Sebastian with his probing gaze. "There's something different about you today. Can't figure out what it is."

"I changed my shirt?" Sebastian offered helpfully.

Tully's thick brows formed a straight line over his green eyes. "That spinster with angel wings got to you, didn't she?"

"Yes, I do believe she did."

"Thought so." Tully leaned over to light his pipe with the tinderbox, then puffed until a halo of smoke hovered around his broad head. "What are you going to do about her, yer lordship?"

"Nothing."

"Nothing?"

Sebastian frowned at his meddling friend. "Don't badger me out of the good mood I'm in. Just fetch me some leather straps and a drill. I could use some help designing this contraption."

Tully clamped the pipe between his teeth and lumbered into the cabin. When Sebastian sank back to give his arm a rest, Tully ambled outside to pluck up the wooden leg. "Let me try my hand at smoothing off these rough edges."

While Tully applied elbow grease, Sebastian studied the scooped basin he had carved in the top of the stump. He envisioned the straps needed to secure the artificial leg, wondering how to make the appendage as comfortable and efficient as possible.

After several minutes, he fashioned the straps into a harness that would allow James Pike to conceal the partial appendage inside his pant leg, rather than displaying it to the world.

It was a matter of masculine pride, Sebastian mused. It would also provide James with an extra boost of confidence, added to the heaping doses delivered by the Angel of Pembrook.

Who would've thought that woman with a smile of molten gold could've melted his defenses.

Sebastian had become hardened the past five years. He had been so determined of purpose that he had refused to let sentiment influence him. He had lived with deception, learned to lie without batting an eyelash. It was necessary for survival, necessary to perform the tasks demanded of him.

Very soon, he predicted, Eden would begin to question him about his past and his present occupation. And what would he tell her? Another set of lies, like the ones he fed Micah Bancroft?

Sebastian had deceived dozens of men the past few years, but the thought of deceiving Eden played hell with his conscience. She had touched him in some elemental way, exposing emotions he preferred to keep sealed off. That kind of emotion could be dangerous. It could cause complications . . .

"Yer lordship?"

Sebastian, disturbed from his musings, glanced over to see Tully holding up the wooden appendage and smiling. "Smooth as a baby's bottom. Now here's a leg a man could wear with pride. It beats the hell out of those pegs. Why, you could even put a stocking on this smoothed leg and it would be difficult to tell—"

"That's it!" Sebastian burst out. "Tully, help me fetch a few more hollow stumps. I have another idea."

When a flash of color caught Eden's attention, she glanced up from the ledgers that cluttered the office desk. "Bet? Where are you going so early this morning?"

Elizabeth pulled up short, muttered something under

her breath, then reluctantly pivoted to met Eden's curious stare. "I'm going for a ride."

"It seems that you have been going on, or coming from, rides these past two weeks." Eden laid her forefinger on the numerical column to mark her place, then peered at her sister for a long moment. "You have decided daily rides in the fresh air are doing wonders for your disposition," she presumed.

Elizabeth grinned. "Nothing like the inspiration of the great outdoors."

Eden scrutinized her sister carefully. "Is there something you want to tell me?"

Elizabeth flashed the kind of smile her sister was famous for. "Yes, good-bye. Don't wait lunch for me. My commune with Mother Nature might linger past noon."

With that, she sped off as she had so many times the past two weeks. Eden refocused her attention on her mathematical calculations. Balancing books was giving her a ferocious headache. Perhaps when she tallied these tedious columns she would follow Bet's practice of enjoying the wide-open spaces. Her headache could certainly use a break.

Eden mopped the perspiration from her brow and dug up a few more weeds that were taking over the gardens that encircled the back lawn. Carnations, nasturtiums, alpine strawberries, gardenias, and grapevines formed pockets of glorious colors, amid the thick greenery of vegetation. Unfortunately, the weeds seemed to be flourishing better than the flowers shipped to Eden from all corners of the world.

"Tsk, tsk. How many times must I remind you, my dear Eden, that you are a proper aristocrat." Micah Bancroft sauntered out the back door, a glass of mint julep clasped in his hand. "The gentry isn't supposed to rise from bed before nine. Then one is supposed to stroll to the stables before returning to the house for a leisurely breakfast. After catching a nap, *then* one is supposed to consider what task—if any atall—one intends to tackle in the afternoon."

"Thank you for the dissertation on proper conduct for Virginia aristocracy," Eden teased as she uprooted another weed.

Micah sipped his drink as he strolled down the flagstone path. He halted beside Eden who was hunkered over, waging war on the weeds. "You really should leave these rigorous chores to your servants. Genteel ladies were not born to crawl on hands and knees, but rather to rule from their tufted thrones. You're giving the rest of us a bad name."

"The servants are tending my errands for me," she said as she climbed to her feet, then sank down on the bench beneath the mulberry tree.

"So, you are still providing food and supplies to the neighbors whose husbands and sons are fighting with the militia," he presumed as he flicked back his coattails and parked himself on the bench beside Eden.

"I know you practice the same policy."

Micah shook his head in contradiction. "I provide living expenses and supplies for the families of the two men who are fighting in my stead."

Eden blinked, appalled by his confession. She'd heard that some of the gentry who had no wish to enlist in the Army had made such arrangements. But *Micah?*

"Don't look so shocked." Micah squirmed uneasily beneath Eden's disappointed stare. "Besides, it is common practice, you know. Those of us with sprawling plantations to manage have too many families depending on us, don't we? It's not as if I have someone I feel confident in turning my plantation over to, you know."

Eden held her tongue while Micah made his excuses.

She knew he employed a very competent, reliable overseer. Truth was, Micah wasn't about to sacrifice his life of leisure, unless battle broke out on his front lawn.

Which it might very soon.

Micah sprawled on the bench and sighed heavily. "Lord, I'm still incapable of functioning normally, even two weeks after the fair. I must have drunk three gallons of that punch!"

At least three gallons, Eden agreed silently. "You certainly seemed to be enjoying yourself that day."

"I did indeed. Watching you beguile my cynical cousin was the highlight of my day. Saber, of course, had the crazed notion that he would be immune to your charms, while you fell head-over-heels for his. I, of course, bet him that he was wrong."

Eden did not appreciate learning she had become the object of such a ridiculous wager. But it explained Sebastian's attitude toward her. What a cruel thing to do, she thought.

"Just where does your cousin call home?" Eden asked. "I don't recall your mentioning him before."

"He's a distant relative on my mother's side of the family—I think." Micah frowned. "I must admit my mind was a mite fuzzy when Sebastian arrived to introduce himself. He looked me up when he arrived in Williamsburg three weeks ago."

Eden frowned. "You mean you never met him until three weeks ago?"

Micah dismissed the question with a flick of his wrist. "It is not easy to become well acquainted with one's relatives when they are scattered hither and yon. And with this dreadful war going on, who has time to keep in touch with the outspread branches of family trees?"

Eden smiled in amusement at Micah's nonchalance.

"I see the red raspberries and blue grapes that I had shipped from France to decorate your botanical gardens are flourishing," he said. "And Carlyle's camellias are coming right along." He frowned thoughtfully as he glanced at Eden. "Now, let's see, was Carlyle your fourth or fifth fiancé? My, one does tend to lose track."

Micah *always* amused her, and that endearing quality had carried her through their two-month betrothal, before she realized she couldn't marry him. She had outgrown her need for Micah's constant companionship. It wasn't Micah's fault she had grown bored with him. Once she learned all he could teach her about plantation management, they had little common ground left.

Grinning, Micah gazed across the sloping meadow. "I see you made off with Sebastian's prize stallion. The blood line should make a fine addition to your stock."

"The Arabian is utterly magnificent, and Sebastian was a wealth of information about the progress being made to improve livestock on grain formulas."

"Sebastian seems to be an authority on a number of subjects. Except women, of course," Micah put in.

Eden watched Micah fluff his ruffled sleeves. "What do you mean?"

"I mean, he doesn't hold ladies of the gentry in high esteem. According to him, most of them are frivolous social butterflies. But that was before he met you. I thought he needed to change his perspective, so naturally, I introduced him to you."

Eden would have been happier if he hadn't. Thoughts of Sebastian had crept, uninvited, into her thoughts. She found herself anticipating his next visit, galling though it was to admit. Sebastian had stopped by three times the past few days to visit with her patients, treating her with the utmost kindness and respect. He never overstayed his welcome, never ventured close enough to retest her startling reaction to him, and then he left without announcing when he would return.

"Just where is my cousin anyway? I thought he'd be here,

since he packed up and left before I returned from the
fair."

"I can't say. Sebastian simply entrusted the Arabian to
my care. He arrives to check on his stallion, tarries for no
more than an hour, then rides off."

"He must be gathering wagers for prospective races in
the area," Micah speculated. "Sebastian insists that horses
are his greatest passion in life."

When Micah stood up, Eden rose to escort him to his
carriage.

"I would like you to accompany me to the church social
on Sunday," he requested as he strolled leisurely down the
flagstone path.

"Well, I—"

"You are in desperate need of diversion," he diagnosed.
"You shoulder entirely too much responsibility for a
woman. You need to set aside your obligations occasionally
and enjoy yourself, Eden. I'll come by for you in time for
church."

Without allowing her to accept or decline, Micah placed
the empty glass in her hand, dropped a kiss to her lips,
then climbed into his coach.

As he drove away, Eden traced her lips with her fingertips. Nothing. No tingles, no warm, splintering sensations.
For some unexplainable reason, Sebastian Saber was the
only man who could turn her into a living flame and leave
her to burn.

Eden turned back to her battle with the weeds, refusing
to let herself dwell on that fact.

"You're leaving?" Eden stared up the flight of steps to
where James Pike stood, dressed in a handsome blue waistcoat, breeches, stockings, and polished shoes . . .

Shoes and stockings? Eden gaped at the artificial leg
hidden beneath the breeches. Befuddled, she watched

James, who grinned with newfound confidence, descend the steps.

He drew himself up proudly in front of her, then doubled over in a courtly bow. "Good afternoon, Eden."

"Where? How?" was all she could get out.

James pretended to flick a speck of lint from his sleeve, then straightened his cravat. "The new leg and clothes were gifts from Sebastian Saber. He delivered them while you were counting casks of grain in the storage barn." He opened his expensive jacket to reveal a small pouch of coins. "And he also gave me traveling money."

When Eden continued to stare at him with her jaw sagging, James bent over to push down his white silk stocking, then tapped his knuckle on the oiled and polished appendage. "A hollow leg with a hollow foot hinged to it. A rather grand likeness of a foot, don't you think? Sebastian is a man of many talents, it seems."

Eden was speechless. Why had Sebastian taken it upon himself to design an artificial leg and purchase clothes for a man he had only known for a few weeks?

"It seems I have two guardian angels to thank for my new lease on life," James said. "I will never be able to fully repay either of you."

After James pressed a kiss to her forehead and ambled out the door, Eden sank down in the chair in the foyer, shaking her head in astonishment. James's attitude had improved drastically the past few weeks. He had arrived a bitter, tormented man, and he had left with a fresh outlook on life. Amazing!

"Amazing!" Maggie materialized in the hall to echo Eden's thoughts. "I think that man is going to be all right now. And there are a few more young men upstairs who have had their spirits lifted."

When Eden peered curiously at her, Maggie giggled. "That Mr. Saber arrived with crates of body parts while you were gone. There was a partial arm and harness for

Benjamin, a foot for Timothy and a leg for Andrew. Mr. Saber also brought several sets of clothes for our patients." Maggie shook her frizzed head. "You would have thought it was Christmas upstairs with all the laughter and shouts of delight. Saint Sebastian, they called him when he came bearing gifts for one and all."

Was Sebastian trying to compensate for the grief he had initially caused her? Eden wondered. She recalled that he had said he planned to reverse his fall from grace and make amends. He had done that the past two weeks, Eden realized. Boosting the spirits of her wounded patients, and treating her with charm and politeness had gone a long way in altering her first impression of him.

She would have to thank him—from a distance, of course. She couldn't trust herself within three feet of him. Yet, he had kept his word and had ceased taunting her, had kept a polite distance from her each time he came to call.

That was what she wanted . . . wasn't it? She had no room in her hectic life for involvement with the mysterious Sebastian Saber. But why did that handsome, midnight-haired fortune hunter keep showing up as regularly as clockwork in her dreams?

Eden wished she had a logical answer to that question.

Sebastian propped himself against the door of the improvised schoolhouse that sat in the central square of slave cabins at Pembrook Plantation. Maggie, the housekeeper, had given Sebastian directions to locate Eden, and to his surprise, he found Eden sitting on the wooden floor, her colorful green skirts in a rippling pool around her. She was reading to the children of slaves who were working in the fields.

Sebastian watched Eden with the children. She definitely had a way about her that made each child feel special, wanted. She used that same technique to lift the spirits, and rebuild the self-esteem, of the injured soldiers.

While Eden read a story to a group of toddlers, the older children were reading aloud to each other from a book that was being passed around the circle.

Each time Sebastian happened by the plantation, he gained more insight into this complex female's character and personality. It never failed to amaze him how many lives Eden touched with her kindness and generosity. It was vividly apparent that the needs and concerns of others were foremost in Eden's mind.

While most plantation owners frowned on teaching slaves and servants to read and write, Eden saw to it that hers received an education. He wondered what motivated her, drove her to add this duty to her many daily good deeds.

When Eden glanced up to see him lounging in the doorway, she called to one of the older children to replace her. Rising, she strode toward Sebastian, gracing him with her characteristically sunny smile.

"Did you come to retrieve your Arabian?" she asked as she stepped outside.

"No, I was visiting with the wounded soldiers and I thought I would stop by to see you before I left."

Eden strolled beneath the canopy of trees that shaded the cabins, and Sebastian fell into step beside her. "I haven't had the chance to thank you for the gifts you brought to James Pike before he left yesterday," she said. "It was exceptionally kind of you to think of him and the other men. And where on earth did you find those unique artificial appendages for the amputees?"

Sebastian shrugged nonchalantly. "I made them."

Eden blinked, stunned. "You did? My gracious, you are a man of many hidden talents!"

"Since your generosity has rubbed off on me, I thought I would do what I could for the men in your care."

Eden peeked up at him through that fan of thick lashes and smiled wryly. "In that case, I suppose I should forgive you that ridiculous bet you made with Micah the day of the fair."

Sebastian would have preferred that Micah kept that shameless bet to himself. "It was a stupid thing to do," he admitted. "Micah was three sheets to the wind when he challenged me to make an impression on you. That was *his* excuse. *I* was sober, so I have only the arrogant side of my nature to blame for rising to his taunts. I hope you realize how much I regret my conduct that day."

"We didn't get off to a good start, did we?"

Sebastian shook his head, and couldn't resist reaching out to trace the delicate line of her jaw. He hadn't dared to touch her in almost two weeks.

To Sebastian's surprise, Eden didn't pull away from his touch. She stared at up him with those luminous blue eyes and he felt himself tumbling into their enthralling depths. He realized, and not for the first time, that offering Eden polite respect, and nothing more, left him feeling empty. Portraying the gentleman she expected him to be was playing hell on his male body.

"I want very much to kiss you," he murmured suddenly, his voice rustling, "but I don't want to spoil this truce between us."

Eden saw the flicker of desire in his eyes, felt the pull of attraction that always niggled her when she was with Sebastian. "I don't think a respectable kiss would ruin our truce," she replied, her voice unsteady.

Sebastian moved a step closer, his arm gliding around her waist. He realized just then that he had never been so cautious with a woman. For the past eleven years, it had never mattered much to him whether he made a good impression on the females who came into and went quickly from his arms. But Eden was different, and he was beginning to understand why her previous beaux were reluctant to annoy her. It seemed a sacrilege to do so, because facing her disappointment seemed unthinkable.

When Sebastian simply stood there, staring intently at her lips, and *not* kissing her, Eden frowned curiously. Twice before, he had taken her in his arms and kissed her breathless. Now, he hesitated.

"Perhaps you should be the one to initiate this kiss," he whispered. "I don't want to overstep my bounds and end up back where we started—with you hating me until the day you die."

Eden laughed lightly. "I was sorely irritated at you when I said that."

"And you had every right to be," he murmured, his sensuous lips only a scant few inches from hers.

Eden felt the familiar tingle of desire spreading through her, along with the warmth of satisfaction that he was allowing her to decide how and when she wanted to be kissed.

Rising up on tiptoe, Eden pressed her lips to his, and felt a hungry desire rising. Eden wanted to affect Sebastian as strongly as he had affected her since the day of the fair.

And suddenly, nothing mattered, except tasting him, holding him, exploring these fascinating sensations that riveted her when she kissed Sebastian—and he kissed her back.

When Sebastian gathered her tightly in his arms, Eden felt the bold evidence of his need, felt his heartbeat pounding against her breasts. Instinctively, she deepened the kiss, aching to be closer, wanting what she had told herself that she shouldn't have. And so she yielded to the sizzling sensations Sebastian so easily stirred in her, longing for just a glimpse of her secret dreams.

For that instant, Eden gave herself up to temptation and forbidden desire, reveling in the pleasures she had never experienced with any other man.

When Eden kissed Sebastian without one ounce of reserve, as if she were starving for the taste of him, desire exploded through him. When she leaned into him, he completely lost himself in her.

And then common sense reared its head to remind Sebastian where he was.

Long before Eden would have broken the kiss, Sebastian set her away from him. "Lord, woman," he rasped. "You are hell on a man's good intentions."

Eden stared up into his ruggedly handsome face, feeling oddly disappointed that he had retreated. Though she knew she was playing with fire, it was becoming increasingly more difficult not to step into the compelling flames.

Spellbound by this growing attraction, Eden lifted her hand to limn the curve of his full lips. She wanted to invite Sebastian to stay for dinner, to spend more time with him, but she didn't dare. She had chosen her course in life, and her interest in this fortune hunter would only complicate matters.

"I must go," Sebastian murmured as he curled his hand around her wandering fingertips. "Five more minutes alone with you and I am liable to take liberties that will have you back to hating me again."

"I don't think I could ever bring myself to hate you again," she told him honestly. "You have proved yourself to be a tender, caring man." She smiled impishly at him. "And I must confess that I was being purposely cruel and spiteful the night I claimed it would be more enjoyable to kiss your horse than to kiss you."

"I'm glad you think so." Chuckling, Sebastian turned and walked away.

The temptation to call him back was strong, but Eden resolutely held her tongue. She knew the children would expect her to return momentarily. If she tarried long, some of the toddlers would come searching for her. It would never do to have the children see her draped in Sebastian's arms, sharing kisses that carried enough steam to brew a sky full of clouds.

After Sebastian strode toward the barn to retrieve his mount, and Eden hiked back into the meeting hall to read to the children, Elizabeth stepped out from behind the tree. When she accidentally happened on the distracted couple, Elizabeth had confirmed what she expected was true. Eden was developing a romantic interest in Sebastian—an interest that looked to be eagerly returned.

Finally, a man had come along to catch Eden's eye. And this time, Elizabeth promised herself, Eden's feeling of responsibility to her younger sister was not going to stand in her way. This time, Eden was going to have the opportunity to enjoy this budding romance. Elizabeth was going to see to that!

"I don't think this is a good idea," Maggie protested for the third time. She watched Eden fasten herself into men's clothes and stuff her chestnut-colored curls inside a tricorn hat. "You should send out some of the men to search for your foolish sister. It's long past dark, and *you* could get into serious trouble, if *she* hasn't already!"

"I'll be fine, Maggie," Eden insisted as she sank down on her cot to pull on her riding boots. She scolded herself for waiting so long to investigate Elizabeth's lengthy absence, but then Eden reminded herself that Bet had made a habit of being away from the plantation a great deal lately. Eden had become accustomed to that and had failed to become alarmed until darkness settled over the countryside.

"Besides, this is my fault," Eden said. "I was too busy with my chores to realize how much time had passed."

"There you go again, accepting the blame for everybody else's actions," Maggie scolded. "If your sister has landed in trouble, then it is her fault, not yours. You are not responsible for everything that foolish girl does wrong."

"Aren't I?" Wide blue eyes transfixed on the housekeeper's disgruntled frown. "I am obligated to protect and care for everyone at this plantation, my sister included. Papa isn't here to provide guidance for a young lady who is standing on the threshold of womanhood." Eden frowned thoughtfully. "I wonder if her disappearance has anything to do with Peter Dalton. His name has been the first word out of her mouth for a month."

"Dear God!" Maggie howled. "You don't think she is gallivanting about unchaperoned with that man, do you? She will ruin her reputation!"

Resolutely, Eden headed toward the staircase.

"When you find Bet, *I* am going to mete out her punishment for a change," Maggie insisted as she scurried at Eden's heels. "I intend to paddle her backside good and hard. You are not going to pat her hand, like you usually do, and share her blame. That sister of yours needs to be taught a stern lesson."

Eden hurried on her way. Punishing Bet was the least of Eden's concerns. Finding Bet before disaster struck was tantamount. Where could she have gotten off to?

A flashback of memory burst through Eden's mind. She recalled the night she had decided to walk home from the fair and heard the nickering horses and hushed voices of the men who had gathered beside the marsh. Eden was sure she had stumbled onto a den of thieves—or at the very least, a troop of reconnoitering Tory scouts who gathered information for British intelligence.

Eden knew that both the Patriots and Tories had networks of spies infiltrating the area that might become a battlefield. These days, it was difficult to tell friend from foe, when covert operations were being conducted by both armies.

And when times were hard, and economy struggled, desperate people resorted to robbery and sold information for the coins needed to line their empty pockets.

Thieves might have apprehended Bet while she was riding in her buggy. British guerrilla bands might have overtaken her . . .

Eden swallowed apprehensively as she swung onto the saddle. She was not going to think the worst, she told herself. There was probably a logical explanation for Bet's lengthy absence. Eden would simply trace Bet's usual steps of visiting friends. Bet was around here somewhere, oblivious to the fact that her family was fretting about her.

Eden touched her heels to the bay gelding's flanks and trotted down the road. Bet may have stayed for supper at Daphne Cunningham's plantation. That would be Eden's first—and hopefully *only*—stop.

When flashes of lightning illuminated the sky, Eden swiveled in the saddle. The murmur of distant thunder pierced the damp night air. She had scads of time before the approaching storm arrived, she assured herself. She and Bet would be enjoying the comforts of their home long before the first raindrop fell.

Despite her optimism, Eden felt an eerie shiver snake down her spine when the wind howled. She had never liked the darkness, but *enclosed* darkness, now that was something else again.

Eden inhaled a steadying breath and bolstered her courage. After seventeen years, she hoped those tormenting memories would have vanished. Instead, they subtly ruled her life. No one had guessed to what extent, until Sebastian Saber came along to question the shield of her sunny smile.

"Don't be a ninny," Eden chastised herself as she quickened her pace. No one knew the truth of what had happened all those years ago—not her father, not Maggie, and especially not Elizabeth. No one would ever know Eden's horrible secret. It was just that Sebastian was a natural-born "prober". His cynicism provoked him to look deeper than most folks bothered to do.

Determined to concentrate on her mission of locating Elizabeth, Eden cast thoughts of Sebastian and her living past, aside. This was not a good night to be out and about, and the sooner Eden returned home with her sister in tow, the better she'd like it!

Eden arrived at Cunningham Keep, heralded by a flash of lightning and the belated rumble of thunder.

"Miss Eden?" The servant staggered back a pace when Eden removed her hat and graced him with her characteristically cheerful smile.

"Good evening, Raymond. A lovely night for a ride, don't you think? So invigorating." She glanced inside the dimly lit vestibule. "Is Daphne here? I need to speak with her."

"Yes, but she is—"

Eden whizzed inside when she heard Daphne's laughter wafting from the parlor. She pulled up short when she realized she had barged into the room that had been re-arranged to accommodate two drop-leaf tables that were surrounded by guests who were studying their hands of cards. Eden nodded politely to the two gentlemen and young ladies in attendance. Curse it, Elizabeth was nowhere to be seen.

With coiled red curls bouncing around her ivory face, Daphne scurried toward Eden. "What are you doing here, dressed like that?" Daphne whispered as she towed Eden back into the hall.

Eden had no time for impertinent questions. "Have you seen Elizabeth?"

"She came by this morning," Daphne revealed. "She wanted me to help her select a new gown in Williamsburg. Something about a celebration she planned to attend this evening. We drove to Bostick's Millinery to pick out a gown. I invited her to join us tonight, but she said she had a previous engagement."

Celebrate? Celebrate what? Bet was showing a streak of independence, what with all these jaunts around the countryside. Although Eden encouraged Bet's autonomous thinking, she obviously had not convinced her younger sister that responsibility was attached to it. Out of consideration, Bet should have let her family know where she was and what she was about.

Damnation, where was Bet? Maggie would tan the girl's hide when Eden hauled her home.

Daphne grinned impishly as she appraised Eden's outlandish attire. "I know you don't give a fig about convention and fashion. I also realize you have used your public declaration of spinsterhood so you can tramp about whenever, and however, you please. But really, Eden, don't you think this is a bit much? A saint in breeches?"

Eden had never been annoyed about being referred to as an angel or saint—until Sebastian Saber mocked her for it. Lately, however, she winced when someone made such references. "I am not a saint, Daphne."

"Of course you aren't," she said with a patronizing smile.

Eden turned toward the door. Thunder grumbled. It had nothing on Eden. She was fast losing her cheerful disposition.

Eden galloped away, mentally clicking off the various invitations she and Bet had received while attending the fair. The Muldorphs were entertaining kinfolk from . . .

Well, wherever. They had asked the Pembrooks to attend. The Gannons were hosting a dinner party to announce the betrothal of their daughter Amelia.

That must be where Bet had gone. Peter Dalton was Gannon's nephew. Bet undoubtedly planned to make herself available for Peter's courtship. The poor girl was in love, and her life had begun to evolve around Peter. Bet mentioned the man of her dreams every other minute.

Man of her dreams. Eden sighed. The man of *Eden's* dreams kept hounding her. Her instantaneous responses to Sebastian's touch had shocked her. His ability to irritate her was disconcerting.

And then he began changing personality right before her eyes. He had gone from bitingly sarcastic to respectfully tender, from mocking to humble, to courteous and unbelievably generous to the men under her care. Sebastian was a chameleon, she decided. She had seen him in so many moods the past month that she wasn't sure which image was the real Sebastian Saber. He was an enigma that constantly drew her thoughts.

"Get out of my mind," Eden muttered as she raced toward Gannon Plantation.

An hour later, Eden reversed direction and swore under her breath. Bet and Peter weren't attending the Gannons' betrothal dinner, and Eden had looked like an idiot perched on the stoop in her outrageous attire. But she couldn't have made this urgent ride with full skirts and petticoats billowing around her, now could she?

Eden gouged her heels into her mount and sawed on the reins, anxious to pursue the lead the Gannons had offered. She rounded the bend of the road that was lined with cypress and black cedars—and found three riders trotting toward her.

"Hold up, boy" came a gruff, authoritative voice.

Eden skidded to a halt when three masked riders blocked her path. To her disbelief, the riders closed in around her to search her person!

"Unhand me!" Eden protested when she was grabbed from three directions at once.

"Why, the boy ain't no bigger than a mite. He couldn't be—"

"We'll search him anyway." The burly man, who appeared to be in charge, groped at the pockets of Eden's topcoat.

Eden yelped when a meaty fist collided with the underside of her breast. She recoiled, only to have the appointed leader jerk her up by the nape of her coat and plunk her down on his lap.

"A woman!" Gerard Lockwood exclaimed, then chuckled. He yanked the hat from her head, allowing a tangle of curls to cascade over her shoulders. "Pembrook . . ." he choked out.

"Let me go," Eden demanded. "I have done nothing to warrant this disrespectful treatment. Now, if you will kindly replace me on my horse—"

"Surely the lady ain't carrying anything we need," one of the men spoke up when Eden squirmed away from Lockwood's groping touch.

"Maybe not, but I'd best search her," he said with another lewd chuckle.

Eden's skin crawled with revulsion when the masked man shoved his hand under the hem of her shirt. Realizing that he intended to molest her—while his companions watched—caused her to stiffen in alarm. There was no time for subtle persuasion, she realized. She would have to fight to save herself!

Her hand snaked out to claw at the mask covering the man's face. When Lockwood roared in fury, Eden smashed her elbow into his soft underbelly and bucked to free herself from his grasp. But Lockwood clamped a painful hold on her, refusing to let her go, and Eden panicked when she realized she was about to be attacked and there was nothing she could do to prevent it!

Five

"Hey, gov'nor! That's no way to treat a lady!"

The booming voice caused Lockwood to twist around in the saddle. He snatched his hands away from Eden and reached for his flintlock.

"I wouldn't if I were you!" came an ominous growl from the man who approached on horseback.

Eden half twisted to appraise the voluminous form of a man swathed in a billowing black cape and dark mask.

Lockwood muttered as he tucked his pistol away. "Let me remind you that I am in charge around here. My orders are to stop suspicious travelers who might be carrying rebel dispatches."

Eden grimaced. If bands of Tories were swarming this area, then the threat of war *was* imminent. Sweet mercy, there was no telling what might have become of poor Bet!

Bold as you please, the cockney-tongued giant reined his horse over to pluck Eden onto his lap. "I've got a sister about the size of this little lady. I wouldn't hold with any man roughing her up, no matter what side of the war I favored. Women aren't spoils of war," he said, his attention fixed on Lockwood. "You'd best remember that."

Eden wondered if her rescuing knight was associated with these thieving Tories. The man seemed to be acquainted with them, and he, too, was wearing a concealing mask. Eden wondered if she would fare better with this gargantuan man, though his comments could have been a ploy to drag her off and molest her himself.

When the threesome rode away, Tully Randolph shifted Eden to a more comfortable position on his lap. "Lady, ye're in dire need of a keeper," he scolded. "You've got a bad habit of thumbing yer nose at possible disaster and roaming around on nights when you'd be safer at hearth and home."

"I agree that I was careless, but citizens should not have to contend with raiders and thieves," she said as she crammed her shirttail into her breeches. "I am indebted to you for showing my captor the error of his ways. I'm sure he will regret his behavior once he has a chance to think about it."

A deep, resounding chuckle vibrated in Tully's chest. "Lady, that rascal knew what he was about. He's not the repentant kind, and you're lucky I happened along." He scooped up Eden and deposited her on her horse. "Point yerself toward home and be quick about getting there. It's dangerous to be out and about at night these days."

Eden had no time to properly thank the man before he thundered off in the same direction the Tory band had taken. Eden contemplated his advice, rejected it, then rode off to find her sister.

Thunder exploded again, and Eden nearly jumped out of her skin. The Lord, it seemed, was trying to tell her something. Unfortunately, she had a flighty horse on her hands and she didn't have time to listen. The gelding shot off at breakneck speed, leaving Eden holding on for dear life!

"Whoa!" Eden practically threw herself backward trying to rein the horse to a halt. Her hat blew off with the wind when the horse took the bit in his teeth and ran hell-for-leather. Eden clamped hold of the animal's neck—and prayed.

Amid the flare of lightning and the crash of thunder,

Eden heard the pounding of another set of hooves in the near distance. Dear God, what now? Another assault?

She glanced back to see a rider racing toward her. His dark cloak caught in the breeze like outstretched bat wings.

Raindrops pattered on the overhanging leaves, and lightning sizzled into the clump of trees. Eden swore she had been struck, for at the same moment, she was jerked off her horse and slammed into yet another masculine body.

This stormy night, she decided, had disaster written all over it!

"Hell and damnation, woman! What is it going to take to make you realize you are not indestructible?" Sebastian scowled down at the dripping-wet female he had hauled off the runaway horse.

For a half hour, Sebastian had been hiding in the cypress thicket, cursing several blue streaks. He had made contact with Gerard Lockwood, before the unidentified rider came barreling down the road, accompanied by lightning and rolling thunder. Sebastian and Tully had taken cover moments before this brainless female ran amuck. Eden, no doubt, was on some saintly quest—regardless of personal danger.

Sebastian couldn't risk having Eden discover his connection to the Tory patrol. And he couldn't leave her in Lockwood's hands—one situation Eden couldn't have smiled her way out of. So Sebastian had done the next best thing. He sent Tully to rescue her. And things would have turned out fine if Eden had reined toward home instead of tearing off on that skittish horse.

Eden marshaled her resolve, vowing not to show fear, though her heart was beating madly. "Good evening, Sebastian. What are you doing here?" she asked as calmly as she could.

"Guarding the idiot angel, it seems." He scowled irritably as he chased down her mount. "What are you doing here? Battling the demons of the night to make Virginia a safer place?"

"If you are going to be snide, then set me back on my horse," she requested.

Raindrops pelted Eden, making her unbound hair cling to her head like a wet mop. Cursing, Sebastian grabbed her horse's reins, jerked his cape over Eden and tucked her protectively beneath his arm. "I ought to throttle you for being out here alone. Now tell me what the sweet loving hell are you doing here?"

"I can't breathe," she wheezed, squirming to remove her head from the suffocating cloak, since closed spaces made her nervous. Eden flipped back the hem of Sebastian's cloak and inhaled fresh air.

As rain poured down on them, and the wind wailed, Sebastian guided his horse toward the glowing lights of the roadside inn. His first order of business was to get this fool of an angel dried off. Then he was going to put a safe distance between them. Having her sprawled on his lap was the kind of temptation that could get him into trouble.

Sebastian reined into the stable to shelter the two horses. Before Eden's head popped up again, Sebastian removed his hat and stuffed it down around her ears to conceal her identity from the groom who swaggered toward them.

"A bad night for traveling, eh, friend?" the groom said as he grabbed both sets of reins.

"A bad night all the way around," Sebastian mumbled. Assured that Eden's long hair was tucked under the hat, Sebastian flung back the cloak to grant Eden breathing space. "See that our horses are brushed and well fed." He tossed the groom a coin. "The lad and I will be staying the night."

"I am not a—"

Sebastian clamped his hand over Eden's mouth. Keeping her tucked under her cloak, he dismounted. As he strode toward the inn, Eden jerked upright, nearly throwing him off balance.

"That's her buggy!"

"Whose buggy?"

"Elizabeth's."

"At least she had the good sense to stop for the night when foreboding weather threatened," Sebastian snapped. "A pity some of Elizabeth's close relatives aren't blessed with the same good sense."

Hurrying Eden along beside him, Sebastian stepped into the inn. "I need two rooms for the night," he said to the proprietor, who was sprawled nonchalantly in his chair.

"Don't have two rooms." The innkeeper gestured a stubby arm toward the tavern room, where travelers—all of the male persuasion—were bedding down on the floor. "I've got a little floor space and one suite upstairs. The price of the suite comes steep."

"I'll pay it," Sebastian said without hesitation. "Send up water for a bath." He tossed several coins on the counter.

While Sebastian waited for the lethargic innkeeper to fetch the key, Eden studied the register. Shock settled on her waterlogged features when she found Peter Dalton's name. Dear Lord in heaven, did this mean what she feared it meant?

"Come along, boy," Sebastian said, grabbing her arm.

"I am not—"

"Keep quiet," he muttered as he propelled her toward the steps.

Eden kept her mouth shut until Sebastian ushered her into the room. "Sebastian, my sister is here with—" She swallowed apprehensively, her mind reeling with the shocking possibilities of what Bet was doing. "Dear God!"

Sebastian shrugged off his wet cloak and hung it over the hook beside the door. "What's wrong with you?"

Before Eden could elaborate, a young lad rapped on the door and scurried inside to fill the tub. Two more young men from the bucket brigade trooped inside. Sebastian placed himself between the boys and Eden, trying to conceal her identity. She didn't seem the least concerned about damaging her reputation. Indeed, she hadn't put up the fuss Sebastian anticipated when he rented the only vacant room—a spacious, well-furnished suite usually rented by traveling dignitaries.

The inn sat beside King's Highway, which extended from Savannah to Charles Town, through Williamsburg and all the way up to Boston. Sebastian knew that for a fact, because he'd been up and down the road more times the past five years than he cared to count. Even so, the path he had followed never had the kind of pitfalls he encountered now. A night spent with Eden Pembrook could be pure heaven—or a slow burn in hell . . .

He felt a tug on his coattail and pivoted to see those beautiful sapphire eyes peering anxiously up at him. Gone was the characteristic smile.

Sebastian stepped back apace. He didn't trust himself too close to this woman. She was entirely too good for him. He had discovered that after he toured her home to find the injured Patriot soldiers under her care. He was trying to remain courteous and respectful, but it wasn't easy when his male body kept reacting to her every time they touched.

"Sebastian, I must find my sister," she whispered urgently. "Every moment I tarry could mean disaster."

When the attendants trooped out, Eden bounded up

and headed toward the door, adjusting the lopsided hat on the way.

Muttering, Sebastian followed the determined saint on crusade. "Damn it, Eden, your sister is safe and she's probably already asleep—"

He slammed his mouth shut when Eden burst through the door at the end of the hall without announcing herself.

"Elizabeth Annabelle Pembrook, have you lost your mind!" Eden cried.

Sebastian closed the door before the trumpeting angel awakened the dead—and all the occupants in the inn. He swallowed a smile when he saw Peter Dalton and Elizabeth sitting arm in arm on the side of the bed.

"How could you do this?" Eden railed in dismay.

Sebastian leaned against the wall and watched in amusement as Peter came to his feet and hoisted Bet up beside him. Sebastian was curious to see if Eden accepted the blame for this interesting development as quickly as she did everything else.

"Where did I go wrong?" Eden whispered.

Sure enough, Eden was prepared to shoulder all responsibility.

"How did you find us?" Peter's refined features flushed with embarrassment as he held Bet protectively to him. His gaze darted over Eden's head to focus on Sebastian who was having difficulty controlling his laughter.

"Never mind how I found you," Eden said. "How are we going to deal with reputations ruined?"

Elizabeth, whose face was splotched with embarrassment, squared her shoulders to face her sister. Inhaling a deep breath, she blurted out, "It is because of you, you know."

Things were worse than Sebastian thought. Not only

did Eden accept responsibility, but Elizabeth was ready to lay the blame at Eden's feet.

"It's true," Bet confirmed. "It took me a long time to realize that I was another responsibility that cluttered your life. You refused a half dozen marriage proposals, all because you felt obliged to see to my raising in Papa's absence. You have sacrificed your own happiness for me for the very last time, Eden. Saints lead far too complicated lives as it is. Therefore, I have removed myself from your endless list of duties."

When Bet paused for breath, Peter wrapped a possessive arm around her, then took up where she left off. "And furthermore, I refused to let my parents marry me off to Cornelia Wickleheimer—"

"Cornelia?" Eden cut in, frowning in surprise.

"She's the daughter of one of my father's associates," Peter grumbled. "But it's Bet I want. I acquired a special bann for a marriage license two days ago. Bet and I are man and wife."

When Eden's knees threatened to fold up like a tent, Sebastian reached out to steady her.

"But, Bet, I have never complained about my responsibilities to you," Eden said shakily.

"Of course you haven't. Angels never do."

"I am not an angel," Eden protested.

Elizabeth gave a sniff that indicated she didn't agree. "You never complain about anything. You just do your good deeds, wearing your cheery smile. That is why it took me so long to become aware of the problem and resolve it."

"But you are my sister. We are family. I care about you," Eden said in a rush. "The solution to what you perceive to be a problem may well be the beginning of more problems." She stared meaningfully at Peter and Bet. "Marriage is a serious commitment."

"The deed is done, Eden," Sebastian put in as he shepherded her toward the door. "I'm sure Peter will care properly for his new bride. We are interrupting."

"But—"

Eden found herself standing in the hall, staring at the closed door before she could voice her objections.

"Go take your bath," Sebastian ordered. "It will make you feel better."

"Will it? I think not."

"I'll fetch some brandy while you're bathing."

Stunned, Eden allowed herself to be ushered back to the room. When Sebastian strode off, Eden stared unseeingly at the tub, listening to thunder crash down on the inn. Instinctively, she walked over to open the drapes, allowing the bright flashes of lightning to illuminate the room.

Eden went through the mechanics of bathing, without realizing half of what she was doing. Her thoughts centered around Elizabeth and Peter. She knew Bet had developed a strong affection for Peter, and he to her. But marriage? Elizabeth could not possibly be prepared for matrimony, much less the honeymoon . . .

Dear Lord, Eden had never explained the facts of life to Bet—not that she herself was an expert on the subject. Indeed, watching the Arabian stallion cover the mares was the extent of Eden's knowledge. Now, Bet was fumbling through her wedding night, totally ignorant and ill prepared. Why, at this very moment . . .

Grabbing a towel, Eden bolted from the tub. She had to speak with Bet, to reassure her.

She was so intent on her obligations that she barely noticed Sebastian sail into the room with two mugs and a bottle of brandy.

Sebastian froze to the spot, staring at the enticing feminine form barely concealed in a towel. His hungry gaze roamed over her flesh, watching water droplets sparkle on her bare shoulders and arms like chips of diamonds. To his astonishment, Eden whizzed past him on her way out the door.

"Where are you going?" he croaked.

"I have to speak to Bet. This is her wedding night. There are things she should know and it is my responsibility to tell her."

Sebastian snagged her arm before she reached the hall. "You're going to explain the birds and bees to your sister, dressed in nothing but a towel?"

Eden blinked, then glanced down at her skimpily clad torso. Her eyes rounded as she clutched the towel to her bosom. Embarrassment stained her neck and flooded up to her eyebrows.

Willfully, she regained her composure, reminding herself that Sebastian had probably seen his share of naked bodies. Besides, this was no time to concern herself with her modesty. Bet needed her . . .

When a thought flashed through her mind, Eden glanced over her shoulder at Sebastian.

A devilish grin quirked his lips as his gaze ran the full length of her barely clad body. "You're risking your reputation by being alone in a room with a man. What do you think gadding around in nothing but a towel will do to it?"

"I have declared myself a spinster," Eden said, as if that solved everything. "It is Bet, and what she is about to do, that is the pressing matter here."

Pressing matter? Sebastian could not have put it better himself.

"Sebastian, I need your help," she said as she snatched the brandy and mugs from his hands and set them aside. "Come on, we haven't much time."

"What in the hell—?"

Sebastian found himself bustled down the hall. Scowling, he wormed out of his jacket and placed it around Eden's shoulders. He wondered if she would regret making a spectacle of herself when she had time to think about it. Actually, he doubted it. This self-sacrificing angel of mercy had no time for trivial details when she was on a crusade.

Eden rapped twice on the door, waited all of one second, then plunged inside. She found Bet and Peter sitting on the edge of the bed again. This time they were kissing.

"Eden, for heaven's sake!" Bet's eyes popped when she noticed Eden was wearing a towel beneath the oversize coat. "What are you doing?"

Heedless of her appearance, Eden motioned Bet to her. "You have to come with me. Right now. This very minute."

"Why?"

"Sebastian and I have something to tell you. It can't wait."

Sebastian blinked. "We do?"

Eden strode over to grab Elizabeth's arm, uprooting her from the bed. "We won't be gone long, and Peter will be here when you get back. Won't you, Peter? We need to speak with you immediately," she told Bet confidentially.

Sebastian could think of absolutely nothing he needed to say to Bet. But he'd learned that deterring Eden from her missions was a waste of time. He would simply stand aside and see this madcap misadventure to its conclusion.

"Anything you have to say to Bet can be said to me," Peter insisted.

Eden deposited Bet in Sebastian's hands, then shoved them both into the hall. She turned to her new brother-in-law. "Do you love her, Peter? Truly love her?"

"Of course I do," he affirmed.

Well, that was a relief, thought Eden. "And do you promise to care for her, to treat her with the respect she deserves?"

"I will," he said without hesitation.

Eden nodded. At least Bet's impulsiveness hadn't led her into heartache. "Very well, then, I bless this marriage. I know you will be kind and understanding with Bet. You are a noble young man who honors the bonds of matrimony. You would do nothing to hurt her, would you?"

"Certainly not."

Outside the door, Sebastian was smiling to himself. Eden was using her tactic of listing the behavior she expected from Peter. She was laying the ground rules to ensure her brother-in-law did exactly what she wanted him to do.

When the door creaked open, Sebastian stepped back. Eden surged down the hall, motioning for Sebastian to bring along the bride. The instant the door was closed, Bet glanced from her skimpily dressed sister to Sebastian, then frowned.

"What is going on here?"

Eden waved away her sister's concern, then gently urged her into the chair. Wheeling around, she peered up at Sebastian. "Tell my sister what to expect this evening. I'm sure you are an expert on the subject. I am too ill informed to be of help."

Sebastian staggered back, as if an unseen fist had clipped him in the jaw. "You want me to—?"

"Explain," Eden requested.

Sebastian peered at the Pembrook sisters, then burst out laughing. He laughed alone. Both women awaited answers. Sebastian actually blushed. He hadn't blushed since he couldn't remember when. Despite all the things he had seen and done in life, he realized he had yet to do it all . . . and he wasn't sure he could do this.

"Eden, I don't think—"

"Would you send Bet to her husband unprepared?" she cut in. "Surely there is something you can say to reassure her. What would you have the maiden in your arms know before the two of you—" She halted, cleared her throat and battled down a blush. "Well, I'm sure you know what I mean."

Sebastian mentally scrambled to organize his thoughts. But damn it. This was not going to be easy!

"Passion isn't something to fear," he said for starters. "It can be very satisfying." So far so good, he thought as he stared at the two women who were hanging on his every word. "But one must begin by letting go, by expressing feelings in a physical way rather than fighting them."

Sebastian felt himself blushing again. "There will be initial pain, but there are some kinds of pain that are worth the pleasure to come." He stared solemnly at Elizabeth. "The most important thing for you to remember is that you and Peter should communicate with each other. What your husband offers to you, he would very much like to see returned."

"What does that mean exactly?" Eden wanted to know.

Leave it to Eden to request specifics, thought Sebastian. Shifting self-consciously, he stared at the toes of his boots. "That means learning to pleasure your husband, showing him how to pleasure you."

"But the Arabian stallion didn't—"

"And that is the difference," he interrupted Eden. "There is a great distinction between animal instinct and passionate affection."

"There is?" Eden asked.

"There is," he confirmed.

"I see." Eden mulled over his words for a moment.

"So the thing is to let your body express what you feel inside. Is that what you are saying?"

Sebastian nodded. "Exactly. Passion isn't a duty, but rather a shared enjoyment between husband and wife." He glanced at Bet. "If you feel something special for Peter, then show him. When he—" Sebastian slammed his mouth shut. There were some things Bet was going to have to learn for herself. "Simply trust him, Bet, and the loving will take care of itself."

Bet rose from the chair and ambled toward the door, her pretty features knitted in a pensive frown. "Thank you, Sebastian. I will strive to be a loving wife." She glanced back, smiling gratefully. "I must admit I was a mite nervous and uncertain, though I hesitated to tell Peter that."

She turned to leave, then stared at her sister. "Eden, I really think you should put on some clothes."

"I will see to it immediately," Eden promised. "I'm sorry for interrupting you and Peter, but I needed to speak with you and I was working on a short clock."

Elizabeth pivoted to stare pointedly at Sebastian, then moved closer so that her words would not be overheard. "I think my sister is very fond of you. I hope that whatever is going on between the two of you will be resolved satisfactorily."

Sebastian's lips twitched, noting that Bet had developed the rudimentary skills of persuasion that Eden wielded so well. "I have no intention of dishonoring your sister, Bet. I only came along to offer her protection while she was searching for you."

Satisfied with his reply, Elizabeth strode toward the door.

When Elizabeth left the room, Eden collapsed on the edge of the bed. "Thank you, Sebastian. I don't know how I would have gotten through that situation without you."

It dawned on Sebastian that Eden had come to trust him, depend on him. He remembered what Micah Bancroft said about Eden's habit of searching out reliable sources for information. He shouldn't be surprised that Eden turned to him for consultation. Hadn't she followed the same procedure when she picked his brain to improve livestock productivity?

"I believe I could use some of that brandy now," she said, propping herself up on the bed. "It has been a very taxing evening."

Sebastian steeled himself against the innocently seductive pose she struck on the bed, and a smile twitched his lips as he handed her a mug. She choked down the first swallow while she stared ponderously at the wall. It was obvious she was still stewing about Bet, unaware that she would also be spending the night with a man. He wondered how long it would take for the realization to dawn on Eden.

It had taken Sebastian all of two seconds.

Eden wheezed to catch her breath when brandy seared her throat like liquid fire. "My gracious, this stuff could rust one's pipes."

"Take another drink," Sebastian instructed. "The first is always the worst. In a few minutes, the whiskey will take effect." He sank down on the chair to sip his drink, then grinned as Eden trustingly followed his advice.

It wasn't long before Eden's rigid shoulders relaxed and her arms sagged against the towel she held to her breasts. His gaze lingered on the creamy swells that rose and fell with each breath she took, then he gave undivided attention to her trim but firmly developed legs.

This lovely angel had a body built for sin.

Sebastian looked away when his male body reacted to

that tantalizing thought. He was not going to take advantage of this situation. He was going to play the gentleman.

"Sebastian?" Eden questioned groggily.

"Yes, Eden?"

"Did you truly mean what you said to Bet? Or were you filling her with false hopes? After watching the Arabian stallion—"

"Your sister will be fine," he insisted. "I could tell that Peter was exceptionally fond of Bet by the way he cradled her possessively to him when we interrupted them."

"I suppose I should have seen this coming," Eden mused aloud. "I was simply too busy to question why Bet was flitting off so often the past two weeks. And I should have acquired the information she needed before she approached the marriage bed."

Sebastian made a neutral sound and sipped his drink.

Unsteadily, Eden leaned over to set the empty mug on the night stand. "Earlier tonight, before you rescued me from my runaway mount—and thank you for that—I encountered a ruffian. He—" Eden grimaced, then determinedly forged ahead. "He grabbed me. It was a most unpleasant encounter. I naturally assumed that lovemaking was like—"

"I can imagine what you assumed." Sebastian gnashed his teeth. He would like to tear off Lockwood's arms for groping at this wide-eyed innocent. Unfortunately, Sebastian had business dealings with that boorish bastard.

"I suppose that was a display of animal lust," she said. "Like the Arabian with the mares."

"Did he hurt you, Eden?" he asked quietly.

"Yes." She shivered repulsively at the thought. "And if that giant of a man hadn't shown up when he did, I shudder to think what might have happened. I swear I will have bruises after he pinched and prodded at me."

Sebastian's hands clenched around the mug, wishing he had Lockwood's neck in his grasp. One day, that scoundrel would pay for his oafish behavior, Sebastian promised himself.

Eden snuggled beneath the quilts, then stared at Sebastian. "I hope Peter is tender and gentle. I wonder if he has your wealth of experience."

"How do you know I do?"

Eden smiled sleepily. "A man whose kisses are as potent as yours could not possibly be a novice."

"Thank you . . . I think," he said, grinning rakishly.

"I pray that Peter won't be the kind of man who marries, then takes a mistress," she murmured drowsily. "I don't want to see Bet hurt." Yawning, Eden curled up on the bed, cradling her head on the pillow. "It disturbs me that a man could marry and still keep a mistress. It seems such a contradiction of loyalty."

"And you can't imagine marrying one man and going to bed with another," Sebastian concluded before he swallowed another sip of brandy, looking anywhere except at the tempting woman who had him throbbing with unappeased desire.

Something flashed in Eden's eyes, and Sebastian was quick to detect the return of those secretive shadows.

"I believe the vows of marriage should be a sacred commitment that aren't discarded when it meets a reckless whim. I couldn't live with myself if I made a mockery of those vows."

"You're a rare breed, angel," he assured her quietly.

Eden frowned. "I do wish you would stop calling me that."

It serves to keep me in my place, he thought to himself.

Or at least he was hoping it would . . .

Sebastian inwardly groaned when his gaze settled instinctively on the delicious feminine scenery on the other side of the room. He wanted Eden so badly he could taste her from here. Curly chestnut hair cascaded over her bare shoulders like a waterfall of flames. The satiny swells of

her breasts teased him from the edge of the towel. Stream-
lined legs were bent and resting at an impossibly seductive
angle.

God, have mercy! He didn't want to sit here discussing
the how-tos and what-fors of passion and marriage. He
wanted to experience them! But he had promised to keep
his distance from her. Hell and damnation, he was really
beginning to hate himself for making that tormenting vow!

Sebastian squirmed restlessly in his chair and guzzled
another drink. The passion prowling through his body was
in direct conflict with his noble intentions. Tormented, he
watched Eden for what seemed hours before her long
lashes finally fluttered against her cheeks and her body
relaxed in sleep.

Sebastian breathed a gusty sigh of relief, then polished
off his drink. If Eden had continued with her unsettling
questions about lovemaking, Sebastian wasn't sure he
wanted to be held accountable for what he did.

When Sebastian ambled over to snuff the lantern, shadows consumed the room. A flash of lightning speared
through the darkness, and he frowned at the opened draperies. What provoked Eden's preference for wide open
spaces? he wondered. He had noticed that every window
at Pembrook Plantation flooded the rooms with light, providing an unhindered view of the outdoors. Draperies were
never drawn, not even at night.

And what was the reason for Eden's baffling need to
constantly rearrange the furniture? he asked himself. The
second time he arrived at her plantation, he noticed the
furniture in every room—including the infirmary—had
been rearranged. And each time he paid Eden a call, the
furniture had been moved again. He wondered which part
of those shadows in this angel's eyes were responsible for
that.

His thoughts evaporated when he pivoted toward the
bed to see silvery beams of lightning spotlighting Eden.

Desire struck hot and hard again. Sebastian marshaled his willpower and peeled off his shirt. He was going to be the honorable gentleman Eden expected him to be. He would share the bed with her—but only to sleep. He could lie beside her without touching her, if he really tried. Hadn't he learned the necessity of self-discipline and restraint these past few years?

Of course he had.

After Sebastian shucked his stockings and breeches, he padded around to the vacant side of the bed. The mattress sagged beneath his weight, and Eden unintentionally rolled toward him. Although she didn't rouse, she squirmed into a more comfortable position beside him. Her bent leg slid over his bare thigh, her arm settled on his chest. He heard her quiet sigh against his neck—and felt torturous desire buffet him with the intensity of a cyclone. If Eden's knee had glided a few inches closer to his hardened length . . .

Sebastian flung aside the thought, gritted his teeth, and battled for control of mind over unruly body. He was *not* going to take advantage. He did *not* deflower virgins. He would burn into a frustrated pile of coals first!

Sebastian started counting sheep—hundreds of them—hoping to distract himself. Nothing helped. He could feel Eden's feminine contours molded to his masculine flesh, feel her breath stirring against his shoulder like a lover's caress. Her fresh, clean scent filled his senses, until every breath he inhaled left him so tormentingly aware of her that he felt like howling in agony.

Hell and damnation! He was lying here, suffering for all the sins he had ever committed, plus a few he would have liked to. He was paying his penance for being such a hardened cynic. Damn it, of all the women in this world, why did he have to get tangled up with this do-gooder saint who shattered every cynical theory he had established about women? Eden Pembrook was obviously his curse, his punishment. Wanting her—and not having her—was his hell on earth.

More sheep, Sebastian told himself resolutely. *Count more sheep, flocks of them.*

Hell's fire, this wasn't working. He would never get to sleep. He needed more brandy—the remainder of the bottle, to be exact. He wasn't going to be able to fade off to sleep, he realized. He was simply going to have to pass out.

Six

Sebastian eased off the bed, then groped toward the table, using the occasional flash of lightning to guide him. Grabbing the bottle, he took three long swallows, and inhaled a deep breath, then tipped up the bottle and drained it dry. He was standing there waiting for the whiskey to take effect when Eden's shriek startled him. He fumbled toward the bed as Eden flung herself sideways. She fell on the floor with a thump.

Her towel was gone, and Sebastian was lost. His all-consuming gaze devoured her shapely form, and desire bubbled forth like molten lava.

When Eden's flailing arm slammed into the bed frame, Sebastian scooped her into his arms. She struck out at him in her attempt to escape the nightmare that had apparently entrapped her.

"Eden, calm down. It's only me." When she tried to launch herself from his arms, Sebastian's knees bumped against the edge of the bed. He sat down much sooner than he intended. "Eden! For God's sake, wake up!"

Her eyes fluttered open. When she recognized Sebastian, she collapsed against his chest, breathing in great gulps. "Sorry, I must have been dreaming."

He could guess the reason for her nightmare. Damn that Gerard Lockwood. The scoundrel was haunting Eden's sleep.

"You're safe now," he assured her. "Try to go back to sleep."

Eden nuzzled against his hair-roughened chest, then realized what she'd done. Sensual awareness sizzled through her.

Sweet mercy, she would have expected the effects of drinking to numb her to these strange tingling sensations Sebastian set off. But every breath she took was thick with Sebastian's masculine scent. There was nothing between them but bare skin.

Eden swallowed audibly, afraid to move for fear of triggering even more of these pulse-jarring sensations. "Sebastian?"

"Yes, Eden?" he said, his voice strained.

"You aren't dressed."

"I know."

"I'm not, either."

"I'm painfully aware of that."

"Remember that definite problem we have when we get too close?" she murmured against the pounding column of his throat.

"I remember it very well."

"I think the problem is back. It's getting worse by the second."

"Much worse," he said unevenly.

"What are we going to do about it?"

"I think," Sebastian said shakily, "there is only one thing left to do."

"I was hoping you had a solution. I've had too much brandy to think straight."

"One of us is going to have to go downstairs and camp out on the floor," he rasped.

She moved restlessly on his lap where she had levered herself and his elbow accidentally grazed the taut peak of her breast. She groaned. So did he.

"Eden?"

"Yes?" Her voice was a breathless whisper, her body a quivering mass of sensations. The effect Sebastian had on her was so potent that she fairly shook with apprehension and anticipation.

"I'm not sure I can make it down the steps," he told her.

"Why not?"

"There's something I neglected to explain during our discussion with Elizabeth. Men suffer a different kind of pain from *not* doing the kind of things that cause a woman initial pain."

"They do?" Her voice rose one octave as she sat perfectly still.

"They do," he confirmed.

His noble intentions were perched on the windowsill, ready to take a flying leap. God, what he wouldn't give for another bottle of brandy and an experienced female right about now!

"Then I should be the one to go downstairs. I would if I had a set of dry clothes."

Tremors of heightened awareness rippled through Eden when Sebastian curled his hand beneath her chin and turned her face to his. "I have a confession to make, Eden. I don't want either of us to leave the room. If you don't want what is about to happen between us, tell me now. Another minute may be too late."

Sebastian held his breath, dying in sensual torment.

"I . . . want . . . you . . . ." she whispered.

When his free hand swirled over her hip to trek across her ribs, then lightly skimmed her nipples, delicious heat streamed through her body. This, she decided, was what Sebastian meant by offering pleasure and having it returned. She reached out to emulate the caresses he bestowed on her, wanting him to experience the same sensations that consumed her.

Sebastian groaned in unholy torment. She was killing

him, inch by inch, touch by touch. He wanted to bury himself within her, to feed this maddening hunger that ate him alive. But damn it, she was an innocent, unaccustomed to quick tumbles in bed.

"Did I hurt you?" Her hands stalled on the hard, flat muscles of his belly. "I didn't mean to. I was only trying to return the pleasure, like you said— Oh, my . . ."

Her breath gushed from her lips when his head dipped downward and his tongue flicked at the aching tips of her breasts. Pulsating waves of need pounded through her, and sweet fires of pleasure channeled through every fiber of her being.

Sebastian had dug himself a fine hole when he had described tender lovemaking to Eden and her sister. Now, because he had taught Eden what to expect, he must deliver, even when his own passions were raging like the thunderstorm outside the inn. He wanted to erase Gerard Lockwood's painful touch from Eden's mind, to kiss away the fear the rascal had caused her. Tonight Eden would know the difference between hurtful gropes and gentle passion. And in the process, Sebastian would discover heaven.

Begin by letting go. Don't fight the feelings. Enjoy them. Sebastian's words echoed through Eden's mind as his moist lips and warm fingertips caressed her sensitized flesh. She swore the skin was melting off her bones, and she could feel herself sinking into a blissful dimension of sensual awareness.

Each time Sebastian treated to her to another feathery caress, her body moved instinctively toward him, feeling his bunched muscles flex, then relax. When she reached out to return each tantalizing caress, Sebastian clutched her roaming hand and drew her down beside him on the bed.

"I thought I was supposed to touch you back, when the

feelings overwhelmed me," she said between ragged breaths.

"Angel, you can touch me all you please—later. But for now, let me show you what lovemaking is all about."

His lips slanted over hers, his darting tongue inflaming her with another fiery burst of need. His hands grazed her nipples, then glided ever so slowly down her belly, inciting phenomenal sensations that dissolved Eden into liquid flame. Her breath caught when his fingertips coasted over the ultrasensitive flesh of her inner thighs.

Eden remembered all too well how Sebastian had made her burn the first time he touched her. She had been shocked that night, unnerved by the wild tremors that assaulted her, afraid of the power Sebastian held over her traitorous body. But her perspective had changed since that first night. She had come to realize that Sebastian could be generous, kind, and wonderfully tender. She entrusted herself to this handsome rake, welcoming the knowledge of passion he could share with her . . . if only for this one moment out of time.

Her senses reeled when his fingertips sought the heated coil of longing that pulsated through her. When he gently guided her thighs farther apart, she yielded to him without protest. When he spread a row of kisses over her collarbone, Eden shuddered uncontrollably. Each touch unveiled another electrifying sensation that superseded the previous one. She could feel herself letting go, reaching toward some elusive and oh-so compelling need that hovered just beyond her grasp.

Sebastian couldn't remember being so completely aware or totally enthralled by any woman. After learning the hard lessons of love eleven years ago, he had never had enough respect for women to concern himself with a woman's needs.

Until now, until Eden. He couldn't take his pleasure at her expense. For all the times he had mocked her, insulted her unfairly, scolded her for frightening him, he would compensate tenfold.

It was going to be pure torture to restrain his ravenous needs, but this was one promise Sebastian vowed to keep. He would teach Eden the meaning of exquisite pleasure. And when the moment of inevitable pain came, she would welcome the ecstasy that would follow shortly thereafter.

His lips brushed the dusky crests of her breasts, and he felt her quiver in helpless reaction. It was unbelievably satisfying to know that he, alone, had claimed Eden, that she was learning to respond to only him.

His hands flowed over her belly to knead her breast, and Eden arched toward him like a stroked kitten. He smiled against her silky flesh as he retraced a languid path toward the moist heat he had summoned from her. She shivered and sighed, and his name tripped from her lips like a soft incantation.

Sebastian had never felt so much a man until he experienced Eden's uninhibited responses. He was utterly beguiled, spellbound. He wanted all of her, and he would have all of her, sharing her sweetest, most intimate secrets, touching the very depths of her soul.

To that dedicated purpose, Sebastian shifted sideways. His lips skimmed over her flat belly, his tongue flicking out to taste her skin, arousing her until she moaned his name in litany. His outspread hand swept downward, cupping her, feeling her silky heat burning his fingertips. He delved deeper, sharing the hot sensations that claimed her, stroking her until tremor after tremor shook her. When he withdrew his fingertip with tormenting deliberateness, Eden all but came apart in his arms.

"Sebastian—?" Her voice shattered with torturous longing.

Although he yearned to learn all her body's delicious secrets by taste and touch, the sound of his name was a hopeless lure. She was hot and aching for him, and he wanted to end her torment as well as his own.

Sebastian guided her thighs apart with his knees and settled himself above her, wrapped her legs around his hips. He felt Eden stiffen he as he took ultimate possession—with more eagerness than tenderness. He instantly regretted his impatience, for the sensations he aroused in her had been overridden by pain.

Eden winced. "I don't think—"

"Don't think, love," he commanded hoarsely. "Relax. I don't want to hurt you."

"It's too late. You already have—" She gasped when he plunged deeper, filling her with an unfamiliar kind of pressure.

"This is the pain I told you about," he gritted out, battling like hell for control. "You're going to have to trust me when I say that it gets better."

Eden tried to relax, but it wasn't easy. He surged toward her again and she tried to smile. "I guess that wasn't so bad. Are we finished now?"

He wanted to laugh—he wanted to scream. He did neither. "No, we aren't finished yet, Eden."

"When then?"

Sebastian braced himself above her and stared down into her lovely face. He was going to make her enjoy the ultimate act of lovemaking, even if it tortured him. And there was a strong possibility that it might. His body was so tightly clenched that he shook with restraint. He couldn't hold back much longer, but he couldn't go over the edge unless Eden was with him all the way.

Gently, he leaned down to take her lips. He arched toward her as his tongue thrust into her mouth. He moved in age-old rhythm, gliding to and fro, caressing her intimately.

He felt Eden relax, felt her arms gliding up his chest to curl over his shoulders. Her tongue fenced with his and

Sebastian groaned as she gave herself up to him, trusting him. He clutched her to him and rode out the tidal waves of pleasure that roiled and surged and pummeled him.

Eden felt the initial pain ebb, replaced by the intense sensations that had consumed her earlier. She felt herself melting around the hard, throbbing length of him, met his driving thrusts. And then, from out of nowhere, that wild tremor that had claimed her earlier unfolded like a flower petal seeking sunlight. Eden dug her nails into the whipcord muscles of Sebastian's back when shudder after shudder of rapture engulfed her. She couldn't breathe! She was dying. Sweet mercy, she never expected passion to be anything like this!

When Sebastian convulsed in helpless reaction, Eden held him to her, reveling in indescribable contentment. But her satisfaction was short-lived, because it dawned on her that she hadn't contributed to their lovemaking. She had selfishly savored the pleasure without generously offering it back. She had failed Sebastian, disappointed him—she was sure of it.

"Sebastian?" she whispered against his muscular chest.

He struggled to draw breath. "Yes, Eden?"

"I didn't touch you. I'm sorry. I forgot."

An unseen smile quirked his lips. "You mean I made you forget?"

"No," she contradicted hurriedly. "I certainly don't fault you for it."

"No, I suppose you wouldn't," he said, strangling on a chuckle. "But if it will make you feel better, you can touch me later."

Her face turned to his, the whites of her eyes glowing in the dim flashes of lightning. "You mean we're going to do this again later? Is that a good idea, do you think?"

Grinning roguishly, he propped himself on his elbows. No wonder he had never found so much pleasure in other women's arms. He had never made love to an angel—an angel who was dismayed that she hadn't fulfilled her share of the responsibility in lovemaking. But Eden had done quite enough, and Sebastian had no complaints whatsoever.

"Of course we will do it again," he said before he dropped a kiss to her lips. "It's very necessary."

"It is?"

"Passions takes practice to be perfected, and you still have a lot to learn," he told her, feigning seriousness.

"I do? Oh, of course I do. You would know about such things, being the expert. I'm sorry I have no experience to contribute. I'm sure I would have been much better if—"

"Eden, you did just fine," he assured her, another smile pursing his lips. "Better than fine, actually. You were splendid."

"Thank you, but I didn't do anything at all—"

His lips slanted over hers and he drank the sweet taste of innocence and sensual generosity that was so much a part of Eden. Sebastian swore he would never forget this night as long as he lived. In Eden's naiveté, she had put him in touch with unrivaled sensations, as if her first time was his first time. He had watched her become a woman in his arms, felt her tremble and burn for him.

And he had discovered there was no fire equal to this angel's passion . . .

The thought caused his body to grow rigid with remembered pleasure. His lips trailed over her shoulder and descended to whisper over the taut buds of her breasts. He could feel himself growing hard inside her, assuring both of them that the passion between them needed constant feeding.

"My gracious," Eden gasped as the strange sensations expanded inside her.

She instantly surrendered as Sebastian surged toward her, then withdrew. She could feel the intimate fires consuming her again, and this time she knew what awaited her. She reached toward the pleasure, letting go with mind, body, and soul, to savor the splendor Sebastian had taught her to crave. She was swept away, moving in perfect rhythm, matching Sebastian's penetrating thrusts, clinging to him while the world careened and spun out of control.

In the aftermath of their lovemaking, Eden groaned in dismay. "Sebastian?"

He didn't have enough energy left to lift his head. Her loving generosity had sapped the last of his strength. "Now what, Eden?"

"I forgot to touch you again. I really am sorry about that."

Sebastian chuckled, realizing he had never been so thoroughly sated—and amused—by a woman. "We'll work on that aspect later."

When Eden snuggled trustingly against him and fell asleep, Sebastian pressed a tender kiss to her brow, closed his eyes, and followed her into blissful dreams. Amazing what sleeping beside an angel did for a man's peace of mind.

Sebastian hadn't slept so soundly in years.

As sunlight blared into the room, Eden came awake with a steady throb in her skull, a queasy feeling in her stomach, and soreness between her legs. She stirred, but the uncomfortable sensations didn't ebb. They grew more pronounced as she moved closer to consciousness. She felt the solid presence beside her, and she cuddled toward the inviting warmth. The manly fragrance that infiltrated her senses triggered fuzzy memories of a night . . .

Eden recoiled when reality hit her between the eyes. Good Lord, she thought, panicky. She opened her eyes to see Sebastian sprawled beside her. Her face blossomed with color.

Sebastian grinned broadly. It had been a long time since he woke up smiling. He usually had too much on his mind, but this morning he was anxious to see how Eden reacted to what they had shared the previous night.

Her face flamed with so much color that Sebastian wondered if she had developed a rash.

"Good morning," she murmured self-consciously.

"So it is." He glanced pointedly at the window. "Someone opened the draperies to invite in the sun long before I would have preferred to rise. Why do you do that?"

Eden inched toward the edge of the bed. "Old habit," she said evasively.

"Old habit prompted by what?"

She shrugged a bare shoulder. "I simply like wide-open spaces.

Who, Eden wondered, was supposed to be the first to rise? The thought of standing up, stark bone naked, unsettled her. Lying in Sebastian's arms in the shadows hadn't been disturbing. But in broad daylight? Now that was something else again.

"Eden, about last night . . ." Sebastian said behind her.

Eden swallowed, cleared her throat, then pulled the sheet protectively around her. What was she supposed to say the morning after the night she surrendered to a secret fantasy that had hounded her since the first time this irresistible rake kissed her?

"Are you sore?" he asked as he reached out to trail his index finger over the curve of her shoulder.

Eden turned all the colors of the rainbow. "Yes, are you?"

Sebastian camouflaged a burst of laughter behind a cough. "Umm . . . no."

"Oh." Eden looked around for her clothes. They were draped over the rack of the commode—a good six feet away. Damn.

"I'll fetch them," he volunteered when he noticed the direction of her gaze.

When he peeled back the quilt and stood up, Eden sucked in a startled breath. Her gaze drifted helplessly over his masculine torso, studying each muscle that flexed and relaxed as he sauntered across the room. She noticed the long scar that curled around his ribs—the one blemish that prevented him from being absolute perfection. When her curious gaze dipped lower, Eden turned a darker shade of crimson.

Sebastian retrieved her clothes, then presented them to her, providing a full frontal view of his masculine anatomy. Eden sat there staring at him like a wide-eyed owl. When she realized she was ogling him, she clutched the sheet around her, snatched the clothes from his hand, and darted toward the dressing screen. Her shoulders sagged when she no longer had to face him. She simply couldn't pretend to be casual when intimacy was so new to her.

"I'm really sorry about all this," Eden apologized as she wormed into her clothes. "I was so concerned about Bet last night that I didn't stop to think. Then I started drinking and I . . . Well, things simply happened."

Sebastian grabbed his breeches and stabbed his leg into the garment. He chuckled quietly to himself as he listened to Eden accept full responsibility for what happened. He wasn't surprised. When had she ever foisted off blame on someone else? Her generous nature refused to allow her to place Sebastian at fault, though he was the one who initiated their lovemaking.

She demanded no marriage proposal to salvage her reputation, he noted. Not Eden Pembrook. She was ready to let bygones be bygones and get on with her busy life. Sebastian wasn't sure why he was just a teensy-weensy annoyed that she expected—and demanded—nothing from him.

Eden emerged from the dressing screen to scoop up

her boots. Her gaze drifted to the telltale signs on the sheet. She groaned when she faced the evidence of what she had done.

Sebastian shifted awkwardly. He wasn't sure what to say, but he wasn't going to apologize for the remarkable pleasure they had shared.

"I think we should go downstairs separately," Eden suggested. "I'll go first."

Drawing herself up to dignified stature, she strode toward the door. She paused to glance back at Sebastian with those luminous sapphire eyes that cut all the way to his soul.

"I never did get to touch you, Sebastian. I think I shall always regret that I didn't. I wanted to do my part, you know. I just didn't know how."

And then she was gone, slipping down the hall like a shadow.

"Married?" Maggie half collapsed in the chair. "What can that girl be thinking! Why would Bet run off and do a fool thing like that?"

Eden swept the crumpled hat from her head and sank down on the settee beside the stunned housekeeper. "She wanted to lighten my load of responsibilities."

Narrowed black eyes zeroed in on Eden. "Bet is blaming you for her impulsiveness?"

"Of course not. She cares deeply for Peter Dalton. I was just the perfect excuse."

"Married . . ." Maggie threw up her hands, then let them drop to her sides. "Where are they going to live?"

"I don't know. It was Bet's wedding night. I didn't have the chance to ask for details."

When Maggie muttered under her breath, Eden patted her hand comfortingly. "I'm sure everything will work out for Bet. She will inform us of her intentions in her own good time. Meanwhile, we have injured patients to tend and chores waiting."

Eden surged to her feet and headed toward the hall. But Maggie's question halted her in her tracks.

"Where did you spend the night, Eden?"

"At the same inn where Bet and Peter stayed." She smiled apologetically. "I'm sorry if you worried over my whereabouts, Maggie. As it turned out, I was so concerned about Bet that I didn't think to send a note home. I was as inconsiderate as she was."

"I did indeed fret over you," Maggie grumbled. "And you are very lucky you didn't meet with trouble, dashing off into the night the way you did."

Oh, Eden had met with plenty of trouble, but she refused to confide that to Maggie. The protective housekeeper would be beside herself.

No one would ever know about Eden's misadventures, unless repercussions arose—and those she would take in her stride, she promised herself.

"Did you lose yer way, yer lordship?" Tully snorted, when Sebastian entered the cabin.

Shrugging off his coat—and Tully's disapproving tone— Sebastian ambled over to the kitchen cabinet. "I was caught in the storm."

"Oh? A storm of whose making, I wonder. And what of the daring Miss Pembrook who nearly got herself molested at Lockwood's hands?"

"She's fine, thanks to you." Sebastian busied himself at the stove. He could use a cup of strong tea—and a little less of Tully's lip.

"And no thanks to you, I'll wager" came the snide rejoinder.

Since Tully was in such a surly mood, Sebastian steered

the conversation in a safer direction. "Have we received any messages?"

Tully straddled a chair backward and propped up his bulging arms. "A dispatch arrived early this morning. Cornwallis and his Regulars are on their way to Petersburg to join Benedict Arnold." He cast Sebastian a disgruntled glance. "Since you weren't here, I contacted the agent and had the news forwarded to Tarleton."

Again, Sebastian overlooked Tully's goading remark. "The Rebel Army is going to find itself overpowered, just as it was in the South, if the rebel soldiers are unable to gain French naval assistance."

"The Patriots have been at a disadvantage since the beginning of the war. This could be the end of the road for all parties concerned. I for one am anxious to see it done. Some of us are going to have other obligations to fulfill very soon."

"Meaning?" Sebastian turned from the stove to his longtime friend.

"Meaning Miss Pembrook," he said point-blank. "And don't bother denying the truth. You weren't sleeping on the floor at the inn with the other stranded travelers."

"How do you know that?" Sebastian questioned in surprise as he poured himself his special blend of tea.

"Because I was sleeping on the floor of the inn. The proprietor told me a man and a *boy* rented the last upstairs suite. And *that,*" Tully added sourly, "was not part of our mission in Williamsburg. You, yer lordship, just joined the lowly ranks of our rutting friend Lockwood!"

Having said his piece, Tully got up and stormed outside. Sebastian sipped his tea, staring at the closed door. He had known he would catch hell from Tully who, after encountering Saint Eden, had instantly become her gallant knight. But it wasn't Tully's condemning comments that disturbed Sebastian. It was Eden's quietly uttered words that got to him.

I didn't get to touch you. I think I will always regret that . . .

She had sounded so final. God, he still wanted her, more than before. But like Eden, he was a realist. He knew their midnight tryst was a chance out of time, a whimsical fantasy come true.

He was a man on a secret mission, destined to go where his assignment took him. But he wasn't going to forget that magical night he had spent with Eden.

He wasn't even going to try.

Seven

When Micah Bancroft arrived at Pembrook Plantation early Sunday morning, Eden and her wounded patients were waiting for him. Eden insisted that everyone who was able to travel to Bruton Parish for the church social was going to go. Six young soldiers—some with arms in slings, others on crutches—piled into Micah's coach.

Although Micah had visions of spending the day with Eden, he shrugged, saying saints would be saints and that he had always known she served a higher purpose.

With the church social in full swing, Eden stood aside, watching the soldiers' faces alight with the pleasure of seeing giggling children bound across the lawn and gaily adorned young ladies casting coy smiles. The event was good for her patients, who had spent too many days confined to rooms teeming with other injured men.

Although Eden rearranged the furniture every few days to relieve the men's monotony, and appease her own private need for constant change, this social gathering accomplished what her daily visits and rearranged furniture could not. Here, the men could see what they had been fighting for—the chance to pursue happiness, the freedom of choice, a life unburdened by England's high-handed decrees.

The night she spent in Sebastian's arms was a dream

come and gone. Eden needed to be here to remind her of her true calling in life.

"Eden, look who has graced us with their presence," Daphne Cunningham chortled, drawing Eden from her pensive musings.

Eden glanced sideways to see Bet and Peter climbing down from their carriage. Bet looked the happy bride and Peter the attentive groom.

"Those two really set the community back on its heels," Daphne said. "I should have known by the way they were making sheep eyes at each other at the fair that something was brewing. Isn't love grand?

"I cast Sebastian Saber dozens of interest glances at the fair, but he paid me little mind," Daphne added. "I even invited him and Micah to my card party, but Micah said his cousin had left. Have you seen Sebastian since the fair?"

Eden smiled. "Not lately."

"If you learn where he's staying, let me know," Daphne insisted.

Eden waited for the crowd of well-wishers to scatter before she approached Bet and Peter. The instant Bet and Eden were alone, Bet's smile faltered.

"Eden, you have got to do something!"

"What's wrong?" Eden asked in alarm. "Are you and Peter already having problems?"

"We are wonderful," Bet assured her. "It's Angus and Catherine Dalton who are causing problems. They are threatening to have our marriage dissolved. Angus still wants Peter to marry Edwin Wickleheimer's daughter to promote their merchant business. Angus refused to allow us to live in their home until we can find a suitable cottage. We have been staying at the inn, but it's draining Peter's savings. Eden, what am I going to do? I have made a terrible mess of everything, and my in-laws despise me because the Pembrooks are strong supporters of the rebellion!"

Eden gave her sister a consoling hug and a cheery smile. "I'll speak to the Daltons on your behalf. I know they have tried to remain neutral to attract business from rebel and Tory supporters in the area, but they need to understand that you and Peter have made your choices. In the meantime, you and Peter will come to live with us."

"No," Bet objected. "The whole point of my marriage was to relieve you of one of your responsibilities so you could pursue your interest in Sebastian. I know you are taken with him, because I have seen the two of you—"

"The whole point?" Eden cut in quickly, steering the conversation away from her relationship with Sebastian. "You didn't marry Peter because you loved him?"

"Well, of course I did, but—"

"And you wanted to be with him, didn't you? To care for him, to encourage and support him in all his endeavors."

"Well, naturally—"

"And you knew that because of the war a long engagement might mean months of separation when the future is uncertain."

"Actually, I never really thought—"

"Of course you did," Eden assured her sister. "I am quite certain that thought was in the back of your mind, driving you to make the most of the moment."

"Well, maybe the thought did enter my mind," Bet said, more to herself than to her persuasive sister.

"And I shall be sure to bring up your logic when I speak to Peter's parents. Now don't fret about a thing. You and Peter will come home and that is the end of it. Maggie will be delighted. She was—"

"Furious?" Bet ventured, daring Eden to deny it.

"I think stunned would be more accurate," Eden said smoothly. "She will be thrilled to have you home. Why, just this morning she was saying how much she missed you."

"I doubt that. Maggie thinks I'm a spoiled brat, because I haven't done enough to assist you with all your good deeds and endless chores."

"Nonsense. You know how Maggie likes to fuss at both of us." Eden clasped her hands on Bet's shoulders and turned her around. "Now, enjoy the church social and tell Peter not to worry about a thing. His family will soon realize the two of you were meant for each other. I will see to it that they do."

"Eden, you're a veritable saint, and I don't know what I'd do without you." Her spirits rejuvenated, Bet swept off to rejoin her husband.

"I do wish people would stop calling me a saint," Eden muttered to herself.

Her friends wouldn't think of her as a saint, but rather a soothsayer of doom, once she worked up the nerve to relay the information Daniel Johnston had delivered to her the previous day. Eden had waited as long as she dared to announce the approach of the British army. But she wasn't saying anything to anybody until after Micah loaded up the wounded soldiers and drove them home.

And sure enough, the news put a damper on the last few minutes of the church social. Eden, however, finished with a rousing oratory on patriotism, reminding the good citizens of Virginia of the wounded soldiers who had fought for their families' freedom, then calling for provisions and moral support. To Eden's relief, the church social evolved into a rally that inspired contributions of food and supplies for the Rebel Army.

Now that Eden had notified her fellow countrymen of possible British invasion, her next order of business was to convince the Daltons that love was a far better reason for marriage than a mere business merger. She wondered if Angus Dalton would understand, since it was hardly a secret that he had married Catherine for wealth and position in society, and that he kept a mistress in Williamsburg.

According to rumor, Catherine Dalton found consolation in the arms of other men. Neither Angus nor Catherine appeared to advocate loving marriages.

Eden would simply have to find the right words to convince the Daltons that love wasn't such a bad bargain.

Eden glanced skyward. She could use a little divine inspiration for this one!

When Eden returned from the church social to check on the soldiers who hadn't been able to attend, she was stunned to find Sebastian visiting with her patients. It was the first time she had seen him since the night of the storm a week earlier. Summoning her composure, she pasted on a smile and sallied forth.

"I wish all of you could have joined us this afternoon," she said to her patients. "But for those of you who weren't up to the outing, I brought some refreshments and gifts from your appreciative supporters who send their warmest wishes."

Eden paused to nod slightly to Sebastian, who appeared to be a damned sight better at pretending nothing had happened between them. He seemed calm and nonchalant, while she felt as if butterflies were rioting in her stomach. Her hands shook faintly as she placed home-crafted gifts and pastries on her patients' laps.

"Everyone at the church function asked me to convey their deepest gratitude for supporting the Patriot cause," Eden said as she made her rounds.

Sebastian lounged in his chair, watching Eden deliver her treats and gifts. It was difficult to mask the pleasure of seeing her again, difficult not to react to the memories of the night he had spent in her arms. Sebastian knew she'd had a staggering effect on him, but he hadn't realized how lasting that effect would be, or how much he had missed seeing her until she walked into the room.

He shifted in his chair, battling the warm throb of desire that rippled through him. Damnation, here he sat, savoring the sight of Eden in her bright pink gown, wanting her all over again. He was beginning to think there *was* some mystical quality about this woman, even if she did have secrets lurking behind her sunny smile.

After Eden passed out her gifts, Sebastian followed her down the hall. "Where do you sleep now that you have opened your home to the wounded soldiers?" he asked curiously.

Eden gestured toward the storage closet that contained a wide-open window.

Sebastian did a double take. A prison cell offered more space. "In the *closet?*"

"Our soldiers have bedded down in worse places," she maintained. "This is a small sacrifice, don't you think?"

"It is a small *room,*" Sebastian corrected. If he had any visions of rediscovering the pleasure he had shared with Eden that stormy night, they vanished immediately. There was no privacy to be had in this house.

"I'm not complaining about the arrangements," she said as she continued on her way.

"You wouldn't," he muttered to himself.

"With our home filled to capacity, I'm not certain what to do with Bet and Peter when they arrive."

"Arrive?" he repeated as he watched Eden all but float down the staircase.

Eden glanced over her shoulder, then clamped down on the arousing effect this handsome rogue was having on her. He looked good. He smelled wonderful. He . . .

Control yourself, Edeline Renee. You sound like a lovestruck idiot!

"Peter's parents objected to the elopement," she explained, forcing herself to concentrate on the topic of conversation rather than dwelling on the sensual effect Sebastian had on her. "Angus and Catherine Dalton want to end the marriage so their only son can wed the daughter of another prosperous Williamsburg merchant who has also catered to Patriots and Tories alike. Peter's union with one of the daughters of the militia commander has the Daltons up in arms."

"Financial gain is more important to some people than happiness," Sebastian said on a bitter note.

Eden studied him astutely, wondering at the source of irritation she heard in his voice. "The Daltons married for wealth and connections and intend to arrange a union that will benefit both families. They have refused to allow Peter and Bet to live with them until the newlyweds can find a suitable cottage."

"And naturally, the benevolent angel spread her wings and welcomed the prodigal sheep back to the flock."

"Naturally. Bet is my sister."

"And your generosity knows no limits."

"What would you have me do, Sebastian? Turn them out on the street?"

"You could let Bet and Peter handle their problems," he suggested. "How do you expect them to become independent if you let them run to you each time they stumble over one of life's pitfalls?"

"In this instance, I have already offered the invitation. Bet and Peter will arrive first thing in the morning. I volunteered to speak with Angus and Catherine tomorrow night. Hopefully, I can persuade the Daltons that marrying for love is far more noble than wedding for financial profit."

Sebastian chuckled sardonically. "You are forever the idealist, always rushing off to defuse volatile situations. But I warn you that more hearts are ruled by money rather than love."

Her chin snapped up. Eden was no longer smiling indulgently. "And you are forever the cynic, aren't you? However, some skeptics can be persuaded to believe that goodness and love are far better rewards than monetary gain."

"Are you trying to convert me to your noble ideals, angel?" he teased her.

Eden appraised him for a ponderous moment. "Just what kind of ideals do you have, and where do your loyalties lie? For all the things I have come to know about you—" Eden blushed profusely, then plowed ever onward. "I don't really know you at all. Micah Bancroft tells me that you are his long-lost cousin. I find it odd that you have just appeared to renew broken kinships."

"And you are striving to establish a new kinship with the newlyweds and the disgruntled in-laws," Sebastian countered. "Where are you going to stash the bride and groom? In an extra closet?"

Though Sebastian had evaded the questions about his background, Eden set aside her curiosity. She did indeed have a dilemma to resolve—and quickly.

"Come along, Eden. I would rather help you find the space to accommodate your ever-growing family than debate my honorable virtues, or lack of them."

Eden scurried to keep up with Sebastian's long strides. He paused at the door of every room on the ground floor, carefully appraising each one.

"The ballroom has definite possibilities," he said, gesturing toward the spacious area that was flooded with sunlight. "This would make a perfect location. It offers privacy and space.

"Move the settee and end tables to the north corner and arrange the furniture like a drawing room. Leave the space at the south end for a bed, dressers, and wardrobe. The bed will be far enough away from the entrance to prevent passersby from—" He paused, then grinned wryly. "I think you get my meaning."

Eden blushed beneath the intensity of his rakish smile, knowing why the bed shouldn't be placed near the doorway. Flustered, she peered at the room instead of Sebastian. "I . . . um . . . see your point."

Eden pulled up her sleeves, then began carrying the end tables to the north side of the room.

Sebastian gaped at her in astonishment. "What the hell are you doing?"

"Following your suggestion and moving furniture," she threw over her shoulder. "Before Bet and Peter arrive I want to have their room prepared. I want them to think we are looking forward to having them in our home and that it was no inconvenience to make a place for them."

Sebastian sighed, then reminded himself that Eden never expected anyone to do what she wasn't prepared to do herself. While her servants delivered daily rations of care packages to neighbors, Eden proceeded with her projects without waiting for reinforcements to arrive. And, although most individuals expected to be given credit for efforts made in behalf of family and friends, Eden downplayed her good deeds. She truly was one of the most generous, kind-hearted individuals Sebatian had ever met, and she had gone a long way in restoring his faith in the female gender.

When Eden tried to drag the heavy settee by herself, Sebastian hurried over to lift the opposite end. He knew Eden was accustomed to moving furniture. He just hadn't realized that she actually moved it all by herself! And why, he wondered, did she rearrange things so often?

The question reminded him of the comment Micah had made about Eden outgrowing her ex-fiancés. Frowning, Sebastian pondered her fetish about leaving draperies wide open. What motivated her? he wondered. Did this need for constant change, and open spaces have something to do with the shadows he had seen in her eyes when troubled thoughts bombarded her?

"And now for the bed and dresser," Eden announced, her customary enthusiasm bubbling at full capacity. "I think you're right, Sebastian. This will make a practical but luxurious suite for the newlyweds. I will move Bet's belongings down from her niche in the attic and we will have a grand homecoming!"

When Eden whirled around and scuttled off to gather more furniture, Sebastian shook his head in disbelief. The dignified members of Virginia aristocracy would be horrified to see Eden behaving like a common servant, especially at this time of night, when most of the gentry were lounging in their parlors, or amusing themselves in coffeehouses and pubs.

Eden was the personification of energy and industriousness. And though her shapely derrière would be dragging when the newlyweds arrived, they would never know how much effort Eden had expended on their behalf. She was, as Micah claimed, in a class by herself.

Sebastian went in search of Eden. By the time he caught up with her, she was yanking drawers from the walnut dresser in the attic. While she lugged the drawers downstairs, Sebastian reversed direction to summon assistance. Several wounded soldiers volunteered to move the furniture down two flights of steps.

Eden stumbled to a halt when she saw the troop of men carrying furniture. "You shouldn't be taxing yourselves," she protested. "You are supposed to be resting in bed."

"For you, angel, I would carry this wardrobe all the way to Williamsburg," Henry Maynard assured her.

The rest of the wounded army seconded the notion.

Eden stood aside as the men, led by Sebastian, hauled the furniture to the new honeymoon suite. In less than an hour, the bed stood near the south wall and the beautifully

crafted furniture was arranged according to Eden's specifications.

"You were absolutely right, Sebastian. This makes a
grand honeymoon suite," she said, appraising the room.

Sebastian stared at the delicate lace bedspread, envisioning someone other than the bride and groom using the
accommodations. "I think Bet and Peter will be pleased.
Who wouldn't be?"

"Oh, dear!" Eden stared at him in concern. "You must
have had a reason for stopping by this evening. I was so
preoccupied that I forgot to ask. What was it you wanted,
Sebastian?"

You. He smothered the erotic thought. "I came to fetch
my stallion. I have obligations elsewhere, and so does the
Arabian."

Eden's spirits dropped several notches. Sebastian was
leaving. She had prepared herself for the possibility, but
she hadn't expected to feel such a strong twinge of disappointment.

"Let me pay you for the Arabian's services."

When she lurched around to retrieve her purse, he
grabbed her arm to detain her. "I don't want your money."

Eden stiffened. If he was implying that the night they
spent together was payment she would clobber him!
"Nonetheless, you will be paid your due," she insisted.

"No, this is yet another example of how your generosity
has rubbed off on me. As you said, monetary profit should
not always be a man's primary motive."

When he smiled that devastating smile, Eden had
trouble faulting him for much of anything. She had come
to feel a strong attachment for Sebastian—too strong for
her own good, it seemed.

It hurt to know she cared so much for a man who didn't
equally return her affection. She didn't expect anything
from this handsome adventurer—refused to let herself expect anything except the pleasure of the moment.

"Good-bye, Eden," Sebastian murmured, lifting her hand to his lips.

Eden knew she should have bid Sebastian farewell on the front steps, but impulse prompted her to follow him out into the darkness. In silence, she watched him walk into the pasture where the Arabian grazed with the mares.

She was going to let Sebastian go without stipulation, Eden told herself. But ah, if only there was time enough to return all the wondrous pleasure he had given her. If only . . .

Have you taken leave of your senses? Eden admonished herself. What she and Sebastian shared was gone like the storm that had rolled across the countryside. She was never going to have the chance to explore the muscled contours and hair-roughened planes of his magnificent body . . .

Stop that, you ninny! Eden gave herself a mental shake, appalled at her wanton thoughts. She couldn't seem to look at Sebastian without wanting him. Had she no shame left?

It was a good thing that Sebastian was walking out of her life, she told herself. There was no telling what might become of her noble intentions if he stayed.

Sebastian's sharp whistle brought the Arabian's head up, but the stallion was content where he was. Sebastian knew the feeling. He was in no hurry to leave Pembrook Plantation. When he called to the horse again, the Arabian tossed his head and glanced at the mares surrounding him.

"The Arabian seems to have a contrary streak," Eden noted.

"He's with his harem," Sebastian said as he grabbed the lead rope and then opened the pasture gate. "The Arabian isn't one to take his duties lightly."

Sebastian walked up to the mare the Arabian had been favoring and led her toward the gate.

Eden stared admiringly as the magnificent stallion circled the pasture, racing against the last crimson and gold rays of sunset. When the Arabian trotted up to check on the mare, Sebastian grabbed the halter and tied the lead rope in place.

"This sorrel mare is the Arabian's downfall. She means more to him than his freedom."

"Only for the moment," Eden amended. "There will be other mares in greener pastures that will draw his attention. Life, after all, is a series of phases through which we pass. What seems essential today may only be a fleeting memory tomorrow."

Sebastian clenched his teeth, annoyed by Eden's casual acceptance of change. True, Sebastian had done his share of walking away without looking back, but he couldn't walk away from Eden with that same kind of indifference.

And in Sebastian's opinion, Eden seemed eager to close this chapter of her life. The thought pricked his male pride. He felt as if he had just been categorized with Eden's former fiancés.

"This is how it was with the others, isn't it?" he questioned as he led the stallion through the gate.

Eden frowned, bemused. "What are you talking about?"

Sebastian tethered the Arabian, then pivoted to confront Eden. "Your seven ex-fiancés. Once you acquired all the knowledge they could offer, you convinced them that they would be better off without you. Then you sought a new diversion."

Eden gasped. "You make me sound like a scheming shrew!"

"Not a shrew," he clarified. "A shrewd saint who subtly convinces her jilted suitors that it was their idea to call it quits. Your comments about the Arabian are your way of telling me that what we shared was just another phase you have passed through."

Eden clenched her fists in the folds of her gown, forcing herself not to take a swing at Sebastian. "May I remind you that you are the one who is leaving, and by your own choice. I've made no attempt to hold you, because that is not what you want."

"Or is it that you have outgrown the need for my company?"

Her gaze locked with his as the faint rays of twilight dissolved into shifting shadows. He was very wrong. He was the one man she didn't know how to handle effectively. He was the one man who stirred her, aroused her, even when he irritated her.

Saying good-bye to Sebastian was killing her by inches. She longed for one last kiss before he left, one last taste and touch before he walked out of her life.

Despite what he seemed to think, nothing was the same as it had been with the stuffy dandies who bored her with their predictability. She couldn't seem to get enough of Sebastian. And damn it, she didn't want him to leave! She wanted to be selfish and hold on to Sebastian, because he had come to mean more to her than she had ever imagined possible.

"Oh, to hell with it," Sebastian muttered to himself as he took a step closer. He wanted to hold her just once more before he left, and that's exactly what he was going to do.

So what if this lovely little elf had outgrown him, as she had all the others. But she was *not* going to forget her first lover!

When he took Eden in his arms, his body reacted as it always had—explosively, instantaneously. The burning memory of their night together was enough to send Sebastian up in flames.

When Eden's arms curled around his neck, and she pushed up on tiptoe to accept his kiss, desire pounded through his blood.

"I need to be alone with you," he rasped when he came up for air. "Where can we go?"

Eden pointed a trembling finger toward the back of the mansion. "The garden. We'll have privacy there."

He grabbed her hand and strode off, zigzagging around the shrubs and magnolia trees. Sebastian paused beside the wooden bench and hurriedly peeled off his jacket. The garment wasn't a soft pallet, but it was the best to be had.

Eden's bubbling laughter skipped through the garden. "On the ground, Sebastian?"

It suddenly struck Sebastian that a pallet on the grass was the ideal place to make love to Eden—because it was a *change* from the bed where they had first made love.

He took her hand, drawing her down beside him. His hands didn't still for a moment as he mapped the shapely curves and swells of her body.

"I want you to know that I'm leaving here tonight because I have to, not because I want to. If not for other obligations, I—"

Her forefinger brushed his lips, shushing him. "It's all right. You don't have to explain. All that matters is . . ." Eden peered into his shadowed face, suddenly aware of why this one man was capable of triggering so many emotions inside her, why she was so vulnerable to him, so vividly aware of everything he said and did. He had touched her in some elemental way that breathed life into her heart and soul. "All that matters is that I love you . . ."

Sebastian had heard those three little words whispered

a dozen times, but never with such sincerity and conviction as Eden said them. She did care, he realized, awed
and humbled. *More* than cared. She really didn't want
him to leave.

Groaning, Sebastian clutched Eden to him, savoring
the taste and feel of heaven on earth. But when he tried
to caress her, she stilled his roaming hands.

"I want to touch you, to return the pleasure you gave
me."

It took all the self-control Sebastian could muster to lie
there while Eden unbuttoned his shirt, then trekked her
fingertips across his hair-roughened chest. He felt his
muscles contract, then dissolve beneath the gentleness of
her untutored touch. When her lips skimmed his skin
and her tongue flicked at his male nipples, he asked himself how much of this sweet, arousing torment he could
endure before savage need overwhelmed him. She had
only just begun to explore the contours of his body and
he was already throbbing with need.

As she caressed him, Eden became enthralled by the
power she seemed to hold over him. She could feel his
accelerated heartbeat, hear his quick intake of breath.
She wanted to learn how and where he liked to be
touched, to make him burn as she had burned beneath
his masterful caresses.

When her hand glided along the band of his breeches,
she felt the hard muscles of his belly clench, heard him
hiss a breath through his teeth. Fascinated, she bent to
trace a path of kisses over his skin, savoring the taste and
scent of him.

"Eden?" Sebastian moaned when her hand swept over
the fabric of his breeches, tracing his hard length. "This
will not do."

"Am I doing something wrong?"

"No, you're doing everything superbly, but—" His

voice dried up when her hand dipped beneath his waist-band and she enfolded him in her fingertips.

"But what, Sebastian?"

Eden opened the placket of his breeches to glide the tip of her tongue over his satiny tip, stroking him, plea-suring him, driving him mad with wanting.

"You're killing me," Sebastian groaned as his body arched instinctively toward her hands and lips.

"Am I?" She smiled as she nipped his sensitive flesh.

When she took him into her mouth and gently suckled, fire raced through him. Sebastian could barely breathe beneath the onslaught of riveting sensations.

"Come here. I need you," he said in desperation.

Urgently, he drew her on top of him, pushing away the barrier of skirts and petticoats, aching to burying himself inside her and hold on to her before the world went up in flames.

"Aren't we going about this backward?" Eden asked. Her breath hitched as his hand glided up her thigh, strok-ing her, arousing her. "I . . . thought you were supposed to be up here."

Knowing Eden's penchant for change, Sebastian had no intention of loving her the same way twice. He shud-dered at the thought of Eden becoming bored with his intimate techniques.

"There are dozens of ways to do this—"

When her silky body brushed against his aching length, all thought whirled off in the evening breeze. He curled his hands around her hips, lifting her exactly to him, sinking into her as she sank onto him.

A wild rush of pleasure surged through Eden as Se-bastian taught her to move with him in perfect rhythm. Her senses reeled, and her body splintered into one in-effable sensation after another. She could feel herself coming uncoiled like a clock spring as the heat of passion blazed higher and higher.

Intense heat boiled inside her. And then it came, that helpless feeling of falling through time and space. Waves of splendor buffeted her and Eden clung tightly to Sebastian, not able to let go, because of the desperate need to hold on to him.

As ecstasy tumbled over her, Eden felt a deep affection whispering through her heart and murmuring in her soul. She felt far more than a fierce physical reaction to Sebastian. When she was in his arms, torments of her past faded like shadows absorbed by sunlight. This was most definitely love, Eden diagnosed. This was what had been lacking in her life.

In the aftermath of passion, Eden nuzzled against Sebastian's chest. She wondered how long love lasted. Nothing remained the same forever. Time changed everything. So didn't it naturally follow that love changed with the passage of time?

Eden rested her chin on her folded hands and stared down into Sebastian's face. She truly did love this man, but he was going away. So why delve into questions that needed no answers. She must simply enjoy this moment while it lasted, because tomorrow would bring drastic change.

"What are you thinking?" Sebastian whispered.

Eden smiled. "I'm thinking how incomplete my life would've been if I had never met you."

For the first time in five years Sebastian cursed the double life he had chosen to lead. He wanted to ask Eden to come with him, to turn his back on his obligations, but he knew he couldn't do that. Nor could she walk away from her responsibilities.

Damnation, Sebastian thought as he eased away to

gather his clothes. He wanted to stay—he had to go. He wanted to take Eden with him—he couldn't.

Heaven and hell in one.

Eden rearranged her gown and rose to her feet. Silently, she watched Sebastian fasten his breeches and shirt. "If you ever happen by this way again . . ." Her voice trailed off when he stared at her with those silvery eyes that glowed like starlight. God, letting him go hurt worse than she dreamed possible!

"I'll be back," he assured her.

"When, Sebastian?"

He framed her face in his hands and tilted her head to his kiss. "I wish I could say for certain," he murmured before his lips brushed hers in the tenderest whisper of a kiss. "Will you be waiting for me?"

"Yes, because I love you."

Sebastian stared into her expressive eyes, aching to the depths of his soul. "Do you love me enough to wait forever, if that's how long it takes?"

Why was he tormenting her like this? She had said words to him that she had said to no other man. Did he want to add her name to his chain of broken hearts?

"I believe I could have loved you long and well," she admitted.

"At least remember me, Eden," he whispered. "Remember what we might have had if things were different." He smiled faintly as he peered at her. "I swear, each time I glance at the morning sky, I will remember these glorious angel eyes."

Eden's heart twisted in her chest when Sebastian walked away. At least she had these precious memories, she consoled herself. She had discovered what her own parents never had, and now she understood what her sister and Peter Dalton shared.

The thought strengthened Eden's resolve. She would

see that Bet and Peter lived out their dream, even if Bet's stiff-necked in-laws opposed the marriage. If Eden couldn't enjoy her own secret fantasy, she would ensure her sister did. Eden was going to give Elizabeth the chance to find out if love could endure forever. That, Eden decided, was going to be her next crusade.

Eight

Gerard Lockwood rapped at the cottage door. He and his companions had set a hectic pace to deliver the dispatch to the Tory sympathizer who deciphered and relayed messages through the network of secret agents in Virginia.

"Come in, gentlemen." Thaddeus Saber stepped aside to let his guests pass. "The coffee is simmering on the stove."

Gerard lumbered inside and plopped down at the table. His squint-eyed gaze darted to the closed bedroom door. "I don't suppose your grandnephew is around."

Thaddeus hobbled over to retrieve four mugs from the cabinet. "Afraid not. He is tending to some business at the moment."

"Then you will have to deliver his new orders to him," Gerard insisted.

Thaddeus studied the disgruntled expression on Gerard's coarse features. "What is brewing in Virginia besides my coffee?"

"Something big, old man, something very big, but I should have been in charge of this new operation because—" He broke off in a scowl.

"Something big has already occurred," Thaddeus said. "Lieutenant Colonel Banastre Tarleton almost pulled off the capture that would have left the Patriots in a frenzy."

The comment brought a faint smile to Gerard's puckered expression. "Indeed, if one of those rebel spies hadn't overheard our plans at the crossroads inn near Charlottesville, and rode off to alert the Virginia Assembly, Tarleton's men would have captured Thomas Jefferson, Patrick Henry, and the Virginia governor, Thomas Nelson, Jr."

Thaddeus served his guests, then sipped his coffee. "We could have had the most prominent citizens of Virginia for bargaining power, if not for that pesky spy."

"But Tarleton did take seven legislators captive," Peyton Haines spoke up. "Too bad those men don't carry the same prestige as Jefferson, Henry, and Nelson."

Thaddeus shrugged a thick shoulder. "Ah, well, since the British are closing in on Virginia, we will have other opportunities."

"If we can keep those sneaky rebel spies from learning our plans," Gerard grumbled. "I don't know how the Patriots got word of Tarleton's surprise attack at Charlottesville."

"What of this important plot you mentioned?" Thaddeus prompted Gerard. "Is Tarleton planning another surprise visit to the esteemed assemblymen?"

Gerard grinned devilishly, displaying the gap between his two front teeth. "Fetch me some brandy for my coffee and I will give you the message to deliver to Lord Saber. We have plans to make this evening."

Thaddeus levered himself out of his chair, then shuffled over to retrieve the liquor. "Where does my grandnephew fit into this scheme?"

Gerard feasted greedy eyes on the full bottle of whiskey in the old man's hand. "Lord Saber is going to ensure British victory. It was my plan, but the British high command decided to put your grandnephew in charge. We are going to follow Benedict Arnold's example."

"After Arnold's betrayal, I would think Washington would be wary of a man planted in his immediate circle.

I don't think the Patriot general will be as gullible a second time."

"Washington has nothing to do with this mission, but rebel defeat will come from within, nonetheless." Gerard sipped his spiked coffee. "This plan will break the Patriots' back during the heat of battle.

"It's not *who* we are going to plant among American troops, old man. It's *how* we are going to twist the arm of the rebel's trusted commander."

Thaddeus frowned impatiently. "Spit it out, Lockwood. You've piqued my curiosity. What does British high command want my grandnephew to do for them this time?"

Gerard smiled wickedly. "The illustrious General Leland Pembrook, commander of the Virginia Militia, is our target. When his two daughters are taken captive, Leland will become an agreeable participant to treason."

Thaddeus went very still. He stared at Lockwood from behind his wire-rimmed spectacles. "We are seizing women to use as leverage?"

"And no one is more deserving of capture than the Rebels' Angel and her sister," Gerard insisted. "Besides, I have an old score to settle with Eden Pembrook."

Thaddeus stroked his gray beard as he eyed his companions consideringly. "What demands must General Pembrook meet when his daughters are taken captive?"

Gerard took another swallow of his drink and wiped his mouth on his sleeve. "Pembrook will give us information about the strength and weaknesses of the Patriot defenses and relay rebel strategy to us. When the British and Patriots clash in Virginia, Pembrook will retreat, giving our armies a route to divide and conquer the enemy."

"I'm surprised British high command would agree to this underhanded scheme," Thaddeus said.

"This is war, old man."

"I don't think my grandnephew will approve of his orders. He became acquainted with the Pembrooks when he established himself in the area."

"Why do you think he was ordered to infiltrate Pembrook Plantation, where rebel soldiers are recovering from their battle wounds? We were laying the groundwork. Now that Lord Saber is familiar with the area, we can put my plan into action, though I damned well should have been in charge of it!" His fist hit the table, rattling the mugs.

Clearly, Gerard wasn't happy that he had not been given control of his own scheme.

"Tell Lord Saber to meet me at our usual rendezvous point tomorrow night. The abduction must take place quickly, because Cornwallis has already joined Benedict Arnold at Petersburg and intends to march to the new base of operations.

"Once we have Leland Pembrook at our beck and call, we will break the economic backbone of rebel resistance. This is the stronghold we need to win the war. If Lord Cornwallis takes Virginia, and Sir Clinton retains his hold on New York, the rebels will have to surrender."

"The situation is changing daily," Thaddeus reminded him. "The Marquis de Lafayette and his French troops have been putting up noticeable resistance. Considering the strength of the Virginia militia, this colony may not be the easy target you think it is."

"It will be, when my scheme is put into action," Gerard maintained. "Remember, Thaddeus, you can write your own ticket when England wins this war. You will have your pension and prestige in the reconstructed colonial government, and I will have a powerful position.

"The colonies don't have the military strength and financial backing to oppose the Crown indefinitely. It was a foolhardy proposition from the onset. I saw the idiocy of joining the rebel cause early on."

When the three Tory soldiers trooped out, Thaddeus scowled to himself. The citizens of Williamsburg would be outraged when the daughter of their local military hero disappeared. And worse, Eden Pembrook was considered the guardian angel of the rebel cause.

Thaddeus cursed foully. It seemed to him that Gerard Lockwood was a mite too eager to abduct Eden Pembrook. Thaddeus didn't have a clue why, but he was certain this underhanded plot would lead to disaster!

"So, yer lordship, how are you going to wriggle out of this predicament?" Tully Randolph questioned as he watched his friend wear a path on the grass.

Sebastian wheeled around to stalk in the opposite direction. "Hell and damnation!"

"Cursing won't solve the problem," Tully snorted. "And this is one ticklish situation. You have been ordered to abduct the very woman you recently seduced." Tully propped himself against a tree and crossed his arms over his massive chest. "I can't wait to see the look on Eden's face when she realizes ye're riding with the Tory patrol."

Sebastian let loose with several colorful expletives. Never in his worst nightmare did he dream he would be placed between the devil and the deep. The prospect of having those lovely blue eyes staring up at him in wounded betrayal was eating him alive. What he and Eden had shared that stormy night, and again in the moonlit garden, was about to be destroyed forever. She would never forgive him for this.

"What are you going to do, yer lordship?" Tully prodded when he heard the hoof beats in the distance. "Lockwood and friends will be here shortly."

"You know I have no choice but to accept this assignment," Sebastian muttered. "I sure as hell can't leave Lockwood in charge of it."

"And the lady is going to despise you," Tully prophesied. "Ye're gonna cut yer own throat where the Rebels'

Angel is concerned. This time there will be no returning to Miss Eden's good graces."

"I am vividly aware of that," Sebastian ground out.

He felt as if a team of horses had been hooked to each arm, yanking him in two. He was damned if he obeyed the offensive orders, and damned if he didn't. If Lockwood was put in charge, he would treat Eden and Bet as cruelly as he treated all women.

Sebastian hoped he would be able to protect Eden and Bet from harm during this distasteful assignment. For sure, he was going to insist that the abductors conceal their identity behind hoods and cloaks. He also warned himself not to revert to that slow, southern drawl he employed while he conducted his business in Virginia. Eden would hear only his clipped British accent and see the sophisticated manner and gestures exemplary of a titled lord in English court.

No way in hell did Sebastian want to be recognized and left to face Eden's condemnation. Knowing that he was about to betray her was torment enough!

A brisk wind whipped around Eden's ankles, causing her skirts to billow as she scurried down the front steps—without alerting anyone to her departure. So far so good, she congratulated herself.

Eden had sent off a note to the Daltons, announcing her arrival. She had managed to sneak from the house without alerting Bet and Peter to her early departure. They had wanted to accompany Eden, but she thought it better to handle this situation alone.

With one last glance toward the lamplight glowing in the window of the new honeymoon suite, Eden scuttled into the stables to fetch the carriage Jacob Courtney had readied for her.

Eden stared at the parading clouds that played hide-

and-seek with the moon. If not for her crusade to repair broken relations between Peter Dalton and his parents, she wouldn't have gone out tonight. With the blustery wind howling in the trees, it would be difficult to detect trouble before it was upon her.

Eden shivered. She remembered the night she had gone in search of her missing sister and stumbled onto the Tory patrol—or rather a pack of thieves. She suspected those hooligans were responsible for the rising number of robberies in the area.

"I should drive you to town," Jacob insisted. "It's an eerie night, what with the wind howling like a banshee."

"I'll be just fine," Eden said as she hoisted herself into the carriage.

Eden hadn't gone thirty yards before two cloaked figures darted from the line of trees to waylay her.

"Edeline Renee Pembrook, you are too saintly to be sneaky," Bet scolded her sister.

Eden clutched her chest. "You scared ten years off my life. What are you doing out here?"

"What are you doing trying to flit off without us?" Peter questioned, then lifted Bet onto the seat. "I am grateful that you intend to speak in our behalf, but I will not hide behind a woman's skirts, Eden."

Eden muttered at her foiled plans of laying the groundwork for reconciliation before Bet and Peter arrived. "How did you know I left early?"

"Maggie saw you skulking out of your closet of a bedroom and asked us why we weren't going with you," Bet explained.

"I should have expected as much," Eden grumbled. "That dear old woman has eyes like a hawk."

"And more sense than you do," Bet chided. "I am a married woman now, Eden. You don't have to treat Peter and me like helpless children."

"I still think the best approach is for me to confer with the Daltons first."

Bet elevated her delicate chin. "Peter and I don't agree."

Resolved to the situation, Eden handed the buggy reins over to Peter, then mentally edited the comments she intended to make to the Daltons.

Sebastian scowled while he watched the threesome speed down King's Highway. He had hoped Eden would be traveling alone so he could leave Peter and Bet out of this disastrous mess. He was sure he could have appeased British high command by simply taking Eden captive.

"We should take them now," Gerard insisted as he stirred restlessly beside Sebastian.

"We will wait until the return trip or we will call off this absurd mission here and now. Make your choice, Lockwood."

Scowling, Gerard glared at Sebastian. He resented this handsome aristocrat's lordly airs, his polished British accent and fine cut of clothes. It also irritated the hell out of Gerard that Sebastian was reportedly related to some highfalutin earl in England. That was why high command had given this mission to Lord Saber.

Even if Saber had a pedigree as long as his leg, he was not going to treat Gerard like a lowly lackey! Here was one British spy whom Gerard would like to see haul his lordly ass back to England—and stay there. Gerard and Sebastian had crossed swords more than once since their first meeting.

Tully Randolph leaned close to convey a confidential comment to Sebastian. Gerard glared at both men. "If you have got something to say, just come out and say it instead of mumbling in our lordship's ear."

"Suit yerself, Lockwood," Tully accommodated as he

turned to stare directly at Gerard. "I think ye're a royal pain in the ass."

When Gerard doubled his fist to strike Tully, Sebastian snaked out his hand to grab the knuckles headed for his friend's jaw. "Easy, Lockwood. Dissension among the troops only causes complications. Like it or not, I am in command and we will handle this situation my way."

"Fine, but I don't have to tolerate your mouthy friend's comments. He got on my bad side when he interfered the night I encountered the Pembrook wench while on patrol."

"You should be thanking Tully for showing good sense," Sebastian replied. "We don't molest innocent women. You had best remember that when we take the Pembrooks captive. You put your hands on either woman and Tully will have to wait his turn to take his anger out on you. Do you understand me, Lockwood?"

Gerard cursed under his breath. "Yes, your lordship, I understand."

Gerard cast Sebastian a resentful glance. He should be the one in command here. But of course he was colonial born and bred. He didn't have a blue-blooded pedigree like Lord Saber.

Those English lords stuck together, didn't they? Well, very soon Gerard would have as much power and position as this British dandy . . . and he vowed to ruin this high-handed bastard the first chance he got!

"Let me do the talking," Eden requested as she hopped from the carriage. The wind swirled, and she had to grab hold of her skirt to prevent it from swelling like a sail and sending her stumbling backward. "Your greatest contribution will be sitting in silence, looking hopelessly in love."

Eden rapped at the door and was met by a somber-faced

butler. His eyes widened when he saw Peter on the stoop. "I don't think—"

"I wish to see Catherine and Angus," Eden cut in, flashing a cheery smile. Before the butler could object, Eden breezed inside to see Catherine lounging in the parlor.

The older woman's eyes rounded when Bet and Peter invited themselves inside. "What are they doing here? Come to announce the end of this preposterous marriage, I hope."

"Is your husband here?" Eden asked. "I was hoping to speak to both of you."

"My husband has been detained at the shop," Catherine muttered, casting her son a belligerent glance.

Eden suspected Angus's mistress had detained him, not business. "I wish to discuss the marriage. I understand that you and Angus might be upset, since you had other plans for Peter." Eden sank down on the couch beside Catherine, then patted her hand consolingly. "I was surprised, too, but we have to learn to adjust to life's surprises, don't we?"

"I—"

"By now, I'm sure you and Angus have had time to rethink your position. You've come to realize that we can't always predict or shape the future, especially when it comes to matters of the heart. Peter and Bet have found something rare and special together." She paused to glance at the lovebirds who were staring starry-eyed at each other, as prompted. "I myself envy their mutual devotion. To love and be loved in return must be a rewarding experience. Would that each of us could find our soul mate, as Bet and Peter have. Don't you agree, Catherine?"

"Yes, but—"

"I was pleased that Bet and Peter came to live at Pembrook. Peter has taken charge of the accounts and has set them in proper order. It was a great relief to me, what with other obligations to occupy my time. Peter has such a good head for business that I expect he will have our budget balanced within the week. He also shows great promise in business management, don't you think?"

"Yes, but—"

"Since Angus has been managing his shop without Peter the last few days, I'm sure he would like to have his son back on the job." Eden smiled warmly. "I understand if Angus wishes Peter to return to the shop—"

Heavy footsteps thudded in the hall. Angus Dalton appeared, looking slightly rumpled and glassy-eyed. Eden doubted the wind was responsible for leaving his periwig askew and putting a flush on his doughy face.

"Good evening, Angus," Eden greeted with her customary smile.

"What are they doing here?" Angus growled at his wife.

Eden was not to be ignored. "I was just telling your wife how pleased I am to have Bet and Peter living at the plantation and helping me with my duties. I am sure Peter regrets that he hasn't been at the shop to assist you. No doubt, you wouldn't have had to work so late if Peter had been there."

Her pointed glance caused Angus to shift awkwardly from one foot to the other. *He* knew that *she* knew what kind of inventory Angus had taken after work hours.

"This family misunderstanding has caused you inconvenience," Eden went on. "You have been short-handed at the shop, have you not?"

"Yes, but—"

"I'm sure Peter will agree to return to work."

"I don't—" Angus burst out.

"I don't want hard feelings, either," Eden inserted quickly.

"Now wait just a blessed minute," Angus growled. "You are not getting me to agree to anything. I want this marriage dissolved immediately. I expect Peter to honor the arrangement I have made for him."

When Peter rose to confront his red-faced father, Eden grimaced. She had intended to take the brunt of any anger directed at the newlyweds. If Peter overspoke himself, family fences might never be mended.

"Just as you have honored your marriage vows, Angus?" Eden asked, cutting Peter off at the pass. "I admire Peter for following his heart rather than the almighty coin purse. Honesty and sincerity are qualities becoming a gentleman. Peter is that and more. You could learn from your son."

"How dare you insult me in my own home!" Angus blustered.

"Would you prefer to hear the well-deserved insults outside?"

Angus gasped and staggered back a pace, shocked by the sarcasm in Eden's voice.

Eden suspected Sebastian's influence on her prompted the snippy remark. He had taught her to unleash her temper occasionally. Besides, she reminded herself, it was better to have Angus angry at her than Bet or Peter.

Elizabeth was so shocked by Eden's uncharacteristic retort that she swayed on her feet. Peter lunged sideways to offer support.

"Now see here, Eden," Angus sneered. "Just because everybody considers you some sort of saint does not give you the right to sit in judgment."

"Nor you," Eden parried quickly. "That is exactly what you have done in Peter and Bet's case. What right do you have to deny them love and happiness?"

"I'll tell you what right I have." Angus roared. "Peter's association with your Patriot family is damaging my business. I have tried to remain neutral. I do not want to lose my Tory patrons because my son married into a den of rebels. Despite you and your father's belief that the colonies can withstand a charge from Lord Cornwallis—whose seasoned Regulars have been victorious in dozens of European wars—I'm not so certain. Before the year is out,

Cornwallis, Tarleton, and Arnold might secure Virginia. The war will be over. When it is, I intend to be in business while your rebel plantation lays in ruin!"

"I believe in fighting for what is necessary and right for the good of all colonies," Eden countered. "You, on the other hand, are simply protecting profits. Your coin purse means more to you than your own family and friends. You have already forsaken your wife and your only son because of your selfish desires. Now you plan to forsake the very colonies that provided you with profit.

"And you speak of honor, sir?" Eden eyed Angus with disdain. "You don't know the meaning of the word. If you were half the man your son is, you would understand patriotism, loyalty, and honor. You should be ashamed of yourself, Angus!"

Elizabeth fainted dead away when Eden's voice rose to match Angus's loud pitch. Catherine wilted on the couch, shocked by Eden's audacity.

"And I," Peter said with great conviction, "am officially announcing my loyalty to my bride and to the rebel cause!"

Angus stumbled back as if he had sustained a body blow.

"I would rather starve than live in the strained atmosphere of this house," Peter proclaimed. "Having learned what love is *not,* I want what love *is.*" He glanced down at his wife who hung limply over his arm. "If it means disinheritance, then I have made the better bargain, Father."

Nonplused, Angus gaped at his son. "You would sacrifice wealth for the love of this little rebel?"

Peter scooped Elizabeth's body into his arms and spun toward the door. "Bet is my first consideration, because I love her. If you can't accept that, then we having nothing more to say to each other."

He glanced back at his thunderstruck parents. "Eden accepted me as I am. She opened her house to me as if I were family. She has been warm and generous, understanding and kind. Now she is my family."

When Peter stalked off, Eden followed in his wake, mentally kicking herself every step of the way. Her good intentions had gone awry, and she had left a path of ill feelings behind her.

"I'm sorry, Angus," she murmured, pausing in the doorway. "I preferred a different outcome. My sister is very much in love with Peter. My own mother lived in misery because her family contracted her marriage. Bet and I both suffered because of her unhappiness. If my father had it to do over again, I think he would have married a woman who truly cared for him."

Her eyes filled with anguish as she stared at Angus. "Don't deny your son's happiness. You cannot imagine what misery you might cause if you do."

Eden walked outside to meet the fierce blast of wind. She inhaled a fortifying breath and climbed into the buggy. The mention of her mother and father unearthed ghosts she had valiantly tried to lay to rest. But memories swarmed around her.

Too much misery led to disaster. Eden knew that all too well. But by God, Elizabeth would not live with anguish and despair. At least one Pembrook offspring would find true happiness and know mutual love. Peter and Elizabeth would have their chance, Eden vowed resolutely. She would see to it!

Elizabeth groaned groggily, then cuddled against Peter's chest.

"I apologize for botching up," Eden told Peter. "I don't know what came over me."

"I thought you made several legitimate points," Peter said. "You inspired me to take a stand for what I believe in. If Virginia becomes a battlefront, then I will take arms against Cornwallis and his Regulars, even if my father paid two young men to take my place in the Army—one to fight for the rebels and the other for the Tories."

Somehow that news didn't surprise Eden. Angus Dalton was determined to keep his mercantile store in operation, refusing to offend rebel or Tory customers.

"Peter?" Elizabeth stirred against Peter's shoulder. "I had the worst nightmare. I dreamed my sister the saint breathed dragon's fire on your family."

Peter glanced at Eden and grinned. "It wasn't a dream, Bet."

Bet levered herself upright and blinked owlishly. When she saw Eden controlling the reins, she groaned in dismay. "Oh, my God!"

"It's too bad you fainted," Peter said, cuddling his wife close. "You missed Eden's grand finale. She is every bit as effective in fiery confrontation as she is at diplomacy."

"I am?"

"Absolutely. Patrick Henry has nothing on you. You are the female orator for Virginia—"

The thrashing of underbrush and thunder of approaching hooves caused Peter's voice to dry up. Five darkly clad riders swooped down on the carriage like angry hornets. The startled horse reared up, and the buggy lurched forward, flinging Peter off balance. Elizabeth shrieked when she landed at Eden's feet.

Outraged, Eden slapped at the muscled arm that snaked around her waist, jerking her off her perch. Before Eden could wrest free she was planted on the lap of one of the masked riders. The horse beneath her pranced sideways to avoid colliding with the buggy, where Peter floundered to upright himself.

Elizabeth screamed bloody murder when she was snatched up and hauled onto the back of the second rider's horse.

"Elizabeth!" Peter yowled as he bolted to his feet.

Horrified, Eden watched moonlight reflect off the flint-lock Peter pulled from beneath his jacket. Peter was bravely trying to rescue his screeching wife. But defying five masked men was inviting suicide!

"No, Peter!" Eden screamed at him.

Five pistols appeared from beneath the swirling cloaks their captors wore. Eden was so terrified she couldn't breathe!

"You take him out, yer lordship. Ye're the best marks-man of the bunch." This from the gargantuan man who held Elizabeth so tightly to his chest that she passed out for the second time that night.

Eden made a lunge for the flintlock in her captor's gloved hand. Yer lordship—as he had been called—aimed and fired before she could put a hatchet chop to his wrist.

Peter howled in pain and spun like a top. The blast startled the horse, and the carriage rolled off. Elizabeth roused in time to see Peter stumble and pitch forward on the seat. She let loose with a bloodcurdling scream—and fainted again.

Eden stared after the carriage in outraged disbelief. The brute who was holding her had shot Peter down. The murdering bastard!

Something inside Eden snapped. Her emotions had been whirling since the unpleasant encounter with the Daltons. This was simply too much. Furious, she clawed at her captor's masked face.

"Bloody hell!" The growled curse carried a heavy British accent. "Hold still, wench, or you'll end up like your friend in the buggy."

At that moment, Eden's only concern was vengeance. She was going to make "yer lordship" pay for killing poor Peter, who was only trying to save his distressed wife.

When Eden gouged her captor in the belly, he doubled over, sandwiching her between him and his high-stepping horse.

"I told you she was a handful," Gerard Lockwood snorted. "Give her to me. I'll teach her some manners."

"I can handle the chit."

To Eden's dismay, "yer lordship" twisted her arms behind her back until they nearly popped from their sockets.

"Damn your black souls to eternal hell!" Eden spluttered. "If it's the last thing I do, I will—"

Her spiteful vow drowned beneath the gag that was crammed into her mouth. She was shoved head-down, left to dangle over the horse like a feedsack. Outraged, she jabbed her elbows into her captor's belly and rammed her toes into the horse's flank.

When Eden tried to somersault off the horse, while her captor tried to calm down his mount, she found herself pressed to the horse. "Yer lordship" slid his booted feet from the stirrups and curled them over her dangling arms and legs, pinning her in place.

Eden muttered unladylike oaths into her gag. Her chin rubbed against the leather of the saddle, and the awkward position left blood rushing to her head as the horse thundered into the underbrush. Eden tried to remain conscious, but darkness swirled around her, drawing her into its murky depths.

Sebastian sent a prayer heavenward when Eden finally passed out. Who would have thought this dainty female could fight like a tigress? She had become one hundred pounds of seething fury and fierce determination. Sebastian had sustained several painful blows to the midsection and groin, not to mention bites and scratches.

Too bad Eden wasn't as easily subdued as Elizabeth, who simply fainted in Tully's arms.

Sebastian cursed this distasteful mission a dozen times over. He hated to restrain Eden. But better him than the ruthless Gerard Lockwood. Lockwood had the brutal habit of backhanding resisting females. Although Eden wouldn't believe it, Sebastian and Tully were her protectors in this misadventure.

And God help him if Eden discovered that Sebastian was involved . . .

Not so long ago, Eden had put her faith and trust in him, had confessed to love him. Saint Eden would never forgive him for this betrayal if she knew the truth. Her generosity wouldn't stretch that far.

Sebastian vowed, there and then, never to face Eden without the shield of his cloak, mask, and the staunch British accent she wasn't accustomed to hearing from him.

Sebastian slowed his mount to a walk as the cavalcade followed the narrow path beside the swamps. Unseen creatures slithered into the murk, sending silver ripples fanning in all directions.

Peter Dalton was the lucky one, Sebastian mused as he led the way to the obscure cabin. Sebastian had only winged the bridegroom to protect him from death at Lockwood's hands. If not for Tully's comment, Lockwood would have taken the shot—and shot to kill. A wounded left arm was a damn sight better than a bleeding heart.

Yet, Sebastian doubted that Eden would see the deed as an act of mercy. In her eyes, it was another reason to despise her captor.

Sebastian squeezed his eyes shut and cursed mightily. He wondered how much more hell had to teach him before this despicable mission was over and done.

Peter floundered onto the seat of the runaway buggy and groped for the reins. Stabbing pain shot down his left arm. He was losing blood by the pints, he was certain of it. His jacket sleeve was wet and sticky, and the coppery scent of fresh blood filled his nostrils. His stomach lurched, but he struggled to keep his wits about him.

Inhaling a fortifying breath, Peter cradled his injured arm against his ribs and turned the buggy toward his parents' home. He held his composure admirably . . . until he stepped beneath the lamplight on the stoop and saw the blood saturating the left side of his linen shirt.

He was a dead man walking! No one could lose this much blood and survive. How could he rescue his wife if he died!

Frantic, Peter plowed through the door, calling his father's name.

Angus Dalton scrambled down the steps in his nightshirt. Catherine followed at his heels. When she saw her son bleeding all over himself, her wild scream echoed around the foyer.

"Father." Peter propped himself against the wall. "Fetch Doctor Curtis."

Angus reached out a shaky hand to touch the ragged edge of Peter's sleeve. "What happened?"

Peter's blue-tinged lips curled with disdain. "Tory renegades shot me and abducted Bet and Eden. *Tories,*" he emphasized. "I kept wondering if those five bastards were patrons of Dalton's Mercantile.

"Ironic, isn't it? Those who we have been so careful not to offend have turned on us like rabid wolves." Peter coughed—the melodrama of it all quite intentional. "I suppose you think I got what I deserved for marrying the only woman I will ever love . . ."

When Peter collapsed in a lifeless heap, Catherine sank down beside her son and wailed hysterically. Angus buzzed out the door in his nightshirt, dashing down the street to rouse the physician.

This was Angus's penance for turning away his only son and daughter-in-law. Peter was going to die in the foyer, and his young bride would be beaten, molested, and raped. Angus, who had bent over backward to remain politically impartial, had cursed his own son for joining the rebels.

Dear God in heaven! His world was crumbling around him. His own frivolous dalliances had sent his wife into other men's arms. His attempt to pressure Peter into a contracted marriage had torn the family apart.

Angus was truly and surely cursed! He should have known that the instant he raged at the angel of mercy who had come to talk sense into him. Angus hadn't listened . . . and now it was too late!

Nine

Jacob Courtney stared down the road, anxiously waiting Eden's return. Although she hadn't asked him to wait up for her, he couldn't sleep until she was home, safe and sound. An uneasy feeling had been nagging Jacob for the better part of an hour. He had checked his timepiece several times, wondering what was keeping Eden. It was the witching hour and she still hadn't returned. Something was wrong.

In hurried strides, Jacob headed to the house to alert Maggie.

"Give me a moment to dress," she said, "and I'll help you look for her."

Doffing her robe, Maggie wriggled into her clothes. When she scurried down the hall, she noticed the wounded soldiers who congregated at the head of the stairs.

"What's going on down there?" Henry Maynard questioned, and Maggie explained the situation.

Scrabbling noises echoed in the darkness. Every injured soldier who could stand on his own two feet trooped down the steps.

"We are joining the search party," Henry announced. "If Eden is in trouble, we'll find her. I've had training in scouting, and so have some of the other men."

"I don't think Miss Eden would want you risking further

injury on her account," Maggie protested. "You know how she fusses over you."

"That is the whole point, Miss Maggie," Artemus Riley spoke up. "If Eden can open her home to tend to us, we can damn sure come to her aid."

While the rescue brigade tracked the route Eden had taken, Maggie kept asking herself how she would cope if she found herself in charge of Pembrook Plantation. The guardian angel always saw to every detail and considered the needs of everyone under her care. Maggie wondered if she would be able to fill Saint Eden's shoes if . . .

Maggie clamped down on that pessimistic thought. Eden, Bet, and Peter were perfectly fine, she reassured herself. They had simply been delayed . . .

Air froze in Maggie's lungs when Henry Maynard lifted a bandaged hand to halt the procession of riders. He dismounted to pluck up Peter's jacket and Eden's beaded reticule that lay in the middle of the road.

"Light the other torches, Artemus," Henry ordered.

When the torches blazed to life, the group of wounded soldiers surveyed the area, finding five sets of hoof prints that disappeared into the thicket of cypress trees.

"It's no use," Artemus said bleakly. "We can't follow these tracks through the bushes in the dark. We will have to wait until first light."

Maggie bit back her tears. Eden didn't deserve to endure another terrifying ordeal! Eden had learned to cope with her childhood nightmares, and Maggie had gone to her room to soothe her time and again, wondering what secrets tormented Eden so. Blast it, now what anguish was Eden suffering?

Thieves were said to haunt the forests and prowl the marshes, preying on Patriots and Tories alike. Bands of reconnoitering troops lurked about, spying on one another. The countryside teetered on the brink of war, and Eden, Bet, and Peter had vanished into the night!

With that thought Maggie could no longer control her tears.

"Now don't you worry, Miss Maggie." Henry leaned out to give the weeping housekeeper a consoling pat on the shoulder. "We will find our guardian angel. Every man who can crawl off his cot will be ready and willing to help with the search. We'll bring all three of them back safe and sound, you'll see."

Maggie sincerely hoped so. She didn't even want to think about sending the grim news to General Pembrook that his family had vanished in the night. The poor man had enough trouble on his mind already!

Eden roused to the feel of strong arms lifting her from the saddle and draping her over a sturdy shoulder. She would have kicked "yer lordship" once or twice for good measure, but he had bound up her wrists and ankles.

Fuming, Eden surveyed her surroundings from her upside-down position on "yer lordship's" shoulder. She was being toted inside a shabby cottage near the swamps. She wasn't sure where Elizabeth was, but muffled feminine sobs could be heard in the near distance.

"Yer lordship" placed Eden in a chair, then quickly lashed her to it. She peered up at the looming figure whose voice held an eerie familiarity, though she couldn't imagine where she had met him.

"Tie Elizabeth in bed," Lockwood ordered Tully, who lumbered inside with his captive doubled over his burly shoulders. "The oldest wench is the one I want to question."

Eden refused to let herself show a smidgen of fear to these men. She rubbed her cheek against her shoulder until the gag sagged around her neck, then stared defiantly at the masked man looming in front of her. "What do you want with us?"

"I will get what I want from you later, wench," Lockwood smirked. "Right now, I am more interested in what you can get for us."

Eden glared at the masked man who loomed in front of her. "You aren't making sense, though braying asses rarely do."

Lockwood cocked his arm, only to have "yer lordship" block the oncoming blow.

"I warned you what would happen if you laid a hand on the women." The heavily British-accented voice was as soft as velvet—but cut like steel. "If she can provoke you so easily, then she holds the greater power."

Lockwood wheeled around. He slammed his fist into his left palm to vent his anger. "If you think you're so damned smart, your lordship, then you deal with this snippy chit."

"I had planned to." A wry smile twitched Sebastian's lips as he strolled around behind Eden. The straight-backed chair had nothing on this angel-turned-hellion. Her body was as rigid as stone. Sebastian decided to ply Eden with the same cunning tactics she had used on him the first time they met.

"I can understand that you are upset, Miss Pembrook," he said. "And believe me, I sympathize with your distress."

"Do you?" Eden glowered at the rough-hewn wall, since the present source of her irritation was standing behind her.

"Of course I do. You are feeling positively murderous, but you realize hostility will only aggravate the situation."

"How incredibly astute of me."

"You consider yourself a keen-witted, intelligent woman, do you not?"

Eden gnashed her teeth. "No, I consider myself a cretin for being captured by a brigade of buffoons. And you may as well know that subtle suggestion won't work with me. I have practiced the tactic far more successfully than you, 'your lordship,' and I am far better at it."

Lockwood smirked when Lord Saber was slapped with the insult. "Looks like you can't outsmart the chit, either. Violence, she will understand. She will tell us what we want to know after I use my brand of persuasion on her."

Eden elevated her chin and glared rebelliously at Lockwood's hooded face. "You could twist off my arm and I still wouldn't tell you anything except where you can go and what you can do with yourself when you get there."

Sebastian decided Eden Pembrook was extraordinarily adaptable. The butterfly had emerged from her self-controlled cocoon to fight back.

Although he did admire Eden's spunk, he wished she wouldn't antagonize Lockwood. The man was too cruel and impatient to provoke.

"Miss Pembrook, you and your sister will be treated with respect and courtesy, in exchange for a few tidbits of information," Sebastian bartered. "It has come to our attention that your father is in charge of the Virginia Militia."

"Any idiot could have read that in the Virginia *Gazette*. Who, I wonder, *read* that information to you and the rest of your masked cretins?"

Tully laughed aloud, but quickly swallowed his amusement when Sebastian sent him a silencing nod.

"Where is your father, Miss Pembrook?" Sebastian asked point-blank.

"In bed at this late hour, I hope." She glanced toward the closed door, behind which Elizabeth had been stashed. "I wish to retire for the evening, your lordship. I become irritable and cranky when deprived of sleep."

Another muffled snicker rumbled inside Tully's concealing hood.

In hostile defiance, Eden rocked forward and stood up—partially—the chair hugging her back. "I hope we have suitable accommodations. A clean feather tick with recently laundered quilts will be acceptable. I prefer to eat breakfast immediately upon rising. I will take my meal in bed tomorrow morning. See that your lackeys have my bath prepared shortly thereafter."

She glanced sideways at "yer lordship." "If you haven't thought to gather decent clothes for me and my sister, see to the matter post haste. I refuse to wear the same set of garments two consecutive days."

Eden pivoted toward one of the men who had yet to utter a word. "Untie me," she commanded.

Jonathan Baxter reflexively did as he was told.

"Damn it, you fool! You don't take orders from this chit!" Lockwood snapped.

Jonathan snatched his hands away from the coiled rope, as if he'd been snakebit.

"It's all right," Sebastian assured Jonathan. "She can't sleep with a chair tied to her back. I'm sure she has enough sense to realize she can't escape while surrounded by an army of men." To Eden he said, "You are aware of that, are you not, m'lady?"

"Am I, your lordship?" Eden glared daggers at the man who refused to react to her snide retorts.

"I do believe you are," he said very deliberately. "I wouldn't think to speak for you. But if the situation were reversed, I would realize that hostility might cause unpleasant repercussion. I would ask myself if rebellious conduct might provoke my captors into seeking out a route of less resistance." He moved a step closer to Eden, forcing her to look up at him. "I'm sure it has occurred to an astute woman like yourself that if you don't cooperate, we will be forced to apply pressure to your sister—the path of least resistance."

A cold chill slithered down Eden's spine as Jonathan removed the chair from her back. The thought of Elizabeth being used as leverage against her was unacceptable. "In that case, I might propose a bargain."

"What kind of bargain, m'lady?" This from Tully who

had propped himself against the wall to listen to Lord Saber match wits with a very worthy opponent.

Eden glanced at the familiar hulk of man who had once rescued her from these wretches—and now betrayed her. "We will discuss negotiations in the morning. After my breakfast and bath."

With regal aplomb, Eden strode toward the bedroom, only to find "yer lordship" a step behind her. When Eden disappeared from sight, Tully plucked off his hood and tossed it on the table.

"Where the hell are you going?" Lockwood demanded as Tully ambled toward the front door.

Tully turned around, glancing at Lockwood as if he had asked a stupid question. "Where else but to fetch the lady's tub and a change of clothes."

"Now she has you fetching and heeling like a handmaid," Lockwood said sarcastically.

Tully grinned wryly. "Better a handmaid than a braying ass."

Lockwood took a threatening step forward, but Tully directed him toward the cabinet. "Go brew yourself a pot of coffee and fetch his lordship's special blend of tea."

"His highfalutin lordship can fix his own goddamn special blend of tea!"

Lockwood jerked off his hood and hurled it at the table as Tully ambled outside. He had had his fill of that arrogant giant and his cocky lordship!

As for that sassy Eden Pembrook, she was going to pay for the insults, Lockwood vowed spitefully. The minute Lord Saber's back was turned, Lockwood would see that Eden learned to keep a civil tongue in her head!

Eden surveyed the crudely furnished room, then stared at Bet who had sobbed herself to sleep, strapped to the bedpost. Cold fury froze Eden's veins when the image of

Peter tumbling across the carriage seat flashed in front of her eyes. Now, Eden knew how Patriot prisoners of war felt when they were marched away. Anger, resentment, and frustration were only a few of the emotions churning inside her.

Wheeling around, Eden stared at "yer lordship" who was appraising her through the narrow slits of his hood. "What do you expect to gain from this scheme?" she demanded to know. "It can't be information, so don't insult my intelligence with that flimsy excuse again."

Sebastian chortled wryly. "As I recall, m'lady, you are the one who has been flinging insults around here."

"Surely you aren't so naive to think that I am privy to military secrets. And I can't imagine that you Britishers have become so desperate that you have stooped to interrogating women about campaign tactics."

Sebastian ambled forward. "Your father's whereabouts, the number of men under his command, and his plan of attack aren't difficult to obtain, it's true," he admitted.

"Then why are Bet and I here?"

"I'm sure the answer to that question will come to you soon enough, m'lady," he replied. "I certainly don't intend to insult your intelligence by explaining the obvious."

Eden tilted her chin a notch higher. "And don't think I'm swayed by your charm, your lordship. When you shot Peter and took us hostage you became my mortal enemy. Nothing is going to change that."

Sebastian stared into those animated blue eyes and couldn't resist reaching out to touch this proud, defiant beauty. Watching Eden change to suit this new situation was as fascinating as staring into a kaleidoscope. This iron-clad daisy could be gentle and understanding, fiery and tenacious, or shrewd and cunning.

She was also determined not to admit defeat.

When his gloved hand cupped her chin, Eden slapped it away. "And don't think you can seduce information from me, either. Having recently discovered what love is, I would never settle for your tawdry imitations of affection."

"What makes this man you love so special? Does he grovel at your feet? Does he fulfill your every whim like a lackey?"

"If you have to ask, then you know nothing about love."

"I don't?" Sebastian was grateful that his hood concealed his wide grin.

Her chin elevated another notch. "Kindly untie my arms so I can retire for the night," she demanded.

"Do I have your word that you won't attempt escape?"

"Would you give your word if the situation was reversed?" she parried.

"Yes, then I would set about to plan my escape."

"Then why should I lie when we both know I would escape the first chance I have?"

"Then why ask if I will untie you?"

Eden smiled mockingly. "Because I was testing your character, or lack of it."

"Did I pass your test, m'lady?"

"What do you care if you did or didn't?" she shot back.

This time, when his gloved hand skimmed her cheekbone and limned her lips, Eden forced herself to stand her ground. Something about this calm, self-assured aristocrat disturbed her. Her captor seemed adept at the same mental subterfuge she had learned to use. He challenged her, fascinated her with his polished manners, his husky voice and sophisticated British accent.

She allowed her captor to trace her features for several moments, then peered at him with cool disdain. "Therein lies the difference between you and the man I love."

The comment seemed to puzzle him. "Your meaning escapes me, m'lady."

"Even without your glove, your touch would leave me cold, unaffected," she told him. "A man without character is like a lover wearing gloves. You can't touch what I feel, and I cannot feel what you touch. Take off your hood and gloves, your lordship, and let's see if there is truly a *man* hiding behind this disguise."

"Why should I bother?" he countered smoothly. "You see only what you have decided to see in me. You believe your cause is far nobler than mine. I believe just as strongly in what you oppose. What we have here, m'lady, is simply a difference of opinion."

Eden contemplated that, but decided she wasn't going to soften her feelings toward him. He was her sworn enemy and that was the beginning and end of it.

"I'm ready to go to bed." Eden held out her bound wrists. "Untie me, your lordship."

Sebastian simply turned on his heels and walked away.

"Good night, 'Duke,'" she called after him. He stopped abruptly but didn't look back. "Have my breakfast ready by six. Bet prefers to wait until eight to eat, though I doubt she'll be hungry while she mourns her husband's death."

"Your brother-in-law is alive," he assured her. "I only shot to wound him, before my trigger-happy cohort could do his worst. Be grateful for small favors, m'lady," he murmured before he opened the door. "My loyal servant and I are the best friends you have right now."

"Then I am indeed in perilous straits," she flung at him.

"That you are. Think of that while you lie abed."

"And no matter how charming and gallant you try to be, I will not cooperate. Think of that while *you* lie abed."

When her captor closed the door behind him, Eden eased down on the bed listening to Bet's steady breathing. Just why the devil had they been abducted? Eden frowned. She was going to puzzle out the answer to that question, even if it took the rest of the night!

* * *

Peter Dalton groaned when pain burned through his arm. Suddenly, he was reliving the attack and abduction "Bet!" he yelled hoarsely.

Angus and Catherine bounded from their chairs beside the bed when Peter's shout broke the silence.

"You're going to be all right," Angus assured his son.

Peter lifted heavily lidded eyes to see his parents hovering over him. "What happened?"

Another face appeared above him. "I gave you a dose of laudanum before I cleansed your wound," Dr. Curtis explained. "The superficial wound looks worse than it is."

That was all Peter needed to know. He would survive and he was going to locate his missing wife—immediately!

When Peter tried to roll from bed, Dr. Curtis held him in place. "Whoa, young man. I said you would recover, but I didn't mean instantly."

"I have to find my wife," Peter insisted.

"Lie down, Peter," Angus ordered. "I have contacted the constable. He and his men are combing the countryside."

"Bet needs me," Peter said, trying to squirm free of his father's restraint.

"If you insist on going, drink this." Dr. Curtis shoved a glass under Peter's nose. "It will get you where you need to go."

Peter swallowed the sedative unknowingly. Within seconds he wilted back to the bed, oblivious to the world.

"As I said, the brew will get you where you need to go— to sleep," Dr. Curtis said wryly. He pivoted to fetch his medical bag, then strolled across the room. "By the time Peter wakes up, he'll be in better shape for his rescue mission. Hopefully, his new bride will be returned to him before he rouses."

Dr. Curtis half turned in the doorway to smile at Angus and Catherine. "I neglected to congratulate you. Peter has chosen a fine wife. And it doesn't hurt to have a guardian angel like Eden connected to your family. I pity the wretches who abducted Bet and Eden. The whole town will be up in arms when the word spreads."

Angus didn't comment—couldn't. He was so ashamed of himself that his heart had leaped up to clog his throat.

"Oh, my God!" Eden bolted straight up in bed. She had lain there for the longest time, trying to puzzle out why she and Bet had been taken captive. The answer crashed down on her like a ton of rocks. These Tories didn't need information about General Pembrook. They were holding Leland's family hostage as leverage against him!

Once Eden arrived at that alarming conclusion, she contemplated a half dozen ways the Tories could strong-arm Leland into providing confidential information about the Patriot Army. Leland might even be ordered to sabotage weapons and artillery in exchange for his daughters' lives. He might be coerced into turning traitor.

Although Benedict Arnold had willingly turned against the Continental Army and blackened his name, Leland Pembrook would not betray his country, Eden vowed fiercely. She would not let it happen!

"Bet, wake up. We have to get out of here," Eden whispered urgently.

Bet tried to roll over, but her manacled wrists wouldn't budge from the bedpost. "What does it matter now? Peter is dead. I have no reason to live."

"Peter isn't dead," Eden told her. "He only sustained a wound on the arm."

Bet swiveled her head to stare at her sister. "How can you be certain Peter is alive? Are you simply trying to make me feel better?"

"The leader of this Tory band assured me that he shot Peter to slow him down." Eden pushed up on her knees and maneuvered herself over Bet's sprawled form. "I'll try to untie you so we can make our escape during the night."

Bet sent Eden a skeptical glance. "How do you intend to untie me when your hands are bound behind your back?"

"I'll figure something out," Eden said as she sidled backward toward the bedpost.

Several minutes later, Eden paused to rest her cramping arms. It would have been infinitely easier to untie Bet if she could see what she was doing.

Eden heard footsteps in the outer room, then the whine of door hinges. She didn't know if her captors were coming or going. Coming, she hoped. The last thing she and Bet needed, if they managed to escape, was to run headlong into posted guards outside the window.

Despite aching muscles, Eden strained to untangle the knots that bound Bet's wrists to the bedpost. Finally, Eden felt the ropes sag. When Bet jerked her hand loose, Eden slumped tiredly against the bed, waiting for Bet to free herself completely. Once Bet was free, she released her sister.

"Now what?" Bet rose up on her knees and glanced toward the window. "Do you have the slightest idea where we are?"

"Not a clue."

Bet came off the bed to stare out the window. Her shoulders slumped as she surveyed the moonlit swamps and gnarled branches of cypress trees.

Eden joined her sister at the window. Perhaps Swamp Fox could slither through such a slimy maze, but Eden had her doubts about her navigational abilities.

"We'll be lost forever in these swamps and become food for gators," Bet said grimly.

Eden unlatched the window. When a thought suddenly occurred to her, she wheeled around and scurried back to the bed.

"What on earth—" Bet gaped at the garment Eden had fashioned for herself from the ropes.

Eden had tugged up the back hem of her skirt, wrapped it between her legs and draped the trailing fabric over her rope belt. "Breeches," she whispered, then tossed a piece of rope to Bet. "Take off your petticoats and tie your skirts out of the way."

Bet did as she was told, and when Eden flung a leg over the windowsill, Bet grabbed her arm. "If we don't make it home alive, I want you to know that I have finally grown up enough to appreciate all you've sacrificed for me. There were times when I selfishly wished you weren't such a tireless saint—"

"I do wish you would stop calling me that," Eden muttered in interruption. Quickly, she turned her attention to the problem at hand. "According to the information I have read about celestial navigation—"

"Oh, Lord," Bet whispered.

"Have faith, Bet."

"Faith in stars I can't see?" she smirked. "Unless you can spread your angel wings and fly, we don't have a prayer of coming out of this alive. I will never see Peter again. His parents will marry him off to Cornelia Wickleheimer and they will have a passel of frightfully homely children."

When Eden frowned disapprovingly and started to speak, Bet flung up her hand. "Possum Face Wickleheimer is ugly to the bone, with a personality to match. But, of course, what difference will it make to me that Cornelia will make Peter a horrible wife? I won't be around. I will be wandering around this hellish swamp until I die of starvation—if I'm not eaten first."

"This is no time to wallow in pessimism," Eden insisted as she crept away from the shack, watching carefully where she stepped.

Bet fell into step behind her. "Do you have any idea

why we were kidnapped?" she whispered as she followed
Eden's cautious path.

"I believe we were going to be the leverage to blackmail
Papa into joining the ranks of the enemy."

"Dear God!"

"My sentiments exactly." Eden picked her way around
a clump of slimy underbrush. When a bird fluttered up in
front of her, Bet screamed in alarm. Eden clamped her
hand over the lower portion of her sister's face, then gave
her an abrupt shake.

"Don't do that again," she whispered. "We'll never be
able to sneak away if you scream our whereabouts every
other minute."

Eden vowed to remain calm—if only for Bet's sake. If
Eden panicked in the face of adversity all would be lost.

Truth was, Eden was as terrified as Bet. Childhood nightmares tapped at the underside of her mind. Eden could
feel herself trembling with each carefully placed footstep.
She had to swallow her own terrified gasp when something
slithered into the swamp, only inches from her foot.

"It's going to take a miracle to navigate through these
swamps," Bet murmured.

Eden prayed long and hard for that miracle.

When Gerard Lockwood tried to snatch one of the biscuits Tully had removed from the stove, Tully whacked his
knuckles. "Fix yer own breakfast," he snapped. "This is
for the ladies."

"Those chits aren't our guests, they are captives," Gerard scowled, shaking the sting from his hand.

"They will be treated with courtesy and respect," Tully
contended as he pulled his hood over his bushy head of
hair. "Those were his lordship's orders before he rode off
to report that our mission has been accomplished."

"I don't take orders from his high and mighty lordship," Gerard sneered.

"You do for now." Tully plucked up the steaming biscuits and arranged them on a tin plate. "His lordship is in command, whether you like it or not."

"Which I damned well don't," Gerard muttered sourly.

Tully stepped over the two sleeping men sprawled on pallets, then rapped quietly on the bedroom door. "Miss Eden, yer breakfast is ready."

Silence.

"Miss Eden?" he prompted.

Gerard surged forward, not the least bit apologetic when he tromped on Peyton Haines's hand. The man awoke, howling in pain.

"Just open the goddamn door, man," Gerard hissed at Tully. "We're not running an inn for visiting royalty—"

Gerard burst out in foul curses when he opened the door to find the Pembrook sisters gone! He dashed across the room to stare through the window. Still swearing, he lurched around to glower at the towering giant in the doorway.

"If those women escape, I will make damned sure Saber's head rolls. We will see if our superior officers still want to sing his praises after he botched up our mission."

"If heads roll, yours will be one of them, Lockwood," Tully promised. "His lordship put you in charge during his absence. The women certainly didn't escape while his lordship was in command."

Lockwood barreled toward the main room, attempting to shove Tully out of his way. Tully didn't budge an inch. He merely stuffed the plate of biscuits into Gerard's inflated chest.

"You can have the biscuits. I'll track down the ladies."

Snarling viciously, Lockwood hurled the biscuits against the wall and ordered his men to their feet. "I'll teach that

woman a lesson she won't forget!" he roared as he stalked
outside.

"Fetch yer masks," Tully ordered the men. "His lordship said we were to conceal our identity at all times."

As the men scrambled to give chase, Tully swore under
his breath. Tramping through the swamps didn't bode well
for the Pembrook sisters, especially with Lockwood vowing
vengeance. Tully prayed like hell that he would be the first
to overtake Eden and Elizabeth.

The golden rays of dawn drifted through the window,
bringing Peter Dalton awake. He groaned when he realized he had slept through the night. His beloved Elizabeth
was either dead, dying, or suffering the torments of the
damned. Peter cursed Dr. Curtis for deceiving him into
drinking that sleeping potion!

Grimacing, Peter thrust his injured arm into the sleeve
of his jacket. When he bounded to his feet, the room spun
around him. Staggering, Peter braced against the wall for
support, inhaled a steadying breath and vowed to let nothing deter him from finding Elizabeth.

When he stumbled out the door to descend the mountain of steps, Angus Dalton appeared in the hall.

"Peter, get back in bed. You aren't well enough to be
up."

Peter stared curiously at his father who had appeared
from Catherine's bedroom. It looked as if Saint Eden's
dissertation on loyalty and faithfulness had influenced Angus. Peter knew for a fact that his parents hadn't slept
together in years.

Casting aside his wandering thoughts, Peter grabbed the
banister to make his descent. "I'm going after Bet and
nothing you can say is going to stop me."

"Then I'll go with you," Angus volunteered.

"And who will mind the shop?" Peter questioned.

"Hang the shop, ' Angus mumbled.

Peter very nearly fell off his feet. Apparently, Eden had worked miracles on Angus and Catherine.

"Be careful, both of you," Catherine said as she appeared at the doorway, wrapping her robe around her.

Peter strode off, assured that his family now supported him rather than opposed him. If only he could find Bet, if only she was all right, he thought as he clambered into the carriage and drove toward the site of the abduction.

Ten

Eden quickened her step when she heard wild thrashing and furious curses behind her. A flock of herons soared over the canopy of trees, warning Eden that her captors were closing in.

"Hurry, Bet." Eden leaped over the slimy cypress roots and dashed toward the sunlight beaming through the jungle of vines.

Bet's muffled shriek halted Eden in her tracks. She lurched around to see Bet stumbling over the slippery roots. Bet grabbed her ankle as she collapsed on the ground.

When the thrashing in the underbrush grew louder, Eden scurried back to lend Bet a supporting arm.

"Leave me here," Bet whimpered. "I will only slow you down. One of us has to escape."

"Then it will be you," Eden declared as she shepherded Bet toward a thick clump of bushes.

"No, I—"

Eden grabbed Bet by the shoulders and gave her a firm shake. "You want to see Peter again, don't you?"

"Yes, but—"

"And I want that for you." Eden cast an apprehensive glance at the tangled jungle, expecting to see the masked demons leaping at her. "Now listen to me carefully, Bet. You hide in the brush until I lead the men in the opposite direction." She gestured toward the sunlight sparkling through the trees. "Make sure you walk straight toward the sun."

"I can't—"

Eden gave her sister another shake. "You can and you will," she ordered sternly. "You are going to make it out of the swamp, even if you have to crawl. You and Peter deserve a chance at happiness, and by damned, you are going to have it! And you must tend to the wounded patients while I'm gone."

Eden gave her reluctant sister a backward shove into the underbrush, then hurriedly rearranged the branches to conceal the hiding place.

Mustering her courage, Eden waited until her masked pursuer spotted her before she broke into a run. Eden swore under breath when she recognized the man who was hot on her heels. The man's black mask and Tory-green jacket assured her that this was the same scoundrel who had tried to molest her the night of the storm—the same man who would have backhanded her last night if "yer lordship" hadn't intervened.

Eden bounded off, praying she could lead her enemy away from Bet. If Eden's life was the sacrifice that had to be made to help Bet and Peter then so be it.

On that determined thought, Eden splashed through the mud and murk, making enough noise for any cretin to follow her trail.

And Lockwood was only a few yards behind her . . .

Sebastian reined the winded horse to a halt and peered at the cottage by the swamps. He sensed trouble at first glance. The place was entirely too quiet. Apprehensive, Sebastian leaped up the steps and rushed through the door. The tangle of pallets on the floor, the heat radiating from the unattended stove, and the open bedroom door testified to disaster. A deep sense of foreboding settled over Sebastian.

Damn it, he should have tied Eden to the bedpost instead of binding her hands behind her back. He hadn't wanted to make her uncomfortable, but hell, if he'd known she had the talents of an escape artist he would have tied her in knots!

Muttering, Sebastian spun on his heels and stalked outside. In swift strides, he circled the shack to look for tracks. Sure enough, two sets of female-size shoe prints led into the swamps. Sebastian trotted off on foot, retrieving his hood from his pocket as he went.

Sebastian didn't know how long he darted in and out of the maze of trees and vines—cursing and mentally kicking himself every step of the way. It seemed like a century before he heard muffled sounds in the near distance. He plunged through the thickets to see Tully lumbering ahead of him. By the time Sebastian caught up with his friend he was panting for breath.

"What . . . happened?" he wheezed.

Tully reported the news of Eden and Bet's escape as he leaned against a tree trunk to catch his breath between words. "I think I heard a sound coming from over there." He gestured a brawny arm to the west.

Sebastian noticed the faint rustling of underbrush, then motioned for Tully to circle behind the clump of bayberry trees.

Elizabeth swallowed her tears and drew her legs beneath her, vowing not to make a sound, though her ankle was throbbing something fierce. She had limped eastward, clinging to the cover of the bushes until her gimpy leg gave out and she twisted her ankle—again.

The pain was nauseating, but Bet was determined not to succumb. She shrieked instinctively when a muscled arm stabbed into the bushes to pluck her up by the nape of her gown. Her firm resolve evaporated, knowing that she could never match Eden's unswerving determination. She had bungled her escape attempt!

Sebastian found a bawling female on his hands. Bet soaked the front of his cloak with her humiliated tears.

Tully called Sebastian's attention to Elizabeth's injured leg. "Hasn't this gone far enough, yer lordship? This poor girl must have crawled through the swamp. It's bad enough that men have to endure the hell of war, but must we foist it on the womenfolk, too?"

Sebastian watched Tully melt like lard in a hot skillet. Damnation, Bet's tears were getting to him, too. Sebastian didn't want to see this young woman suffer more than she already had.

"Yer lordship, isn't there some other way?" Tully beseeched. "Can't we let one of them go? This one doesn't have the same fierce spirit—"

Elizabeth wailed louder. "Go ahead and say it. I'll never be my sister's equal. I'm worthless—" Her voice dissolved into hiccuping sobs.

"You aren't worthless," Tully soothed her. "I think you have held up remarkably well, don't you, yer lordship?"

"Remarkably," Sebastian seconded.

"No, I haven't," Bet yowled.

She heaved a shuddering breath, then pushed away from Sebastian's chest. Until now she had failed, but she was going to make the personal sacrifice to save Eden. "Take me back to the shack and let my sister go," she ordered.

"Where is your sister?" Sebastian questioned.

Elizabeth tilted her chin in a manner that would have done her sister proud. "Call off your Tory dogs and keep me as your hostage," she demanded.

Tully muttered under his breath. "Let this one go, yer lordship. We will tell General Pembrook that we released one of his daughters in good faith. Miss Bet won't jeopardize her sister's life."

Sebastian made a quick decision. "We will return Elizabeth to her husband."

"I do not want to be released!" Bet all but yelled at her captors.

Sebastian thrust Bet into Tully's bulky arms. Despite her struggles and objections, Sebastian tore strips of fabric from her tattered gown to make a blindfold and improvised ropes to bind up her wrists.

"Take Elizabeth to the spot where she was abducted," Sebastian instructed. "Make sure she loses all sense of direction."

"Eden and I know what you're planning," Bet blurted out. "But my father will never betray his cause. Never!"

Sebastian didn't argue the point. He already knew what General Pembrook would—and wouldn't—do. The contacts had been made. The scheme had already been set in motion.

"For your sister's sake, keep your speculations to yourself," Sebastian warned. "Your sister's life hangs in the balance."

"Damn your black soul to the farthest reaches of hell," Bet muttered at Sebastian before Tully carried her away.

His soul was already condemned to hell, Sebastian thought as Tully and his captive disappeared from sight.

Glancing grimly around, Sebastian sloshed through the marsh, pausing at regular intervals to listen for sounds that might alert him to Eden's whereabouts. He prayed that he could locate her before Lockwood did.

Eden bit back a scream when the horror of the present collided with nightmares from her past. Her entire body ached from her wild run through the swamps. Her captor had overtaken her, tackling her legs, causing her to slam her head against a tree trunk. Eden couldn't recall the exact procession of events that followed. The blow she sustained left her drifting in and out of consciousness.

Time and again, the swirling darkness parted like a black cloud, but pain exploded in her skull, sending her back into the disoriented silence. Even now, waves of nausea threatened to wash over her as she strained against the confining rope that held her fast.

Eden allowed herself the luxury of a sob as she curled up in a tight ball and shivered in her damp clothes. She wasn't sure where her captor had stashed her. In a smokehouse perhaps.

An eerie shiver snaked down her spine, remembering other instances when she had been trapped in uncertain darkness. Torturous memories from childhood assailed Eden, and she trembled uncontrollably.

She couldn't let the past overwhelm her, she told herself fiercely. She had put the torments of yesteryears behind her—and there they would stay. She couldn't allow herself to fall apart. She *would not* dwell on that tragic day when she had . . .

Eden squeezed her eyes shut. Her body quivered, despite her resolve. If not for this surrounding darkness, she could have controlled her fears. She needed sunlight—a sky full of it—to chase away those haunting shadows and tormenting voices.

Eden sagged against the wall and tried to stretch out her aching leg. There was barely room to move—only room enough for the suffocating darkness and terrifying memories.

Curse it! Hadn't she compensated for her awful crime? Hadn't she made amends every way she could?

She should have known she could never completely absolve her sins, that they would return to haunt her. The past never died, so long as the memories lived and breathed.

Eden had flitted from one phase of life to another, hoping to forget what she didn't want to remember, determined to put emotional distance between herself and her tormenting past, but the memories rose up in dreams, lurking like phantoms in the darkness, waiting, always waiting.

Shadowy images leaped out at Eden as she fought to keep her wits about her. The haunting scene unfolded around her, voices echoed in her throbbing skull. Eden recoiled and screamed, but the blows came repeatedly. She huddled deeper into the very darkness she hated—feared. She tried to fend off the blows, but pain rained down on her with every resounding curse . . .

In Eden's disoriented state of mind, the past merged with the present. The interceding years faded away, as if they had never been. Nothing could hold the truth of the past at bay. She had hoped each change in her life would be an effective barrier to separate her from the hounding nightmare, but there was nothing to protect her from her sinful past. Her defenses were broken down, one by one, until there was nothing left between her and her secret sin . . .

Eden flinched when the door rattled. She shrank back when the voluminous shadow towered over her. Then her masked captor swooped down at her.

It was the man who always wore a mask and Tory-green jacket, she realized vaguely.

"Time for you to learn another lesson in humility," Lockwood sneered as he grabbed a handful of Eden's unbound hair and hauled her to her feet.

Eden staggered, stumbled, and fell into Lockwood's arms.

"You will learn this lesson well," he vowed as he dragged her to the shack. "His high and mighty lordship, and his devoted lackey, won't be here to protect you this time. You have caused too much trouble, and when I'm through with you, you won't dare escape again."

The world spun crazily around Eden. Dizzy and nauseous, she vowed she wouldn't allow this bastard to break her spirit. She would focus on the precious memories of her times with Sebastian. His memory would become her salvation. She would conjure up the vision of his handsome face and lopsided smile and refuse to let her captor's cruelty penetrate her thoughts. Thoughts of Sebastian would protect her from whatever horrors were to come . . .

After two hours of futile searching, Sebastian turned back to the cabin. By now, Tully should have delivered Bet to safety and returned. If Lockwood had arrived with Eden in tow, Tully would be there to protect her.

And if Eden eluded captivity, what then? Sebastian asked himself. Although Sebastian disapproved of this mission, the arrangements had been made. This operation hung in delicate balance—like so many of the assignments he'd undertaken the past five years.

This could be the determining factor in the war, he reminded himself. Cornwallis was marching his men to the new British base, and Sir Clinton was holding on to New York. The nineteen-ship fleet was on its way to reinforce the land corps.

George Washington was scrambling, begging for Admiral de Grasse's twenty-four ships to sail up from the French Navy headquarters in the West Indies.

And in the middle of these strategic maneuvers, Sebastian was trying to carry out this underhanded scheme. Eden Pembrook had become the weight that could tip the scales from one opposing army to another . . .

The whimper of a feminine voice caused Sebastian to freeze in his tracks. The sound went through him like rolling thunder. When the tormented cry came again, Sebastian instinctively dashed toward the shack.

The terrified shriek that met him at the door had him

boiling with fury. He glanced around the outer room to find Haines and Baxter downing mugs of whiskey and casting uneasy glances at the bedroom door.

Tully was nowhere in sight. Cursing murderously, Sebastian stalked toward the bedroom.

When Sebastian opened the door, he saw a nightmare about to take place. Eden was strapped spread eagle to the bed, her soiled skirts riding high on her bruised and scratched legs. Lockwood straddled her, clearly intent on ripping away the bodice of her gown.

Sebastian pounced on Lockwood, knocking the vile brute to the floor. Then, swearing viciously, Sebastian grabbed Lockwood by the front of his shirt and yanked him to his feet. He hammered the bastard with repeated blows to the jaw. Lockwood reeled away, then recoiled to strike out, but Sebastian's doubled fist slammed into Lockwood's menacing snarl.

When Lockwood staggered back, Sebastian buried his fist in the man's soft underbelly. Lockwood doubled over, and Sebastian struck with a forceful uppercut that knocked the air from Lockwood's lungs. He dropped to his knees, blood dribbling from the cut on his lip.

But Sebastian wasn't satisfied. He hauled Lockwood to his feet to deliver another round of punishing blows.

"Yer lordship!"

Tully's booming voice shattered the furious haze that clouded Sebastian's thinking. With one fist curled in the lapels of Lockwood's coat, the other cocked in midair, Sebastian glanced back at Tully.

"Ye're making it too easy on the bastard," Tully said as his gaze leaped from Eden's demoralizing position on the bed to Sebastian's ominous stance. "If you kill him where he stands, there will be questions to answer."

Sebastian knew Tully was right. Reluctantly, he stepped back, then gave Lockwood a shove toward Tully.

"Get this cretin out of my sight. Send Haines and Baxter

to Yorktown with Lockwood in tow. If Lockwood isn't in the stockade, dishonorably discharged and waiting court-martial, I will make certain Lord Cornwallis brings the case to trial immediately."

Haines and Baxter hovered in the doorway, listening to Sebastian spout his explicit orders.

"Lockwood better be in the stockade when I arrive in Yorktown," Sebastian snapped. "If he isn't, I will come looking for the two of you, is that understood?"

The men nodded, then herded Lockwood away.

"Dear God," Tully whispered as he stared at Eden. "Look at the size of that knot on her head. She looks as if she's been dragged to hell and back."

Sebastian yanked off his hood, cloak, and gloves, then sank down beside his unconscious captive. He grimaced as he traced the purple bruise on her skull.

"Fetch some water from the well and fill the tub," he requested of Tully. "Did you find some garments for Eden?"

"I took care of that last night," Tully replied.

"Good."

"I knew this cursed mission was headed for disaster," Tully muttered. "We should have refused to be a party to this."

"And leave Lockwood in charge?" Sebastian asked. "Things would have been ten times worse than they are now."

When Tully shut the door behind him, Sebastian spat every oath he'd ever heard. His anger gave way to despair. He could spend the rest of his life trying to compensate for the torment Eden had endured at Lockwood's hands and it still wouldn't be enough to ease his guilty conscience. She was injured and unconscious because of him. Lockwood may have mistreated her, but Sebastian held himself personally accountable for her pain and anguish.

As gently as he could, Sebastian peeled away Eden's grimy

garments. He muttered to himself when he saw the bruises and scrapes on her arms and hips. Damn that Lockwood!

Tully rapped quietly on the door, then stuck his head inside. "The lady's bath is ready. The clean clothes are on the table. I'll be outside if you need me."

As if he were handling delicate crystal, Sebastian scooped Eden into his arms and carried her to the outer room. She stirred momentarily when he eased her into the tepid water, then she slumped into oblivion.

When Eden roused momentarily as Sebastian trickled water over her bruised skin, he quickly shifted position so he was behind her. He couldn't bear for her to know he was a party to this nightmare.

"Sebastian . . ."

When Eden breathed his name on a wobbly sigh, Sebastian felt an invisible knife twisting in his heart. He knew Eden hadn't recognized him, but it was obvious he was in her thoughts.

"I'm here," he whispered in the southern drawl she could recognize. "Just rest. I'll take care of you."

A feeble smile touched her lips before she sank limply in his arms.

Sebastian lifted Eden from the tub. He noticed the muslin gown Tully had placed on the table, but he decided Eden would be more comfortable wearing nothing at all. It wasn't as if she would be getting up and going anywhere for a good long while.

He tucked her in bed and stared down at the bump on her forehead, the scratches and discolorations on her cheeks. His heart turned over in his chest, imagining the pain she had endured during her escape attempt—and recapture.

Eden's flawless beauty had been marred. Eyes that once sparkled with inner spirit were closed against pulsating pain. Lips that once curved into a dazzling smile were cut and swollen.

Damn Lockwood to eternal hell! Sebastian raged silently.

Sebastian reached out to comb his fingers through the damp chestnut tendrils that coiled around her face. "I am dreadfully sorry, Eden," he whispered. "You will never know how deeply I regret this." His lips feathered over her mouth, ever mindful of her injuries, wishing he could heal her with just a kiss.

Sebastian glanced at the window, noting that Lockwood had drawn the curtains before stretching Eden on her torture rack. Sebastian didn't know why Eden had such a penchant for open windows and streaming sunlight, but he refused to let her wake up in the darkened room.

Rising, he drew back the curtains to let the pale shafts of sunlight flood the room. And then he cursed again his involvement in this nightmare. Hell did have a great deal more to teach him than he possibly imagined.

Elizabeth Pembrook Dalton stood in the foyer at Pembrook Plantation, leaning on her crutch and directing traffic with her free hand. After Tully deposited Bet beside the road, she sat there for only thirty minutes before she was rescued by her husband, a search party of wounded rebel soldiers, and the constable's posse. It has been an emotional reunion that had Elizabeth weeping in relief. When she saw for herself that Peter had only sustained a superficial wound, she limped into his arms and held on to him for dear life.

Since the day Elizabeth returned home, she had been acting in Eden's stead. And all the while that Elizabeth saw to the obligations at the plantation, she had prayed for Eden's safe return.

"Rodney, see that all the supplies we can spare are taken to the storehouse for the Continental Army," Bet instructed. "Pass along the news that Lord Cornwallis has set up headquarters in Yorktown. Rebel troops are converging on the area and we need food and clothing to sustain our fighting men."

Maggie smiled proudly as she watched Bet fill her sister's shoes with determination and efficiency. Bet had obviously paid more attention to Eden's daily procedures than anyone thought. If Maggie hadn't known better, she would have sworn Eden was standing there rapping out orders with a smile.

"I have also been notified that John Brady has returned home, wounded during the skirmish near Richmond," Bet reported, her voice strong with self-confidence. "We will make certain there is plenty of food on the Bradys' table. We want John to know how much we appreciate his efforts on our behalf."

Bet pointed her uplifted crutch at Maggie. "Doctor Curtis sent a message that more wounded soldiers will be arriving. We need more cots. Please have some of the servants see to the accommodations of the new arrivals."

After the staff trooped off to tend their tasks, Bet slumped tiredly against the wall. "I won't fail you this time, Eden, I swear it," she whispered.

While Bet was throwing herself into one crusade after another, Peter was showing his support for the American cause. At the moment, he was at the mercantile shop, loading up goods to be delivered to the storehouse.

Angus Dalton had shifted his full support to the rebels. He had donated clothing, blankets, cooking utensils, and staples to the approaching Patriot troops. And furthermore, Angus and Catherine had apologized to Bet for causing her anguish.

The phenomenal turnabout in the Daltons' attitude was Eden's doing, Bet reminded herself. She smiled ruefully when the image of her sister materialized before her. Bet wished Eden were here to witness the changes she had instigated.

And Eden damned well better be safe. Otherwise, Bet would track down "yer lordship" and skin him alive! He promised Eden wouldn't be hurt, and Bet intended to hold the man to his vow, because she had kept hers. She had told the constable that she had been blindfolded during her captivity and didn't know where she had been taken. Bet had done nothing to jeopardize her sister's life, and "yer lordship" damned well better not, either!

Thaddeus Saber set the mug on the table and levered his bulky body into the chair across from his guest. "You look exhausted, young man."

Lyle Hendrick, the British courier, nodded his dark head and eagerly reached for his ale. "Things haven't been going well of late, Thaddeus. The Americans, with their backwoods warfare, hounded every step of our march to Yorktown. The young French marquis joined forces with Anthony Wayne's hard-bitten veterans and von Stuben's well-trained brigade. We hadn't anticipated that."

"Perhaps you and Lord Cornwallis can catch your breath now that you've reached your destination."

Lyle took another sip of ale. "Our men could use a rest while we wait for Sir Clinton to send the British fleet down from New York."

"Yorktown will serve the British well," Thaddeus said. "Soon, the British Navy will be at Lord Cornwallis's back. With nineteen ships adrift in Chesapeake Bay, we shall soon have control of Virginia."

"I would feel more at ease if Sir Clinton would send part of his army south," Lyle replied. "But Sir Clinton intercepted a dispatch from the Americans that claimed they planned to lay siege to New York. Sir Clinton can't divide his forces with General Washington breathing down his neck."

"I doubt you will need reinforcements." Thaddeus

handed the tattered leather pouch to the British courier. "According to reports from our informants, American morale and supplies are low. Their numbers are too small in Virginia for a major offensive. Lord Cornwallis has seventy-five hundred soldiers under his command. The American have only one-fifth that number."

"I hope you're right, Thaddeus. Our armies have been on the march for months. We need time to recuperate."

Lyle finished off his drink, then rose to his feet. With the leather pouch containing official dispatches tucked in his jacket, he ambled toward the door. He paused to glance at the old man whose out-of-the-way cabin had become central headquarters for information relayed between scattered British troops.

"Cornwallis, Arnold, and Tarleton appreciate your help, and I appreciate the mug of ale."

"I do what I can for the cause," Thaddeus said humbly.

Lyle reached in his pocket to retrieve a coin, then tossed it to Thaddeus. "Keep up the good work. With luck, we will suppress these ragtag rebels before the year is out."

When the emissary went on his way, Thaddeus unfolded the new dispatches that had been left in his care. Retrieving his code book, he deciphered the messages sent by British high command. Then he strode over to fetch the bottle of cobalt chloride from the cabinet.

For more than two hours, Thaddeus labored over the parchments, rewriting his invisible messages between the lines of the dispatches. With his task complete, he folded the letters and stuffed them in separate pouches to be delivered to their respective destinations.

Thaddeus gathered the pouches and hobbled outside. Glancing cautiously around the thicket, he dropped the first pouch in the bucket, then lowered it into the well. The second set of orders was left hanging inside the smokehouse. He tucked the third packet inside his boot before he climbed atop his horse. With a nudge, Thaddeus sent the plodding mare off to rendezvous with another courier who would be awaiting his arrival.

Eleven

"It's about time you got back, yer lordship," Tully muttered as Sebastian came through the cabin door. "The lady has had one nightmare after another for the better part of the day."

"Have you kept her under heavy sedation?" Sebastian asked as he closed the door.

"I gave her a sleeping potion every time I forced her to sip water," Tully reported. "But I don't think the dosage is strong enough. She may be oblivious to pain, but she has been flouncing around and shrieking at irregular intervals."

"Does she recognize you?"

"No. If she opens her eyes, she looks right through me." Tully poured himself a tall drink of brandy and guzzled it in three gulps. "I'll be damned glad when this ordeal is over. How much longer do we have to hold Miss Eden hostage?"

"Thaddeus received news that Lord Cornwallis is settling in at Yorktown. The general has sent reconnoiters to watch Pembrook's militia. Pembrook knows what he has to do."

"Well, I'm glad somebody around here does," Tully grumped. "This whole affair makes me uneasy. I'm leaving the lady in your care while I get some fresh air." He ges-

tured toward the tray of food he had prepared for Eden.
"You can force food down her throat this time."

"And you can gather the new dispatches coming in from
Thaddeus's cabin," Sebastian requested.

"Expecting something important, yer lordship?"

"Very." Sebastian pulled the hood over his head and
grabbed the tray. "If things go according to plan, you're
going to be making the ride of your life very soon, Tully."

"And I'll be damned glad to do it," Tully said. "Playing
nursemaid, after Lockwood dragged that poor girl around,
is making me twitchy. It tears me up inside to see her like
that."

When Tully exited, Sebastian strode to the bedroom. It
sickened him to see Eden in such a weakened condition,
too. He had only to look at her and cold fury iced his
veins. Curse Lockwood's black soul!

Eden's terrified scream caused the hair to stand up on
the back of Sebastian's neck. He stared into Eden's ashen
face, watched her thrash in bed, as if she were fending off
painful blows.

"Damn him!" Sebastian muttered venomously.

"Mama, no! Please, not again!"

Sebastian froze to the spot. He assumed Lockwood's
rough treatment was responsible for Eden's nightmares,
but now he had the feeling that her wild flailing and whim-
pers had more to do with the shadows of misery she tried
to hide behind her sunny smiles.

"Please don't put me down there!" Eden whimpered,
clawing at the invisible image above her. "I hate the darkness . . . please!"

During the next half hour, Sebastian listened to bits and
pieces of tormented conversation and private thoughts
that tumbled from Eden's lips. What Sebastian discovered
about Eden's past shocked and saddened him. It also
dawned on him that the nightmare that had awakened her
at the inn, the night they had waited out the storm, was

triggered by these same torturous memories that haunted her now.

When Eden floundered on the bed, crying out in fear, Sebastian's heart went out to her. "It's all right, angel," Sebastian murmured as he eased down beside her, holding her protectively against him. "No one is going to hurt you. You're safe."

The deep baritone voice triggered other memories—far more pleasant memories—for Eden. The specters faded, replaced by a darkly handsome face and teasing grin. This was the vision that had been her salvation during those hellish hours of captivity. Eden reached toward the captivating voice, the tender smile, the gentle hands.

"Love me, Sebastian . . . love me . . ."

When tangled lashes swept up and tortured blue eyes looked right through Sebastian, he felt his heart give a fierce and mighty tug. He couldn't resist Eden's anguished plea, and pulled off the black hood and bent to press a kiss to her lips. He spoke to her without the polished British accent, reverting to the southern drawl she had come to recognize. "I'm here, Eden. I will always be here for you."

Eden melted beneath the touch of sensuous lips. Her arms wound around his neck and she held on to him as if he were a forbidden dream floating somewhere beyond reality.

"Please don't leave me this time," she whispered, staring sightlessly up at him.

"I'm not going anywhere," he assured her as he cradled her trembling body against his chest.

"I love you, love you . . ." she said on a drowsy sigh.

When she fell asleep in his arms, Sebastian held her— and prayed she would never realize that he and her captor were one and the same. God, how had fate managed to tangle their lives into such a hopeless knot?

An hour later, Eden groaned softly and turned away.

Sebastian glanced at his timepiece, wondering if the sedative was beginning to wear off. He couldn't risk being recognized. Eden was in no condition to deal with *that* deception at the moment.

Cringing at the thought, Sebastian retrieved the supper tray. "Wake up, m'lady. Your supper awaits." His cultured British accent was back in place—and so was the black hood that concealed his identity. When Eden stirred, he propped a pillow behind her head and gave her a gentle nudge. "Eden?"

Eden blinked. Where was she? A nagging throb drummed at her skull. Her head felt as if it were crammed with wool, and her mouth was as dry as dust. She desperately needed a drink. When a cup pressed against her lips, she eagerly accepted the warm brew, though it had an odd undertaste.

"Feeling better?"

"I'm not sure," Eden said groggily.

"Take another drink."

She obeyed. When she sank back against the pillow, pain pulsated through her rib cage and she shifted uncomfortably. It was difficult to tell where she hurt the worst. In her attempt to escape she must have slammed against the tree so hard that every bone and muscle had been bruised.

"Eat this. It will help you regain your strength."

As Eden munched on the biscuits without tasting them she wondered where she had heard that heavily accented voice before.

Oh, yes, now she was starting to remember. It was "yer lordship." But where was that vile monster who locked her in the darkness, then dragged her out by the hair of her head?

"Rest now, m'lady. You're safe from harm."

Eden sighed audibly, then yielded to the drowsy effects of the sleeping potion Sebastian had added to the tea. He covered Eden with a quilt, then ambled to the main room, hoping Eden would sleep through the night without being disturbed by more nightmares.

Sebastian had heard more than enough about the haunting ghosts that tormented Eden. What she unknowingly revealed to him explained a lot. Now, he understood the deep-seated reasons for her obsessive need to control her emotions. He knew why she disliked the darkness and grew apprehensive in confined spaces. He realized why she was eager for constant change. It was her desperate attempt to put distance between memories she did *not* want to remember—and obviously could never forget. One day, Sebastian would learn the whole truth, he promised himself.

Sebastian missed a step when he saw Tully lounging in the chair. "You're back."

"Sure looks that way, doesn't it?"

Lord, thought Sebastian, he had been so attuned to Eden and her needs that he was oblivious to what was going on in the outer room.

"Did you retrieve any new messages?" Sebastian questioned as he set the tray on the counter.

Tully fished into the leather pouch that was tucked inside his shirt. When he produced the dispatch, Sebastian lit the lantern, then unfolded the parchment. When he held the letter over the lantern globe, the words that had been written in lemon juice appeared, as if by magic.

Sebastian read the message and smiled in satisfaction.

"Good news, yer lordship?"

"Indeed," Sebastian confirmed. "You do have a long ride ahead of you, Tully. There will be a fresh horse waiting at each relay station en route." He gestured toward the cabinet. "Fetch the cobalt chloride. I have a message to include with this dispatch."

Sebastian sank down at the table to compose the invisible letter that would accompany this important dispatch.

"What are we going to do about Thaddeus?" Tully questioned.

"I'll deal with my great-uncle," he said, without glancing up from his work. Though he wrote quickly, no words appeared on the page, nor could this message be deciphered without the necessary chemical sprinkled on the parchment.

"How are you going to handle Thaddeus while Eden is in yer care?"

"We'll take up residence at Thaddeus's cabin while you're away," Sebastian insisted.

Tully frowned warily. "I think ye're asking for trouble. If Miss Eden finds out—"

"She won't," Sebastian cut in.

Tully scoffed. "You've been deceiving Miss Eden, but now ye're deceiving yerself."

"In a few more days, Thaddeus will no longer be needed here."

Tully smiled wryly. "I've grown fond of the old man."

Sebastian nodded, distracted. "So have I, but Thaddeus needs to make himself as invisible as the ink on this paper."

Stashing the completed message in his shirt, Tully strode off to fetch his horse.

Eden clawed her way through the groggy darkness when an insistent voice commanded her to do what her sluggish body could not.

"Come on, m'lady. I need your cooperation," Sebastian grumbled as he placed Eden's arm around his neck, only to have it drop limply to her side. "We're going for a midnight ride."

Eden's eyes fluttered shut as sleep called to her.

"Confound it, Eden." Sebastian gave her a gentle shake. "You have to wake up."

She didn't wake up.

Muttering, Sebastian scooped Eden into his arms. She hung there like dead weight.

Maneuvering Eden's unresponsive body onto the Arabian's back took more time than Sebastian estimated. He finally had to drape her over the saddle like a feedsack, then resituate her once he mounted up. When he trotted off, Eden bounced on his lap like a rag doll.

Several minutes into the cross-country jaunt, Eden roused to consciousness—slightly. Sebastian propped her head against his shoulder, but it slid down his arm. Finally, he hooked his arm around her waist and turned her to face him. Once he had settled her legs over his hips, he could hold her against him and still control the high-stepping stallion that was itching to run with the wind.

Sebastian was a mile from Thaddeus's cabin in the pines when Eden mumbled incoherently. He tensed, knowing she was trapped in another nightmare. When she squirmed for release, the Arabian pranced sideways.

"Calm down!" Sebastian snapped at the horse.

"Yes . . ."

"Not you—"

Eden shrieked suddenly. When she tried to launch herself away, Sebastian clamped his arm tightly around her to prevent her from somersaulting to the ground.

"Easy, Eden. It's only me," he murmured against her ear.

"Your lordship?" Eden opened her eyes, staring owlishly at her surroundings.

"Bad dreams?" he asked.

"The worst."

When Eden slumped against him, Sebastian sighed in relief. He didn't need Eden to battle nightmares while they were atop this spirited stallion. If the Arabian took the bit and ran with it, Sebastian wasn't sure he could control the willful animal and keep Eden tucked safely in his arms.

Thankfully, Eden didn't rouse again until Sebastian dismounted. He managed to catch her before she slid off the saddle onto the ground.

"It won't be much longer before you're nestled in bed," he assured her softly.

"That's nice," Eden mumbled.

Sebastian glanced down into her pixielike face that was surrounded by tangles of chestnut hair. The bruises had begun to fade, and Eden was beginning to look her old self again. Within a few days, the pain would also ebb and she could function without heavy sedation.

By then, this ordeal should be over, Sebastian assured himself. Also by then, there would be no need for Eden's captivity. The message Sebastian had delivered earlier in the week would accelerate the arrangements he and the other agents had made. With luck, Eden would be returned home without knowing that he was involved in this underhanded scheme.

By the time Sebastian tucked Eden in her new bed, she was sleeping soundly. He doubted she would remember being transported by horseback to a different cabin. She had been asleep more than she had been awake.

Smiling, he leaned over to trace Eden's heart-shaped lips. He would decrease the dosage of sedatives during the day so she could function normally. It was time to get Eden back on her feet. But at night, he would have to continue heavy sedation. He wasn't going to risk another escape attempt.

"Sebastian . . ." Eden whispered, then reached up to recapture the memories swirling around her.

The temptation to make love to her was nearly impossible to resist. Sebastian wanted nothing more than to lose himself in her arms, but he couldn't bring himself to take advantage of her when she didn't have full command of her mental faculties. He had deceived her enough without adding seduction to the list of regrets on his guilty conscience.

Furthermore, there was always the risk of unexpected visitors in Thaddeus's cabin, Sebastian reminded himself. He had to remain alert, in case a courier came to call.

Even so, Sebastian couldn't resist easing down beside Eden, enjoying their privacy while he could. When she inched toward him, his hand ventured off in a leisurely caress. "What do you want, angel?" he murmured against that sensitive spot beneath her ear.

"I want you . . ."

"I'm all yours, love," he assured her huskily.

And he was—for the duration of the night. But only in her whimsical dreams. And his . . .

Eden came awake after what seemed a century-long nap. Despite the annoying thrum in her skull, she lifted her gaze to see sunlight spraying through the windows—that were on the wrong side of the room.

She rolled onto her side to study her surroundings. Where the devil was she? The last thing she remembered . . . Good Lord, what *was* the last thing she remembered?

Very soon, Eden was wishing she hadn't remembered being tossed in the smokehouse, then dragged to the bedroom. A shudder rippled through her, wondering what had happened after she lost consciousness. She had conjured up Sebastian's image and clung to those cherished memories in order to survive.

A muddled frown knitted her brow as she propped herself up on the unfamiliar bed. She had dreamed the strangest dreams while she drifted beyond reality. She could almost swear she had actually felt kisses and gentle caresses skimming over her responsive flesh . . .

Eden gulped as she stared at the closed door. She had dreamed it all . . . hadn't she?

When the door whined open, Eden saw the familiar figure swathed in cloak, hood, and gloves. "Yer lordship" had arrived, bearing a tray of food.

"Good morning," he greeted cheerfully. "I thought I heard you stirring around in here."

"Where am I?"

"Back in merry old England it is considered proper etiquette to return a greeting before firing questions," he said as he approached.

Eden levered up against the wooden headboard. "We are not in merry old England, though I sincerely wish *you* were."

"I see you're in a sour mood this morning," he noted as he set the tray on her lap.

"This is as good as my mood gets," she declared, flinging her nose in the air. "I have no intention of being a gracious captive who is being used to blackmail my father."

Eden shot a glance toward the door, wondering about her chances of escape. Despite her nagging headache she seriously considered making a run for it.

"Don't even think about it," Sebastian warned, following her gaze. "You have yet to recover from your last escape attempt and your unpleasant encounter with Lockwood."

"Where is he?" Eden questioned as she picked up a slice of ham and chewed on it.

"Serving time in the stockade," Sebastian reported. "I'm dreadfully sorry you had to suffer the brunt of his wrath."

"Are you truly? What difference does it make to you what happens to me? I'm only a means to an end."

"I don't share the man's policy of terrorizing hostages."

"Always the gentleman, your lordship?" she asked flippantly. "I suppose you have visions of being knighted by the good King George if the British win this war."

Sebastian chuckled as he leaned over to trace his gloved finger over her cheek. "If I were to become a knight, would you be my lady?"

Eden jerked away from his caress, stunned by the most unsettling feeling. *The dream . . .*

Her wide-eyed gaze lifted to the hood that concealed her captor's identity. Good gad! Her dreams had seemed so lifelike that she could have sworn she remembered kissing . . . Eden swallowed with a gulp. No, surely she hadn't accepted "yer lordship's" kisses and caresses, thinking he was Sebastian . . . had she?

"Is something amiss?" Sebastian questioned when her face drained of color.

Eden shifted awkwardly, then glanced toward the wall. She wasn't sure she wanted to know if her suspicions were correct. Was it possible to kiss one man while imagining oneself in the arms of another? While under sedation—and Eden was positively certain she had been sedated—had she invited a total stranger to . . . ? Good Lord!

"Your lordship?"

"Yes, m'lady?"

"Did you . . . or rather did I—?" Eden massaged her aching temples and stared at her plate of food, as if the perplexing answers were printed there. "Did we—?"

"Eat your breakfast," he insisted.

Eden couldn't eat a bite until she knew if she had betrayed the precious memories of the only man she would ever love. "Did you and I—?" Curse it, she wasn't sure how to pose the embarrassing question.

"Did you kiss me and I kissed you back?" she blurted out.

Sebastian said nothing.

Oh, God, they hadn't done more than that, had they?

"Did we . . . was there more?" Eden wheezed, appalled at the thought.

When he didn't respond, Eden stared at him with her face blazing with embarrassment. "Answer me truthfully," she demanded. "Did we . . . or didn't we?"

Sebastian nodded slowly. "Yes, we did."

Eden collapsed on the pillows and squeezed her eyes shut in mortification. "I was afraid of that."

She had been betrayed by her own method of surviving her ordeal. She had whimsically wished for Sebastian to rescue her from her living nightmare and she had obviously superimposed his face and body on another man. *This man!* Her captor! Dear Lord!

Eden took several deep breaths and composed herself. "I think I should explain."

Sebastian grinned beneath his mask. He couldn't wait to hear this.

Eden folded her hands in her lap, gathered her thoughts and proceeded. "I was clinging fiercely to the memory of one very special man in order to survive the injuries I sustained at your cohort's hands."

"Power of mind over body," he supplied helpfully.

Eden nodded. "I've heard many of my wounded patients say that they conjured up images of loved ones when pain and terror became unbearable. I also know that I was given a sedative which made it difficult for me to know my own mind. The potion leaves patients with an insatiable thirst."

Eden shifted awkwardly on the bed. And now for the embarrassing part. "I don't wish to sound insulting. I'm sure the women who have ended up in your bed enjoyed themselves—"

Sebastian burst out laughing, then clamped his mouth shut when Eden frowned at him. "Excuse me. Do go on. I didn't mean to interrupt."

Eden was back in usual form, Sebastian realized. She

was trying to explain—diplomatically—what had happened on those nights when she had surrendered to his kisses and caresses.

"If I responded as willingly as I think I did, it was because I believed you were someone else," she explained.

"I see."

"Do you?" Eden stared at the concealing black hood. "Have you ever been in love, your lordship?"

"Well, I thought I was, but it turned out that I was wrong."

"I *was* in love," she emphasized, anxious to conclude this awkward conversation. "I was very much in love once. Although it wasn't meant to be, my feelings were strong. When I reached out to you in a haze of pain and sedation, I was reaching out to *him*. I realize that isn't flattering, but it's the truth. I believe it is important to be honest."

"Thank you for that," he replied. "If I am to be used, I prefer your reasons to women who use seduction for financial gain and social position—like the English ladies in court. Some women will do anything for the sake of wealth and title. They even go so far as to swear undying love while they go behind a man's back to take other lovers."

Eden was surprised by the intensity of his voice. She suspected he spoke from firsthand experience. "I agree that if there cannot be honesty and loyalty between a man and woman, there can be nothing at all. If you can't expect the truth from those you love, there can be no trust. Without trust there is nothing."

Sebastian winced. The comment struck too close to home. He hastily steered the conversation back in its original direction. "Being the honest individual you are, you are saying that I shouldn't read overly much into your eager response to me."

Eden turned ferociously pink. "That is exactly what I am saying."

Sebastian couldn't resist teasing her. "Then I should disregard everything you said and did and think nothing of the extraordinary moments we've shared."

Eden turned fuschia. "It wouldn't be fair to you. I wasn't myself when we—" She cleared her throat, then plunged on. "More to the point, you weren't actually *yourself* in my dreams, if you see what I mean. We should forget the incident happened, don't you agree?"

"No."

Her head snapped up. "No?"

"I enjoyed rare, magical moments with you."

"But I just explained all that," she burst out.

"No, you explained what you felt," he clarified, smiling outrageously beneath his concealing hood. "As for myself, I've never known such a tender, responsive lover."

Eden wished the floor would open so she could drop through it. This conversation was not going as planned.

He leaned closer, his gloved hand trailing down her arm in a familiar caress. "You are welcome to use my body anytime you want to pretend I'm someone else, m'lady."

"We are total strangers!" Eden chirped, shying away from his touch.

Sebastian chuckled as he came to his feet. "Not anymore, my dear. As the saying goes, we know each other's most intimate secrets."

Eden crammed a slice of bread in her mouth, swallowed, then stared at him. "There will be no repeat performances."

"Why not?"

"Because I don't wish to deceive you. And anyway, now that I know it was you, I wouldn't be the least bit responsive."

"Are you certain?" he challenged. "Perhaps this Prince Charming you think you love is only your excuse to explain your reactions to me. Perhaps it is only guilty conscience at work. Did you think of that?"

"No, I—"

"Maybe my kisses and caresses were more pleasurable than you expected. Perhaps recent memory overrode the old memory. Is that not a logical possibility?" he asked, grinning widely beneath his hood.

"Well, I suppose—"

"If that's true, wouldn't you be deceiving yourself by letting the man from your past take credit that isn't due?"

"Yes, but—"

"Being an honest woman, don't you owe it to yourself to find out for certain?"

Eden munched thoughtfully on a bite of ham. Whatever else "yer lordship" was, he was a man of keen intelligence. He left Eden questioning her loyalty to a man who hadn't returned her love. If Sebastian Saber had truly cared for her, wouldn't he have said so?

Was "yer lordship" correct in thinking she had over-dramatized her feelings for Sebastian in order to survive? Had she really immortalized his memory?

Eden was jostled from her pensive thoughts when her captor's hand grazed her lips. She glanced up at the hood that disguised his appearance, wondering what he would look like without his black hood and shapeless cloak.

"Perhaps an experiment is in order," Sebastian suggested.

Eden eyed him warily. "An experiment? Are you suggesting that I retest my reaction to you?" Her gaze narrowed. "Perhaps the truth is that you're trying to take advantage because I'm convenient."

"Make no mistake, m'lady, this has nothing to do with convenience," he told her. "That is *my* truth. You must find *your* truth—"

The pounding of hooves caused Sebastian to curse under his breath. Damnation, he didn't need company right now. Tully had warned him that life could get complicated with Eden underfoot while he was staying in Thaddeus's cabin. Couriers were known to arrive unexpectedly. Hopefully, this emissary would leave the message in the bucket at the well, or in the smokehouse, then be on his way.

To Eden's amazement, her captor bolted off the edge of the bed and snatched up the sheet. Hurriedly, he grabbed her wrists and bound them together. Eden was still staring goggle-eyed at him when he stuffed a gag in her mouth. Her charming captor had changed personalities in the blink of an eye, and she was left with her arms secured behind her back and tethered to the bedpost like a horse!

"Get some rest," he ordered. "I'll check on you later."

Eden stared at his departing back as he swept out of the bedroom with his cloak swirling around him like a tornado. The key rattled in the lock, then brisk footsteps clicked against the planked floor of the main room.

Maybe Eden couldn't shout for assistance, but she might be able to eavesdrop. She might happen on to tidbits of information that would serve the rebel cause.

Eden eased off the bed and tiptoed to the end of her makeshift tether. Sinking down on the floor, she tried to peer through the keyhole. She muttered a curse into her gag when she realized she wasn't close enough to the door to see into the outer room.

She glanced behind her at the bed, then tugged steadily on the sheet. The bed scraped against the floor, but inched forward. Eden repeated the procedure until she was close enough to the door to squint through the keyhole.

What she saw had her staring in stunned disbelief. "Yer lordship," with his back to the bedroom door, peeled off his cape and mask, then rummaged through the cabinet to grab a tattered gray coat, wig, and false beard! When he shucked his linen shirt to don homespun garments, Eden felt as if an unseen fist had slammed into her gaping jaw. There, on her captor's back, was a scar identical to Sebastian Saber's!

Eden nearly fainted in shock. It couldn't be, she tried to tell herself. It was only coincidence.

It's no coincidence came the quiet voice of reason.

Seething with anger, Eden watched her captor—alias Sebastian Saber—and only God knew what other names he went by—thrust a sinewy arm into the gray jacket that was lined with enough padding to make him look as if he had gained an instant twenty pounds. He pulled on a pair of padded breeches over his pants and fastened them into place—fifteen more pounds!

Silently smoldering, Eden watched him paste on his mustache and beard, then jam a gray wig on his head. He barely had time to arrange his clothes before someone knocked on the door, and a British courier handed the "old man" a leather packet. "I hope you have some ale, Thaddeus. There's a storm brewing outside. I could use a drink to ward off the oncoming rain."

In the bedroom, Eden peered through the keyhole and steamed like a clam.

"I had to dodge rebel patrols," Lyle Hendrick said as he plunked down at the table. "Those cunning rascals hide in mulberry thickets and try to pick us off with flying musket balls."

Eden glared at Thaddeus, "yer lordship," and Sebastian Saber—the treacherous trio of deception. Damn him!

"American troops are pouring into Virginia to stop Lord Cornwallis's attempt to set up his stronghold in Yorktown," Thaddeus said as he retrieved the jug of ale.

Eden noted the deep, gravelly voice with its heavy British accent. Sebastian played the role of a crippled old man as if he were born to it.

Lyle reached eagerly for his drink. "This area is jumping with Patriot guerrilla bands. The French marquis has joined forces with the Americans to establish a post near Williamsburg. I think the Americans plan to concentrate all their strength against Lord Cornwallis."

"Has Cornwallis set up redoubts around Yorktown?" Thaddeus asked.

"Yes, the soldiers are ankle-deep in sand. The choking clouds of sand make it difficult to dig our trench barriers. Rebel snipers are roosting in the cypress and cedars to take pot shots while we construct our defenses. But at least the rain will settle the sand and make it difficult for the snipers to do their worst."

"The Americans won't be an equal match for Cornwallis and his seasoned Regulars, especially if this scheme works as expected. The Americans have their weaknesses, and we will prey heavily on them."

Eden knew Thaddeus was referring to her captivity. But she would find a way to escape and alert her father. General Pembrook was not going to be coerced into turning traitor!

Lyle took another sip of his drink, then wiped off the ale mustache on his upper lip. "Do you have dispatches to be relayed to Cornwallis?"

Thaddeus nodded, then hobbled off to retrieve the leather pouch. "According to the latest report, the Americans won't be receiving reinforcements from the French fleet that is docked in the West Indies. Cornwallis should have British frigates in the bay beside Yorktown. The Americans appear to be putting up a bold front, but without the strength of Washington's seasoned army, the south will fall to the British."

"I hope your information is correct, Thaddeus." Lyle fished into his pocket, then placed a coin on the table.

Eden glared at the old man who snatched up the coin. Sebastian Saber accepted money from the British in exchange for passing along information. He was a spy! Sweet merciful heavens! She had been deceived. Sebastian had betrayed her trust and used her for his own purpose. The very thought sickened her.

Eden had never been so outraged. Sebastian had lied

and schemed and manipulated her—and all the while she had been falling in love with that sneaky lout! He would pay for this, she promised herself. She would see to it!

Damn, that was close, Sebastian thought to himself as he watched the emissary ride away. Hurriedly, he peeled off the frazzled wig and itchy beard. After doffing the jacket and breeches, Sebastian grabbed his hood and cloak.

He would be glad when Tully returned so he could run interference. Sebastian had several close calls the past few months, but none were as potentially dangerous as today's.

A wry smile came to Sebastian's lips when he recalled his conversation with Eden. It had been entertaining to listen to her explain her response to him. When he suggested an experiment to test her reaction, he had rendered her momentarily speechless. Of course, Eden would never agree to the absurd experiment, he assured himself. She was too loyal to his memory. And though it was dishonest of him, he had been inclined to test her faithfulness to him. It was gratifying to know there was one woman on the planet who cared for him because of what he was inside, not what he had acquired in the way of wealth and titles.

Grinning in satisfaction, Sebastian sank down at the table to decipher the coded messages he had received.

Twelve

Eden pretended to sleep each time Sebastian checked on her. Indeed, she had dozed off once or twice. She needed her rest, because it was going to be a long night.

The storm had descended on the drafty cottage. Wind whipped through the cracks in the wall, bringing with it a damp chill—like the one that had settled in her heart and soul. She had been deceived and betrayed by the man she loved. The cherished memories that had sustained her this past week were built on cunning lies, she realized.

First, Sebastian had preyed on Micah Bancroft's generous nature to gain a foothold in the area. No doubt Sebastian had made note of every storehouse stacked with American supplies and ammunition. Then Sebastian had turned his abundant charm on General Pembrook's older daughter. God, what a fool she had been!

Eden lay in bed, staring at the ceiling. She remembered the night of the country fair when she had taken the short-cut home and happened onto the group of men in the thickets. Sebastian had arrived shortly thereafter. He had been swapping information with that pack of hounds, she was sure of it.

Sebastian *just happened* to be nearby the night Eden stumbled onto the Tory patrol while she was tracking down her missing sister. Sebastian's Goliath of a friend had rescued her, then Sebastian accompanied her to the roadside inn to wait out the storm.

That devious scoundrel had taken advantage of every situation, Eden realized. She had been seduced, blithely unaware that Sebastian was on a fact-finding mission for the British.

Eden muttered a curse when she remembered the seemingly innocent questions Sebastian posed to the wounded soldiers in her care. He had been gleaning information about the strength and location of American troops! And she, naive fool that she was, had told Sebastian of her plans to travel into Williamsburg to speak with the Daltons. She had provided Sebastian with the perfect opportunity to abduct her. Lord, she was responsible for her own kidnapping and Peter's subsequent shooting!

When Eden remembered how Sebastian had taunted her about her responses to him while she was sedated she wanted to wring his neck! No wonder she had the feeling she was kissing the man of her dreams. She had been! But her dreams had evolved into bitter irony. The gallant lord of the British realm had made an absolute fool of her. It would serve him right if he found himself deceived . . .

She smiled as she pondered that possibility. Nothing would be more gratifying than deceiving a master deceiver.

And love, Eden realized, was the grandest deception of all. Now she despised Sebastian. She had outgrown her need for him and there was no going back.

Very soon Sebastian Saber was going to fry in hell . . . and Eden was going to furnish the kindling for the fire . . .

Garbed in his hood and cloak, Sebastian poked his head around the bedroom door. "Are you awake?" he asked Eden. "Since you slept through lunch, you need to eat supper so you can regain your strength."

"I'm famished," she said, then silently added, famished for revenge.

Eden glanced at the steaming cups of tea that sat on the tray, wondering if hers contained a dose of sedative. Somehow, she would see to it that *he* drank from her cup.

"Has it been raining all afternoon?" she asked, staring at the raindrops that splattered against the window pane.

"The rain began late this morning," he said as he set the tray aside to unfasten her wrists from the sheet. "I'm sorry I had to restrain you. I had an unexpected visitor to contend with."

"Did you?" she asked in feigned innocence. "I must have dozed off."

"Exhaustion," he diagnosed.

Eden suspected it had to do more with the sedative in the tea.

When Sebastian offered her the cup of tea, she smiled gratefully. "Could I trouble you for another quilt. There's a chill in the air."

While Sebastian was doubled over the storage trunk in the far corner of the room, Eden exchanged tea cups. And when he spread the blanket over her, she sipped her steaming brew.

"Better, m'lady?"

"Much better, thank you."

Sebastian picked up his cup and took a sip, and Eden smiled over the rim of hers. She reached for the two slices of bread, then offered one to him. Hopefully, the bread would disguise the undertaste of sedative in his tea.

"You are in a cheerful mood," Sebastian noted.

"I'm feeling better. I have also been giving serious thought to the past few days." Eden continued while Sebastian drank his tea and munched on the bread. "Although we hold opposing views on the war, and I don't approve of this underhanded scheme, I must admit that you have treated me with kindness and courtesy."

"I assured you from the onset that I had no intention of hurting you."

"I am grateful, despite this distasteful situation."

Sebastian offered Eden a slice of cheese. "You won't be detained much longer, I promise."

No longer than it takes to outsmart a clever British spy, she said to herself.

"I have been considering the suggestion you made this morning," Eden announced.

"My suggestion?" he repeated cautiously.

Eden looked away. She didn't want to appear too eager, for fear he might become suspicious. "I have been pondering your theory about . . ." She paused, cleared her throat, then added, "About . . . what transpired between us."

Sebastian shifted onto the edge of his seat. "Yes?"

"I think you might be right in thinking I made too much of a man who has come and gone from my life."

"Has he? Come and gone, I mean."

"I'm afraid so." Eden tried to look the part of a woman who pined for lost love. "Truth is, my affections were not equally returned."

"I see." Sebastian bit into a chunk of cheese, then chased it with tea.

"I think I simply got carried away. My reckless surrender weighed heavily on my conscience—just as you said. I made a foolish mistake, and he left without any promise of returning to make a permanent commitment to me."

"Perhaps he couldn't give you a definite time because he didn't know when he would be back," Sebastian said in his own defense.

Eden smiled wryly. "I think that now *you* are giving the man more credit that he deserves. He toyed with my affection, and you have convinced me that I simply fancied myself in love. But all my perspectives have changed now.

Life, after all, is but a series of phases we pass through. I have outgrown my need for the man I thought I loved."

Outgrown. There was that infuriating word again. Sebastian wanted to reach over and shake Eden. Instead, he took a sip of tea, wishing he had taken the time to mix his own special blend. This colonial brew had an odd taste.

"So now that you have entered a new phase of your life, you have no need for the man who left you behind," Sebastian paraphrased.

"Precisely." She graced him with a blinding smile. "I knew you would understand."

"And where does that leave the two of us?" he managed to say without growling at her.

"I was just coming to that." Eden drained her tea, then offered the cup to him. "Could I have more tea. I'm incredibly thirsty."

Sebastian grabbed both cups and stalked off.

Eden grinned. She hoped Sebastian Saber was frying in his own grease. It was what he deserved. When she was through with this crafty scoundrel, he would know that she no longer fancied herself in love with him.

Meanwhile, Sebastian was in the main room, using a heavy hand on the sleeping potion. Eden's twisted logic exasperated him. He, the former love of her life, had been shunted aside. He should have kept his mouth shut this morning. His ornery prank had backfired.

Yawning, Sebastian returned with two cups of tea. He had to find a way to convince Eden that she hadn't outgrown her need for Sebastian, that she still cared for him, that striking up an affair with her captor was ridiculous!

"Thank you for the tea." Eden eagerly took the cup, then peered curiously at him. "Do you have more cheese? I'm still hungry."

Sebastian stared at her in surprise. "You have already eaten all of it?"

The cheese was tucked beneath her quilt—to be used as a midnight snack after she escaped from this devious spy.

"Yes," she lied with a smile. Thanks to him, she had learned to lie without batting an eyelash. "I really am hungry tonight."

When Sebastian set his tea aside and reversed direction, Eden switched cups.

"Your cheese, m'lady," he said as he set the slices on her tray.

Sebastian sank heavily into his chair. The tension of dealing with Eden and British emissaries was obviously taking its toll on him. He would like nothing better than to climb into bed beside Eden, ease his craving for her, then drift off to sleep. Unfortunately, he needed to restore his name, and his memory, to Eden.

"Now then," Eden said, nodding decisively. "About our experiment."

Sebastian silently groaned. He was feeling sleepier by the minute. "I don't think this is a good idea."

"It was your idea," she was quick to remind him. Then she lowered her lashes and looked away—for effect. "Perhaps I have leaped to ill-founded conclusions here. Perhaps you have already grown bored with what we shared."

"You don't bore me." Sebastian's yawn belied his words.

Eden set aside the tray and flipped back the edge of the quilt. "Come to bed, your lordship," she whispered invitingly.

Drowsy, Sebastian did as she requested. When Eden cuddled up next to him, he tried to remember what it was that he wanted to prove to her, but he couldn't seem to recall.

When her hands glided over his chest, and she bent to press a tender kiss to his throat, Sebastian felt himself sinking into the mattress. A strange kind of drugged pleasure flooded through him . . . and then he was drifting into peaceful darkness . . .

When Sebastian's arm fell loosely to his side, Eden tapped him on the chest. "Yoo-hoo, your lordship."

His muffled snore mingled with the patter of raindrops.

"Can't handle a dose of your own medicine, can you?" Eden asked wryly.

Rolling from the bed, Eden removed his cloak and hood. For spite, she tugged off his breeches and flung them into the corner. She shook out the hood and draped it over his bare hips, then retrieved the rope to tie him to the bed.

He was going to wake up, realizing he had been deceived and humiliated. Then he would know exactly how she felt.

"Sleep well, your lordship," she smirked as she plucked up his cloak and ambled from the bedroom.

Despite the drizzling rain, Eden hiked off to retrieve Sebastian's horse from the shed.

Two horses were tethered inside the lean-to shed. Eden took the Arabian. She didn't have the faintest idea where she was, or how to reach home, but anywhere was better than being confined to a cabin with a man who had betrayed her, used her, and deceived her.

Touching her heels to the stallion's flanks, Eden thundered off in the rain, hoping to come across a path that might lead her to the Virginia Militia—or home. She had to get in touch with her father as quickly as possible, to assure him that he didn't have to agree to any British demand.

A shiver trickled down Eden's spine as she wandered through the darkness, looking for a trail. Nightmares from her past threatened to torment her, but she battled the unreasonable fears. If she could outwit Sebastian Saber, then she could hold her composure, even when she flinched at every sound that came from the darkness. If she could find her way to the American Army's encampment, she would soon be reunited with her father, she told herself. Ensuring that Leland didn't betray the rebel cause was tantamount.

As for Sebastian, he could roast in hell!

"Married?" Leland Pembrook stared incredulously at Bet, who was propped up on her crutch. "You are too young to be married. Fourteen is—"

"I just turned eighteen," Bet reminded her father.

Leland blinked. "Eighteen? When did that happen?"

Peter Dalton smiled at his bewildered father-in-law. "You've been away for more than three years, sir," he prompted.

Leland shook his silver-gray head in disbelief. "Has it been that long?"

His gaze circled the immaculate parlor, noting the wide-open windows and new furniture arrangement. Eden's influence, Leland suspected.

Thoughts of Eden put a frown on Leland's weathered features. He wondered how his elder daughter was faring during captivity. Confinement had never suited Eden. She was too spirited and energetic by nature. Yet, she was also made of sturdy stuff—a chip off the Pembrook block. Eden was nothing like her mother—thank God. Eden had ensured that Elizabeth was nothing like her mother, either.

"Peter, would you give Papa and me a few minutes of privacy?" Bet asked her new husband.

Peter frowned at the request, but Bet reassured him with a smile. He nodded, then walked from the parlor without taking offense.

Bet maneuvered onto the couch, then elevated her bandaged ankle. When she had formulated her thoughts, she stared into her father's intense blue eyes. "I know you are in one devil of a predicament because of Eden's abduction."

Leland plunked down in what had been his favorite chair, still unable to believe it had been three years since he had been home. "Yes, the situation is extremely awkward," he admitted.

Bet leaned forward, her green eyes brimming with concern. "Papa, what are you going to do? Eden insisted that you protect the cause of freedom, no matter what sacrifice had to be made. She can't bear the thought of soldiers' lives being forsaken in exchange for her safe return."

"Your sister has always put the needs of others above her own," Leland concurred.

"You have fought too long and hard for colonial independence to betray the cause at this late date. A man of honor could never do what that traitor Benedict Arnold did!" Bet said emphatically.

"Arnold's treachery was unforgivable. Washington would like nothing better than to capture that double-crossing scoundrel. Unfortunately, Arnold took his regiment north to Connecticut. The turncoat raided, burned, and butchered prisoners in New London. Personally, I want to see him hung for treason!"

"Eden and I don't want you forced into the same category with a man like that. So what are you going to do, Papa?"

Before the general could reply, a young soldier appeared at the doorway. "Forgive me for interrupting, sir, but a courier arrived from Marquis de Lafayette's camp. The commander requests a conference with you."

Leland patted Bet's knotted fists, then came to his feet. "Don't fret, dear. I will take care of it. In the meantime, you will be in charge of the plantation. Our home is about to become military headquarters. See that tomorrow's meals accommodate at least a dozen officers."

Leland strode off, and Bet slouched on the couch. She

had tried to fill Eden's shoes, but there were times when Bet felt overwhelmed by all the responsibility heaped on her.

Snap out of it, Eden would say. *We don't have time to dawdle when chores need to be done.*

Bet grabbed her crutch and stood up. Eden would not have taken time out to wallow in unproductive thought. She would attack the mountain of duties awaiting her. And so would Bet.

Things could be worse, Bet consoled herself. She could have been called upon to fill Leland's shoes. The poor man was faced with the tormenting choice of defending his country or saving his elder daughter. It was a choice Bet wouldn't have wished on anyone, least of all her father. For if Leland defied the British he might be signing Eden's death warrant!

Tully Randolph propped himself up in the saddle and gave himself a pinch, in hopes of staying awake. He had fallen asleep twice during his long ride and had toppled off his steed.

Just a few more miles, Tully encouraged himself. He could catch a catnap before dawn, then deliver the dispatch to its next destination.

Relief washed across Tully's craggy features when he spied the cabin nestled in the pines. He longed for the warmth of the hearth and a set of dry clothes.

When he reached the shack, he dismounted and grabbed his saddlebags. His steed would have to wait to be unsaddled until Tully caught a nap. After all, the horse was in better condition than its rider. Tully had switched mounts at every relay station en route. *He* was the one who was dead on his feet.

Tully pushed open the cabin door. The logs in the hearth had burned out, and the room had an icy chill.

After starting the fire, Tully rolled out his pallet and collapsed upon it. He would speak to Sebastian after he slept, Tully decided. From the look of things, Sebastian was making himself at home in Eden's bed.

And Tully had a thing or two to say about that! And he would—as soon as he caught up on his sleep . . .

Eden reined the Arabian to a halt and stared in confusion across the meadow. Twilight glowed on hundreds of canvas tents. Campfires lit up the countryside. Never had she seen such an overwhelming concentration of military troops! There were thousands of silhouettes moving around the encampment.

Were they friend or foe? Eden wondered. She couldn't tell.

A bugle sounded in the distance. Eden watched, with a growing sense of pride and relief, as the American flag was run up the pole to wave in the wind.

As the sun winked through the cover of gray clouds, Eden surveyed her surroundings. The swamps and thickets of mulberry and pines lay to the northwest. Williamsburg and Pembrook Plantation must be to the southeast, she deduced. And someone among these troops could tell her where to find her father.

Eden felt an urgency to locate Leland and notify him of her escape. She couldn't delay, not when Leland was faced with the choice of betraying his cause to save her.

Pulling the dark cloak around her, she nudged the Arabian toward the guard post. Muskets snapped into firing position as she approached, greeted by loaded weapons and suspicious frowns. She tried out her polite smile as she pushed the cloak from her head, allowing the tangle of chestnut hair to spill over her shoulders.

"What are you doing out here alone, miss?" the lieutenant questioned in concern.

"It's a long story, sir. I need an audience with your superior officer. I'm General Pembrook's daughter."

"The Rebels' Angel?" The lieutenant lowered the barrel of his musket.

Eden gnashed her teeth. She didn't feel like anybody's angel. She felt like a churning mass of conflicting emotion. Learning that she had been deceived and betrayed had done nothing for her disposition. Even now, knowing Sebastian had purposely deceived her, she was frustrated that she still had tender feelings for the man.

The lieutenant led Eden to the central square where three large tents had been pitched around the campfire. Dozens of coffeepots simmered above the flames. Eden stared wistfully at the pots. She would love to have a warm drink to thaw out her cold flesh.

"One moment, Miss Pembrook." The lieutenant bowed politely. "I will inform Marquis de Lafayette of your arrival."

The soldier ducked beneath the tent flap, then returned a moment later. Eden was escorted inside to meet the red-haired, freckle-faced, and hazel-eyed Frenchman who looked to be her age.

So this was the famed young man who was a member of one of the oldest families in France—a family who could trace its lineage back to the year 1000 and boasted an ancestry of brave warriors and noblemen.

Lafayette had offered his services to the American cause, endearing himself to General Washington because of his tireless energy, dependability, and loyalty. It was said that Washington treated the marquis like his son, teaching him all he knew about commanding soldiers in battle. The marquis had won a place in the hearts of Americans, who hailed him as one of their heroes.

Too bad Sebastian Saber didn't possess the marquis's sense of integrity, Eden thought bitterly.

"Miss Pembrook, may I present Marquis Marie Joseph

Paul Yves Roch Gilbert du Montier de Lafayette," the lieutenant said.

Eden smiled at the long-winded title that denoted enough pedigrees to stagger the crowned heads of Europe.

The marquis chuckled good-naturedly as he motioned the lieutenant on his way. "I think the overzealous soldier is trying to impress me with his ability to remember my full name." He bowed slightly, then lifted Eden's hand to press a kiss to her wrist. "My friends call me Gilbert. How may I be of service to you, mademoiselle?"

"My friends call me Eden," she said, then sank wearily into the chair Gilbert offered to her. "I'm in search of my father's infantry. I have a message of utmost importance. Do you know where he is?"

"*Oui.*" Gilbert poked his head outside to request a cup of coffee for his bedraggled guest, then turned back to Eden. "I was in contact with your father yesterday evening. He has been setting up accommodations for headquarters at your plantation."

"He has?"

Gilbert nodded his red head. "Our staff will meet there for conference this afternoon. We are planning to seal off Lord Cornwallis in Yorktown."

"I would like nothing better than to see the British commander waving his white flag of surrender," Eden insisted. Now, all she had to do was speak to her father before he succumbed to the British!

Gilbert offered Eden a cup of coffee and a smile. "You are to be commended on your contribution to the cause of liberty. I have heard a great deal about the Rebels' Angel. You have established a hospital for the wounded in your home and sent supplies to feed and clothe soldiers."

Eden took a sip of coffee, savoring the warmth that spread through her. "I have done what I can," she murmured.

"And I hope this war will end here and now," Gilbert said. "And by the grace of God, the end will come soon."

After a few more minutes of talking, Gilbert checked that Eden had finished her coffee, then drew her to her feet. "Though our accommodations are meager, you can rest before we journey to your plantation," he said.

Gilbert escorted her to an evacuated tent near the campfire. Eden stretched out on the cot and sighed. For the first time in two weeks she felt safe and secure. She was miles away from the deceitful Sebastian Saber. As far as she was concerned, Sebastian and Lord Cornwallis could slink back to England, never to be seen or heard from again. Sebastian was a tormenting reminder of the foolish mistakes she had made—mistakes she would never make again!

Tully was jolted awake by a quiet rap on the cottage door. He hauled himself to his feet to answer the knock. The Tory courier blinked in surprise when someone other than Thaddeus greeted him.

While Lyle Hendrick stood there, dumbfounded, Tully grabbed him by the jacket and pulled him inside. "You'd be looking for the old man, I expect."

"Yes, I—" Lyle clamped his mouth shut, refusing to speak.

"Not to fret, lad," Tully assured him. "I'm one of Thaddeus's emissaries. I just rode in from the north and camped out on the floor."

"My orders were to deliver my messages directly to Thaddeus," Lyle said stiffly.

Tully strode toward the bedroom. He inched open the door—and his eyes nearly popped from their sockets. Sebastian was staked out half naked. His black hood had become his loincloth and he was snoring up a storm.

"Holy—" Tully shut his mouth and closed the door.

Composing himself, he pivoted to face the courier's curious stare. "Thaddeus isn't here. He must have ridden off to gather supplies."

"But my orders—"

"Well, boy, you have a choice," Tully told him. "You can leave the pouch in the bucket at the well or try to track Thaddeus down. It won't do any good to give the dispatches to me, because I'll be leaving soon myself. I have messages to deliver this afternoon."

Flustered, Lyle considered his options. He decided to break the rules—just this once. "I will see to the matter," he said as he wheeled toward the door.

"You do that," Tully grunted.

Impatiently, he waited for the young soldier to stash the leather packet in the well, then ride away.

Muttering, Tully strode to the bedroom.

Sebastian moaned groggily when Tully jostled him with all the gentleness of a grizzly bear.

"Wake the hell up, yer lordship!" Tully shouted.

Sebastian tried to turn away from the blaring voice, but he found himself immobilized. He raised heavily lidded eyes—and sucked in his breath when his gaze landed on his naked torso. "Hell and damnation!"

Tully untied the restraining ropes. "I can't wait to hear how you got yerself into this predicament."

Suddenly, it came back to Sebastian with startling clarity—the drowsiness, the lure, the deception. Damn it to hell! If Eden foiled his plans at this late date, he was going to choke the life out of her!

"Some cunning master spy you turned out to be," Tully said, and scowled. "You couldn't keep one dainty female under wraps for two weeks."

"I can do without your commentary," Sebastian muttered irritably.

"But you couldn't do without the lady, now could you?" Tully eyed him with disapproval. "I can hazard a guess about what went on in here before you ended up tied to the bedposts. If you ask me, you damned well got what you deserved."

"Nobody asked you," he muttered irritably.

Sebastian snatched up his clothes in fiendish haste. When he jerked up his breeches—backward—he swore colorfully.

"Eden must have switched the cups of tea so I ended up with the sedative," Sebastian mumbled.

"Clever of her," Tully's lips twitched as Sebastian stabbed his arm through his shirtsleeve—backward. The man's head was so full of cobwebs he could barely function. "Must be damned humiliating to wake up to find yerself half naked, tied to a tether."

Scowling, Sebastian fought a clumsy battle with his boots. "We've got to find Eden, and quickly! If she disrupts our plans, we face disaster."

"You can bet that she'll be headed straight for her father," Tully predicted.

"Hopefully, it will take her awhile to find him. Maybe I can keep one step ahead of her."

Sebastian dashed outside to find his stallion gone. Swearing, he saddled the extra mount. As he led the way through the pines, Tully erupted in a shout behind him.

"I almost forgot!" He reined back to the well to retrieve the dispatch from Lyle Hendrick. "This message arrived before I found you staked out in the bedroom."

Sebastian wheeled his horse around to double back to the cabin. He gathered his code book and mounted up. He would have to decipher the messages en route. He didn't have a minute to spare for fear the unflappable Eden Pembrook would find a way to thwart the intricate network of arrangements he had made.

Eden must have overheard his conversation with Lyle Hendrick, he speculated. She had disguised her outrage and anger behind that disarming smile—and then tricked

him into drinking the sedative. And now that she knew
who he was, she would never speak to him again!

"Yer lordship?"

"Yes, Tully?" Sebastian murmured, distracted.

"You really are going to have to do something about
Eden Pembrook. You've got responsibilities where she is
concerned."

"I'm aware of that."

"Then you will take care of the matter properly?"

"I doubt she will be receptive to anything I have to say
now that she's discovered who I am."

"Nonetheless, you have to do the right thing," Tully
insisted.

"And I keep telling you that Eden is going to be difficult
to deal with."

"Ye're very good at difficult situations," Tully encouraged him. "Or at least you used to be, until you ran amuck
with that pretty little saint of a female. I'm beginning to
think she is more woman than even you can handle, yer
lordship."

Sebastian muttered sourly. *He* was beginning to think
Tully was right.

Thirteen

Eden left the rebel encampment, escorted by the crème de la crème of military echelon. Marquis de Lafayette rode at her side. Anthony Wayne and von Stuben were behind her. To her right, General de Kalb sat atop a strapping bay gelding.

Just let Sebastian Saber try to snatch her away from these competent officers, she thought. She was going to spoil his devious plans so fast it would make his head spin.

"I appreciate your efforts to our cause," Anthony Wayne said gratefully. "You have become a legendary inspiration to the troops."

Eden smiled. "Thank you, General. I wish we could do more. If we had more space in the house for the wounded—"

"You are entirely too modest, my dear," General de Kalb interrupted. "I can't imagine how you find the time to do all the miraculous things you do. Thanks to your pleas for support our storehouses are heaping with supplies to feed men who have gone hungry. Our wounded return to their units, singing praises of an angel of mercy who watches over them and offers the comforts of her own room. Families in need have found baskets of food on their doorsteps. You have single-handedly boosted morale. Your father has been proud as a peacock each time your name passes a soldier's lips. Legends of the rebels' guardian angel are widespread."

Eden shrugged off the glowing accolades and focused her attention on the tents that dotted the meadows around Pembrook Plantation. It looked as if the entire Patriot Army had camped out in her backyard!

"It is a grand sight, is it not?" Gilbert de Lafayette said with pride. "So many men gathering to repel the British and fight for their freedom. We have taken a beating for the last time. Victory will be ours if we can seal off Lord Cornwallis in Yorktown."

"If General de Grasse and his French fleet from the West Indies arrive for reinforcement we can anticipate a major victory," von Stuben put in.

Eden's thoughts wandered away from the exchange between the high-ranking officers when she feasted her eyes on home. She had never been so glad to see the sprawling brick mansion and those split-rail fences that lined the driveway in all her life. Home. Sebastian Saber couldn't touch her now, not with an army camped by her doorstep. She would expose Sebastian for the cunning spy he was, and he would be tossed in a musty dungeon for the rest of his miserable life.

Eden set aside her bitter thoughts when she saw her father stride across the lawn. Eden dismounted and sailed into his outstretched arms.

"Eden, it's so good to see you!" Leland enveloped her in an affectionate bear hug.

"All is well now, Papa," she confided quietly. "You don't have to fret anymore. I escaped my captors, so you don't have to bend to their demands."

Leland stepped away, staring solemnly at her. "Eden—"

"Dear Lord, it isn't too late, is it?" She searched his face intently. "You haven't done anything to betray the cause, have you?"

"No, but—"

"Miss Eden, thank God you're back safe and sound!" Maggie interrupted as she rushed outside to squeeze the stuffing out of Eden. "Bet and I have worried ourselves sick, and the wounded soldiers have been moping about for two weeks. One look at you will send their spirits soaring again."

Before Leland could manage another private conversation with Eden, the Patriot officers converged on him. Maggie propelled Eden inside to receive Bet's smothering embrace.

"Thank the Lord!" Bet gushed. "Oh, Eden, I'm so sorry you couldn't escape when I did. It was my fault you had to endure such a long captivity. How did you elude them? Are you all right? Did they—?"

"I'm fine." Eden broke through Bet's barrage of questions. She didn't want to discuss her captivity. Her dreams had been shattered, and she had discovered she was a poor judge of men's character. Sebastian Saber was—without question—the worst mistake she had ever made.

"Monsieur Saber! It's a pleasure to see you again," Gilbert Lafayette called from the doorway.

In shocked amazement, Eden pivoted to see the dark-haired scoundrel standing in the doorway of her dining room, as if he belonged there. He looked as suave and self-assured as ever, damn him! Where did he learn such bold audacity?

His skills of deception were obviously so well perfected that he had gained the confidence of the most exalted leaders of the American cause. This clever British spy was being paid to relay American battle strategy to his fellow Englishmen, yet the rebels seemed to think he was one of them!

Sebastian had to be stopped, and he had to be stopped now!

Eden pointed an accusing finger at the man who had deceived and betrayed her. "Trai—"

"Hello, Miss Pembrook." Sebastian clasped her out-stretched hand, bowed gallantly and pressed a kiss to her wrist. "It is a pleasure to see you again." He flashed her a charming smile. "You look a mite pale. I hope you have been feeling all right."

Her nails bit into his hands, and she flung him a glare that was hot enough to melt the iron off a skillet. "As a matter of fact, Mr. Saber, it has been a most unpleasant couple of weeks."

"I'm sorry to hear that." He practically squeezed her fingers off her hand, daring her not to make a scene.

When Eden glowered murderously at him, then opened her mouth to voice her condemnation, Sebastian's lips narrowed into a grim line. "I *wouldn't* if I were you," he whispered for her ears only.

Eden decided that she most definitely *would* speak her piece. Sebastian couldn't threaten and intimidate her while she was surrounded by military upper echelon. The only one around here who was going to be dreadfully sorry was Sebastian—the spy—Saber!

"Papa, you have a devious traitor in your midst," Eden blurted out. "This is one of the men who held me hostage under British orders."

Eden swore she could have heard a feather drop to the floor of the crowded foyer. To her shocked disbelief, no one but Maggie and Elizabeth seemed to be stunned by her announcement. Indeed, the illustrious Patriot officers stifled smiles and glanced from one to another. That was not the reaction Eden expected.

"Well, aren't you going to arrest him?" she sputtered.

"Um . . . Eden, I tried to explain a few minutes earlier, but we were interrupted." Leland strode forward to take Eden's hand, then led her into the dining room. "I'm afraid there has been a slight misunderstanding."

"I assure you, Papa, there is no misunderstanding—" Eden's voice dried up when Tully Randolph stepped from the shadowy corner of the room. She would have recognized the brawny man anywhere. This was the man who once rescued her from disaster, and then betrayed her to "yer lordship's" cause. This scoundrel was obviously Sebastian's accomplice to treason!

Before Eden could spout another accusation, Tully bowed politely. "Good afternoon, Miss Pembrook."

When Eden glanced between Tully and Sebastian, clearly overwhelmed, Leland turned to his fellow officers. "Gentlemen, under the circumstances, I think my daughter should be allowed to sit in on the conference while Colonel Saber presents his report."

Colonel Saber? Was this another alias?

Eden stared at Sebastian in wary consternation. Dear God, the Patriots truly had been deceived into thinking that "yer lordship" was one of *them!*

"We have no objections," Gilbert Lafayette said. "In fact, I would consider it an honor and good omen to have an angel in our midst."

While the officers took their seats at the table, Eden glared venomously at Sebastian. This was going to be one of his finest efforts of deception, Eden predicted. She couldn't wait to hear the crock of lies he fed to the military's upper echelon. She was going to contest everything this sneaky spy had to say!

"Permit me to seat you, Miss Pembrook," Sebastian offered cordially.

Eden sank down in the chair he pulled out for her. "Of course, why shouldn't I allow it? I have already permitted you to betray, use, and deceive me. I am anxious to hear you twist the truth to suit your purpose this time. But be warned, your lordship," she hissed, "I am going to expose you for the treacherous spy you are."

Sebastian grimaced as he stared down at Eden. She was positively furious. She tried to hide it, but it showed.

There were dozens of things Sebastian wanted to say to

Eden, but he didn't have the chance. Of course he knew she would never forgive him—even saints had their limitations. If the murderous expression in Eden's eyes was any indication, she had been pushed beyond her limit.

Well, hell, thought Sebastian. There was nothing for him to do but present his report and hope he would have the chance to speak to Eden alone when the conference ended.

Standing at the head of the table, Sebastian focused his attention on the officers who anxiously awaited his report. "Most of you have already been informed of the British plot to abduct General Pembrook's daughters and hold them for bargaining power," he began. "Tully and I played out our roles and tried to prevent the women from coming to harm during their captivity. Our objective was to leave Cornwallis with the impression that Pembrook would provide information about America's weaknesses and upcoming battle strategy."

Eden frowned dubiously. Sebastian Saber was exceptionally good at twisting lies into convincing truths. He had also dropped his staunch British accent, as if he never had one! Even his gestures, mannerisms and the way he walked changed, when he wasn't portraying "yer lordship!" How did he do that?

"Because the British thought they had Pembrook in their pocket, Lord Cornwallis decided not to engage Lafayette and press for absolute victory against the rebel forces at Richmond. Cornwallis fell back to establish his stronghold at Yorktown, choosing to wait for a dramatic conclusion to this war.

"By doing as General Washington suggested, Lafayette was able to prevent the junction of Cornwallis's Regulars and Phillips's army, buying us the precious time needed to put our reinforcements in place for a major offensive.

"Our intelligence network has been feeding Cornwallis false information through Pembrook. The British have accepted the messages as truth, because Eden's life supposedly hung in the balance."

"What other distorted truths has the exalted Lord Charles Cornwallis been fed?" von Stuben inquired, smiling wryly.

"The British assume the Patriot numbers are only half their actual size and that Pembrook's militia will fall back during the upcoming skirmish, allowing the British to advance and penetrate American lines at Yorktown."

Sebastian unrolled his sketches on the table, then pointed out the sites he had located during his reconnoitering missions. "Cornwallis has erected forbidding fortifications on the riverbank, above and below Yorktown," he told the officers. "The redoubts are protected by rows of sharpened logs and heavy artillery. Beyond Yorktown creek, with its deep ravines, lies the inner line of British defense. Our reports indicate that Cornwallis has seven redoubts and a half dozen gun batteries in the second barrier of defense."

Eden silently wondered if Sebastian was misrepresenting the facts to the rebel command. She still wasn't certain whose side he was on—if any side at all. More than likely, this mercenary's loyalties lay with the highest bidder.

"The only access for British retreat will be across the bay to Gloucester Point, where a long palisade has been erected," Sebastian noted. "I believe we can blast Cornwallis into submission and prevent him from crossing the bay to rejoin Clinton in New York. But we will have to strike hard and relentlessly if we hope to keep him bottled up between the sea and the sheer bluffs on the riverside."

Sebastian grinned. "Lord Cornwallis will be in for a shocking surprise very soon. I have been altering his dispatches, leading him to believe that Admiral de Grasse's French fleet will not arrive in time to come to our aid. He thinks he will have the British Navy at his back."

"Will the French fleet arrive in time?" Anthony Wayne asked anxiously.

Sebastian nodded. "De Grasse, and his twenty-four men-of-war, are carrying three thousand French troops. They will completely seal off the bay within a few days, making it impossible for the British Navy to come to Cornwallis's defense. The news has been coming up through our network of agents this past week, and Tully took the report directly to General Washington, who has been staging his own clever deception against Clinton in New York. The Continental Army left thousands of campfires burning in the darkness in order to mislead Clinton. Then Washington and his soldiers beat a hasty march south during the night. Clinton didn't know the rebels were gone until long past daylight. Washington will soon arrive to take part in the siege of Yorktown."

The officers eased back in their chairs, smiling in satisfaction.

Eden watched Sebastian carefully, wondering if this was another pack of misinformation that would lead to the rebels' downfall.

Sebastian unfolded the message Tully had delivered from the commander-in-chief, then read it to the officers. " 'We are on our way to you and we expect the pleasure of seeing your encampment. I hope you will keep Lord Cornwallis safe, without provisions or forage until we arrive.' "

Washington's request drew a round of snickers from the military high command.

"We will indeed keep the illustrious Lord Cornwallis safe," Leland Pembrook said. "He can sit on his Yorktown throne and watch the French fleet bottle up the bay, cutting him off from the British frigates. We will seal him off by land, cut off his incoming food and supplies, and he will have nowhere to go, nothing to do but surrender."

Eden glanced curiously from one officer to another.

Were they actually swallowing this nonsense Sebastian was stuffing down their throats? Didn't they realize this was another clever ruse, designed and engineered by a master spy? Why, they were as gullible as Eden had been!

"Do not let this man deceive you into thinking you have cornered the British!" Eden erupted as she bounded from her chair. "The rebels are the ones who will—"

"Eden, sit down," Leland Pembrook ordered in his most authoritative voice.

Eden's chin tilted to a determined angle. "I most certainly will not sit by and listen to this traitorous spy fill our heads with cunning lies. I saw a Tory courier hand a pouch of coins to this British spy in payment for information about Patriot troops. I also saw him disguise himself as an old man who relayed messages—"

"Eden, confound it," Leland blustered. "Saber is a double agent who has purposely falsified information that is supposed to fall into British hands. He was hand-picked by General Washington himself, after serving with our commander-in-chief during the first year of the war. In fact, Sebastian was a charter member of Washington's Life Guard. It was his duty to screen visitors and check background information. Washington and Saber have been neighbors and friends for a decade, and Saber is in charge of military intelligence."

Eden's thoughts and emotions were being twisted into tangled knots. She didn't know what to believe, especially when Sebastian could be so convincing and persuasive, no matter what role he chose to play.

"I have received many messages from Chameleon—as Saber has become known, because he has been a man of so many faces," von Stuben said in Sebastian's behalf. "I was once visited by a shabbily dressed old farmer with wiry red hair who carried a basket of eggs into which messages had been rolled up and inserted into the shells."

"I once received a Bible in which the words of sentences were underlined in invisible ink. They were delivered by a half-crippled preacher last winter," Lafayette spoke up. "Monsieur Saber is presently heading the network of agents in Virginia and Carolina. He is the very man who escorted me to General Washington when I arrived to pledge my services to the American cause." Lafayette smiled in amusement as he glanced at Sebastian. "As I recall, Saber was posing as a Tory blacksmith at the time."

Eden's mouth dropped open.

"As you see, Miss Pembrook," Anthony Wayne said with a grin, "one can't always trust our perceptions. If not for men like Saber and Randolph, we wouldn't have succeeded in luring our enemy into our hands for this siege at Yorktown. It has taken months of meticulous planning."

Mortified, Eden rose from the table. Whether Sebastian was for or against the American cause, he had succeeded in making her look the fool in front of these esteemed officers—and her own father.

"Forgive me for my ignorance and my accusations," she murmured before she turned on her heels and swept out of the room.

There and then, Eden vowed never to speak to Sebastian for the rest of her life—or his, whichever came first. If he was supporting the British, then she would have to find a way to prove that her accusations were correct. If he sided with the Americans, then his conduct implied that he considered her such an imbecile that she couldn't be trusted with Patriot secrets—*her*, the daughter of a general!

No doubt Sebastian had found amusement in watching

her make an absolute fool of herself in front of her father's peers—men she idolized. Damn Sebastian Saber! How many more ways could he humiliate her? How could he be so cruel and uncaring of her feelings?

And how could she have fancied herself in love with a man who obviously had so many faces and personalities that no one truly knew who he was?

Eden stepped into the vestibule and paused to inhale a steadying breath. She was not going to let Sebastian disrupt her life for another minute. She was going to put him completely out of her mind, forget he even existed. She would carry on as usual, making her personal contribution to the American war effort.

Resolved to that purpose, Eden squared her shoulders, bolstered her resolve and marched upstairs to check on her patients.

The smiling faces that greeted Eden did wonders for her flagging spirits. She was touched beyond words to learn that the wounded soldiers had attempted to rescue her the night she had been abducted. Yet, Eden was concerned that her patients had put their own health in jeopardy for her sake.

"After all you've done for us, how could you think we would abandon you in your hour of need?" Henry Maynard questioned as he propped up on the edge of his cot.

"I appreciate the fact that you cared enough to organize a search party to look for me," Eden replied. "But I'm hardly worth risking setbacks in your conditions."

"Hardly worth the risk?" Artemus Riley hooted. "Nobody would turn his back on an angel in need."

Eden was growing annoyed at being constantly referred to as an angel. She wasn't deserving of the title. Less deserving than these soldiers could possibly imagine. And furthermore, her ordeal with Sebastian Saber made her feel like the very devil.

"Eden, my dear?" Leland Pembrook poked his gray head around the door. "I wonder if your patients could spare you for a few minutes. There is a matter we need to discuss."

Eden followed her father down the hall. "I assume your conference has adjourned."

"Yes, and I will rejoin my men in camp shortly," he informed her. "But I wish to put our business in order before I leave."

Eden frowned, puzzled. "What business?"

Leland descended the stairs, Eden one step behind him. When Leland strolled leisurely into the parlor, where Sebastian and Tully lounged on the sofa, Eden screeched to a halt in the doorway. The very last thing she wanted to do was be in the same room with the very last man she ever wanted to see again.

"Come sit down, Eden," Leland requested, when his daughter refused to budge from her spot.

Eden stared at Leland, as if he had just asked her to swim through shark-infested waters. She would have to walk past Sebastian to reach the vacant chair.

"I can hear you perfectly well from here, Papa," she replied, refusing to glance in Sebastian's direction. "What do you wish to discuss with me?"

"Sebastian Saber has asked for your hand," Leland announced proudly.

A puff of wind could have blown Eden down. What absurd nonsense was this? "Oh, he has, has he? And does he wish for me to chop off my hand at the wrist or the elbow?"

"Eden!" Leland stared aghast at his daughter. "I never thought I would see the day when a sarcastic word flew out of your mouth. You have always been the epitome of courtesy and politeness. What the devil is the matter with you?"

"I am sure the disreputable company I have been keeping lately must be to blame," she explained.

Sebastian bit back a grin when she aimed the barb at him and hit her mark. Rising, he sauntered over to Eden, then dropped into a spectacular bow. "Let me assure you, Miss Pembrook, that I have no intention of separating you from your hand at wrist, elbow, or anywhere else." He smiled politely, though she glared pitchforks at him. "The fact is, I am interested in the whole of you. Will you do me the honor of marrying me?"

"Why? Can't you find anyone else who is foolish enough to wed you, *your lordship?*" she asked flippantly.

Tully choked in amusement while Leland stared at Eden in shocked astonishment.

"Eden, for God's sake, what has gotten into you? I thought you would be pleased with the proposal. You are twenty-one years old—"

"I'm twenty-four," Eden corrected her father. "The rest of us haven't been frozen in time while you were away, though I must admit that I am beginning to wish I would have been."

"Twenty-four? Good gad, things are worse than I realized. It is long past time for you to take a husband and begin your own family."

Eden elevated her chin and stared past Sebastian as if he were empty space. "I have decided to become a spinster," she informed her father. "In fact, I made the decision several months ago."

"That is preposterous," Leland objected. "Your loving, caring tendencies are qualities that will make you a wonderful wife and mother."

"Is it preposterous that I want to enjoy my personal independence, without a man telling me what I can do

and when I can do it? Is it preposterous that I am perfectly satisfied with my life just the way it is?" Eden gave
her chestnut head a firm shake. "I have no intention of
marrying Sebastian Saber, or any other man, now or
ever."

"Whyever not?" Leland demanded to know. "Saber
won't restrain your self-reliance and independence. He is
a fair, reasonable man. Otherwise, I would not have given
his proposal my blessing."

Eden fixed her gaze on Sebastian's darkly handsome
face. "I feel restricted already." Indeed she was. It was all
she could do not to pound this scoundrel flat and mail
him back to England—where she wished he would have
stayed in the first place!

"I am offering wedlock, not human bondage," Sebastian clarified.

"And I am supposed to be flattered, I suppose." Her
tone of voice indicated that she was anything but!

"It would be nice if you were," Sebastian said, smiling
engagingly.

"Well, I'm not. I am offended that you think I would
even consider accepting such a ridiculous proposition in
light of everything that has happened."

"Eden, I thought we satisfactorily explained what happened and why," Leland broke in.

Sebastian pivoted to face Tully's amused grin and
Leland's befuddled frown. "Perhaps if Miss Pembrook
and I were allowed a few moments of privacy we could
come to an agreement."

"I doubt it," Eden muttered obstinately.

When she wheeled away, intent on making a run for
it, Sebastian latched onto her satin-clad arm and drew
her deeper into the room.

"I have to return to my troops. I hope you will resolve
this matter quickly." Leland informed his daughter, then

flashed her a cajoling smile. "I would like to have this engagement on the home front resolved before we *engage* the British at Yorktown."

Eden was not amused by her father's pun. What she was was incensed that she was being left alone with the man she had sworn to hate—for a thousand legitimate reasons!

Fourteen

The moment Leland and Tully left the parlor, Eden jerked her arm from Sebastian's grasp, then retreated to the furthermost corner of the room.

"If you have suddenly been struck by the need to do the right thing by me, I guarantee that the gesture is not only unnecessary but unwelcome," she hissed at Sebastian. "This marriage proposal was not prompted by your strong sense of integrity, because you have none."

Sebastian surveyed her belligerent expression. "Why is it that your seven would-be fiancés were treated to your courtesy and cunning powers of suggestion, while I am lambasted with insults?"

"Isn't it obvious?" she parried. "You bring out the worst in me. That in itself is proof that a marriage between us would be disastrous."

Sebastian begged to disagree as he edged ever closer. "I think interesting would better describe a marriage between us."

Eden took one giant step back, refusing to be taken in by that sensual aura of masculinity that surrounded Sebastian. "I don't want to marry you under any circumstances. I want you to leave this plantation and never come back."

"Why?"

"Because I don't like you very much."

One dark brow arched in contradiction. "You have said you loved me more than once."

"That was a lifetime ago. Things have changed, and so have I. Now I have outgrown my need for you. You have nothing of interest to offer me—"

Sebastian snaked out his hand and drew her into his arms. He had come to despise that word, and upon hearing it, he grew instantly irritated. "We have not *outgrown* each other, Eden. Now kindly tell me the real reason you are dead set against accepting my offer?"

"Take your hands off me," she hissed at him.

"Not until you tell me why you won't marry me."

"I will explain nothing until you back off and give me breathing space."

Sebastian dropped his arms to his sides, then retreated.

Eden made a spectacular display of fluffing the wrinkles from her sleeve. "Although I can't imagine why you offered the proposal in the first place, I refuse because you deceived me, lied to me, and used me. And furthermore, I cannot imagine how you can be so arrogant to think I would accept, given the situation."

"Eden, I had no other choice in the matter—"

"We always have choices," she argued. "But you have been at this spy business so long that lies come easier for you than the truth, I suspect. I suffered nine kinds of hell because of you. And for your information, I'm not sure I believe everything you told the military commanders."

"It was the truth," he maintained.

"Was it? You seem to be the only one who knows for certain. How very convenient, just in case your wavering loyalties should suddenly lean toward the British."

"Damn it, Eden, what would you have me do, when faced with the choice of accepting the British assignment to take you captive? If I left Lockwood in charge, you would have suffered nines times the torment. I couldn't reject the assignment, because the British would have become suspicious of me. I couldn't take that risk, not with the situation in Virginia starting to fit together like a jigsaw puzzle."

"You could have confided your purpose and plans to me," she snapped.

"And how would you have reacted in Lockwood's presence?" he questioned. "Would you have conducted yourself as if there was no possibility or need for rescue, because you believed you would come to no harm? Would you have behaved as if you knew for certain that your father's integrity and reputation wasn't about to be torn asunder? Would you have accepted your captivity and calmly waited for the charade to end?"

"Yes, I wouldn't have worried unnecessarily. Furthermore, I would never have tramped through the swamps, and Bet would never have been injured—"

"And your calm acceptance would have aroused Lockwood's suspicions," Sebastian contended. "All the arrangements I have made to turn this war to the rebel advantage would have been in vain. We have arrived at this point in the battle strategy of the war because the hostage situation is believed to be successful."

Eden glared at him. "Essentially, you are saying that my pea-size feminine brain could not assimilate the facts and respond with the kind of behavior the situation demanded."

"I'm saying nothing of the kind."

"The crux of the problem is that you didn't trust me with the information," she accused. "You believed me to be incapable, so you lied to me, used me to suit your purpose, seduced me while I was under sedation."

"I didn't seduce you under sedation," he contradicted.

"You said you did," she was quick to remind him.

"I lied, just to see how you would react to the possibility. I'm ashamed to say that the mischievous part of my nature got the better of me at that moment."

Her gaze narrowed on him. "If you lied to me then, why should I believe anything you have to say now, Sebastian?"

Sebastian winced. He should have known his ornery prank would return to haunt him.

Eden spun around and stared out the window, her nose in the air. "I refuse to marry a man who has no faith in my abilities or my intelligence. You have teased, insulted, and lied to me for the very last time. Now kindly leave. We have nothing more to say to each other—ever. And if I happen to see you fighting for the British at some time in the near future, I can't say I will be surprised."

Sebastian hadn't wanted to press his advantage, but Eden was being excessively stubborn and close-minded. He was determined to resolve the situation—any way he could.

"If reasoning won't work with, you force me to apply other methods to gain your cooperation."

Eden tossed her head and stared out the window. "There is absolutely nothing you can say to make me change my mind."

"No?" he challenged.

"No," she said with firm conviction.

Sebastian circled around to face her. "There is the matter of what really happened to your mother those many years ago, is there not?"

Eden's flushed face turned milk-white instantaneously. She staggered back as if he had struck her. "How—?" was all she could get out before her throat closed up.

Sebastian cupped her chin in his hand, forcing her to meet his unblinking stare. "You talk in your sleep, Eden. I noticed the shadows of carefully guarded secrets in your eyes when we first met, heard the catch in your voice when a dark memory from the past slipped past your self-control. I remember the first nightmare I witnessed while we were at the inn, and I recall the ones that followed while I held you captive.''

With each comment, Eden's face paled even more.

"Does your father know what happened to his wife, or did *you* twist the truth for your benefit? Did you deceive Leland into thinking you and your mother were something you were not? And whose charade testifies to the greater sin, I wonder? Yours or mine?''

Eden felt as if ice water was flooding through her veins. Sebastian couldn't possibly know her terrible secret. He was bluffing. Even under heavy sedation she wouldn't have . . .

When those silver-gray eyes bore into her, Eden swallowed hard. *Dear God, he knew!* She had betrayed herself to him!

"Now, will you set our marriage date or shall I?" he asked very deliberately.

"I . . . will . . . consider your betrothal," she said shakily, her eyes flashing with resentment.

Sebastian shook his head. "No, not this time, Eden. I will not give you time to beg off as you have done seven times before. And you are not going to use the power of suggestion to persuade me to retract my offer. I am not like the rest of your suitors."

He certainly had that right! The other men were gentlemen. Sebastian Saber was a devilish scoundrel, and he was still playing games with her. He was going to use his private knowledge to punish her for her sins, even after she had spent a lifetime atoning for her crime.

"Shall we seal the engagement with a kiss?" he whispered as his dark head moved steadily toward hers.

Eden stiffened, refusing to feel anything except outrage. But her resistance wavered when his full, sensuous lips glided over hers. She didn't want to expose her vulnerability to this man, but the tenderness in his kiss assured her that he still had the power to stir her. Despite their conflict,

there was still this fierce attraction that had been her downfall since she met him.

Eden couldn't imagine why Sebastian wanted to marry
her. He must have another wily scheme in the making.
She was to become his pawn again, she suspected. Why
else would he insist on a hasty wedding? It wasn't because
he loved her and was impatient to be with her. No, he
definitely wanted something from her, Eden was certain
of it.

"Yer lordship?" Tully's voice wafted across a room that
had plunged into silence.

Eden lurched back, ashamed of herself for accepting his
kiss—and enjoying it. Damnation, she simply could not
trust herself when she got within three feet of this sensual
wizard. She was too susceptible to his masculine charms.
And now that he knew the truth of her past, he would
hold it over her for the rest of her life, forcing her to
become an accomplice in whatever treacherous scheme
he devised.

No, she could not possibly think of marrying this man.
There had to be a way out, Eden told herself, and she
would think of one as soon as Sebastian gave her enough
space to gather her scattered wits.

"The marquis requests our presence in his camp," Tully
continued when Sebastian pivoted to face him. "I think
another mission awaits us."

Sebastian glanced back at Eden and scowled. He didn't
trust her to graciously accept his proposal, and he hated
himself for pushing her into a corner. Yet, if he left Eden
alone, he knew she would devise some way to escape him—
just as she had eluded her former fiancés.

"I will be along in a moment, Tully," Sebastian murmured.

When Tully lumbered off, Sebastian focused absolute
attention on Eden. "I want you to set the wedding date—
now."

"I think the week after the war ends would be an appropriate time for a wedding, your lordship."

Sebastian refused to be deceived by a comment that was loaded with double meaning. "Which war, angel? The one between England and America or the one between us?"

"We are at war?" she asked with feigned innocence. "Good gracious, you should have said so. I will need extra time to gather my weapons and ammunition."

Sebastian was not about to give her time to gird herself up for battle. He wanted the situation resolved here and now. "The wedding will take place at the first of the week. You aren't going to spend your time dreaming up ingenious ways to avoid your eighth betrothal."

"Ingenious?" Her perfectly arched brows lifted in mock surprise. "You give too much credit to an empty-headed twit who could not possibly be trusted with military secrets."

"No, Eden, I know you well enough to give you full credit for your keen wit and intelligence," he said, eyes narrowed on her.

She stared pensively at him. "Do you really?"

"Yes, and furthermore, I think I know you better than you know yourself."

"And I suppose you think I should leave it up to you to know what is best for me. That sounds like something an egotistical male would say. But I feel that I am at a tremendous disadvantage in this matter, because I don't know the real Sebastian Saber at all. In fact, were we to wed, I'm not sure which personality I should expect to encounter—the cocky adventurer, the soft-spoken Thaddeus, or the sophisticated Lord Saber."

"You will have a lifetime to get to know the real me," he said.

"Naturally, I am intrigued by that prospect," she said flippantly, then shooed him on his way with the flick of her wrist. "Now you best hurry along. You are keeping Gilbert waiting."

"*Gilbert?*" Sebastian repeated.

"Gilbert," she confirmed. "And the French marquis is one of the most sincere gentlemen I have ever had the pleasure of meeting. He is dedicated, loyal and honest—the endearing qualities I admire in a man."

"In other words, everything you have decided I am not."

"You said it, I didn't," she flung back at him.

"Yer lordship!" Tully prompted from the foyer.

Sebastian scowled in frustration. "I'm coming, damn it."

He didn't want to leave, because he didn't trust Eden to her own devices. He had twisted her arm a dozen different ways, and yet she refused to submit. But no matter what, Eden was going to be his wife. He needed time to reassure her that he did care about her, that he truly regretted what he had been forced to do. Somehow, he had to convince her that his marriage proposal was honest and sincere.

"Eden, I—"

"Dear, sweet Gilbert is waiting," she cut in.

"About the marriage—"

"Duty calls," she persisted. "You said yourself that patriotic duty must be your first priority and that my personal feelings cannot stand in the way."

Sebastian gnashed his teeth. Eden had an unsettling way of reminding him of every conflict, every mistake he had made.

"I'll be back," he said as he spun on his heel.

"Thank you for the warning, your lordship."

Sebastian broke stride, then glanced over his shoulder to pin her with a probing stare. When she smiled that cheery damned smile, Sebastian scowled to himself.

Eden stared pensively after him. She couldn't marry the man. It was out of the question. He held too much power over her.

In her opinion, a good marriage required a delicate balance of power. Man and wife had to trust and respect each other. A man who tried to blackmail his would-be bride would never respect her, never look upon her as his equal partner. And more to the point, Sebastian would never love her as she had once loved him.

Eden sat herself down to contemplate the problem. She could pack up and run. She could join a nunnery . . . Now there was a good idea. Perhaps she could rely on the fact that she had been referred to as an angel and a saint. She could claim to have heard the calling. Who would dare dispute that?

But what if . . . Eden knotted her fists in the folds of her gown. What if she carried Sebastian's child? Then she wouldn't be suitable nun material.

There had to be other options, Eden assured herself. All she had to do was calm down and think. And that, she realized a good while later, was easier said than done!

"Well, yer lordship, did you and Miss Eden set a wedding date?" Tully questioned a mile down the road.

Sebastian frowned. "I'm not sure."

"How can you not be sure?" Tully asked.

Sebastian let out his breath in a rush. "If I am not mistaken, Eden views my marriage proposal as a declaration of war."

"War?" Tully parroted. "When a man tells a woman he loves her and that he wants to marry her, how can that possibly be misinterpreted as grounds for battle?"

Sebastian scowled. "Who said anything about love?"

Tully scowled back. "Apparently *you* didn't."

"I have been down that road before, as you well know. And you also know where that forthright declaration of sentiment got me."

"But Lady Penelope was a bird of a different feather,"

Tully contended. "Miss Eden isn't a selfish social butterfly craving titles and wealth."

Sebastian waved off his well-meaning friend's arguments. "It wouldn't have mattered what I said to Eden. She thinks I deceived her and betrayed her. *That* she cannot forgive."

Tully swore aloud. "I knew that damned assignment was trouble. But surely Miss Eden realizes that, under the circumstances, marriage is the only logical solution."

Sebastian barked a laugh. "Eden assured me that there were always choices, no matter how far one is backed into a corner."

"What are you trying to say, yer lordship?"

Sebastian peered bleakly at his friend. "I'm saying that Eden Pembrook—for all the saintly qualities she exhibits toward the less fortunate of the world—is the stubbornest, most contrary creature God placed on the planet. She refuses to make concessions for my conduct, though she unconditionally forgives everyone else for their shortcomings. In fact, she claims that I bring out the worst in her. Therefore, I don't possess any of the qualifications for a tolerable husband."

"And if you can't come right out and admit that you love her, perhaps you aren't acceptable," Tully remarked.

"I told you that Eden wouldn't believe it, even if I said it. For me, love has turned out to be a double-edged sword."

"And because you were wounded by the blade more than a decade ago, you are too much the coward to risk injury again, eh?"

"I am not a coward," Sebastian snapped.

"No? Then why is it that you can't even admit the truth to yerself, even while you are busy trying to conceal it from everybody else."

"I am many things, several of which Eden just finished pointing out to me, but I am not in love. I will admit that

I have fond affection for Eden and that I believe we can have a workable marriage."

"If you say so, yer cowardly lordship," Tully taunted. "But a man who doesn't even know his own heart is a sad sight to see, to my way of thinking."

"Your way of thinking appears to be warped and twisted," Sebastian flung back.

"Fine then, become ex-fiancé number eight. At least you won't be alone in your unsuccessful mission to marry Miss Eden. Maybe after all the ordeals she's been through the past two weeks she has outgrown her need for you."

Tully smiled shrewdly when Sebastian snarled a curse. "I guess there are some challenges that can't be met, and some women who can't be tamed. Though I think you are obliged to meet yer responsibilities for compromising the lady, I suppose a man can only do so much, given his limitations. And I also think, yer lordship, that you have not only *met* yer match, but *lost* it."

"And *I* think *you* think, and speak, too damned much on subjects you know nothing about," Sebastian muttered.

"Then that makes two of us, yer lordship," Tully insisted, grinning wryly.

Sebastian gnashed his teeth. He had been frustrated when he left Pembrook Plantation—and he was still frustrated. Tully was badgering him unmercifully.

Hell and damnation. One minute Tully was trying to convince Sebastian to accept his obligations, and the next minute the man suggested that Sebastian admit defeat. Eden and Tully were both making him crazy and he had a mission to fulfill. He didn't need distractions right now.

And he was not in love, Sebastian assured himself a mile later. He wasn't going to stumble into that humiliating trap again. Confessing to love made a man vulnerable. Being vulnerable to a strong-willed, independent woman like Eden Pembrook was asking for trouble. Vulnerability, Sebastian was certain, was what earned Eden's ex-fiancés the ax. They had fawned over her, plied her with doting affection—and she had left her footprints on their backs when she waltzed away.

No, a man couldn't handle Eden the same way he dealt with typical females. Eden reacted too differently. She was highly intelligent. If she thought she held the upper hand with a man, then she would grow as bored with Sebastian as she had with the other seven casualties of betrothal. Now, if only Sebastian could figure out how to handle Eden he would be able to accomplish the impossible.

Sebastian set his mouth in a grim line. No matter what, Eden was going to become his wife the following week. They shared passion, the likes of which he had never known, and her astute wit fascinated him. Sebastian could not imagine any man wanting a mistress when a wife like Eden could stir such a kaleidoscope of emotions inside him. Already, Sebastian felt as though Eden belonged to him—with him—in every sense of the word. They had shared the best—and worst—of times and he never grew tired of her companionship.

When she got over being angry at him, she might realize there was something special between them. And she was going to marry him so they would have the time to explore all the emotions they aroused in each other, even if he had to resort to blackmail to get her to accept his proposal . . .

Sebastian inwardly winced when the image of Eden turning as white as flour when he mentioned her secretive past rose in his mind. He hadn't wanted to excavate the ghosts that obviously tormented her. But damn it, he had been desperate to gain her cooperation.

Sebastian frowned. Perhaps he had gone about the proposal backward. Maybe he should have . . .

"Ah, there you are, Colonel Saber." Gilbert Lafayette stepped forward to grab the Arabian's reins. "We have one more assignment for you, before we send our regards to Lord Charles Cornwallis in Yorktown."

Dismounting, Sebastian forced himself to set aside his thoughts of Eden. But she was very much mistaken if she believed he was going to let her wriggle loose from this betrothal!

Sebastian stared at the map that pinpointed the location of each Patriot encampment. Gilbert Lafayette stood beside him, studying the information that had been prepared for General Washington's pending arrival.

"If your numbers are accurate, we will have almost nine thousand American soldiers, volunteers, and militiamen ready to join forces with the eight thousand French troops under my command," Gilbert said. "With the overwhelming number of French seamen and cannons that will soon be riding anchor in Chesapeake Bay we will have Cornwallis in a fine fix."

"Have you made all the necessary preparations for the siege?" Sebastian questioned the marquis.

"*Oui*, our infantry is in the process of digging trenches so our cannons and mortars can be moved into place. Our strength of manpower has already forced Cornwallis to abandon two of his redoubt outposts near the York River."

"And just what is it you want me to do?" Sebastian asked.

The marquis's hazel eyes sparkled devilishly. "Take word to Lord Cornwallis that he has been sealed off from his food supplies and that the rebels are gathering more reinforcements than the reports projected. Now is the time for him to recognize the gravity of his situation."

"And you want me to find out what the inestimable Lord Charles plans to do about it."

"Precisely," Gilbert confirmed. "I received another dispatch from General Washington an hour ago. He will be arriving very shortly. Considering the speed at which he abandoned his deception of attacking Sir Clinton, and hightailed it south, I expect that he and his troops will be exhausted. While Washington rests, my soldiers will provide cannon and mortar fire to force the British deeper into Yorktown and ensure that they abandon their outposts."

"I deciphered a message sent out by Cornwallis, requesting assistance of the British Navy," Sebastian informed the marquis. "I think Cornwallis is counting on the English fleet to guard his back, but I didn't send out the dispatch in time for the English frigates to weigh anchor and set sail."

"If we storm Yorktown, Cornwallis will have no choice but to evacuate his troops by ferrying them north across the bay. We will have to make certain he isn't able to do that," Gilbert said.

"Cornwallis doesn't know the strength of the forces gathering around him yet. I have falsified as many reports from Tory couriers as I could get my hands on," Sebastian confided. "Cornwallis still believes the Patriots are bluffing, and that General Pembrook will lead a rebel retreat."

"That is why Pembrook placed the Virginia Militia in a strategic position," Gilbert said. "Until the very last moment, we want Cornwallis to assume that Pembrook's division will become the gate that opens for him. When Cornwallis realizes Pembrook has no intention of cooperating, he will realize the desperation of his situation. Very soon, Cornwallis will discover that Pembrook only pretended to cooperate. You can tell Cornwallis that Pembrook has decided not to turn his back on the men under his command, in exchange for one life. I want to know Cornwallis's reaction, and his counterstrategy."

Nodding, Sebastian spun on his heels.

"Saber?" Gilbert called after him.

Sebastian halted beside the tent flap. "Yes?"

"You are aware, are you not, that you will be accompa-

nied to Yorktown by a barrage of gunfire. Hopefully, it will
be launched over your head."

Sebastian smiled dryly. "I doubted that a cease-fire
would look convincing. Nor would I expect your cannons
to remain silent while I am in conference with our friend
Cornwallis."

"That would look a trifle obvious, would it not?" Gilbert
chuckled. "We wouldn't want Cornwallis to think we are
exceptionally fond of you and Tully.

"You are to report to General Pembrook's regiments at
the front line. He will provide you with believable reasons
to escape from the American lines and seek refuge with
the British."

He extended the rolled document that bore his seal to
Sebastian. "I advise you to make your way from Yorktown
by sea. This message to Admiral de Grasse will grant you
and Tully safe passage through the French fleet. I do not
suggest that you allow your British associates to see the
document. You might find yourself hung for treason."

Sebastian flattened the document, then threaded it
through the lining in the crown of his tricorn hat. "You
will have your information about Cornwallis's countertac-
tics before nightfall," Sebastian promised. "But I intend
to travel alone to the enemy camp. I have another assignment for Tully."

"I do not advise walking barefoot into a den of coiled
snakes alone," Gilbert insisted. "One needs a big stick, or
Tully Randolph close at hand. He could prove invaluable
with his imposing size, stature, and his unwavering loyalty
to you."

Sebastian walked out of the tent without responding to
the comment. After all, Sebastian answered only to General Washington himself. And in this instance, Sebastian
didn't intend to answer to anyone at all.

Tully Randolph was needed elsewhere—to spy on Sebastian's reluctant fiancée, whom he doubted was anx-

iously making wedding plans. More than likely, Eden was plotting her escape from the betrothal. Sebastian wanted Eden under surveillance until he got back—*if* he got back. There was a strong possibility that he could be trapped in the cannon fire and have to wait out the siege with Cornwallis.

Fifteen

While Tully was reluctantly trotting back to Pembrook Plantation for his stakeout, Sebastian was paying a visit to Leland Pembrook.

Sebastian purposely maneuvered Leland into revealing information about his problems with his wife during the early years of his marriage. From what Sebastian could ascertain from Leland—and from recalling Eden's haunting nightmares—he began to form a broader understanding of Eden's past. Armed with the needed information to help him deal with Eden, Sebastian channeled his thoughts to his assignment so he could portray the role Pembrook had devised for him.

An hour later, Sebastian was dodging the musket balls of guerrilla bands who were pounding British redoubts with heavy fire. The gunplay, though purposely aimed over his head, came damned close to blowing him out of the saddle more times than he cared to count. Pembrook's militia was staging a very convincing act of attacking the escaped British spy who was headed for Yorktown.

The English officer who halted Sebastian's flight across the sandy knolls became a confirmed believer, when General Pembrook himself rode out into view just beyond musket range.

Pembrook stood up in the stirrups and brandished his sword at Sebastian's retreating back. "And you can tell

Lord Cornwallis what I think of his underhanded tactics!"
Leland said in a booming voice. "Nothing will stand in
the way of our cause of liberty. Tell his lordship that while
you're at it!"

Sebastian smiled to himself. Leland Pembrook showed
commendable acting ability, what with all his blustering
and sword swishing.

"Your escort is waiting to take you to Lord Cornwallis's
headquarters," the British lieutenant informed Sebastian.

Sebastian glanced over the soldier's head. Discreetly, he
appraised the fortification around Yorktown. Sebastian was
sure the newly elected governor of Virginia was going to
be fit to be tied when he learned the British high command had ensconced themselves in his home. Sebastian
made a mental note not to spend more time than necessary in Governor Thomas Nelson's house. Nelson was an
avid Patriot who would turn a cannon on his own home
if it would route the British from the colonies.

When a musketball zinged past them, Lyle Hendrick—
the courier who frequented Thaddeus's cabin—flattened
himself on his horse. "Bloody hell! I'm afraid this is the
beginning of the end! Those rebels have been trying to
pick us off all afternoon. Half our men sneaked off during
the cover of darkness last night to turn themselves over to
the enemy."

"Yorktown looks as if it is fast becoming a sealed tomb,"
Sebastian agreed as he nudged the Arabian into a trot.
"Now that Pembrook has defied the pressure to betray his
cause, we have no choice but to try and hold our position,
hoping for reinforcements from the north."

When a cannonball exploded near the redoubt that Sebastian had evacuated a moment earlier, cries of agony
rose from the British trenches. Pembrook and the Virginia
Militia were providing protective fire, while the French infantry stormed the outer lines of British defense. His Maj-

esty's men fell back immediately, abandoning their cannons and ammunition.

The closer Sebastian came to town, the more he realized that Lord Cornwallis had backed himself into a precarious corner. Chesapeake Bay's blue-gray waters were crowded with two dozen French ships. Their wooden masts stood out against the horizon like a swamp of barren tree trunks.

The French naval strength made it impossible for Sir Clinton's British frigates to reach Lord Cornwallis. Sebastian could barely make out the British men-of-war that were sailing toward the bay.

Sebastian rode toward British headquarters, wondering how long he had to glean information before the second wave of artillery blasted this town to smithereens. Considering how quickly the rebels were shelling and seizing the outer redoubts, Sebastian wasn't sure he had much time.

In the past, the British had shown no mercy when they attacked American troops. General Tarleton—or Bloody Tarleton as he had come to be known—had massacred prisoners on numerous occasions, and the Patriots hadn't forgotten their fallen friends. Banastre Tarleton and Lord Cornwallis were about to experience the full force of rebel wrath.

And Sebastian could be caught in the cross-fire if he wasn't fast. This assignment hadn't come without a word of warning, Sebastian reminded himself grimly.

Dismounting, Sebastian approached the young guard who stood on duty at the foot of the steps. Within a few minutes, the guard relayed the message to Cornwallis, then reappeared at the door.

"The general will see you now," the soldier told him.

Sebastian strode into the foyer of Governor Thomas Nelson's confiscated home, noting that the British had rearranged the furniture to suit themselves. The new Virginia governor was not going to be pleased to hear that the redcoats had overrun his home!

The minute Sebastian walked into the office, Cornwallis's fist hit the desk. "What the bloody hell has happened?" he demanded.

"Pembrook double-crossed us," Sebastian told him.

"By God, 'tis the man's own daughter whose life hangs in the balance. How could Pembrook turn his back on his own flesh and blood? I was certain we had his full cooperation."

Sebastian sank down into the chair beside the desk. "I think the news of General Washington's southward march was the determining factor in Pembrook's decision. The Patriot forces are gathering faster than our agents believed possible. Every able-bodied man in the area has outfitted himself with weapons and joined the rebel forces. To quote Pembrook: 'The lives of so many, in a cause so noble, demanded personal sacrifice from all of us, and generals are no exception.' Pembrook insists that nothing is going to stand in the way of Patriot victory. He emphasized his point by letting loose with his cannon. I think he had every intention of sending me to you in several pieces."

"Bloody hell," Cornwallis muttered. "I suppose you took time to glance seaward before you came in the door."

"The sight was hard to miss. I think the rebels have been using devious tactics on us for the past month," Sebastian replied.

Cornwallis frowned. "What do you mean, Lord Saber?"

"I think the rebel emissaries who were captured by Tory patrols might have been *ordered* to be caught and searched. I think the rebels wanted us to intercept those falsified documents. The message that stated the French fleet would not be leaving the West Indies was an outright lie. I'm certain those brigantines that are floating in Chesapeake Bay aren't a figment of our imagination."

Sebastian eased back in his chair to watch Cornwallis guzzle his glass of brandy—confiscated from Governor

Nelson's wine cellar, no doubt. "Your request for Sir Clinton's naval assistance did not arrive in time, I'm afraid."

"No, damn it," Cornwallis said, and scowled. "The French blocked the British fleet before it could reach port. If I could ferry my men across the bay, the same way General Washington escaped from Long Island when he faced defeat, we might be able to regroup at Gloucester and march north to rejoin Sir Clinton in New York."

"We are already surrounded," Sebastian reminded him. "The Patriot forces are twice as strong as we were led to believe. Their men and artillery are securely in place. I saw their impenetrable strength for myself. In fact, I came dangerously close to being tossed into the American stockade." He frowned, pretending to mull over a sudden thought. "Or perhaps the truth is that Pembrook wanted me to escape so I could bring the information to you."

"What would the Americans have to gain from that?"

Sebastian shrugged. "Scare tactics, perhaps. Maybe the Patriots want you to know that they intend to seal off Yorktown and then shove us right into the sea to be gobbled up by that French fleet that waits like hungry sharks."

"Hell and damnation." Cornwallis levered out of his chair and paced the room. "We have already lost one hundred men. Our outer defenses keep falling back at the first sign of cannon shelling. Desertion has become the rule rather than the exception."

"I know," Sebastian said quietly. "More than a dozen redcoats emerged from the thickets this morning, holding their muskets high above their heads. Last I saw of them, they were being marched to the crowded stockade at Williamsburg. Soon there will be more redcoats with arms raised in surrender than soldiers under your command—"

Whistling rockets soared overhead. Seconds later, the earth shook and a deafening explosion rattled the windowpanes. Dust dribbled from the woodwork.

Wide-eyed, the young guard burst into the room. "Sir,

the French fleet is pouring murderous fire on our entrenchments!"

Another messenger arrived shortly thereafter, bearing news of an infantry attack. " 'Tis said that the Marquis de Lafayette himself is leading the strike force," the soldier reported breathlessly. "They mean to butcher us all!"

When a string of grim-faced officers filed through the door, Sebastian took his cue to leave. He stepped outside to see that Yorktown was being blown apart at the seams. From all indication, General Washington had arrived, and he had wasted no time in sending his regards to Cornwallis, via Lafayette. Seventeen thousand rebel soldiers had converged on Yorktown.

Sebastian strode down the street, veering around piles of rubble. Cornwallis was left with only two options—flight or surrender. Victory was out of the question and Cornwallis knew it. Eighty pieces of French siege artillery were being moved toward the front lines. Soon, Cornwallis would try to exercise his first option—retreat across the bay to Gloucester during the cover of darkness. Sebastian would see to it that Admiral de Grasse was ready and waiting to greet the British general. It would be a long way across the bay, with twenty-four French frigates breathing down British necks.

While Sebastian was scurrying along the wharf to confiscate a fisherman's skiff, Gerard Lockwood was ducking in and out of niches to conceal himself from view, keeping surveillance on Saber.

For two weeks, Lockwood had been under military guard, confined in a cell, nurturing a murderous hatred for the high and mighty English lord. If not for the barrage of gunfire that sent soldiers scrambling for their lives, Gerard could not have escaped from the stockade. But a cannonball had blasted a hole in the side wall of the prison, and Gerard had squeezed through the opening to gain freedom.

If Gerard would have had the slightest inkling the Patriots had a chance of winning this war, he would never have given his allegiance to the king! Now, his hopes of a high-ranking position in the army of occupation were dashed. The British were doomed, and there wasn't a man in Yorktown who didn't know it.

Lockwood glanced at the town that lay in ruin, then glowered at Sebastian's departing back. He had a score to settle with that cocky English lord. It was time Saber received his due.

Skulking along the wharf to avoid gunfire, Lockwood followed Saber. If Saber intended to escape this hellhole, Lockwood was determined to follow the same route, then finish his ongoing feud with him. That arrogant Englishman was going to pay dearly for having Gerard stripped of his commission and left to rot in the stockade!

"Edeline Renee Pembrook, you are mad!" Elizabeth declared as she stared at her sister. "Why would you not want to marry Sebastian Saber? I know you have a fond attachment for him. I could see it every time he paid a call at the plantation."

"I can't marry him, because, against my better judgment, I think I might still be in love with that scoundrel."

Bet plunked down on the settee in her spacious suite and watched her sister wear holes in the carpet with her restless pacing. "You are afraid you love him, so you cannot possibly marry him? What kind of twisted logic is that? The whole idea is to love the man you marry. At least that is what you have preached to me for the past four years."

Eden wheeled around to pace in the opposite direction. "You simply don't understand, Bet."

"Obviously not," Bet replied. "If Peter had followed

your absurd theory, he would have married Cornelia Wickleheimer. And may I remind you that you spoke to his parents on our behalf. If you believed everyone should marry someone he, or she, didn't love, you should have spoken in Cornelia's defense!"

Eden paused to glance down at her sister. "There is much you don't know about Sebastian Saber. He was 'yer lordship,' the very man who held us captive."

Bet blanched. "Dear Lord, are you certain? Then is he really a British spy? What—?"

Eden waved her arms, demanding silence. "He is supposedly a double agent, though how anyone can trust a man of such complicated deceptions to stand *for* or *against* anything, I cannot fathom. I suspect that Sebastian is a turncoat whose loyalties lie with the victor of this war. If the British had sealed off the Patriots in Yorktown, I imagine Sebastian would have changed colors rather quickly."

"Good gad," Bet wheezed, trying to digest and analyze the information. "He was 'yer lordship?' Then that explains why he let me escape, why he promised that you wouldn't come to harm."

Eden frowned, bemused. "Sebastian recaptured you, then let you go?"

Bet nodded. "He and Tully spotted me after I twisted my ankle a second time. I insisted that they take me to the cabin and let you go free, but 'yer lordship' ordered Tully to take me back to the spot where we were abducted."

Eden was grateful that Sebastian had been sympathetic and generous to Bet, but the truth was, Eden still wasn't certain she trusted the man's ultimate motives. "If I could figure out what Sebastian thinks he has to gain by marrying me, perhaps I could spoil whatever wily scheme he has dreamed up."

"Perhaps he is simply fond of you. After all, he isn't the first man who has tried to claim the elusive title of your husband," Bet pointed out.

"Do not be deliberately dense, Bet," Eden grumbled. "The man has to be up to something." She drew herself up in front of her sister who reclined on the settee, elevating her swollen ankle. "I didn't call you in here to persuade me to marry Sebastian, but rather to inform you of my plans. I have no intention of alarming you when I turn up missing. You scared me half to death when you eloped with Peter. I refuse to put you, Maggie, and Papa through that."

"I said I was sorry about that," Bet murmured.

"And you have been forgiven. Your in-laws have accepted you, and Angus has made a stand for the Patriot cause. The only one suffering is poor Cornelia, but I'm sure her father can afford to buy her a husband after things simmer down."

"I'm sure Possum Face will have a dowry large enough to attract one of her own kind," Bet put in.

"Elizabeth Annabelle, mind your tongue," Eden scolded, but she couldn't contain the smile that pursed her lips. "Even if Cornelia Wickleheimer does bear an astonishing resemblance to a possum, we should not hold that against her. It is hardly her fault that she looks the way she does. Now, as I was saying, I'm going to use a similar approach to avoid marrying Sebastian Saber. I'm—"

"Godamercy!" Bet interrupted, when she concluded where this conversation was headed. "You don't mean you are going to *buy* a husband, do you? If you are, then you *are* utterly insane!"

Eden flung up her hands in frustration. "I wish you would stop questioning my sanity and simply pay attention. I'm bound for Micah Bancroft's plantation tonight to convince him that he needs to marry me."

"Marry Micah Bancroft?" Bet rolled her eyes in disbelief. "Really, Eden, you know that would be a mistake."

"Micah has many good and decent qualities. He is manageable, predictable, and easygoing."

Bet eyed her sister speculatively. "And you have decided to settle for a tolerable arrangement, just so you can avoid marrying the man you love. I think that is preposterous."

"It is wiser to marry a man I can handle than one I cannot," Eden reasoned. "Besides, I know very little about Sebastian Saber. He has told me too many half-truths since the day I met him. Now, when I do not return home this evening," Eden began her explanation, "I want you to tell Maggie that you know of my whereabouts, and my plans, but that I swore you to secrecy. Papa will be far too occupied to know I'm gone. Once the deed is done, Papa will accept my decision, just as he accepted your decision to marry Peter."

"You are going to regret this," Bet predicted. "I can say from experience that mutual love in marriage offers the kind of happiness you can only begin to imagine."

Eden smiled ruefully at her sister. "Mutual," she emphasized. "That is the point I have been trying to make. I can't marry a man who doesn't love me."

"But you think it's perfectly acceptable to marry a man you don't love," Bet said. "You will be practicing the kind of deception you accused Sebastian of using on you. In your attempt to defy him, you are going to become just like him."

Eden winced, then cast off the stab of guilty conscience. "I will be a good wife to Micah," she insisted.

"Of course you will, because you are an angel of goodness and mercy. But you will be living a lie." Bet stared grimly at her sister, then shook her head. "I'm sorry, but I can't be a party to your scheme, Eden. I think it would be a disastrous mistake that will make you miserable."

"I will be just as miserable if I marry Sebastian," Eden assured her.

"That is nonsense, and I will not condone this foolishness about marrying Micah!"

Eden knelt before her sister, taking Bet's knotted fists in her hands. "Bet, there are times when one has to choose between the lesser of two evils. I have made my choice and I can live with it. You must accept it."

When Eden left the room, Bet flounced against the back of the settee. The haunted look in Eden's eyes indicated a sense of urgency and apprehension was spurring her. But Bet couldn't understand what could possibly be troubling Eden so deeply. There was something Eden wasn't telling her, and that something had caused Eden to behave irrationally.

After thinking the matter through, Bet decided to send off a note to Micah, asking him to escort Eden home the moment she arrived. Eden was not going to marry one man while she was in love with another. Hypocrisy simply did not fit Eden's saintly image, and Bet was not going to allow her sister to make this crucial mistake!

Eden scurried down the back steps of the second-story gallery. She had checked on her patients, announcing the exciting news that General Washington had arrived to commandeer the siege of Yorktown. Although Eden had left her patients in high spirits, her emotions were in turmoil. Elizabeth had called her crazy for marrying one man while she was in love with another.

Eden preferred to think of it as necessary for survival.

Riding the mount she had stashed from sight earlier in the evening, Eden reined toward Micah's planation. What was she going to say to Micah? she asked herself.

I have changed my mind and I think the two of us should marry immediately. Is tonight too soon for a wedding?

Eden's shoulders slumped. Micah would be curious to know why she had reversed her decision, why she was in an all-fired rush. And what, Eden wondered, would she reply to those sensible questions? If she lied to Micah, she would be no better than Sebastian Saber. The man had perfected the technique to such incredible extremes that he could stare her squarely in the eye and lie through his pearly white teeth. Sweet mercy, in order to save herself from a man she knew she couldn't trust, she would have to become like him—just as Bet said.

Eden yelped in sudden alarm when a shadow pounced from the trees near the garden. A steely hand shot out of nowhere to pull her from the saddle. Eden toppled into muscular arms, while her mare—the traitor—reversed direction and trotted back to the barn.

Eden swung her satchel wildly, to pound the head of the man who held her directly in front of him. The latch of the satchel sprang open, spilling the contents over the man's face and shoulders.

When he tried to shift her in his arms, Eden launched herself away. She glanced back to see the masculine form covered with her petticoats and gown. Bounding to her feet, she tried to dash off, but a muscular leg coiled around her knees, flipping her off balance. She landed with a thud and a groan.

Her assailant stepped into the moonlight that sprayed through the opening in the trees, then yanked the petticoat off his head and shoulders. Silver-gray eyes bore down on Eden.

"Going somewhere, my dear?" Sebastian questioned sarcastically as he glared at her.

Not to be outdone, Eden glared right back.

"As a matter of fact, I am," she said as she climbed to her feet to dust herself off. "I am on a crusade of the utmost importance. As soon as you chase down my horse, I will be on my way."

Sebastian surveyed the scattered garments and frowned suspiciously. "From the look of things, I would say you are trying to run away . . ." His voice trailed off when the thud of hooves heralded the approach of another rider.

Tully jerked his steed to a halt when he saw Eden and Sebastian squared off in the clearing beside the creek. "Miss Eden, are you all right?" Tully questioned.

"You were supposed to be keeping an eye on my bride-to-be," Sebastian scowled at his friend.

"I was. I am," Tully insisted.

"I thought it was understood that you were to prevent Eden from doing something foolish. Late-night rides do not qualify as suitable evening amusements," Sebastian snapped irritably.

"She sneaked down the back steps," Tully informed him. "I expected her to leave by the front door if she tried to escape."

"You had Tully spy on me?" Eden asked in outrage. "How dare you treat me like a witless, incompetent child!"

"How dare you behave like one," Sebastian flung back. "I don't know why I credited you with a smidgen of sense. Don't you remember what happened to you the last time you went tearing off in the middle of the night without an escort?"

Eden didn't have to stand here and tolerate his scathing comments, especially with Tully as a witness, she muttered to herself.

Wheeling around, Eden stalked off. "I am leaving. I have someplace else I prefer to be."

Sebastian latched on to her arm and spun her to face his scowl. "Where the hell are you going?"

Her chin tilted to a hostile angle, and she gave no answer.

"Eden . . ." he said warningly.

She glared at him in defiance.

"Miss Eden has decided the best way to avoid marrying you is to wed Micah Bancroft," Tully revealed.

Eden's smoldering glower branded Tully as a traitor. It

was obvious the man had eavesdropped on her conversation with Bet. The man was as sneaky as Saber!

"Tully, I have a message for you to deliver while my intended bride and I discuss her plans of marrying one of her many ex-fiancés," Sebastian said, bracing himself when Eden tried to twist free of his grasp.

"We are not having a discussion on any topic," Eden bit off, glaring at the hand that restrained her.

"Yes, we are," he contradicted. "If you don't feel like talking, then you can do all the listening. I, on the other hand, have a great deal to say to you."

Sebastian shot Tully a sideways glance. "Take word to General Washington that I have made contact with Cornwallis. The British general is aware of his grave predicament. The French fleet has effectively blocked the channel so the British men-of-war can't reach port to provide reinforcement or carry off the troops to safety. Cornwallis confided that he intends to cross to Gloucester during the night—if and when surrender becomes his last option. I have alerted Admiral de Grasse of the possibility."

Tully smiled in satisfaction. "So this war is almost over, is it? Cornwallis has met his fate at Yorktown."

"Yes, after a few days of heavy artillery and decreased rations, I think Cornwallis will accept the inevitable, but he intends to put up a good fight."

While Tully whirled his steed around and galloped away, Eden stared up into the shadowed face that haunted her dreams. "A man who can feed a pack of lies to his comrades, then betray them, has no conscience, no integrity. As much as I yearn to see this war end, I pity Cornwallis for putting his faith and trust in you."

Sebastian flinched as if he had been slapped. "You're wasting your sympathy on a man who ordered the burning and pillaging of homes and farm fields. Do you condone his methods in wartime over mine?"

"No, but I despise your deceitful games," she countered.

Sebastian used Eden's arm like a rope to tow her resisting body against his. "It seems to me that the rebels' beloved angel has no qualms about using deceit when it suits *her* purpose."

Eden felt the traitorous stirrings trickle through her body when she came into familiar contact with Sebastian's masculine physique. Damnation, why did he have to be the only man who aroused her, even against her strong will? Why was he the one her aching heart desired? Maybe Bet was right. Maybe Eden was a little mad.

"I . . . don't . . . trust . . . you," Eden said in raspy spurts. "I will never trust you. I don't know you at all—"

Sebastian silenced her with a searing kiss that stole her breath away. His arms glided around her hips and he pulled her full length against him, letting her feel his hungry desire for her.

No matter what else was between them, no matter how hard Eden tried to deny him, Sebastian knew there would always be this white-hot spark of attraction. One kiss and his senses reeled in long-awaited pleasure. One caress and his body clenched with overwhelming need.

Why couldn't Eden accept the passion bubbling between them and be content with it? Why couldn't she confess her love for him as freely and openly as she once had? And why couldn't *he* set her free when she fought so hard to escape him?

"Eden, for once, don't let yourself be sidetracked by what you *think* you know about me. Rely on what you feel," he whispered against the pulsating column of her neck. "Does Micah make you feel this way when he touches you?"

When Sebastian traced the scooped neckline of her gown, Eden trembled uncontrollably. He pressed his advantage during her silence. "Can Micah spin the stars around when he kisses you?" His forefinger traced her heart-shaped lips before his mouth slanted tenderly over hers. His hand brushed lightly over the blue satin that strained against the taut peaks of her breasts. "Perhaps Micah, and the others, treated you like a lady, but could any of them really make you feel like a woman?"

Eden had trouble thinking straight. Sebastian had the infuriating knack of spinning her noble theories into tangled webs. Eden was so frustrated by the quivering sensations of her betraying body that she didn't know what she wanted, didn't know how *not* to react to the hot, tingling sensations that burned in every part of her being.

She was afraid, she realized. She was afraid that Sebastian would be like her mother—unfaithful, deceitful. Eden couldn't endure that kind of torment in her own marriage. Knowing how Victoria Pembrook had betrayed Leland had been a living hell for Eden. If Sebastian married her, then took his affection elsewhere, Eden couldn't bear it.

"I can provide you with all the luxuries Micah can afford," Sebastian whispered, cutting effectively through her thoughts. "But more than that, Eden, I can give *you,* give *us,* this . . ."

Sixteen

When Sebastian's moist breath whispered over the thrusting crest of Eden's breast, her knees buckled. She felt as weightless as the air drifting past her. Then she was lying upon a bed of scattered clothes, unsure how and when she had gotten there, yielding to the delicious sensations spreading through her.

Wild ripples of pleasure skittered through her as his lips closed over her nipple. His hand glided up her thigh and his skillful caresses practically melted the skin from her bones. Her responsive body arched toward his seeking lips and questing fingertips, reveling in the sensations he called from her.

Eden could no more control her wanton needs for Sebastian than she could swim all seven seas. He made her forget her firm resolve, made her crave him to mindless obsession.

"I want you as I have never wanted another woman," he murmured against her silky flesh. "Some things have never changed, Eden. My desire for you can be appeased temporarily, but it demands constant feeding. I swear, I can't get enough of you."

Ever so slowly, his kisses drifted over the lush texture of her body, memorizing the taste, scent, and feel of her, wanting her to want him so desperately that even her fierce denials would burn in the fires they ignited in each other.

Tonight he would love her in all the wildly intimate ways he had always dreamed of. The memory of this night beneath a canopy of twinkling stars would haunt her when she sought out the arms of another man.

Eden could run to the ends of the earth to avoid him, spout her claims that she had outgrown her need for him, but she wouldn't be able to outrun this memory, never be able to forget the feel of his hands and lips sensitizing her flesh and bringing her feminine body to life.

His hand glided between her legs to cup her. His lips coasted over the flat plane of her belly and he felt her body quiver with anticipation, heard her breath catch.

He loved the way she responded to him. Touching Eden was his heaven on earth. He savored the taste and scent of her, let his senses fill with the very essence of her. She was like a long-awaited feast, and he was starving for her.

When his kisses drifted over the inner curve of her thighs, and he nudged her legs apart with his elbow, Sebastian felt Eden tense, as if she intended to deny him such intimacy.

"Yield to me, angel," he whispered as he traced the heated petals of passion's most delicate flower.

"No, it's too—"

His tongue flicked out to tease her, sending shards of shimmering pleasure bursting through her body—and echoing into his. He delved deeper with his fingertip and felt her body quiver with the hot need he had called from her.

"Sebastian, please . . ." Eden drew a ragged breath and tried to ease away from his wildly erotic touch. But he eased his leg over hers, refusing to let her deprive him of the intimacy he craved to obsession.

"I'm trying to please you." His husky laughter floated above them. "But you aren't cooperating. Obviously, you need more convincing that I am not the insensitive, deceitful monster you want to believe I am."

Eden didn't need to be convinced—she needed relief from the sensations that bombarded her like a volley of cannonballs. She tried to cling desperately to her sanity when he caressed her with lips and fingertips and evoked the most indescribable sensations she had ever experienced. A soft cry of disbelief tumbled from her lips when he took her so near the edge of oblivion and left her dangling in midair.

"Dear Lord—" The world spun out of control, taking Eden with it.

Sebastian felt the convulsive tremors consume her, as if each shivering sensation was his very own. Yet, he wasn't satisfied. He wanted to take Eden to towering heights of passion, then call her back from the breaking edge to shower her with splendor all over again.

When his thumb stroked the bud of her feminine desire, he heard her breath break and he smiled against her scented flesh. "Shall I take you back to paradise again, angel?"

"No, I swear I can't survive it," Eden said raggedly.

"Yes, you will," he insisted as he dipped his fingertip into her moist heat, feeling her burning him with her liquid fire, feeling her body returning his caresses in the most intimate ways. "And I promise you that you'll die to live again, Eden."

"No, Sebastian, I mean it, I can't—"

His lips and tongue whirled over her sensitive flesh. Her raspy words became a breathless cry of immeasurable pleasure. He tasted the essence of her, stroked her until she shattered around him, teased her until every shudder became another hot cascade of ecstasy. He held her while she sobbed for him to ease the aching emptiness that his kisses and caresses couldn't satisfy completely. And then he sent her reeling again and she died another wild, sweet death without him.

"Sebastian, stop! There's a limit to—"

"Is there? Reach beyond that supposed limit and tell me what you find," he challenged her. His fingertips parted her delicately as he bent his head. "Can you give so much to me and still insist on marrying another man when we both know that you are mine until long past forever?"

Eden could do nothing but surrender to the kaleidoscopic sensations that assailed her. Quite honestly, she hadn't expected to survive this long, not when she had come so close to dying thrice . . .

Her thoughts wobbled away when Sebastian caressed her with such unbelievable tenderness. She knew she could never outlive the wild, sweet memories he was spinning around her, never be able to tolerate another man's touch but his. She would never be able to close her eyes without seeing those entrancing silver pools glowing in his darkly handsome face. She would feel Sebastian's masterful caresses flowing over her body, and she would be living a lie if she tried to make love to another man. She could never love anyone but him, though she could never marry Sebastian. She was destined to survive on the bittersweet memories of this one man, of this one night . . .

Tidal waves of rapture swept over Eden as she felt Sebastian's sinewy body uncoil upon hers. When his lips slanted over hers, she tasted her need for him—a need that refused to be denied, despite her strong will. Her arms curled around him involuntarily and she held him to her as he became the searing flame inside her. Eden met each penetrating thrust without an ounce of reserve. She was a woman hopelessly yielding, matching the cadence of his ardent passion.

Sebastian moved with breathless impatience, aching to bury himself so deeply inside her that he couldn't tell where her luscious body ended and his began. Though he was afraid he was going to smother her in his crushing embrace, he couldn't let go. His male body was so tightly clenched that desire made him a prisoner of his own turbulent needs. It was true, he wanted Eden the way he had never wanted or needed another woman in his entire life.

Sebastian groaned when he felt the last surge of passion engulf him, stripping away his strength. He collapsed upon Eden, desperately trying to catch his breath.

Sweet mercy, making love to Eden might one day be the death of him, he decided. His heart had actually stopped beating once or twice, and it was a wonder he had a pulse left. It was definitely going to take a few minutes to recover his energy after this kind of all-consuming passion!

When the clouds of blinding passion finally parted, Eden felt herself crashing back to reality like a blazing comet. Had she no shame whatsoever? No willpower? Dear God in heaven, the things she had allowed Sebastian to do to her! Their lovemaking had been so intimate that she had no secrets from him.

"Confound it, let me up!" she burst out, on the verge of tears. "Now look what you've done."

She *was* in tears!

"Eden, I—"

"I said . . . get off," she spluttered, shoving at his muscular shoulders. "You have ruined just about everything!"

Sebastian rolled away. To her irritation, he grinned while she groped for the first article of clothing in her reach. Refusing to look at him, she yanked her chemise over her head, then grabbed her petticoats in an angry huff.

"What is it you think I have ruined?" he asked, fighting back a smile.

"Any chance of my finding happiness, that's what!"

Sebastian came to his knees, then to his feet. "Eden, you are being overly dramatic." He scooped up his clothes and hurriedly fastened himself into them, then plucked up the assortment of weapons he had tucked in his jacket.

"I am not being overly dramatic. Elizabeth is the one

who is melodramatic," Eden declared loudly. "I am calm, rational, and sensible!"

If the dead weren't awake, Sebastian knew they would be very soon. Eden could be heard from here to high heaven. He couldn't remember hearing her ever yell like this.

"You don't sound all that calm and rational to me," he pointed out.

Eden rounded on him, her breasts heaving beneath her skimpy chemise. "And that pleasures you immensely, doesn't it? You delight in exasperating me until I lose my temper. You laughed yourself silly while I was suffering through my captivity and you pretended to be a Tory sympathizer who collected dispatches from both American and English soldiers, then deciphered them to meet your own whim. Maybe my father, and the other Patriot officers, sing your praises, but I don't trust your hidden agendas. You lie as easily as you speak the truth, and I can't tell which is which!"

"And trust and devotion are tantamount to you, aren't they?"

"They are everything," Eden insisted. "Because I know exactly what can happen when one practices to deceive—" She slammed her mouth shut, then busied herself by gathering her discarded garments.

"And because your mother was unfaithful and lied her way through her torrid affair behind your father's back, you're afraid you'll turn out to be just like her? Is that it, Eden?"

The emotions Eden was trying so hard to control came bursting out on a sob. "I won't live through that kind of hell again, not with you or any man."

"And you've punished yourself for years on end because of what happened seventeen years ago," Sebastian murmured, pressing her for the truth of the misery he had seen in the depths of her luminous eyes. "That's what all this noble generosity of yours is all about, isn't it? You think you are atoning for your sins. But are you absolutely certain you are responsible? Maybe—"

The crackling of twigs caused Sebastian to wheel toward the sound. He muttered a foul curse when the looming shadow hovered like a demon rising from hell.

Grimly, Sebastian stared at the musket—with its deadly sharp bayonet protruding from the muzzle—that was aimed at his chest.

"You conniving bastard," Gerard Lockwood snarled at Sebastian. "You betrayed our cause to those goddamn rebels. While we were sending dispatches through Thaddeus, you were selling the information to the Patriots! Your deception caused the English to be backed into that doomed fortress in Yorktown and you have spoiled my chance of wealth and prominence. Damn you, Saber, you have become the bane of my life, and I intend to break this damnable curse once and for all!"

Eden reflexively sidled against Sebastian when the masked man sneered at her. Although Eden had never actually seen Gerard Lockwood without his concealing mask, she recognized his gruff voice and imposing stature. The mere sight of this cruel heathen was enough to activate nightmares.

Sebastian wrapped a protective arm around Eden's trembling shoulders. Clearly, she was terrified of this brute who had treated her so roughly during captivity.

Sebastian had to do something, and he had to do it quickly. Otherwise, Eden was going to suffer because of this ongoing feud between him and Lockwood.

"Lockwood, you and I—"

"Don't ply me with more of your cunning lies, Saber," Gerard spat hatefully. "I overheard enough to know that you were playing both sides of this war to your financial advantage. I have spent a fortnight rotting in the stockade, and I have bruises and scrapes as souvenirs of the night you tried to beat me to death so *you* could have this sassy chit beneath you."

Gerard took an intimidating step forward, his weapon shifting back and forth between Sebastian and Eden. "You have spun your last web of deceit, Saber. While you are bleeding all over yourself, you are going to watch me take this wench the way I planned to take her the night you interfered. This time there won't be a damned thing you can do except listen to her beg for mercy."

"If you want enough money to—" Sebastian tried to bargain. It was a waste of breath.

"Shut up, Saber. I will have all the money I need very soon. I am willing to bet your life that Pembrook will pay a ransom to get his daughter back, even after I have used her for my pleasure a few times."

There was no reasoning with him, Sebastian realized. But no matter what else happened, Eden wasn't going to suffer for it. He would make damned sure that she had a sporting chance to escape.

Sebastian could feel his flintlock resting heavily against his hip—the same hip, unfortunately, that Eden was cuddled against. Sebastian made a pact with himself, there and then, that if he managed to survive this crisis, he would keep Eden on his left side henceforth and forevermore so his gun hand would be accessible.

He wondered if he would have the opportunity to put that policy to future use. Gerard seemed hell-bent on making this the last night of Sebastian's life.

Eden marshaled her courage, willing herself not to fall apart in this crucial moment. She couldn't bear to watch Sebastian be gunned down in cold blood without making an effort to dissuade Lockwood from doing his worst. Even though she was terrified of this merciless beast, she had experience in converting people to her way of thinking. If ever there was a time when subtle persuasion was vital, it was now!

"Mr. Lockwood, I understand that you are upset with Sebastian's deception. And rightfully so. But you must consider the consequences of what you are contemplating—"

"Silence!" Lockwood boomed at her.

Eden was not to be silenced. Sebastian's life was at stake, and hers as well. "This area is jumping alive with rebel soldiers who could pounce on you before you have time to escape, especially while I am putting up a fuss. And I assure you that I will be putting up a fuss," she insisted, willing her voice not to waver. Miraculously, it held firm and convincing. "Killing Saber will only bring down the wrath of his allies on you. If you spare him, I will go with you without protest, and you will have your ransom. My father will pay for my return."

"I'm not interested," Gerard snorted, shifting his attention to Sebastian. "I plan to settle my grudge with Saber, here and now."

"What good is revenge if you don't survive to enjoy it?" Eden questioned, frantic. "The sound of a discharging musket will draw a unit of soldiers who will be armed to the teeth."

Sebastian waited until Lockwood's attention turned back to Eden. He knew Lockwood was intent on murder. The man was not to be dissuaded, even if Eden talked herself blue. Although Sebastian knew she was terrified, she was trying to spare his life—even when she was the sacrifice to be made.

This woman was forever the martyr, Sebastian decided. She had trained herself to put the needs and concerns of everyone else first—even him, the man she believed had forsaken her.

Sebastian could name dozens of men who would have knuckled under the pressure of staring down the spitting end of a musket to save their own hide. But Eden had tenacious fortitude. If Sebastian had ever doubted that before, he knew it now for a fact.

"You must listen to reason, Mr. Lockwood,' Eden implored. "If you don't, you will be signing your own death warrant. You—"

While Lockwood was focused on Eden, Sebastian shoved her sideways, hoping to draw Lockwood's gunfire and spare Eden's life. He prayed she would hit the ground running and never look back.

"You bastard!" Lockwood roared as he snapped the musket into firing position, then fired.

Sebastian swung up his flintlock to answer the bark of the musket, despite the searing pain that exploded in his shoulder and streamed down his shooting arm like fire. Gritting his teeth against the pain, he squeezed the trigger. His shot was slightly off the mark, catching Lockwood in the arm rather than his black heart.

Sebastian staggered to keep his feet, and the world tilted on its axis. His eyes blurred, his pulse roared in his ears, and his chest ached like a sonofabitch. Eden's horrified scream mingled with Lockwood's roar of rage. The sounds seemed to come to Sebastian from a hazy, echoing tunnel.

"Eden, run!" Sebastian rasped as his knees folded beneath him. "Run . . ."

Horror flooded through Eden's veins like ice water when she saw the bloodstains saturating Sebastian's jacket. She had seen too many serious wounds on the soldiers in her care not to recognize this for what it was. Sebastian was losing precious amounts of blood with each pulse beat.

At that moment, Eden knew without a single doubt that she loved this man with all her heart and soul. Despite her mistrust, despite her injured pride over his betrayal, despite everything, she loved this man who had tried to spare her life by sacrificing his own.

She couldn't leave Sebastian to die alone—if that was what was about to happen! But it would not happen, Eden told herself fiercely. She wouldn't let it happen!

Her gaze fixed on Sebastian's crumpled form, Eden crawled on her hands and knees toward him. Her breath caught in her throat when Lockwood's demonic shadow fell over her. The murdering bastard wasn't satisfied to let Sebastian die from one wound, she realized. The man was reloading his musket to deliver the killing shot at close range.

"No!" Eden bolted to her feet, launching herself at Lockwood with the kind of outraged anger she hadn't allowed to slip past her defenses in seventeen years. Her hatchet chop to Lockwood's elbow caused the shot to go astray, thudding in the grass beside Sebastian's shoulder.

"Meddling bitch!" Lockwood sneered as he swung the butt end of his musket at her.

The blow to Eden's head caused a blinding, disorienting pain that left Eden teetering on her feet. She staggered, tripped, and fell facedown onto Sebastian's sprawled form. Her arms dangled off Sebastian's shoulders, her breasts pressed to the pulsing wound on his chest, her cheek resting against his ashen cheek.

Gerard hissed at the pain in his arm as he fumbled to pour powder down the barrel of his musket. His fingers were becoming numb from the shot Saber had delivered, but Gerard was determined to finish this feud by blowing the devious bastard straight into hell. Then he would have his revenge on Eden Pembrook, he promised himself.

Gerard reached down to drag Eden's limp body off Sebastian, but he heard the clatter of approaching hooves, saw the glowing torchlight appearing and disappearing in the trees behind Pembrook Plantation. Behind the floating torchlight appeared another, and another.

Gerard cursed furiously. He had no time to put a bullet through Saber's skull and drag Eden away. There was only time to scurry down to the creek and tend to his wound. He couldn't risk firing another shot, because he might not have time to reload to protect himself from the rescue brigade.

Gerard, his injured arm dangling at his side, sprinted toward cover. Judging from the number of thundering hooves, he predicted every able-bodied man at the plantation was coming to Eden's defense. While hoof beats amplified in the night, Gerard scrabbled down the cliff beside the creek and buried himself in the underbrush.

"Oh, my God!" Elizabeth wailed at the top of her lungs when she saw her sister's unconscious body draped over Sebastian's lifeless form.

Her heart pounding with overwhelming fear, Bet slid off her horse and dashed toward Eden. She grabbed Eden's shoulders and rolled her to her back. Blood saturated Eden's clothes from neck to waist.

Bet screamed bloody murder.

Peter dismounted, then knelt beside his hysterical wife, who cradled Eden in her arms. He grimaced when he spied Eden's stained chemise and the bloody gown that had been pressed to Sebastian's chest. Peter squeezed his eyes shut and fought down a wave of grief.

A flood of torches encircled Eden and Sebastian, and it was into that scene that Tully Randolph rode hell-for-leather. He, too, had heard the shots and the terrified scream when he was returning from General Washington's encampment. Tully's senses reeled when the glowing torches spotlighted Sebastian's deadly wound, and the bright red stains that drenched Eden's clothing.

Tully was off his horse in a single bound, pushing bodies out of his way to reach Sebastian. "We'll take them back to the house. Get the beds readied and have plenty of boiling water and bandages on hand. And fetch Dr. Curtis from Lafayette's camp," he ordered the servants who stood paralyzed in horror. "I said, *move!* We have no time to spare."

Servants scattered like quail.

With sickening dread, Tully knelt beside Sebastian. He scooped up his longtime friend and carried him to the horse.

"I'll help," Peter volunteered when Tully struggled beneath Sebastian's dead weight.

When Tully had settled himself on the saddle and pulled Sebastian onto his lap, his eyes dropped to the expressionless face that glowed ghostly white in the moonlight. Tully was sick at heart to see a man who had once been vibrantly alive flirting so intimately with death. Tully's anguished gaze drifted over to Eden who dangled in Peter's arms. Damnation, that lovely angel had suffered too much already, he thought to himself.

Elizabeth couldn't dam up the tears that flooded down her cheeks as she clung to Eden's limp hand. Each time Bet glanced at her lifeless sister, her heart twisted in her chest. It wasn't fair that this kind and charitable saint should be struck down in the prime of her life. Eden had never harmed a living soul. She was the personification of goodness and generosity.

By the time the grim procession reached the house, Bet had managed to pull herself together enough to take charge—as Eden would have done if she was able. "Put them on our bed, Peter," Bet requested.

"In bed together?" Peter stared dubiously at his young wife. "I don't think it would be proper—"

"Propriety be damned," Bet erupted. "Their lives are far more precious than their reputations. I want them both where I can keep a constant vigil on them."

"You're right, Bet," Peter murmured as he glanced from one pale face to the other.

Tully carefully placed Sebastian on one side of the bed

and removed the stained jacket and shirt. He grimaced
at the gory wound that cut into Sebastian's flesh like jagged teeth. "Dear God," he wheezed.

Bet made the crucial mistake of staring at Sebastian's
wound. The color seeped from her face and her knees
wobbled. She would *not* faint, she told herself. She would
not faint now!

"Oh, Lord!" Maggie howled as she hovered in the
doorway, her arms ladened down with a bucket of water
and a stack of bandages. Water slopped on the Belgian
carpet when Maggie staggered in shock.

Sebastian's thick lashes fluttered up to reveal dazed
silver-gray eyes. Tully's hand stalled above the wound on
Sebastian's chest. "Just rest, yer lordship," Tully murmured. "I will take care of you. Never doubt it."

"Where's Eden?" Sebastian's voice was no more than
a scratchy whisper.

"She is beside you, right where she belongs."

Sebastian closed his eyes momentarily, as if struggling
to summon the energy to continue. His chest rose slightly
as he tried to swallow. "Fetch the parson . . ."

Tully winced. "You want a man of the cloth in here
right now, yer lordship?"

"Yes . . . now . . ."

When Sebastian slumped and fell unconscious, Tully
bounded up to retrieve the water and bandages from
Maggie's shaky hands. "Send one of yer servants to fetch
the clergyman from Lafayette's camp."

Maggie's eyes rounded. "He wants his last rites? Dear
God, Dear *God!*"

When Maggie continued to stand there, absorbing the
full effects of horror, Tully shoved her out the door. Turning back to the bed, he dipped the cloth in water to
cleanse Sebastian's wound.

While Tully tended Sebastian, Bet stared into Eden's

pallid face. Her trembling hand brushed over the goose egg on the side of Eden's head. What brutal beast dared to strike Eden? It was inconceivable that anyone would harm her. Whoever the bastard was, he deserved to be shot, stabbed, poisoned, and hung!

"Where are my patients?"

Bet spun around when she heard Dr. Curtis's voice wafting through the foyer.

"In here!" she called out. When the physician appeared, Bet smiled sympathetically. "I know you have spent a long day administering to wounded soldiers near the front lines, but I'm afraid your day is far from over." She gestured toward the bed.

Dr. Curtis's weary eyes widened in alarm when he spotted Sebastian and Eden. He rushed forward, shooing everyone out of his way as he entered.

Reluctantly, Bet, Peter, and Tully backed toward the door. Bet couldn't bear to leave Eden's side, because she was very much afraid it would be the last time she saw her sister alive.

In tears, Bet allowed Peter to shepherd her into the parlor. When he thrust a glass into her hand, she gulped down the brandy he had offered and promptly requested more.

Three glasses of brandy later, Peter removed the goblet from his bereaved wife's hand. "I think that's enough," he cautioned.

Bet peered at her husband through glazed eyes. "I can still *feel*, Peter. It is not nearly enough."

When Peter hesitated in refilling the goblet, Tully gestured toward the bottle. "Give her as much as she wants. There are times when not thinking and feeling is a blessing." After Peter refilled Bet's glass, Tully snatched up the bottle and drained it dry. "I think I could use a couple of quarts of this stuff myself."

"Damnation, I don't want to be the only sober one around here, just in case the news goes from bad to worse," Peter said as he spun around to retrieve several bottles of whiskey from the cellar.

Seventeen

Eden groaned. Shadowed images, and fragments of disjointed memory leaped around her throbbing skull. When a snarling face loomed over her, she flung up her hand to protect herself from an anticipated blow.

"Argh!" Dr. Curtis caught a fist in the jaw. When Eden's flailing arm shot toward his face again, he grabbed her wrist. "Easy, Eden. It's Doctor Curtis. Just lie still."

It took several moments for the words to register in Eden's pounding brain. When they did, she dropped her arm to her side. She felt the sticky garment being pulled away from her chest and she pried open one eye to see Dr. Curtis dangling the bloody chemise in his fingertips.

The doctor frowned in confusion. There was nothing but red stains on Eden's shoulders and chest. His gaze leaped back to Sebastian, realizing that Eden's bloodstains had come from Sebastian. Dr. Curtis sighed in relief. One seriously wounded patient to attend was plenty!

"You are going to be just fine, Eden," he assured her. "You may be sporting a hellish headache, but otherwise, you are in one piece. I wish I could say the same for Sebastian Saber."

The comment brought Eden onto her elbow to peer at Sebastian through squinted eyes. His chest and shoulder were a mass of stained bandages, and his raven hair accentuated his deathly pallor. Dear God, Sebastian had one foot in the grave!

Eden reached out a shaky hand to clasp his cold fingertips. "Sebastian, can you hear me?"

He had saved her life by pushing her aside and drawing Lockwood's gunfire. Sweet mercy, if Sebastian didn't survive this act of unselfish bravery, Eden would never be able to forgive herself. She didn't deserve to be spared. If she hadn't been ranting and raving at Sebastian like a waspish virago, Lockwood might not have found them. She was responsible for this disaster. She had taken yet another life!

The dismal thought had her sobbing.

"Eden, calm yourself." Dr. Curtis eased her back onto her pillow. "I have tended Saber's wounds and he is resting as comfortably as possible. He has lost a great deal of blood. There is nothing we can do but wait, and you need to rest."

Learning that Sebastian was in critical condition wasn't what Eden wanted to hear. Indeed, she refused to accept the fact that Sebastian might die because of her foolish tantrum. This was yet another lesson that reminded her how costly unleashed anger could be. Hadn't she learned that well enough as a child?

Eden cast aside the tormented thought and concentrated on Sebastian. She was not going to allow him to die. She had always made it a practice to sit beside her seriously injured patients, reading to them, talking to them, encouraging them until the worst had passed.

Sebastian was entitled to those same practices, even if Eden had to prop herself up and pinch herself every few minutes to remain awake. She was going to inject the will to live into Sebastian, and she would not allow him to disappoint her by dying! She hadn't even had the chance to thank him for sparing her life, hadn't had the chance to tell him that she loved him, despite the problems that still lay between them.

Dr. Curtis handed Eden the fresh nightgown Bet had laid out for her. "Put this on while I fetch your sister. Bet is anxious to see you."

When the physician left, Eden wormed into her gown, then clutched Sebastian's hand. "Sebastian, we have things to do," she whispered to him. "You won't allow a scoundrel like Lockwood to defeat you, now will you? Of course, you won't. We can't let him enjoy any satisfaction, now can we? I should say not, and I know you heartily agree."

Eden inhaled a steadying breath and tried to think past the headache pounding at her skull. "I know you don't feel up to snuff at the moment, but you're the kind of man who is bold enough to rise to any challenge. I have always admired that about you, did you know?

"We are going after Lockwood to ensure justice is served. Of course, you will want to rest a few days to regenerate your strength, but we have things to do. Neither of us can lie abed for too many days."

Sebastian lay there, not moving a muscle.

She gave his hand an affectionate squeeze. "For the most part, I have been forgiving and gracious, but I think revenge is in order here.

"What shall we do with Lockwood when we track him down? Shoot him and be done with it? Stab him a couple of times for the pain he caused us? Or maybe we should poison the evil fiend. After what he did to you—"

Eden chastised herself for bringing Sebastian's attention back to his critical wound. The whole idea here was to encourage and distract him.

"Where do you suppose that slimy weasel got off to, Sebastian? He can't have gone far after you blasted him. And a fine shot that was, all things considered," Eden complimented him.

God, she could use a drink. Her mouth was as dry as

the Sahara. Nonetheless, she licked her lips and forged ahead. "Now then, as soon as you are back on your feet, you and I are going—"

"Eden?"

Sebastian's hoarse voice was a manna from heaven. For a moment, Eden became oblivious to the drumming in her tender skull.

"Yes, Sebastian?"

"I have asked you time and again not to use your powers of suggestion on me." The faintest hint of a smile curved the corner of his blue-tinged lips. "You know how I hate it."

"Yes, well, with all the excitement I forgot. This horrendous headache makes it hard to think straight," she explained.

Her heart swelled with relief when Sebastian squeezed her hand in return. Although he hadn't opened his eyes, she knew he was listening as best he could. "But the thing is, we have a crusade awaiting us. I can't go after Lockwood alone. You keep harping on my bad habit of taking matters into my own hands. There is no one else I would even consider taking with me to track down Lockwood. So you'll simply have to hurry up and get well—"

The door flew open to admit a flock of visitors. Eden squinted through the fuzzy blur that impaired her vision to see Elizabeth stagger forward to fling herself on the foot of the bed.

"Oh, Eden, thank God you're alive!" Bet blubbered.

"Bet, you are jarring the bed," Eden scolded her inebriated sister. "Sebastian doesn't need to be jostled." Her gaze narrowed on the elderly, white-haired clergyman who brought up the rear of the procession toting a tattered Bible. "Parson Milbourne, what are you doing here?"

Tully strode forward to tower over Sebastian's side of the bed. He stared at his employer, then met Eden's stricken expression. "His lordship requested a preacher."

"Now why would he want to do that when he is going to be perfectly fine?" Eden demanded. "Tell him, Sebastian. You are going to be up and around in no time atall, aren't you? There is no need for the pastor to speak the rites."

"I asked for a man of the cloth," Sebastian murmured.

Eden's gaze narrowed on him. "Now you listen to me, Sebastian Saber. You aren't going anywhere that needs a preacher to send you on your way, so toss that idiotic notion out of your head this instant—"

"Eden?"

"Yes, Sebastian?"

"Grant my last request . . ."

"I will grant any request you so desire, as long as it is not your last. Do you hear me, Sebastian? Now stop this morbid nonsense before you irritate me. We have business to tend—"

Bet was wailing so loudly that Eden couldn't concentrate. "Stop it," she snapped. "I can barely hear Sebastian as it is." She glanced at her glassy-eyed brother-in-law. "Peter, kindly do something about your simpering wife."

While Peter gathered Bet in his arms, muffling her sobs against his chest. Parson Milbourne stepped front and center.

"What is it you wish, my son?"

"Marry us," Sebastian requested weakly.

"Marry us?" the bystanders chorused.

Eden blinked, stunned. Marry Sebastian Saber? She couldn't do that, though she loved him dearly. If marrying him was his dying wish—and she granted it—Sebastian would think it was perfectly all right for him to flit off to the pearly gates, having done the right thing by her.

Well, Eden would have none of that! She was not going to supply Sebastian with any excuse to sink into oblivion and not fight his way back. She absolutely refused to become a wife and a widow in the same night!

"Sebastian, I can't marry you today. I look a frightful
mess. I am dressed in a nightgown, not a proper wedding
gown. I think we should delay the ceremony until tomorrow. Parson Milbourne can return tomorrow afternoon.
By then, you will have rested, and I will have time to fashion
a gown. I will marry you tomorrow if that is what you wish."

"Tomorrow then, and not a day later." Sebastian lifted
heavily lidded eyes momentarily, trying to locate Tully.
"Take care of all the details for me," he requested, then
sank into the circling darkness that he could no longer
hold at bay.

After what felt like a decade-long nap, Sebastian forced
himself to open his eyes. Staring blankly at the ceiling, he
listened to the cheerful, animated voice that he swore had
been his constant companion, even in sleep.

"Daniel Johnston, my father's courier, reported to me
early this afternoon," Eden said. "Word from the front
lines is that the rebels have been hammering away at the
British redoubts. French and American forces have drawn
ever closer to Yorktown."

Eden squeezed Sebastian's hand and blessed him with
a sunny smile. "Governor Nelson aimed a cannon at his
own house and fired away, after learning that his home
had been used as British headquarters. The French fleet
has been shelling Yorktown from sea, while the rebels close
ranks. Despite the rain, Gilbert Lafayette, and the light
infantry, took one of the redoubts in less than ten minutes.
Another one fell shortly thereafter. The high echelon of
Patriot command is certain it is only a matter of time before Cornwallis is forced to admit defeat—"

"Eden?"

Eden leaned down to press her palm to his fevered brow,
then brushed her lips over his forehead. "Yes, Sebastian?"

"Marry me."

Eden graced him with another radiant smile. "I can't possibly marry you in this cold, drizzly rain. A ceremony with cannons and muskets echoing in the distance is hardly my idea of an orchestrated wedding. Besides, Parson Milbourne has already come and gone for the day. I promise to marry you tomorrow . . ."

Marry you tomorrow . . . The words drifted through Sebastian's mind as he fought to remain conscious . . . and lost the battle . . .

Eden rose from her chair beside the bed to unwrap the bandages on Sebastian's chest and shoulder. The unsightly wound made her stomach roll over. She swallowed hard, reminding herself that Sebastian had taken Lockwood's musketfire in order to spare her life. That could have— and still might—cost him his own life.

Dr. Curtis had offered no guarantee that Sebastian would survive his injury. For three days Eden had kept constant vigil, talking to Sebastian while he dozed, then roused momentarily. She couldn't say for certain that he had heard a word of what she said—until just a few moments ago. It was the first coherent response he had made since he had been shot.

Exhausted, Eden coated the healing salve on Sebastian's jagged wound, and applied fresh dressing. Then she eased down on the bed beside Sebastian and cuddled up against his good side. She would allow herself to sleep for just a few minutes, she told herself. Just a short catnap before she continued her vigil . . .

Tully glanced up from brushing the Arabian stallion to see a woman's shapely silhouette hovering beside the barn door. A backdrop of blowing rain, spotlighted by the glow of the lantern, gave Tully the feeling that he was being visited by an angel. The moment Eden moved deeper into the barn, Tully dropped the brush and rushed toward her.

"Is his lordship—?"

"His lordship is sleeping off another dose of laudanum," Eden told the apprehensive Tully. "I have only come to ask you some questions. Sebastian is too groggy to respond for himself."

The determined expression on Eden's face caused Tully to frown warily. "What is it that you want to know, m'lady?"

"Who is Lady Penelope?" Eden questioned.

"Penelope?" Tully wasn't certain what question he expected, but that wasn't it!

"Sebastian has been mumbling the woman's name for the better part of two days."

"Has he?"

"He has."

"And that's why you keep telling his lordship that you will marry him tomorrow," Tully presumed.

"No, I have been putting him off so he will rouse each tomorrow to propose again," Eden informed Tully. "I won't have Sebastian dying on me, after he thinks he has done the right thing before he departs to a higher sphere."

Tully smiled in amusement. "You are a very shrewd and insightful woman."

"No, I am only being sensible," Eden contradicted. "Sebastian saved my life and I am trying to return the favor."

"But you don't intend to marry him the first tomorrow that he manages to remain conscious for five consecutive minutes, do you?" Tully speculated. "It is a mistake, you know. The two of you should be married as soon as possible."

Eden's sapphire-colored gaze lanced off Tully's whiskered face. "I can't marry a man who dreams of another woman."

"Has his lordship uttered your name as well?" Tully questioned.

"Yes, but—"

"Well then, why does it disturb you to hear him mention a woman from his distant past?"

"Who was she?" Eden asked point-blank.

"Someone he used to know," Tully said with a lackadaisical shrug.

Eden sighed. "I did not tramp out into the darkness and the rain to hear your evasive answers."

Eden was a relentlessly persistent female and was going nowhere until her curiosity had been appeased, Tully suspected.

"I'm not sure it's my place to divulge his lordship's past, but if it means the difference between a marriage taking place or not, then I will tell you what you want to know."

Eden sat herself down on a wooden nail keg and stared intently at Tully. "Very well, then, let's start at the beginning. Where does Sebastian call home?"

Tully scooped up the brush and turned back to the stallion while he collected his thoughts. "Sebastian was British born and bred. He has an impressive pedigree that's well known in England."

Eden frowned warily. If Tully confessed that Sebastian favored the British, after all, her emotions were going to be in turmoil again.

"With his lordship's background, he was able to serve General Washington very well in the war. With his contacts and credentials, Sebastian could go where other Patriot spies could not."

"Right smack dab into Cornwallis's own camp," Eden murmured pensively. "And Sir Henry Clinton's in New York, too?"

Tully grinned. "Earls do have all sorts of privileges, you know."

Eden very nearly toppled off her wooden keg. "An earl?" she croaked.

"Once an earl," Tully amended. "Now a died-in-the-wool colonial who demands, and expects, the same civil rights and personal freedoms in Virginia that he enjoyed in England, though I know you've been given just cause to question where his loyalty lies."

"An earl?" Eden repeated, flabbergasted.

"When the Crown began treating colonists like stepchildren, Sebastian objected. In fact, he was one of the men who urged Washington to take charge of the American Army and fight for our rights. The land that the Saber family purchased as an investment a half century ago lies beside Mount Vernon. Sebastian and George Washington have been acquainted for many years."

Eden stared at Tully. "An earl abandoned his earldom to reside on a plantation in Virginia? Why?"

"It's a long story."

"I have the remainder of the night to hear it," she insisted. "Bet and Peter are sitting with our lordly patient. And I cannot wait to hear how Lady Penelope fits into this."

"She didn't fit in at all," Tully snorted. "That was the problem."

"Tully, you are being deliberately evasive again."

Tully draped his arms over the Arabian's back and stared at Eden. "M'lady, are you always this insistent on wringing information out of everyone you know?"

"Yes," she said. "One cannot understand if one doesn't gather facts. I don't usually meet with such resistance. You and his lordship have proven to be the exceptions. Now then, you were about to tell me about Lady Penelope."

Tully grinned wryly. "I was?"

"You were. You also know that I will never consent to marry a man I don't understand and cannot completely trust. I would make his lordship miserable by pestering him for information for the rest of his life."

Tully didn't doubt it. Eden, despite all her saintly qualities, had a will of iron. Heaving a sigh, Tully resigned himself to the fact that he was about to spill his guts to the lady—and would eventually catch hell from Sebastian, who wasn't in the habit of explaining himself, or his past, to anybody.

"More than a decade ago, Sebastian fancied himself in love with a vivacious blonde who was the darling of the English court. Penelope used her feminine wiles to wrest a marriage proposal from the new Earl of Sabervale. All was well until Sebastian announced to his betrothed that he planned to hand over his title to his younger brother."

"Why was he going to do that?"

"Because, three years earlier, Sebastian and Jarred Saber were in a carriage accident that injured them both. The scar on his ribs is a constant reminder of the disaster that crippled Jarred."

Eden remembered hearing Sebastian mumble Jarred's name while he was trapped in laudanum-induced dreams.

"In England, younger sons do not inherit titles and wealth. Jarred was expected to make his own way in the world and secure his own future. But after the accident, Jarred was in no condition to do anything except learn to walk again.

"Sebastian felt responsible for his brother. Jarred had been a frail, sickly child who had been left in Sebastian's care when their parents perished in a voyage at sea. Sebastian decided to hand down the title and sail for America to oversee the lands his family had purchased."

"And Lady Penelope objected to being dragged off to the backward colonies, away from the glamour and excitement of court," Eden presumed.

"Objected?" Tully chuckled. "That's putting it mildly. The little shrew threw a spectacular tantrum when Sebastian informed her of his plans. Sebastian never liked the pretentiousness of court life that Penelope thrived on. She immediately broke the engagement and turned her fawning attention on Jarred, confirming what Sebastian hadn't wanted to believe was true. Penelope's interest in him went only as far as his wealth, title, and prestige."

Eden sighed. What a bitter blow Sebastian must have suffered when he realized that Penelope had catered to his money and wasn't interested in him, just for himself.

"When Sebastian set sail for Virginia, I, o'course, came with him," Tully said. "I had been in his employ since we were no more than children. It's the kind of loyalty and devotion a woman like Penelope couldn't understand."

Eden stared toward the lights of the house. "He was forsaken because of his generosity to his injured brother, the new Earl of Sabervale. I pity a woman so shallow that she couldn't see the endearing qualities Sebastian possesses."

"Not everyone looks deeper than wealth, m'lady. Certainly not Penelope. A few months after we reached the colonies, his lordship received a letter informing him of Jarred's marriage to Penelope. It was Jarred who got the worst end of that bargain," Tully said, and snorted. "According to Jarred's letters, Penelope has turned into a full-fledged shrew. A pity that he loves her despite her many flaws. And fitting, too, that the lady is barren. It infuriates her to know that it will be Sebastian's children who reinherit the titles."

Tully stared somberly at Eden. "So you see, Sebastian does indeed hold faithfulness and loyalty in the same high regard that you do. Yet, when Penelope betrayed him, after she openly professed to love him, he became cynical and mistrusting of women. Now that he has been deeply involved in espionage, he has been trapped in a world of half-truths and twisted lies. It goes against his grain, even while he performs the duties Washington requests of him."

Tully paused from brushing the stallion and stared pointedly at Eden. "You don't think you can trust Lord Saber, because he was forced to ply you with distorted truths to accomplish his missions. And he isn't certain he can trust you, because you can't completely trust him. It is a complicated tangle, to be sure."

Eden nodded. "And I am most hesitant to marry a man who can't let himself love me."

Tully chuckled, then went back to brushing the Arabian. "Are you so certain of that? Some men have difficulty forcing out the words, but that doesn't mean they don't care every bit as much. Sometimes affection is demonstrated in what a man does, not what he says or doesn't say."

When Eden was silent for a moment, Tully slanted her a glance, then drove home his point. "Take that unpleasant business of your captivity, for example. When Sebastian returned to the cabin to find Lockwood mistreating you, he lost every shred of temper and beat the blackguard to a pulp. His lordship watched over you while you recovered. And more recently, when you both faced death at Lockwood's hands, he chose to risk his life to spare you. Now I ask you, does that sound like a man who doesn't care? Do you still think his lordship has decided to marry you just to fulfill an obligation?"

Eden smiled up at Tully. "How have you become so wise?"

"It is not wisdom, but rather simple observation," he clarified. "I have been with his lordship for so many years that I know him exceptionally well. Better than he knows himself, I think. No man chooses to risk his life for a cause, or purpose, when he has no strong conviction. Sebastian Saber has always been a man of honor and conviction, even when he had to resort to deception to serve his country. General Washington used the same tactic against Sir Clinton before he hightailed it south. And *his* honesty is legendary."

Eden rose to her feet. She glanced toward the door, watching rain swirl in the lanternlight like chips of amber.

"I believe you, Tully. Sebastian is an honorable, generous man. A pity that I'm so unworthy of him."

"A saint unworthy? Nonsense," Tully hooted.

"Believe me, Tully, I am no saint," she said before she walked out into the pouring rain.

Gerard Lockwood erupted in a ferocious snarl that over-rode the sound of raindrops splattering against the windowpane of the cottage in the pines. While searching for food, he came across Thaddeus Saber's disguise.

"That sneaky bastard! May he burn in hell!" Gerard hissed.

For the past few days Gerard had been on the run, living like a scavenger, circling the rebel patrols to reach Thaddeus's isolated cottage. But Thaddeus was not to be found . . . because there was no Thaddeus! That conniving Saber had duped so many British officers with his disguise that it was infuriating. No wonder Sebastian was never around while Thaddeus was at the cabin.

Still swearing profusely, Gerard hurled the padded coat and breeches against the wall, then paced the floorboards. He didn't know if Sebastian was dead or alive. Dead, he hoped. But either way, that sneaky bastard was out of commission. Too bad Gerard had missed his chance to kidnap Eden and hold her for ransom. His funds were dwindling fast.

Pausing, Gerard stared thoughtfully at the window, then smiled fiendishly. No doubt General Pembrook was still occupied on the battlefield. With Saber dead—or close to it—Gerard shouldn't have difficulty abducting Eden.

And when this damned war ended, Gerard would have plenty of funds to set himself up in another colony where he wouldn't be recognized.

The thought put a satisfied smile on his lips. He still had a few axes to grind with Eden Pembrook, ones she knew nothing about. But Gerard did. He had a very long memory.

Very soon he would settle an old score with Eden, then be on his way with a pocket full of ransom money. And at long last, the past would be completely behind him.

Eighteen

"Last night sealed Cornwallis's fate," Eden reported as she sat beside the bed, holding Sebastian's hand. "Just as you predicted, Cornwallis made a last-ditch effort to escape."

Eden pressed her palm against Sebastian's forehead to check for fever. For the first time in days, his temperature appeared to be normal, though he was still weak and groggy from laudanum.

"During last night's storm, Cornwallis tried to ferry his men across the channel to Gloucester, but the high winds and waves scattered his skiffs. At ten o'clock this morning, he called for a white flag and drummer boy to request a parley. We're hammering out the terms of surrender, Sebastian. For all intent and purpose this war is finally over!"

"And what of the war between us?"

Eden started. She hadn't realized Sebastian was awake and listening. He had been lying so motionless that she assumed he was sleeping.

When thick black lashes swept up, and silver-gray eyes pierced her like a lance, Eden felt her heart melt in her chest. After her chat with Tully, she had gained considerable insight about the man she loved. But as much as she savored the thought of spending the rest of her life with Sebastian, there were two obstacles standing in her way—

her blemished past and the absence of his declaration of love.

Tully insisted sometimes deeds, rather than words, testified to affection. Yet, Tully overlooked a crucial fact because of his unwavering loyalty and admiration for Sebastian Saber.

Sebastian was a man of honor. Men of honor always defended those incapable of defending themselves, because their code of ethics demanded it. Eden had no doubt that Sebastian would have saved anyone from Lockwood that fateful night. He had been born and bred a gentleman. She would have expected nothing less of a man with generations of blue blood flowing through his veins. It was Sebastian's strong code of ethics that had motivated him to risk his life for Eden, even if Tully chose to interpret the situation differently.

Furthermore, Eden's past would always be there to torment her. In retrospect, she realized that each marriage proposal she had rejected was spurred by feelings of guilt and unworthiness. She had spent years atoning for her sins, but nothing could rectify what she had done.

Sebastian was the only man who had seen through her cheerful smiles to detect the dark secrets in her eyes. She couldn't take those abominable sins into any marriage, especially one with an earl . . .

"Eden, you haven't answered me," Sebastian prompted.

"I'm thinking. And I think you have misinterpreted the situation. We have never been at war, exactly."

"And we've never been at peace, exactly," he contended. His gaze narrowed on Eden, who looked like a bright yellow ball of sunshine fidgeting in her chair. "You don't plan to marry me at all, do you? Your promise of tomorrow was a tactic aimed at getting me to survive from one night to the next."

Her blue eyes lifted to meet his probing stare. "I can't marry you," she said finally, decisively.

"Why? Because of the mysterious secrets of your past?" he asked, point-blank.

Eden blanched and then stared at the far wall. "Yes and no."

"Well, which is it?"

God, how Sebastian hated being flat on his back and woozy with sedatives. He didn't feel in control, and that was a dangerous prospect when dealing with a woman of Eden's acute intellect.

Rising, Eden paced from wall to wall. "I know of *your* past, Sebastian," she said abruptly.

"I suppose I have Tully to thank for spilling the whole sordid story to you while I was in no condition to stop him," he muttered.

"I was persistent in wringing the truth from him," she said in Tully's defense.

"As always, I'm sure."

"Yes, well, it is one of my many flaws you would grow to dislike intensely if we were to wed. I am also extremely independent and I balk at being ordered around. I am so set in my ways that I tend to think that *my* way is the right way."

Sebastian shifted position—carefully—as he watched Eden wear a path on the carpet. A half-smile dangled on the corner of his mouth. He prepared himself for the rehearsed speech he suspected she had delivered to each of her seven discarded fiancés.

"Knowing about your blue-blooded breeding, I couldn't possibly taint the Saber family name. My ancestors were commoners who sailed to the colonies to make a fresh start. In fact, I am told there were even a few beggars and thieves in past generations. I am sure you wouldn't want my ancestry of outlaws to tarnish your royal ancestry."

Eden shot Sebastian a quick glance as he propped himself against the stack of pillows. "I realize you feel honor bound, because we have been . . ." She swallowed, composed herself, then plowed ahead. "We have been intimate on a few occasions."

"Yes, we have definitely been that," he agreed. "If one tries to ignore all the other facts, one simply can't overlook that, now can one?"

Eden blushed to the roots of her chestnut-colored hair. "No, one can't. But I believe affectionate intimacy should be an expression, an outpouring, of deep feelings which must be the solid foundation of marriage, don't you agree? And without those strong emotions, the foundation would crumble, would it not? So simple sexual intimacy is not really an issue at all, is it? You and I could make love to anyone else for the mere pleasure to be had, couldn't we?"

No, they could not! And Sebastian suspected Eden knew that as well as he did, but he was not going to agree—or disagree—to anything Eden might use against him later. He knew damned well that Eden's previous suitors—in their eagerness to please and accommodate her—had stumbled into similar traps. Sebastian was dodging the pitfalls by refusing to take the bait.

"Well, don't you agree with my logic, Sebastian?" she persisted.

Sebastian swallowed a smile. "Do go on, my dear lady. I am still mulling over the conclusions you have made."

Eden frowned, disgruntled that she hadn't wrested an agreeable answer from him. Sebastian was definitely a cut above the customary male mentality. She was going to have to drag out the heavy artillery to convince him to withdraw his marriage proposal.

"There is another serious defect in my personality that I have never been able to overcome," she continued while she paced. "I am very susceptible to—and eager for— change."

Sebastian knew what was coming next, and he usually lost his temper when she hit on this topic. But he was not going to lose his temper today. There was too much at stake.

Eden paused from circumnavigating the room, then smiled that infuriatingly sweet smile that could drive Sebastian straight up the wall. "If you will note, I have even changed the furniture arrangement in this room twice since I have been nursing you back to health. I simply can't leave things as they are for extended periods of time, because they eventually start to—"

"Bore you," Sebastian supplied through gritted teeth.

"Yes, that is the appropriate word." Eden smiled again, and Sebastian practically ground the enamel off his teeth in an effort to restrain his temper. "You are exceptionally perceptive, Sebastian."

"So you keep telling me."

"You are aware of my numerous flaws, aren't you?"

Who wasn't? Eden threw them up in every prospective husband's face.

"I also have a fierce craving for adventure. I like to broaden my horizons and increase my knowledge. I simply am not suitable wife material, because I never know when the impulse to delve into a new interest will strike."

Sebastian managed to keep his expression blank, though he knew she was purposely trying to irritate him. He kept quiet, unsure where this new line of conversation was leading.

"Take my first fiancé, for instance. Timothy Mason had a penchant for acquiring unusual varieties of flowers for his garden. Once he taught me all he knew about cultivating and caring for exotic plants shipped in from all parts of the world, we had very little to say to each other.

"And when I took an interest in planting crops, other than tobacco, I was inclined to seek out a man who could supply information. But before long, I—"

"*Outgrew* your need for him, and the other men who followed," Sebastian inserted.

"Exactly." She smiled at him.

Sebastian cursed under his breath.

"You see how those quirks of personality could become a problem in marriage, don't you, Sebastian?"

What Sebastian could see was that Eden was annoying the hell out of him! But he would burn in Hades before he let on! And honestly, he thought he deserved a medal for putting up with all this nonsense while he felt so debilitated.

"I am like a child chasing after rainbows, never content with the sameness of life, looking for something I may never find. You would grow tired of my silly whims eventually. You would ask yourself why you chose me as your wife, wouldn't you, Sebastian?"

"Would I, Eden?" Sebastian clenched his fist in the sheet and put a stranglehold on his temper. She had purposely chosen to have this conversation now, because she knew his injury made him irritable and out of sorts. She was purposely preying on his weakness, but he wasn't going to blow his stack and yell at her. He was going to give her no reason to think she could use his temper to her advantage.

"Of course you would," she said with great certainty. "In six months, maybe less, you would start to feel trapped, unhappy. You would be living a lie by attempting to conceal your disillusionment with me, just like—"

Eden snapped her mouth shut before she delved into the forbidden memories that simmered just beneath the surface of her self-reserve. Sebastian's gaze honed in on her, noting the change in her voice, the shadows clouding her eyes.

Eden manufactured another smile. "So you see, eventually those things which form the cornerstones of a good marriage would dissolve like a house built on shifting sand. Loyalty and trust would crumble around us, and we could find no common ground. I am doing you a great favor by

bringing my faults to your attention now, thereby saving
you years of dissatisfaction, am I not? And when you regain
the strength to get on with your life, I sincerely hope . . .
Sebastian, what the blazes do you think you're doing?"

With a mighty heave-ho, Sebastian surged up on the
edge of the bed, his bare feet dangling, his face white as
flour. "I'm getting on with the rest of my life," he panted.
Damnation, it took so much energy to sit upright that he
felt drained of strength!

Alarmed, Eden dashed toward him. "You can't get up
yet. You'll rip your stitches and destroy what little strength
you've recovered."

"Get out of my way, Eden. I intend to rise—or die trying." His voice wobbled. So did his arms and legs.

"I didn't keep constant vigil only to have you collapse
in a heap." Eden placed herself in front of him like a
human blockade. "I absolutely refuse to let you leave this
room until your condition improves."

Gritting his teeth, Sebastian surged to his feet. He lasted
all of one second before the world spun furiously around
him. Instinctively, he reached out to steady himself against
Eden's shoulder. Unfortunately, she was sitting back on
her heels. When he swayed toward her, she stumbled off
balance. They plunged to the floor in a flurry of squawks
and pained howls.

When Eden found herself sandwiched between Sebastian's muscular body and the carpet, she went perfectly
still. She was afraid to move, for fear she would cause Sebastian further discomfort.

This, Sebastian decided, was not discomfort. It was the
inspiration he needed to recover. Having Eden's soft, feminine body beneath his made him feel ten times better.

True, Eden's promises to "marry him tomorrow" had
effectively gotten him from one day to the next, but this
was a sure-fire remedy for recuperation. He could feel his
weak body generating heat and energy the instant his

mouth slanted over her honeyed lips to sip the nourish-
ment that brought his dulled senses back to life.

Sebastian felt whole and alive for the first time in a week.
Content, he closed his eyes and savored the taste of Eden's
kiss, right down to the last delicious drop.

Despite Eden's long-winded soliloquy on why they didn't
suit each other, he felt her arms gliding over his shoulders.
She kissed him back, and he went straight to heaven.

"Dear Lord! What is going on in here?"

Parson Milbourne and Dr. Curtis made an unexpected
entrance. The sound of choked laughter and shocked
gasps indicated that Tully, Peter, and Bet were a few steps
behind the clergyman and the physician.

"Sebastian, you should not be out of bed," the doctor
scolded.

"And you should definitely not be atop Miss—" Parson
Milbourne's face bloomed with color as he glanced heavenward. "Sweet mercy!"

Tully veered around the cluster of bodies clogging the
entrance and hurried over to set Sebastian back on his
feet. As Tully put Sebastian to bed, his lips quirked in wry
amusement. He glanced over to see the blush on Eden's
face.

Someone was going to have to take charge of this situation, Tully decided—and he put himself in command instantly. This matter between his lordship and Eden should
have been settled weeks ago, and it was going to be settled
here and now. Eden and his lordship could grumble over
the specifics of it later.

Spinning around, Tully motioned the clergyman to the
bedside. "I think you should perform the wedding ceremony now. We have the bride, groom, and plenty of wit-
nesses. We need no more than that."

"The special banns—" the parson tried to remind him.

"Are in my pocket." Tully retrieved the papers he had
acquired at Sebastian's request.

"Now wait just a blessed minute," Eden objected.

"No more waiting," Elizabeth insisted. "Every day when Sebastian wakes up and asks you to marry him, you promise to marry him tomorrow. This is the very last tomorrow, Eden. We can't have guests and servants arriving to find you and Sebastian in such compromising situations."

"Curse it, Bet," Eden muttered. "After all I have done for you over the years."

"And now it is time for me to do something important for you," Bet said in the same cheerful tone Eden usually employed. "I will be your matron of honor and Tully can be Sebastian's best man."

Sebastian was losing ground fast. His fall from bed had zapped his strength. The kiss, unfortunately, was effective in rejuvenating his strength only as long as it lasted.

"Get on with the ceremony—quickly," Sebastian said in a hoarse voice.

Tully nudged the thunderstruck parson with an elbow. "You heard his lordship."

"But this is highly irregular."

"Just like the courtship was, and the marriage no doubt," Tully insisted.

The parson took a deep breath and reluctantly began the ceremony. "We are gathered together in—"

"Skip to the I-dos," Sebastian cut in weakly. "I won't last much longer."

"Do you take this woman?" Milbourne said hurriedly, frowning at the lack of color in Sebastian's face.

"I do." Sebastian sank back on his pillow and closed his eyes to save every smidgen of strength he had left.

"Eden, do you take this man—?"

"If I take him, I swear I don't know what I will do with him," Eden grumbled. "This is a terrible mistake. It is never going to work— Ouch!" She glared at her traitorous sister whose heel was grinding into Eden's toes.

"Say it," Bet demanded impatiently.

"In good conscience, I cannot— Ouch!" Eden glowered at her sister, then glanced at the other occupants in the room. There was no support forthcoming. She, it appeared, was the only one here with a lick of sense.

"Marry me, Eden," Sebastian whispered without opening his eyes. "You can outgrow your need for me tomorrow . . ."

Eden made the crucial mistake of peering down into that peaked face that was surrounded by tousled raven hair and a shaggy beard. Sebastian looked so weak and vulnerable, so helpless that it tugged on her heartstrings. She spoke the words from her heart, instead of her head, knowing she would regret her decision later. But not now, not when her betraying body was still tingling from the aftereffects of their unplanned embrace on the floor.

"I do," she whispered, then watched a trace of a smile spread across Sebastian's blue-tinged lips.

"Then I pronounce you man and wife," Parson Milbourne said with a decisive nod. "Since the groom has already kissed the bride, we will dispense with that formality. May this be the beginning of a long and happy marriage." He turned to leave. "Now, if you will excuse me, I have to visit the injured soldiers upstairs and the troops in the field."

"If the rest of you will excuse me, I need to examine my patient," Dr. Curtis announced. "Close the door behind you on your way out."

Smiling triumphantly, Tully, Peter, and Bet ushered Eden from the room.

"I will never forgive you for this," Eden grumbled.

Bet patted her sister's rigid shoulder. "Of course you'll forgive us. That is what saints do best."

"I am not a saint!" Eden all but shouted.

When Tully, Bet, and Peter grinned as they strode off, Eden swore under her breath. She did not appreciate be-

ing forced to do anything—she had been independent far
too long for that!

This was the beginning of trouble, Eden predicted.
When Sebastian was back on his feet, he would be trying
to tell her what to do and when to do it. She was vulnerable, because she cared for him, and he would use that to
his advantage. If they couldn't be equal partners in this
union, then they could not be partners at all.

This marriage simply would not work out. God forgive
her, but she was going to have to make Sebastian's life
miserable until he agreed to a separation. If he couldn't
love her as deeply as she loved him, remaining under the
same roof with him would break her heart and her spirit.

There and then, Eden made a pact with herself. She
had to aggravate Sebastian to the point that he decided
to leave her. Bet, Peter, and Tully would regret intervening
in something that wasn't their concern. And furthermore,
Eden wasn't worthy of marrying a former earl, not with
her checkered past! She was a . . . Well, she simply wasn't
worthy. Enough said.

Sebastian awakened the following morning to find Maggie, rather than Eden, sitting in the chair beside him. He
was congratulated on his recent marriage and then fed
breakfast. One nap later, Tully was sitting beside him. Elizabeth filled in during the afternoon until Peter Dalton returned from the mercantile shop to read the latest copy
of the Virginia *Gazette* to Sebastian.

The only one on the plantation who didn't stop in to
check on Sebastian was his new bride.

Sebastian had a pretty good idea that his new wife was
up to her old tricks. He was being deliberately and obviously outgrown and ignored!

The second and third days of convalescence—following
the wedding—were repetitions of the first. All that kept

Sebastian in reasonably good humor was the news that
Tully brought along with the supper tray.

"The war is officially over and done, yer lordship," Tully
reported as he gently placed the tray on Sebastian's lap.
"I witnessed the formal surrender myself. The American
and French troops marched across the meadow with all
the pomp and pageantry the British would have used if
the war had gone the other way."

Sebastian smiled as he stabbed a slice of potato with his
fork. He could well imagine that the Americans had niggled their British cousins.

"Eight thousand of King George's finest, along with the
kilted Highlanders, the red-coated English Regulars, and
several blond German hirelings, trooped out between the
rows of Americans and Frenchmen. They were accompanied by the tune of 'The World Turned Upside Down.' "
Tully grinned wryly. "The British managed to put in their
own irritating gibe during the ceremony of surrender."

"A humiliating affair for the world's finest army and
navy, I'm sure." Sebastian chuckled, then grimaced at the
pain laughter caused him.

"Humiliating indeed, yer lordship," Tully guaranteed.
"It was mortifying to the point of nauseating, at least in
the illustrious Lord Charles Cornwallis's case. He didn't
show his face. He pleaded illness and sent Brigadier General O'Hara to offer his sword to Washington."

Tully smiled shrewdly at Sebastian. "Pride is a devilish
thing at times, isn't it, yer lordship? Some men can't bring
themselves to face defeat. Lord Cornwallis is one of them."

Sebastian quirked a dark brow and glanced at his friend.
"And I am another, I suppose?"

"Did I say that?"

"No, you let me say it for myself, in order to soften the
blow." Sebastian stabbed a forkful of potatoes and
munched on them. "I swear you've been taking lessons in

subtlety from my wife. She is an expert at planting thoughts in people's heads and putting words in their mouths."

Tully rose to his feet, his hands balled on his hips, and stared sternly at Sebastian. "Why can't you simply come out and tell your new wife what she wants, and needs, to hear? It would solve your problems, I am certain of it."

"You want me to agree to dissolving this marriage? That is what she wants, you know. I suspect her new motto is: Hastily wed and quickly shed."

"Not that, damn it," Tully muttered. "Why don't you tell her you love her and be done with it. I swear, you two are the stubbornest creatures on this earth."

"Thank you, Tully. I have always been exceptionally fond of you, too," Sebastian smirked, then sipped his mint julep.

Tully ignored the flippant comment and forged ahead. "I think you are purposely annoying your new wife. And not to be outdone, she is trying to annoy you right back. That's why she has made herself scarce these past few days."

"Just where is my bride?" Sebastian asked.

"She was outside, riding the Arabian stallion into the ground last time I looked," Tully grumbled. "The stable boys are placing wagers on how long you'll allow your bride to behave like a reckless hoyden." Tully leaned down to stare Sebastian directly in the eye. "Did I mention that she has taken to wearing shirts and breeches during her wild rides over fences and across creeks?"

"A former earl's bride scandalizing the countryside by wearing breeches," Sebastian said consideringly. "I am supposed to be appalled, of course."

"And she has been riding out among the troops, dressed in her outrageous attire," Tully tattled.

Sebastian's eyes narrowed dubiously. "What do you mean out among the troops?"

"I mean she is dispensing all the hugs and kisses that

every conquering soldier deserves in celebration of victory. Your angel is spreading good cheer all around, thick as hasty pudding."

Although Tully appeared to be offended by Eden's outrageous behavior, Sebastian smiled to himself. Truth be told, he preferred this purposeful antagonism of Eden's to mental subterfuge. The feisty spirit Eden usually kept under wraps—in hopes of atoning for past sins—was leaking out and it seemed that Eden's attempt to prove she was outgrowing her need for Sebastian indicated that she was outgrowing her old self. The real Eden Pembrook Saber had begun to emerge. That was the woman Sebastian had come to . . .

Sebastian squirmed uncomfortably in bed and squelched the thought floating around his mind. "Do go on, Tully. I'm sure the whole point of Eden's outlandish antics is to provoke you into tattling to me. I, obviously, am supposed to become so outraged that I confront her in a flash of temper. Then she will insist that I take her as she is—or leave her. And I, in the height of my towering fury, am supposed to announce that I am leaving her. She is using reverse powers of persuasion, it seems."

Tully blinked. "Do you think that is her ploy, yer lordship? You think she is trying to force you to denounce this union that she was hesitant to form?"

"I would bet my life on it," Sebastian confirmed. "You seem to forget that I am not dealing with a simple-minded woman. I swear that she is almost as smart as God."

"But how long do you intend to let her pull these shenanigans before you put a stop to them?" Tully asked. "Riding around on that high-strung stallion is dangerous for a woman. She could get hurt."

Sebastian frowned as he toyed with his food. "Now there is the dilemma. If I try to exert my authority over her, a conflict will inevitably arise and she will put my temper to the test. I'm sorry to say that Eden knows which strings to pull when she purposely sets out to annoy me. And true, if I don't forbid her from these wild antics, she could be injured, or some overzealous soldier who has been too long on the battlefield might take unfair advantage of her."

"So, what do you intend to do?" Tully wanted to know.

Sebastian set aside his tray and scooted to the edge of the bed. "I think it's time I gave Eden the satisfaction of seeing her antics for myself. I suspect the full effect is lost in the telling."

Tully braced his hand on Sebastian's shoulder, detaining him from standing up. "I don't think this is a good idea, considering yer weakened condition."

Sebastian shrugged off Tully's meaty hand. "I don't see myself as having much choice. Help me outside," he requested. "I need some fresh air, if nothing else. These walls are starting to close in on me, even though Eden has sneaked in to rearrange the furniture on a regular basis."

Reluctantly, Tully helped Sebastian to his feet. "I still don't think this is a good idea, yer lordship. I guarantee that you aren't going to like what you see."

"Lord Amighty!" Sebastian choked out when he saw Eden, mounted on the spirited Arabian, leap over the split-rail fence and thunder across the pasture at breakneck speed.

"I warned you," Tully said as he assisted Sebastian into the chair on the porch, then tucked a quilt around him. "I think a strong drink might be in order. I'll fetch you one."

While Tully scuttled off, Sebastian stared across the meadow, silently fuming. Eden's outrageous antics had lost much in the telling. Hearing about it was one thing, but seeing her was quite another!

Dressed in scruffy garments that only a fieldhand at

labor would be seen in, Eden, with her tangled chestnut-colored hair whipping around her like a banner, galloped over hill and dale, taking fences in a single bound and soaring over creek beds. Though she was practicing death-defying maneuvers, she looked as if she were enjoying every blood-pumping, exhilarating moment. And the black Arabian was doing one of the two things he loved best—running.

And here Sebastian sat like a helpless invalid, watching his wife defy good judgment, and propriety, to drive home the point she wanted to make.

When Eden switched direction and caught sight of him sitting on the porch, she waved and smiled that aggravating smile that set his teeth on edge. Sebastian braced himself for the inevitable confrontation with Eden while watching her bypass the open gate and bound over a few fences, just in case Sebastian hadn't witnessed the earlier spectacle.

The woman was definitely handing him plenty of ammunition to blast away at her. No other enemy would be so generous as to supply weapons for the war she fully intended to lose.

"Ah, Sebastian, it is good to see you up and about again." Eden skidded the winded stallion to a halt by the railing. "I'm sorry I haven't had time to stop in to visit you lately. I have been celebrating the war's end and exercising the stallion in my spare time." Smiling nonchalantly, she reached down to pat the Arabian's lathered neck. "I would like to have this magnificent stallion as a wedding gift."

She was resorting to the demanding wife routine, Sebastian realized. But he wasn't rising to the bait. He was going to remain calm and reasonable. No way in hell was Eden going to ruffle his feathers.

"The Arabian is yours," he said.

The comment caught Eden off guard. She knew this

prized animal meant a great deal to Sebastian and she expected him to object. Since he didn't, she would have to find another way to lure him into a verbal skirmish. When she hit an exposed nerve, he would call off this absurd marriage and they could get on with their separate lives.

"Thank you, Sebastian. I was thinking of racing the Arabian at the fall fair in Williamsburg."

Sebastian tightened the tether on his temper. "Ah, so that's what all this riding is about. You're practicing for the upcoming event. I'm sure the Arabian will be in excellent condition by the time the fair rolls around."

Sebastian congratulated himself on sounding so nonchalant. He hadn't said he approved or disapproved of her plans. He had only offered a neutral comment so she couldn't take the bit in her teeth and run with it.

Eden did a double take and stared at Sebastian for a long moment. He wasn't reacting as she predicted. His weakened condition must be affecting his behavior. She would have to try harder to provoke him into an argument.

Swinging down from the saddle, Eden sashayed across the porch to sit cross-legged in front of Sebastian. His dark brows elevated in response to her unladylike conduct, but he didn't say a word.

"There is something we need to discuss—in private," Eden said, glancing every which way before she continued. "Since you are incapable of performing certain duties, and since I have recently discovered the pleasurable benefits of a man's companionship—"

Sebastian clenched his fists around the arms of his chair. A muscle twitched in his jaw, but he forced himself to hold his tongue while Eden went for his jugular.

"When a man can't participate in a sport, he usually sends a substitute to replace him . . . if you catch my meaning," she added with an elfish smile.

"And you are implying that you have found a suitable

substitute among the rebel troops," he managed to say without snarling the words at her. Damn it to hell, she really had her heart set on making his blood boil, didn't she?

"As a matter of fact, I have met a man . . . or ten."

Ten? *Ten!* Sebastian tightened the stranglehold on the arms of the chair and pretended it was his mischievous wife's neck. Eden was really taking her attempt to get rid of him to infuriating extremes—and it was working. He was doing all-out battle with his temper.

When a fleeting thought zipped across his mind, Sebastian frowned. He recalled the conversation he and Peter had the previous night. Peter had mentioned that Eden had asked him to list the qualities he sought in a woman and had found in Bet. Peter had rattled off such things as respectability, loyalty, kindness, and consideration.

Ah ha, thought Sebastian. Eden was going down that checklist, in hopes of disproving her wifely credentials to him. She was trying to ruin her respectability by riding astride the stallion while dressed in tawdry men's clothes. She had been inconsiderate by leaving him alone while he recuperated. Now she was being unkind by suggesting that she might trifle with other men while he was incapacitated.

Sebastian really had to hand it to his resourceful wife. She had gone to considerable effort to irritate him. He should be flattered. How many other brides tried to convince their husbands of the virtues of bachelorhood and estrangement?

Sebastian leaned forward in his chair and graced her with a seemingly sincere smile. "If you feel that it is necessary to continue the intimacy we have come to enjoy together, then do what you must while I am recovering."

Eden studied him ponderously. "Are you saying that you don't mind if I dally with other men?"

He borrowed one of her smiles and tried it out on her.

"I didn't say I didn't mind, only that I understand, my dear."

There. Let's see how she liked a taste of her own saintly generosity.

Nonplussed, Eden glanced away, then refocused on Sebastian. "There is also the matter of where we will live. I have no intention of leaving Pembrook Plantation. I know you have obligations at your own home, so we need to arrange to visit each other on special occasions, don't you agree?"

"Like Christmas?" Sebastian questioned.

She stared at him with feigned innocence. "Do you think once a year will be too inconvenient for you?"

The door creaked and Tully appeared with two glasses of brandy in hand. Eden bounded to her feet to retrieve the drink Tully had made for himself. She guzzled it like a sailor, swallowed a choking cough, then wiped the dribbles of liquor on her shirtsleeve.

"That was just what I needed before continuing my ride." With a wave and a saucy swagger, Eden descended the steps and mounted the Arabian.

Tully winced as Eden and the stallion flew over the fence. "Yer lordship, you really are going to have to do something about that woman."

"I am working on the problem," Sebastian muttered before he downed his drink.

"I suggest you work faster. At this rate, yer wife won't survive the week."

Sebastian reviewed the incident, deciding this first skirmish had ended in impasse. He had not gained any ground, but neither had he lost ground. He would retire to bed and get some rest. Playing mental war games with Eden was exhausting.

Finishing off the last of his drink, Sebastian levered up from the chair. "After you help me back into bed, I would like for you to run an errand for me, Tully. My wife doesn't have a wedding ring. Select the finest ring the jewelers in Williamsburg have to offer, and spare no expense."

Tully scoffed as he lent Sebastian a supporting arm. "You think you can buy her devotion? Three little words would serve far better, yer lordship, and they're not nearly as expensive as a jeweled ring."

"I am trying to make a point," Sebastian said, panting for breath as he wobbled unsteadily on his legs.

"If you say so."

"I do say so." Sebastian eased onto the pillows and let out a weary sigh. Damn, this mending wound was a hellish inconvenience.

"I hope you know what the hell ye're talking about, yer lordship, because I don't have a clue. Are you sure yer fever hasn't returned?"

Sebastian shooed Tully on his way. "Just fetch the damned wedding ring. I want a large, conspicuous one that any man will notice at first glance."

"Staking claims, yer lordship?" Tully grinned slyly. "Considering the effort ye're making to ensure this marriage endures, one might think ye're madly in love with yer wife. Too bad you and the lady are the only ones who can't see it for the truth."

Sebastian didn't hear what Tully said. He was so exhausted that he was asleep the moment his head hit the pillow.

Nineteen

Eden stepped onto the front porch to find a mob of men congregated on the lawn. "What is the problem, gentlemen?" she asked with a smile.

Delbert Gates, a scrawny, beady-eyed little man who ran the blacksmith shop, stepped grandly upon the stoop. "It has come to our attention that you are harboring a traitor in your home. We have come to haul him away and see that he pays for his crime."

"A traitor?" Eden blinked, bewildered. "Every man in my care served the American cause in an honorable manner."

Delbert shook his head. "We have been told that Sebastian Saber was a British spy. As soon as the war turned in favor of the rebels, he made an about-face to save his neck."

Eden scrutinized the tightfisted blacksmith, who had never lifted a hand to support the Patriot cause. In her estimation, Delbert Gates was the traitor here. Eden could also guess who was responsible for spreading that rumor— Gerard Lockwood. Shooting Sebastian didn't seem to have satisfied the vengeful fiend. Now he wanted to see Sebastian hung for treason.

"Mr. Gates, you and the rest of these men know that I have opened our home to tend the brave, wounded soldiers, don't you?"

"Of course. Who doesn't?"

The crowd murmured in agreement.

"You are also aware, I'm sure, that I have supported the war effort in every way possible, unlike some of us who have placed personal profit before God and country."

Gates squirmed when Eden's gaze indicated she thought he belonged at the top of the "unlike some" list. "We know that, but—"

"And I would never permit a man to take shelter under my roof if he hadn't displayed valor to the cause, now would I?"

"No, not on purpose, but—"

"The fact is, Sebastian Saber comes highly recommended by my own father and George Washington himself," Eden cut in. "Furthermore, Sebastian suffered a life-threatening wound while saving me from attack from a British soldier. Were you aware of that?"

The throng of men looked from one to another.

"No, I can see that you weren't. But I am here to tell you that Sebastian is such an honorable gentleman, and dedicated soldier, that I have married him."

The crowd staggered back in surprise. Delbert Gates's jaw scraped his sunken chest.

"Knowing how fiercely devoted I am to the American cause, and to our courageous, injured soldiers, you realize that I would never marry a man I didn't trust completely. Sebastian Saber has risked his life time and again for the Patriots. He left his own home in the hands of his servants so he could donate his time and talents to American victory."

Eden stared Gates squarely in the eye. "No, Mr. Gates, my new husband is not a turncoat, but rather a war hero who deserves your respect. He is to be praised, not condemned. In fact, this ugly rumor sounds like the work of bitter British sympathizers who are searching for a scapegoat to soothe their disappointment."

With hat in hand, Robert Weese moved forward. "We are truly sorry if we have offended you. We heard the alarming rumor and we wanted to protect our angel of mercy, is all."

"I am flattered by your concern, but I am also deeply chagrined that it takes so little to turn you against one of General Washington's hand-picked officers. I had hoped my new husband would be accepted in this community. I wouldn't want his sterling reputation tarnished by lies, not after he has made so many personal sacrifices for the cause of liberty."

Eden graced the crowd with an angelic smile. "And now, if you will excuse me, I must tend to my wounded husband."

When the crowd dispersed, Eden expelled a sigh of relief. Curse that Lockwood character, wherever he was. Sooner or later, he would have to be dealt with. He was hell-bent on causing trouble!

Sebastian eased away from the window and sank back on the bed. He was flattered to see that Eden had come to his defense. Eden refused to allow his name to be slandered, even though she had every intention of escaping marriage to him.

"There, you see, my sister the saint is a defender of truth and justice," Bet teased as she fluffed Sebastian's pillow. "Eden is only being stubborn about this marriage because we rushed her through it. These outrageous antics of hers are merely a statement."

Sebastian looked amused. "You think Eden is staking her territory in this marriage then?"

"Yes," Bet confirmed. "Once she determines how much you will allow her to get away with, the two of you can get on with your life together."

"You don't think her outlandish conduct stems from her past?" he asked, gauging Bet's reaction carefully.

"Her past?" Bet repeated blankly. "Whatever do you mean by that, Sebastian?"

It was unmistakably clear that Bet had been protected from the truth for years. Sebastian wasn't surprised. Eden would never think of upsetting her younger sister. Sebastian suspected that only one person around here knew exactly what happened those many years ago. It wasn't Leland Pembrook. He, like Bet, had been protected. Eden had shouldered all the guilt and shared her terrible secret with no one . . .

"Sebastian, aren't you hungry?" Bet asked, jostling him from his pensive musings. "You need to eat."

Sebastian stared at the tray Bet had placed on his lap. "I will dutifully clean my plate."

"Good. Eden fusses at me each time the tray is returned to the kitchen without being picked clean."

Sebastian cocked an eyebrow. Eden was keeping close tabs on his recuperation? That was an encouraging sign.

When Bet left the room, Sebastian attacked his meal with great relish. His appetite had returned, and he ate like a starving fieldhand. He was anxious to be back on his feet so he could deal with his bride who was staying up nights to devise ways of souring him on marriage to her.

Sebastian tested his tender shoulder, hoping this battle of wills wouldn't come to blows. He didn't want to have to force her to remain married to him. He preferred that she did it willingly.

Tucked into her niche for the night, Eden opened the package Tully had delivered to her. She gasped in disbelief when she saw the gold ring, with enough diamonds and sapphires mounted upon it to choke a horse! Although there was no note of explanation, she knew who had given her this extravagant gift.

Immediately, she felt guilty—an emotion she had lived with for what seemed forever. Even though she had been behaving outrageously of late, Sebastian had sent Tully to fetch a proper wedding ring. But she couldn't possibly accept it. She didn't deserve it, not when she was trying to convince Sebastian of the error of his ways.

She had to return the ring immediately, she decided. Sliding off her cot, she padded down the darkened hall. She would leave the ring on Sebastian's nightstand. He would know without explanation that she refused the gift.

Eden craned her neck around the partially opened door, watching moonbeams spray through the window to spotlight Sebastian. Her heart twisted in her chest at the sight of him. Ah, how she loved this man! If only he had come to love her as deeply as she loved him. If only her terrible past didn't stand between them like an impassable mountain range.

Eden was never going to be able to forget what she had done, never be able to atone for her sins. Sebastian deserved a far better wife than the one he had.

Resolutely, Eden tiptoed into the room to set the ring beside the bed. When she turned away, Sebastian grasped her hand.

Startled, Eden recoiled, clutching her chest. "I didn't realize you were awake."

"I haven't slept well for days," he murmured as he drew Eden down on the edge of the bed. "Lack of companionship, I think."

"I have seen to it that you have had plenty of companionship."

"But not the kind a husband comes to anticipate from his wife."

"Yes, well, I didn't want to aggravate your wound," she replied.

"How considerate of you, Saint Eden," he taunted.

"I am not that considerate, and please do not refer to me as a saint," she muttered.

Sebastian bit back a grin. He had never known anyone to make such a big to-do of denying her endearing qualities . . . And he couldn't remember wanting a woman as much as he wanted Eden. The ache in his loins was beginning to override the pain in his shoulder.

When Eden stood up to leave, Sebastian's fingers curled around her wrist to detain her. "We have to talk, Eden."

"It can wait until morning. You need to rest."

"No, we will talk now," he insisted.

"But—"

"Humor me. I'm not a well man."

"What do you want to talk about?"

There were scores of issues Sebastian wanted to discuss. The first was this exasperating secret Eden had concealed from the world. If he didn't force Eden to confront her hidden torments, Sebastian would never be able to crumble the barriers between them.

"Eden, I want to know exactly what happened the night your mother died."

Eden winced, as if she had been struck. "No—"

"Yes." Sebastian drew her resisting body to his. "You revealed enough in the nightmares you had at the cabin to make me realize you are suffering from unhealed torments. They dictate to you, inhibit you, rule your life. I know these wild shenanigans of yours are designed to drive me away, and I see them as an outpouring of your true spirit. You can't let the past control you any longer. It's time to face it."

When Eden tried to squirm away, Sebastian held her fast. He knew he was digging deep, probing at tender wounds in her soul, but he wanted her to confide in him.

"Let me go. I want to return to my own bed—now!"

Logic and gentle coaxing wasn't proving effective. Se-

bastian was going to have to ignite her temper in order to
loosen her tongue. She might hate him for it, but he had
no choice. She had to get her torments out in the open.

"You aren't going anywhere until I know the truth," he
told her gruffly. "Your mother didn't know the meaning
of loyalty and fidelity. You admitted that much when I pres-
sured you for information before. And I am not so blind
that I can't see that you have an unusual penchant for
open windows and unconfined spaces. Why is that?"

When he felt her tense in his arms, he knew he'd hit
an exposed nerve. Determined, Sebastian pressed on. He
had to know if his presumptions were correct.

"Your mother dragged you with her when she rendez-
voused with her lover, didn't she?"

Eden would have launched herself off the bed if Sebastian hadn't restrained her. When she refused to answer,
he gave her a firm shake.

"Answer me, damn it!"

Flashbacks from the past leaped at Eden. She fought
them—and Sebastian's grasp, but to no avail.

"Your ordeal with Lockwood triggered those childhood
memories, didn't they, Eden? What I heard while you were
talking in your sleep sounded like the outpouring of a
child's fears. Your mother locked you and Elizabeth away
so you wouldn't disturb her while she was with her lover,
didn't she? But Bet was only an infant, and she remembers
nothing of it. You never told her, did you? You have told
no one about your haunting secrets."

"Let me go," Eden whimpered.

"Not this time. We can't ignore your past any longer,
because it threatens to destroy our future together."

When Eden struggled to escape him, Sebastian became
desperate. He didn't have the strength to fight her for
long. If he didn't break her defenses, she would flit
away—forever.

Tonight he would win—or lose—Eden. There would be no in between.

"What makes you so certain you killed your mother?" he demanded bluntly.

There. He had delved into the depth of her darkest secret, and he waited for her to react.

"Damn you, Sebastian," she sobbed. "Damn you . . ."

"You fought her when she locked you in the darkness so she could lie with her lover. You knew Bet was her lover's child, didn't you? I wondered about the lack of family resemblance when I first saw the two of you together."

"Stop it," Eden hissed at him.

Sebastian continued relentlessly. "Your mother carried on her liaison while your father came and went from the battles of the French and Indian wars. Even Leland doesn't know he only has one daughter, does he? You've kept your secret from everyone, haven't you?"

Tears flooded Eden's eyes as the protective barrier crumbled. Old wounds bled, old terror overwhelmed her. Sebastian had stripped away her armor, unveiling the details of her terrible secret. He was cruel and demanding, and she hated him for doing this to her. He was making her face the disgraceful truth again. Curse him!

"Yes, I killed my own mother," she said on a broken sob. "I begged her not to lock Bet and me in that foul-smelling cellar again. But she shoved me toward the steps and I stumbled. I tried to grab hold of her, to plead with her before she locked the door the way she always did when she wanted to be with him!"

Eden dragged in a shuddering breath as the horrible scene unfolded in her mind's eye. "I clutched Mama's skirts and begged her not to go. She pushed me backward while I was still clutching the hem of her skirt . . ."

She trembled uncontrollably in Sebastian's arms, feeling none of his compassion, only the forbidden terror that had been a familiar companion for seventeen years. "She tripped over me and tumbled down the steps. Bet was at the bottom of the stairs in her bassinet. When Mama collapsed, Bet rolled onto that filthy floor . . ."

Although tears roiled down her cheeks, Eden forced herself to continue, exposing her sins so that Sebastian would finally understand that she wasn't worthy of him. "H-he heard the commotion and came running," she said brokenly. "When he saw Mama, he grabbed her reticule and took everything of value from the cottage. He left us there to fend for ourselves."

Eden lifted a shaky hand to reroute the stream of tears. "I scribbled a note, asking for help, giving direction to the cottage. I sent the carriage racing toward home, but none of the servants could read the message. It was hours before we were found. I was afraid to tell anyone about what happened, because *he* vowed to come back and punish me, as he threatened to do before he left."

Sebastian closed his eyes and held Eden close while she dissolved into body-wrenching sobs. He said nothing for the longest time, allowing the pent-up emotion to pour out of her.

"Wouldn't you have spent your life repenting for your sins if you had done what I did?" Eden choked out a few minutes later. "It was my fault. I couldn't face another hour in that dark prison. That crumbling cellar was hell, filled with demons and the sounds of scurrying rats—" Her voice frayed and she shivered as the awful memories swirled around her.

"It wasn't your fault." Sebastian pressed a kiss to her brow. "You were just a child fighting your fear of the darkness. Even soldiers on the battlefield react instinctively to fear. You couldn't have been more than seven years old at the time, Eden. You were at an impressionable age when imagination can run wild. All you were doing was seeking understanding and comfort from someone whose only concern was her selfish pleasure."

"No, I—"

Sebastian brushed his fingertips over her lips to shush her, then framed her tear-stained face in his hands. "If we had a child, would you lock her away while you lay in your lover's arms?"

"Never!" Eden said emphatically.

"Would you deceive me and betray me with another man?"

"I couldn't!"

"But *she* did, didn't she, Eden? You can't understand how a mother could be so selfish and cruel to her child, because you would never do such a thing. And since you can't understand that kind of behavior, you laid all the blame for what happened at your own feet. You've forgiven everyone else for their shortcomings, but you refuse to forgive yourself, refuse to believe that you're worthy of love, because your mother never loved you."

"I was throwing a tantrum and being selfish—"

Sebastian dropped a kiss to her quivering mouth. "Listen to me carefully, Eden. This is the time to confront all truths, no matter how painful they might be. I have the admission from your own father that his marriage was a disastrous mistake. Your mother was ordered to marry Leland for the wealth and prestige the Pembrook family could offer. The marriage wasn't based on love.

"Taking a lover was your mother's way of rebelling against what she couldn't change. You were the symbol of a marriage she didn't want. You were Leland's child, and Bet was her lover's child. Your mother cruelly turned her back on you, just as she did your father."

When Eden burst into tears, Sebastian hugged her to him. "I suspect you tried exceptionally hard to please your mother, but nothing you did was ever enough to win her love. I imagine she even threatened to harm you if you told anyone about those afternoons and evenings she spent with her lover."

Eden reflected on those awful days, envisioning her mother and her lover looming over her, issuing demands and threats. Because of those ordeals, Eden had learned to keep silent, to bury her feelings, her concerns, her fears.

Eden was glad that Bet hadn't been old enough to suffer through those vicious threats and occasional beatings, didn't remember being locked in the musty darkness for hours on end.

Ah, if only Eden hadn't been driven by the hounding torments of her past. Maybe she would have turned out differently if she hadn't been restrained and influenced by those torturous experiences.

"Do you know what became of your mother's lover?" Sebastian asked a long while later.

"No, one could hardly expect him to confide his future plans to the seven-year-old daughter of his dead lover. I don't know where he is, and it torments me to know that he is Bet's father, that he doesn't even care what became of her."

Sebastian was quiet for a moment, giving Eden more time to compose herself. "Eden, have you come to resent me so much that you're afraid you will rebel the way your mother did? You suggested seeking pleasure elsewhere while I recuperated."

"I was only trying to annoy you," she said without thinking. "I would never betray you."

Sebastian hadn't really thought she would, but Eden needed to hear herself say it. "And do I bore you so much that living with me would be comparable to a prison sentence in hell?"

"There isn't a boring bone in your body and you know it," Eden told him. "That isn't the problem."

"Exactly what is the crux of the problem that has you avoiding me every chance you get and romping around on the Arabian? I've been scared to death that you're going to break your neck, just to escape marriage to me."

"It's because you don't love me," Eden burst out, then tried to squirm away.

Sebastian held her fast and smothered a smile. "I see. So, you are saying that all these shenanigans were attention-getters."

"No, I was trying to prove to you that I'm not worthy of being a former earl's wife—"

Eden muttered in exasperation. It was a damned good thing she hadn't been called upon to spy during the war. She would have blabbed information to anyone who bothered to ask.

Sebastian had come at her like a physician probing with a scalpel. He had sliced through her barriers of defense to delve into her tormented soul. One by one, he had analyzed her fears, forcing her to face the reality that a seven-year-old child hadn't been mature enough to understand—and a twenty-four-year-old woman refused to remember because of the anguish.

Yet, Eden had to admit that confiding in Sebastian left her feeling cleansed, drained of tormenting emotion. It was as if a heavy yoke had been lifted from her shoulders.

"Eden, I am the one who is unworthy of you," he murmured.

"Don't be absurd. You're the one with generations of blue blood spurting through your veins. You aren't the one with the tainted past."

"But I haven't been honest with you. I couldn't be, not without threatening military strategy."

"I understand that now and I forgive you," she told him. Eden propped up on her elbow to peer into his shadowed face, watching moonlight reflect in his silver eyes. "Sebastian, will you seek out other women when you grow tired of me?"

Smiling, he reached out to brush away the residue of tears. "Eden, I will never grow tired of a human kaleidoscope."

"But if you did, would you become like her?"

Her, Sebastian presumed, was Victoria Pembrook—the woman Leland claimed was prone to drastic mood swings and unprovoked temper tantrums. From what Sebastian had ascertained, Victoria was borderline insane. Sebastian would never forgive Eden's mother and her lover for the emotional scars Eden had suffered.

Tenderly, Sebastian gathered Eden in his arms, feeling closer to her than he'd ever been. This emotion bubbling inside him exceeded physical satisfaction—it was a spiritual contentment.

When he looked into that angelic face that was spotlighted by silvery beams, Sebastian realized what an overly cautious fool he had become. Because of Penelope's shallowness and self-absorption, Sebastian had become cynical of all women.

Dear Lord, how could he have been so blind, so skeptical? Why had he denied what had been staring him in the face these past few months? When he stared into this angel's eyes, he swore he could see forever.

"Sebastian, you didn't answer my question," Eden prompted as she traced his lips with gentle fingertips. "Would you honor our vows or would you abandon them on a whim?"

"Why would I go in search of what I've already found in you, Eden?"

Eden blinked, stunned. Her breath clogged her throat and her heart skipped a beat. Was Sebastian trying to say he loved her? Were those phrases of love locked as deeply inside him as her tormented past had been buried inside her?

According to Tully, Sebastian had been humiliated when Lady Penelope chose title and wealth over him. She knew it must have been a devastating blow to his pride, a mistake he didn't want to repeat. Could it be that Sebastian had come to care for Eden and was having trouble saying the words?

Eden slid her leg over Sebastian's thigh and sidled closer, feeling him react instantaneously. Careful not to bump his mending shoulder, she pressed her hand against his chest and peered up at him.

"Sebastian?"

"What is it, angel eyes?" he whispered.

"What it is," she said as an impish smile spread across her lips, "is love."

"Do you think so?" He returned her infectious grin. "And what, madam wife, has brought you to that profound conclusion?"

"It has just occurred to me that, although you are a man of honor, you wouldn't have married me if you didn't have strong feelings for me."

"Very true." Sebastian felt gloriously content, lying abed with Eden pressed familiarly against him. She was staring up at him with a sparkle in her eyes that was completely devoid of shadowed misery.

"There is also your reaction to my outlandish behavior," she continued. "But I must admit I got caught up in the mischievous pleasure of doing exactly what I pleased. I almost forgot my original purpose a time or two."

"I came to that conclusion myself when I saw the smile on your face as you leaped my stallion over the fence."

Eden cocked her head sideways and studied him astutely. "You weren't even angry about that. I thought you would be."

"I wouldn't say that," Sebastian murmured as his hand glided down the lush curve of her hip.

"Then what would you say?" she pressed him.

"The truth is that I was doing my damnedest not to become entangled in the snare you designed for me. You, angel eyes, are too damned cunning."

"And that disturbs you?"

"No, it intrigues me."

"So you don't mind if I gad about in men's clothes and romp around on the Arabian."

Sebastian was cautious not to be lured into giving his permission to that! "I'm not overly fond of you wearing men's clothes." His voice dropped to a velvety pitch. "I prefer to see you wearing nothing at all, while straddling the Arabian's master . . ."

Eden grinned at his rakish expression. "I see. Then may I assume that you also enjoy the pleasure of passion we've shared?"

"Absolutely."

Desire throbbed through Sebastian's body, and he cursed his nagging wound. He was eager to show Eden how much he enjoyed making love to her, but his strength was sadly lacking.

Eden glanced over at the ring with its oversize stones sparkling in the moonlight. "Now then, about that ring."

Sebastian jerked up his head. "You don't like it? I instructed Tully to purchase only the best."

"With no expense spared, I imagine," Eden added. "But it's not good enough, your lordship."

"Not good enough?" Sebastian stared incredulously at her. "Tully informed me there was nothing to compare to that ring."

"I'm sure he did his best."

"Of course he did," Sebastian said, irritated. "And what the hell do you mean 'not good enough?' That damned ring cost a fortune!"

"A perfectly good waste of a fortune," she replied calmly. "Had I known of your extravagant nature, I wouldn't have married you."

"You barely married me unawares," he grumped.

Eden was preying on his temper again, he realized. He was having as much trouble handling the new Eden as he had dealing with the old one . . .

Dear God, he thought, suddenly frantic. She was outgrowing him! The realization horrified him. Holding on to a spirited, vivacious woman like Eden was like trying to capture sunbeams in his hand. Now that she had shed all her inhibitions she was going to leave him behind and he would never catch up!

Desperation overwhelmed him. Because of his injury he couldn't match Eden physically. And emotionally? Lord, now that he had unlocked the guilt-ridden chains of her past, nothing would hold her back. He had seen too many glimpses of her blossoming personality these past few days. This spirited angel was spreading her wings, and there was no restraining her now . . .

"Sebastian, you're squeezing the stuffing out of me," Eden croaked.

"Sorry." Sebastian forced himself to relax. He hadn't realized how tightly he had held on to Eden when assailed by his sudden insecurities.

Eden studied the glum expression that claimed his handsome features. "Troubled thoughts, your lordship?"

"Eden, can I ask you something?"

"What is it you want to ask?"

"Have you truly . . . er . . ." Sebastian strangled on the word that always stuck in his craw. "Have you—?" He muttered to himself, then blurted it out. "Blast it, have you outgrown your need for me, just as you outgrew all your other fiancés?"

"What do you think, Sebastian?"

His shoulders sagged in defeat. "I think it's already happened. Your adventurous escapades on the stallion have only whetted your appetite."

"You're right," she admitted, grinning. "Furthermore, our marriage is beginning to remind me of a kite dancing on the wind."

"You, of course, are the high-flying kite," he grumbled.

"And you're the anchor, but the twine that binds us

together is missing. Jeweled rings can't hold kites and an-
chors together, now can they?"

"No, I suppose not." Sebastian was feeling so depressed
that he didn't realize he was being drawn into Eden's
clever subterfuge. He was being lured along like the other
foolish men who fenced words with this astute female—
and lost.

"Fighting the inevitable is a waste of time, don't you
agree?"

"I suppose," he mumbled.

"Then simply say it and let's get this over with, Sebastian."

"No, I will not agree to dissolve this marriage. Damn it,
Eden, I will grant you any wish but that!"

Eden drew her knees beneath her and bent down to
brush her lips across his determinedly set mouth. "That
isn't the wish I want you to grant me."

"Then what the hell is it?" Sebastian scowled in frustration. "Curse it, Eden—"

Her lips feathered over his in the tenderest of all kisses.
Her eyes sparkled as she withdrew to gaze down at him
like an angel hovering just beyond his reach.

"All I want is for you to love me. Love, Sebastian. That
is the tie that can bind us together forever. Loving you the
way I do, nothing is more important to me than knowing
you honestly love me—bad habits, character flaws, and
all."

Sebastian stared up into that enchanting face that was
surrounded by glorious chestnut hair that burned like a
flame in the moonlight. Her flawless skin glowed pale
against the night . . . and his heart flip-flopped in his
chest.

He had but to say the words she wanted to hear and she
would be his forevermore. All the loyalty, faithfulness, and
devotion he would ever want would be his for all time. All

he had to do was unlock the tender emotion trapped in his heart. Heaven was just three words away . . .

"Yer lordship?" Tully whispered as he poked his head around the opened door. "I went to check on Eden for you. She wasn't in her bed. I'm afraid she might be trying to run off again—" He stopped in his tracks when he saw two silhouettes framed by moonlight. "Sorry, yer lordship—"

"Close the door on your way out," Sebastian requested, never taking his eyes off his enchanting wife. "Eden and I are negotiating terms."

Tully thought husband and wife looked poised on the brink of something more physically satisfying than negotiation. He grinned in satisfaction. At long last, Eden was exactly where she belonged. Things were finally looking up at Pembrook Plantation!

Twenty

"Now then, where were we?" Sebastian questioned, his hand drifting over Eden's shapely leg.

"We were waiting for you to say what I need to hear," she whispered, her voice wobbling from the effects of his seductive caress.

"You realize I am going to have to break the solemn vow I made eleven years ago, don't you?" he murmured against that sensitive spot beneath her ear.

"You should have selected a woman who loves you as dearly as I do, so you wouldn't have had to make that vow."

"I doubted that a woman like you waited in my future."

She smiled at him. "And that's why I have seven broken betrothals to my credit. There was never any spark, no fire, no—"

"No kite strings?" he finished for her.

"No kite strings," she confirmed. "I am still waiting, Sebastian . . ."

"The truth is that I never even knew what love was until there was you."

Eden shook her head and chortled softly. "No wonder Washington commissioned you into military espionage. Forcing words from your lips is worse than robbing oysters of their pearls. Now say it before I lose patience with you!"

"You? The saint?" he teased playfully.

Eden swatted his good shoulder. "You're impossible. Why am I wasting my time with you? I should—"

"I love you . . ."

Sebastian felt as if the words had been ripped from his heart. He had become such a private man that revealing soul-deep emotions felt like self-betrayal. Now he understood why Eden had fought so hard to keep her tormenting secret buried. Old habits died hard.

"Oh, Sebastian, I am so proud of you!" Eden flung her arms around his neck and hugged him tightly.

"Ouch!"

Eden freed him immediately. Her heart filled with sublime pleasure when she saw the tender emotion in his eyes, the loving expression on his face. "Let me ease your pain . . ."

Sebastian sucked in his breath when Eden's hand drifted down his neck, over the dark furring of hair on his chest to settle on the aroused flesh where he was most a man. Her fingertips brushed over the pulsating length of him while her petal-soft lips skimmed his cheek, then his shoulder. Sebastian moaned when she stroked and caressed him. His breath hitched as desire raged through him.

"Now, what was that nonsense about being physically unable to perform your husbandly duties?" she teased as she brushed her fingertips over his aching flesh.

Sebastian groaned, then chuckled. "You have become positively outrageous, woman."

"Wait until you see what I'm like tomorrow," she whispered as her lips coasted over his chest.

When her moist kisses flowed over the hard length of him, igniting sensual flames that sizzled through every inch of his body, Sebastian swore he was burning alive. Her flicking tongue grazed the sensitive tip of his manhood, nipping and arousing until he trembled with incredible longing. When she took him into her mouth and suckled gently, he felt himself losing control.

"Eden—"

Her hands and lips moved over him with exquisite gentleness and he couldn't breathe. She was killing him with indescribable pleasure. If she kept this sweet torture up, his wife was going to become an instant widow.

His thoughts whirled into oblivion and his body clenched with ravenous need. When her mouth closed around him again, he knotted his hand in the tangle of chestnut hair that lay over his thigh like silk. He held on to his crumbling willpower—and felt it failing him.

"Eden, I swear you're going to be the death of me," he gasped.

"I'm loving you for all time," she assured him. "And, Sebastian?"

"Yes?" He barely had enough breath to force out the word.

"I love loving you . . ."

When her lips feathered from base to tip, tasting the secret rain of desire she had called from him, Sebastian hissed through his clenched teeth, "Eden, stop!"

Her hands and lips stilled. She felt him throbbing against her and knew she had dragged him to the crumbling edge. She could feel it in the whipcord muscles of his belly that were drawn tight as harp strings. She could detect it in the lines that bracketed his sensuous mouth, the wild glitter in his silver eyes. A satisfied smile crossed her face as she eased over him, guiding him to her, stroking him until he arched toward her and into her.

"I love you, Sebastian," she whispered.

Eden moved above him, with him. She felt the coil of aching need unfurl like rose petals basking in the warmth of the midday sun. She felt his hands clamp onto her hips to set the accelerated cadence that brought them together in a crescendo of ineffable ecstasy. And she let go with heart and soul to assure him that he had become the most important part of her life . . .

* * *

Much later, while Eden nuzzled against Sebastian's good shoulder, she reveled in absolute contentment. After weeks and months of battling this love she thought to be ill-fated and one-sided, Eden knew she was where she belonged. Sebastian loved her, he had offered the words she needed to hear. He hadn't condemned her for her past—he had freed her from it.

"Eden?"

Eden lifted her head to smile up at Sebastian. "Yes?"

"About this business of separate homes and yearly visits. I really must insist on having you in my bed every night."

She grinned impishly. "And I really must accept."

His hand glided over the indentation of her waist, the swell of her hip. "Is this war between us finally over?" he questioned before he pressed a kiss to her forehead.

"Yes, I believe so, your lordship."

"You can stop calling me that now."

"I rather like it," she murmured, then brushed an adoring kiss over his lips.

"And I love the way you love me."

Sebastian shifted on the bed, determined to invent new ways of making love to his wife—given his physical limitations. He abhorred the thought of allowing her to become bored in the bedroom. It was going to require dedicated effort to ensure their lovemaking was exciting and new.

"Sebastian, what the devil are you doing?" Eden peered incredulously at him as he eased onto the chair.

His hand folded around her wrist, drawing her down upon his lap. His lips grazed the crown of her breast, making her arch toward him. "In a chair?" she questioned raggedly.

"Yes, love. And wait until you see what I have planned for tomorrow . . ."

Sebastian smiled against her satiny flesh while he drew

one heated response after another from her. And when
she came to him, whispering her love for him, Sebastian
felt no pain. This was the cure he needed. And why a man
needed to get back on his feet, when the angel in his arms
had taught him how to fly, he couldn't imagine . . .

The following week passed with the swiftness of a dream
for Eden. Sebastian made great strides in his recovery. He
ate like a man who had been on prison rations for months,
and he exercised faithfully to regain the use of his left
arm. As for the midnight hours, her new husband developed a penchant for the erotically unusual. He constantly
astonished Eden with his inventive lovemaking.

Eden smiled as she ambled into the dining room, remembering how Sebastian had drawn her down onto
the . . .

"Thinking pleasant thoughts, sweetheart?" Sebastian
asked as he leaned back in his chair.

Eden blushed profusely when his question drew the cu-
rious stares of her father, sister, brother-in-law, and Tully.
"I was just admiring my new ring," she said. "It's the finest
I have ever seen."

When Sebastian's thick brow arched in knowing amusement, Eden was certain he knew what had inspired the
dreamy smile on her lips. She shot him a mischievous
glance, assuring him that she would get even with him
later. With a rakish wink, he accepted her silent threat.

"Eden tells me you plan to leave for your estate today,"
Leland said.

Sebastian adjusted the sling on his left arm and reached
for his mint julep. "It has been a long time since I've been
home."

"I wish I could stay home," Leland mumbled. "Although Lord North resigned his position as prime minister
of England, and the war is officially over, there is still ran-

dom fighting between our guerrilla bands and the redcoats in the South. My regiment has been ordered to spread the news of the peace negotiations. I will be leaving Peter and Elizabeth in charge until I return."

"Your plantation will be in competent hands," Sebastian assured him.

"Not as competent as my sister the saint," Bet teased. "But Peter and I are willing and eager to do our share."

"If your sister can work miracles on my neglected estate, I will be greatly indebted to her," Sebastian said.

"I hardly think I will have time, what with exercising the Arabian for his scheduled races and—"

"Eden!" Leland crowed. When she smiled playfully, he settled his ruffled feathers. "Thank God you aren't serious."

Eden's shrug could have meant anything, and Sebastian didn't believe for a minute that he had seen the last of his wife in breeches, mounted on that spirited black stallion, leaping fences in a single bound. He would have to find other activities to occupy her time . . . Or maybe the back of a horse would be a scintillatingly unique place to . . .

"Sebastian?" Eden grinned wickedly. "I have noticed these mental lapses you've had lately. I don't think you heard what I said. What time are we leaving for your home?"

Sebastian felt a blush seeping into his cheeks. "One o'clock. I hope you're packed and ready to leave, my dear."

"I'm almost ready, except for digging up the exotic bulbs and gathering seeds from the garden."

"You plan to take Mason's mountain lilies, Bancroft's blue grapes, Dolby's daffodils—both white and yellow varieties?" Bet questioned impishly. "And what of Carlyle's camellia, the ever popular Aldermon anemones, Patterson's peonies, and Newton's nasturtiums?"

Eden squirmed uncomfortably when Sebastian shot her a disgruntled glance, then chuckled. "You named your exotic flowers after your discarded fiancés?" he asked.

"Rather symbolic to bury the poor bulbs, I always thought," Bet inserted, though Eden flashed her a glare. "Most of Eden's courtships came along during the gardening and crop-rotation phase of her life. It was a flourishing five years of blossoming, and wilting, betrothals."

"Bet, isn't there somewhere you need to be?" Eden questioned her loose-tongued sister.

"No, I have finished all my chores, thank you. I can spend the entire day with you until you leave."

"How fortunate for me," Eden grumbled.

"I'm glad those days of broken engagements are over," Leland declared. "My infantry would no sooner pack up and move than my emissary, Daniel Johnston, brought word of another prospective groom who had come and gone." He smiled approvingly at Sebastian. "I'm glad you convinced Eden that it was time to settle down."

"So am I, but I refuse to have the ornamental Saber shrub planted in her garden," he objected.

Eden leaned over to smooth away his frown. "Not to worry, your lordship. I think you would be better suited as a potted house plant."

Tully choked on his laughter, his pleased gaze bouncing back and forth between the newlyweds.

"Miss Eden?"

Eden glanced over her shoulder to see Maggie hovering in the doorway. Rising she strode over to accept the message that had been delivered and frowned at the disturbing news.

"Something wrong, Eden?" Sebastian questioned.

"Dr. Curtis will be tied up all day with the wounded soldiers at the public hospital. He wants me to check on David Holmes, a former patient who has developed a high fever and recurring infection. The family lives a few miles away. I won't be long."

"I'll go with you," Tully volunteered.

"That isn't necessary. I would prefer that you help load

my belongings and ensure his lordship doesn't overexert himself. I will dig up the flower bulbs and gather seeds when I return."

"I'll dig the damned bulbs and collect the seeds," Sebastian insisted.

"But your arm—"

"Hang the arm. This sling is becoming a nuisance."

"Take Daniel Johnston with you," Leland requested. "He has been wandering around outside, waiting for me to compose a message for him to deliver to the military staff in Williamsburg. He may as well be of use to you. He doesn't know what to do with himself, and I have nothing for him to do right now."

Eden nodded, then went on her way. No doubt Daniel would be a source of interesting information. Since the day her father rode off to command the militia, Daniel had been his trusted emissary. Eden was anxious to know how Yorktown had fared, after families had been displaced during battle. She expected the citizens were in need of food and supplies.

She made a mental note to put Bet in charge of caring for families who had been ousted from their homes and trapped in the war zone.

Armed with the medical bag Dr. Curtis provided for her, Eden stepped outside to request Daniel's assistance. He leaped at the chance to occupy the extra time on his hands and in two shakes he hitched up the wagon to drive Eden to her destination.

"Having trouble adjusting?" she questioned the stockily built soldier.

"I am accustomed to tearing off in one direction or the other at your father's command. Now I have been left in one place so long, waiting new orders, that I wonder if I'll sprout roots."

"It will be difficult for all of us to adjust to a world without war, but I am eager to make the change."

"And to settle into your marriage," he said, grinning. "Congratulations, Eden. I never did think spinsterhood was your true calling—"

The crack of a rifle split the air. Daniel doubled over on the seat, clutching his arm. Eden snatched up the reins before the alarmed horse bolted away. Frantic, she tried to determine where the sniper was hiding. She feared that bands of bitter British deserters were exacting their revenge on a soldier in uniform. According to her father, Tory brigades had taken to thieving in order to survive.

Another shot rang through the air, and Daniel clutched Eden's arm. "Get down!" he ordered.

Eden needed to control the flighty horse, but Daniel kept tugging on her arm. Before Eden could turn the buggy toward home, a masked highwayman plunged from the underbrush to block their path.

Daniel reached for his pistol, but not fast enough. The rider lashed out with a whip, sending the flintlock tumbling from Daniel's hand. The second hiss of the whip had Eden shrieking in pain. The whip curled around her waist like a snake, jerking her off the seat. She was flung headlong into the highwayman's horse, then snatched off the ground and clamped in a crushing grasp.

"Leave her alone!" Daniel hissed.

The barrel of a musket rammed against Eden's jaw, forcing her to sit perfectly still in the highwayman's lap. "She comes with me, and if you want to live, you had damned well not object."

The hauntingly familiar voice caused Eden to freeze. Lockwood! The nightmares this monster inspired came rushing back with terrifying intensity. This wasn't just a highwayman in search of coins, but rather a devil on a quest for revenge!

"You can tell that bastard Saber and his cohort, Pembrook, that the price of this chit's life comes high," Lockwood growled as he backed toward the underbrush. "Have five thousand pounds delivered to Thaddeus's cabin by six o'clock tonight or the wench is dead."

Daniel clutched at his bloody arm, then snatched up the reins as the rider thundered away. He had to get help. General Pembrook would never forgive him if Eden perished while in his care!

"Mason's mountain lilies," Sebastian grunted as he plucked up the bulbs and snipped off the leafy vegetation.

"Patterson's peonies." Tully dropped the bulbs in the wooden crate. "Well, yer lordship, that takes care of yer wife's garden varieties of discarded fiancés."

Sebastian shoveled up a bushy plant that Bet had pointed out, while giving instructions on where—and what—to dig. "Here is an interesting specimen we will name after you. Randolph's ranunuluses," he announced.

"Hell, yer lordship, I do not want that glorified weed named after me. I can't even spell it!"

Sebastian thrust the frothy vegetation at Tully. "You don't have to spell the damned thing. Just plant it, nurture it, and water it."

"I am not going to reduce myself to the status of a gardener," he harumphed. "My expertise is with weapons and livestock."

"So it *was*," Sebastian qualified. "Now you have to broaden your horizons."

Frowning, Tully appraised the flowery bush. "I don't think you would have either of us making all these concessions for Lady Penelope."

"You're right." Sebastian uprooted an interesting-looking vine that boasted white blossoms.

"You really do love her, don't you?"

Sebastian kept on digging. "Who? Penelope? I suppose I have to since she's my sister-in-law."

Tully muttered at Sebastian's evasive reply. "I meant

your wife. This isn't the same as it was with that English social butterfly, is it?"

Sebastian refused to glance up at his nosy friend.

"Answer me," Tully demanded.

"No, it's not at all the same," he said eventually.

"Good. I was never fond of that blond twit yer brother married. Yer angel is the true prize—"

Tully frowned when he noticed the buggy that approached the plantation. "Isn't that Dr. Curtis's coach?"

Sebastian dropped the vine like a hot potato and stared down the path. His heart dropped to his stomach when apprehension robbed him of breath. Something was very wrong. He could sense it.

According to the note Eden had received, the doctor had been detained at the hospital. Sebastian had the unmistakable feeling the note had been a clever ruse.

Cradling his tender arm against his ribs, Sebastian jogged around the corner of the house, Tully one step behind him.

The minute Dr. Curtis drew to a halt, Sebastian fired a question at him. "Did you send Eden a note, asking her to check on a former patient?"

The doctor blinked at the abrupt question, then frowned when he noticed the absence of the sling that was supposed to be supporting Sebastian's injured arm. "No, I didn't. And what are you doing out and about? I haven't signed your clean bill of health yet."

"Hell and damnation." Sebastian lurched around, then stopped in his tracks. "Where is the Holmes cottage?"

"Four miles northwest. Why?"

Sebastian had no time for explanation. He rushed off to find Tully, who had darted to the barn to saddle the horses.

"Saber, where the blazes are you going?" Dr. Curtis called after him. "I told you not to engage in rigorous activity until that wound heals properly!"

Sebastian wasn't listening. He and Tully mounted up and blazed off like flying bullets. Slivers of icy fear were riveting Sebastian, and the wary dread got worse when he saw Daniel Johnston racing toward him. The young soldier's shirt was stained with blood and his face was white as salt. Eden was nowhere to be seen.

"A highwayman ambushed us!" Daniel shouted as he approached. "He shot me and absconded with Miss Eden. He wants five thousand pounds delivered to Thaddeus's cottage by six o'clock or Miss Eden—"

"Lockwood," Sebastian snarled in interruption. "Where did that bastard stop you?"

"Two miles west, at the bend in the road. He took off through the underbrush with Miss Eden at gunpoint."

"Take the wagon to the house and alert the general," Sebastian ordered hastily.

When Daniel rushed off, Sebastian gouged the Arabian into his fastest gait. Damn it, this was his own fault. He had been lured into a false sense of security after he and Eden came to terms with their relationship. He had spent too much time nursing his wound instead of tracking down Lockwood. Now that bastard was desperate for money and hungry for revenge. Eden's life hung in the balance, and Sebastian had the unshakable feeling that Lockwood had no intention of permitting Eden to survive this ordeal.

"Do you have a plan, yer lordship?" Tully asked as he raced alongside Sebastian.

"Which plan? The one I use before or after I gut Lockwood and stake him out as a feast for the buzzards?"

Tully winced at the venom in Sebastian's voice. "I'll bet that son of a bitch plans to hole up in the swamps."

"That would be my guess," Sebastian ground out. "There's nowhere he can go in the area without alerting the residents. Eden is too well known."

Sebastian slowed his steed when he saw the hoof prints that veered off the road. Tracking Lockwood would be simple after the recent rains, especially if Sebastian had second-guessed the bastard correctly.

What worried Sebastian was the prospect of Eden putting up a fuss and Lockwood deciding to dispose of her before he reached the secluded shack. Eden was notorious for taking matters into her own hands. He admired her courage in the face of adversity, but this time it could damned well get her killed!

Just as Sebastian had predicted, Eden wasn't taking captivity submissively. She had discovered that Lockwood had trouble holding the rifle barrel to her head while zigzagging his horse through the trees and underbrush. She had no intention of letting this heartless cretin extort ransom money and bait a trap for Sebastian's murder! Furthermore, she knew her chances of survival depended only on her ability to make an unexpected escape.

Eden surveyed the surroundings, trying to devise a way to catch Lockwood off guard. When she saw the drooping tree limbs that formed an archway above the narrow path, a plan hatched in her mind. She forced herself not to tense in anticipation. She didn't want to give her captor the slightest indication she was about to escape. If she couldn't catch Lockwood off balance, she didn't have a prayer.

"Thank God! Help has arrived," Eden yelled out of the blue.

Lockwood glanced over his shoulder, just as his horse swooped beneath the low-hanging branches. Eden's arms shot upward to grasp the limb. Her body slammed into Lockwood's throwing him sideways, and the horse ran out from under them.

Snarling in rage, Lockwood cartwheeled across the ground. Wildly, he groped at Eden, who seemed to have sprouted wings to hover above the ground. Before Lockwood could get his bearings, Eden dropped down on his belly, then bounded a safe distance away.

"Come back here!" Lockwood roared as he came to his knees.

Eden unwrapped the whip from around her waist and turned it on her assailant. When its biting end lashed against Lockwood's thigh, he backed off.

"You are not using me for ransom," Eden told him as she recoiled the whip.

"And you aren't going to deprive me again, damn you." Lockwood jerked off his mask, revealing himself to Eden for the very first time.

Terror nearly took Eden to her knees. A specter from her haunting past rose above her to collide with the present!

"Dear Lord . . ." she wheezed, stunned.

"You remember me, don't you? I thought you might. That's why I have never let you see my face," he taunted her. "I've been waiting for just the right time to renew our acquaintance."

It had been seventeen years since Eden had seen Gerome Locksley. She remembered the man as tall and lean, but the features of his face were the same now as they had been then—coarse, harsh, and angular. The cold black eyes beneath his cavernous brow were the telling truth. Gerome Locksley had become Gerard Lockwood! Years of hard living, and additional body weight, had altered his appearance, but this was the same man Eden had despised as a child.

"Now we will see if you are as much the whore as your mother was." He took an intimidating step forward while Eden battled to shake herself loose from her immobility.

"When you killed Victoria you deprived me of the generous allowance she provided while I was rutting on her," Lockwood sneered. "You are going to pay dearly for that, and for everything else I have tolerated because of *your* interference, because of *Saber's* treason!"

When Lockwood pounced at Eden, she struck out with the whip—and tried to run at the same time. A steely hand clamped in her hair, nearly yanking her head off her shoulders. Wildly, she lashed out with the whip, but it only served to provoke Lockwood.

Before Eden could squirm loose, he shoved her to the ground. Eden fought desperately as he pressed her to her back and plunked on top of her. While they played tug-of-war with the whip, Eden throttled him every chance she got. But, eventually, he managed to rip the weapon from her hand.

Raising the whip, Lockwood snarled diabolically. "Now we'll see if you like the same sadistic pleasures your tramp of a mother did."

With lightning quickness, Eden threw herself sideways and snatched her arm free. Her nails scored his face, evoking his enraged howl.

"Damn you!"

As if time were moving in slow motion, Eden watched Lockwood reach for the dagger stashed in his boot. Sharp steel glinted in the sunlight. He poised the blade above her heaving chest. When the dagger thrust downward, Eden clutched both hands around his fist, swerving the blade toward her shoulder rather than her heart. Her bloodcurdling scream mingled with Lockwood's vicious growl.

Flashbacks of Eden's life paraded across her mind as she battled overpowering odds. Desperate, she raised her knee, gouging Lockwood in the back. He bellowed in rage, and his dark eyes glittered with murderous intent.

"Now you die!" he snarled as he braced himself on his knees, bearing down on Eden to swerve the dagger back to her heart.

Eden screamed at the top of her lungs when she felt

358   *Carol Finch*

her arms shaking beneath the oppressive weight. She saw
the deadly blade bearing down on her, and she knew she
didn't have the strength to defend herself. She was going
to die, and there was nothing she could do to prevent
it . . .

Twenty-one

"Lockwood!"

A voice as cold and hard as a tombstone rumbled from out of nowhere. Lockwood didn't have time to glance over his shoulder. The lethal hiss came at him before he could react. For a moment, he didn't realize what was happening. A strange numbing sensation spread across his back, his shoulder, and then intense pain seared through him.

A startled expression crossed his hatchetlike features when he felt something warm and sticky trickling between his shoulder blades. He glanced back, too distracted by the odd sensations to realize Eden had shoved him sideways. His dagger landed in the mud, rather than in her chest.

Still braced against his dagger, he glanced up to see Sebastian Saber striding around him. Eyes like chips of iron burned into Lockwood as he wobbled, his strength waning.

It dawned on him, just then, what caused the strange sensations in his back. Saber had flung his knife and buried it to the hilt.

"You're mistaken," Sebastian snarled into Lockwood's peaked face. "Now *you* die, and may you burn in hell!"

With one swift kick of his boot heel, Sebastian knocked Lockwood backward onto the protruding dagger. There was no regret, no mercy in his stormy gaze as Lockwood slumped.

Eden stared up at the mass of fury who had come to her rescue. It seemed to take him a moment to compose himself. When he did, he swooped down to hoist her to her feet. Air gushed from Eden's lungs when Sebastian crushed her against him, mindless of his injured shoulder. Her face was smashed so tightly to his chest that she couldn't speak.

"Um . . . yer lordship?" Tully said as he approached. "I don't think Miss Eden can breathe."

Sebastian loosed his grasp and stepped back. "Are you all right, love?"

"Yes, but did you know Lockwood was my mother's—?"

"So I overheard."

After what Eden had confided about Victoria Pembrook, Sebastian had been thoroughly appalled. Now he was sure the woman was utterly mad. Anyone who would take up with a merciless barbarian like Lockwood had to be mentally imbalanced.

God, how Sebastian pitied Eden's miserable childhood. He had grown up in a household that offered respect, encouragement, and affection. He wondered if Leland even realized how cruelly Victoria had treated their daughter.

"Tully, will you take care of Lockwood for me?" Sebastian requested, not taking his eyes off Eden.

"With pleasure. It's not all that far to the swamp, and this cretin deserves to be fed to the gators," Tully insisted.

Her legs wobbling, Eden found herself propelled toward Lockwood's abandoned mount, then gently deposited in the saddle. Sebastian said not one word as he swung onto his Arabian. He simply led Eden away from what could have been the scene of her death.

"You were exceedingly brave, your lordship," Eden murmured. "Thank you for saving my life."

"No, angel eyes, *you* were exceedingly brave. *I* was exceptionally scared," he contradicted.

"How did you become so proficient with a dagger? You must have been at least twenty feet away," Eden speculated. "I would like to learn that skill, in case I am ever in need of—"

"You never will be," Sebastian cut in. "I am never letting you out of the house for the rest of your life. I am not going to risk being scared to death again."

"Don't be ridiculous."

"I am not being ridiculous! I am being the cautious, protective husband I should be!" he shouted.

Eden stared at his grim countenance. "I don't have that many enemies to warrant permanent confinement," she said reasonably.

"Nor will you have the chance to collect new ones."

"Sebastian Saber, you are behaving like a wool-brained idiot, and I have no intention of suffering through protective confinement!"

"Hell and damnation, Eden. I almost lost you!" His voice hit such a loud pitch that birds fluttered from their roosts in the trees. "Do you think I plan to endure that kind of hell more than once in my life?"

"You are overreacting, Sebastian."

"No, I'm not!" he blared.

"You know I thrive on change. How do you think I will fare if I am locked in a tower, wasting away in the same place, surviving under the same mundane conditions for years on end? If you want to sentence me to a slow, torturous death, I may as well have ended it back there with Lockwood. Is that what you ultimately want? To be rid of me?"

"Now you are the one who is being ridiculous."

"Then you agree that you were being ridiculous a moment earlier, is that correct?"

"I—"

"And having the time to reconsider, you realize you were being rash. Not to mention illogical. But now you realize that you were overset by anxiety, don't you?"

"Do I?" Sebastian felt the tension draining away the moment he realized that his shrewd wife was up to her old pranks of subtle persuasion.

"Of course you do." Eden ducked beneath the low-hanging branch she had grabbed on to when she knocked Lockwood from the saddle. "Now, you are ready to retract that unreasonable decree, aren't you?"

"I am? How incredibly generous of me." Sebastian smiled in spite of himself.

"Generous, astute, and understanding," she added.

"A paragon of manly virtue." He sat erect in the saddle. With a flair, he flicked a blade of grass from his sleeve.

"Precisely." She stared at him from beneath a fan of long lashes, an impish smile on her lips. "Now that we have that settled and out of the way, when would you like to begin my lessons on handling a dagger? And while we are at it, I would like to become as skilled with a pistol as you are."

"Putting weapons in your hands—"

"What an excellent idea!" Eden enthused. "Thank you for suggesting it."

Sebastian could see it all now. Eden would drain him of every tidbit of knowledge he possessed about pistols and daggers. She had obviously passed through her gardening, crop-rotation, and livestock phases to take an avid interest in weapons. And why, Sebastian asked himself, had he bothered to debate the issue with Eden? The woman would never be satisfied until she knew everything he knew.

And then what would he do? Damn it, if she outgrew him, he was never going to forgive himself for being so indulgent.

The thunder of dozens of hooves shook the ground.

Sebastian glanced up to see a regiment of militiamen racing toward him. With unsheathed sword held high, Leland Pembrook led the rescue brigade's charge.

Eden giggled at her father's spectacular demonstration. He had always been a flamboyant, dynamic individual. That was why he had made such an excellent military commander. His dedication and enthusiasm were contagious.

What a shame Victoria Pembrook hadn't appreciated Leland. To this day, Eden couldn't understand why her mother despised her father so much, why she had been prone to drastic mood swings and spiteful retaliations.

But it didn't matter now, Eden reminded herself. She had finally laid her tormenting past to rest. She had a bright, promising future awaiting her. Her children would grow up in a loving environment, surrounded by the tender encouragement she had never experienced. When Eden's children tried to please her, tried to be accepted, Eden vowed to let each one of them know they were wanted and cherished.

"Dear God, Daughter, are you all right?" Leland skidded the big roan gelding to a halt beside Eden. "Daniel was beside himself with concern, yammering on and on about how he had failed you in your hour of need. What the devil happened?"

"I'm fine, thanks to Sebastian," Eden assured her father. "It was only a desperate Tory soldier trying to raise funds after his cause had been lost."

Eden would never let her father know who Lockwood was. Knowing Leland's marriage had been an utter failure was enough for the man to live with. And for sure and certain, Eden would never let Leland know that Elizabeth wasn't his child. That was one secret Eden planned to take to her grave!

"You're certain this matter is settled?" Leland asked as

he scanned their surroundings. "Are you sure the man was acting on his own?"

"Yes, it's settled," Sebastian confirmed.

Leland swung his sword in expansive gestures, dismissing his troops. When the soldiers trotted away, Leland gazed fondly at his daughter.

"I was worried about you, Eden. You have endured so much, had mountains of responsibility thrust on you in my absence."

"It wasn't so bad," she assured him. "I was proud to do my part while you commanded the militia. And today, I found myself in competent hands."

"That's a comforting thought." Leland slid his sword into its sheath. "I know I haven't been a good father to you. I shouldn't have expected so much of you all these years."

"I have no complaints. I've enjoyed my independence, my position of authority," she insisted.

That, thought Sebastian, was the understatement of the decade.

"Be that as it may, my child, I feel I have failed you. For that I apologize. I was a miserable husband and father."

"If Washington is being called the father of our country, then you are the uncle," Eden proclaimed. "It is not every man who has unselfishly given of his time and energy to protect our country. Personal sacrifices have to be made to ensure the success of noble causes like liberty, do they not?"

"Certainly, but—"

"And where would we be now, if not for daring, dedicated men like you?"

"Well—"

"We would be wearing King George's burdensome yoke of oppression, wouldn't we?"

"I suppose—"

"It is a far greater deed that you have done for God and country, Papa," Eden broke in—again. "I'm proud and honored to be your daughter. You are responsible for making me what I am today. And speaking of hero worship, you'll probably want to check on Daniel Johnston the minute you return to the house. He looks upon you as the father he never had, you know."

"He does?" Leland blinked, then sat up a little straighter in the saddle.

"Indeed he does," Eden assured him. "Daniel has been faithful to you these past few years, devoted to seeing every dispatch reach its destination. He considered it an honor to serve with you. I would imagine a visit from you would lift his spirits immensely."

"Do you think so?" Dark-blue eyes locked with luminous sapphire. "The son I never had?"

"Precisely. I imagine you have also been giving consideration to hiring Daniel at the plantation as soon as your military duties have been completed. Knowing how devoted he is to you, he will undoubtedly accept."

"That's a good idea—"

"Daniel would make a fine addition to the household, since Peter will have to spend part of his time helping his father at the mercantile shop. It's a grand idea, Papa. I am so glad you thought of it."

"If you don't mind, child, I think I will ride back to the house to see if Daniel's injury has been tended properly."

When Leland trotted off, his male pride having been stroked and fed, Sebastian flung a wry grin at his wife. Ah, he did love to watch this clever female operate.

"Eden?"

"Yes, your lordship?"

"Is there even one man on this continent you haven't learned to manage?" Sebastian asked curiously.

Eden blessed him with a mischievous smile. "With the exception of you, you mean?"

"Including me, I mean." He watched her eyes twinkle with the kind of inner spirit no one else he knew could begin to match.

"Do you honestly think I would have married a man who didn't pose the greatest of all challenges to me?" she questioned. "You are a man who can't be persuaded by mental suggestion, because you know and understand me as well as I know myself. You made that very claim yourself, didn't you?"

Sebastian took a mental step backward, before he tumbled into a cleverly laid trap. His brows drew together in a single line on his forehead as he studied her astutely.

Eden's bright ringing laughter filled the crimson twilight. "There, you see, you have outfoxed me again. You are simply too cunning by half, aren't you?"

Sebastian didn't consider himself all that clever and adroit in comparison to Eden. It was going to take a century of concentrated effort to figure out how to handle Eden competently. It would become his greatest challenge, and his most cherished reward.

Sebastian glanced heavenward, thankful he hadn't given in to Penelope's seductive wiles and let her convince him to retain his titles to the earldom across the sea. Fate had brought him to Virginia to discover a bold breed of individuals who strained against England's heavy hand.

This was the land of purpose, of intriguing challenge, of thrilling adventure. A man could create his own destiny here. He could carve out a life for himself that had meaning and worth.

The superficial court life that Sebastian had come to despise held even less appeal to him now than it had a decade earlier. Here, Sebastian felt whole and alive, free to make his own choices.

Now the only title of consequence to him was that of husband and prospective father. Sebastian would create a world to captivate Eden. He would invent dozens of ways to satisfy this woman whose zest for life rivaled his own. Eden would make Saber Hall radiate with pleasure and excitement, and together they would fulfill every dream.

Of course, some refurbishing would be needed at Saber Hall, Sebastian reminded himself. The dark, suffocating draperies that blocked out sunlight would definitely have to go. The stable also spoke of too much gloom and darkness. The gardens boasted more weeds than flowers. Sebastian would have to hire a gaggle of carpenters to make the necessary renovations and changes . . .

Changes . . . Lord, thought Sebastian. Now Eden had him doing it, too! He couldn't look upon anything these days without figuring out how to improve upon it, how to make things more efficient and organized.

Eden surveyed the stunned expression on Sebastian's handsome features. "Something amiss, your lordship?"

"I was just thinking—"

"What splendid mental exercise. I will have to try it myself," she teased playfully.

Sebastian frowned. "You, madam, do entirely too much of it already."

"Ah, if only I could accomplish so much with thought as you do. Now, about that target practice you mentioned earlier."

"*I* mentioned?"

"Of course." Eden smiled radiantly. "There is just enough daylight left for a little practice, don't you agree? I prefer to begin with a pistol, just to get the feel of that little kick. When I have mastered the flintlock, I will tackle the rifle."

Eden frowned, bemused, when Sebastian grabbed her

horse's reins, then hopped to the ground. "What are you doing? We are still a mile from the house."

Sebastian grinned roguishly as he pulled Eden off the horse and into his arms.

"We aren't having shooting practice, I take it," she presumed.

"No, we're not." He drew her toward the small clearing that was encircled by towering pines. "And then again, you might say we are," he murmured, smiling roguishly.

"I didn't think you had your pistol with you—"

Sebastian's mouth slanted over hers, cutting her off in midsentence. When he raised his head a few moments later, his eyes glittered with mischief. "I thought we agreed that you weren't going to think quite so much."

When he sat her down on his lap, atop a hollow log, Eden eyed him dubiously. "Here, your lordship?"

"Anywhere," he murmured as his nimble fingers worked the stays on her gown. "Everywhere . . . as long as it's with you."

Eden suddenly forgot about target practice and last-minute preparations for their journey to Saber Hall. The moment Sebastian's masterful caresses began to work their potent magic, she did forget to think. All she could do was feel the delicious sensations that elevated her from one heady plateau of pleasure to another.

The world shrank to a space no larger than this seductive wizard occupied. With Sebastian, each voyage into passion was wondrous and new, an indescribably delightful launch of the senses.

Eden gave herself up to him without an ounce of reserve. She returned each worshipful touch, each breathless kiss. Devastating shudders consumed her as the flame of his desire burned through her, the echo of passionate ecstasy vibrating in the depths of her soul. She was so lost in the love she felt for Sebastian that she couldn't imagine life without him.

"And that," Sebastian whispered a good while later, "is what hollow logs are for."

"Very interesting," Eden said, smiling elfishly. "And all these years I thought hollow logs were just a refuge for quarry avoiding a predator."

Sebastian dropped a kiss to her soft lips. "It only goes to prove that there are times when one goes ahunting that one doesn't have to be an expert with pistols and daggers and such."

Eden looped her arms around his neck and moved sensually against him. "I do believe that marriage to you is going to be intensely stimulating—physically, emotionally, and intellectually speaking."

Sebastian muttered in disappointment when he heard the thud of approaching hooves. Tully, no doubt, had arrived. His timing was lousy.

"Yer lordship?"

Tully's voice boomed in the darkness. "Is everything all right? No more trouble, I hope."

"The trouble," Sebastian grumbled as he hurried to rearrange Eden's gaping gown, "is that privacy is damned hard to come by."

Tully grinned outrageously when Eden and Sebastian appeared to retrieve their tethered horses. Eden looked a mite rumpled and self-conscious, and Sebastian looked irritable. As for Tully, he was exceptionally pleased. From all indications, this marriage was progressing superbly. Sebastian Saber had found his match.

"We may as well finish packing," Sebastian said as he helped Eden onto her horse.

"May as well, yer lordship," Tully agreed, still grinning. "I think we should postpone our departure until tomorrow. Why, before you know it, it will be time to retire for the night."

Sebastian smiled at the tantalizing thought. "I suppose it will be that." He would use the next few hours to devise new ways to pleasure his very passionate and exceedingly responsive wife . . .

Twenty-two

Sebastian stared down the hill at Saber Hall. The plantation home, reminiscent of the English estate where he had grown up, was nestled inside a grove of stately trees. *Home.* Sebastian smiled in satisfaction. The plantation, with its redbrick outbuildings, coachhouse, henhouse, smokehouse, elaborate gardens, and private wharf on the river, had come to life. Newborn foals romped beside the mares that trotted across the meadow, led by the prancing black Arabian that won every race he had run at recent fairs.

And not with Eden on his back, either. Sebastian had put his foot down good and hard during that debate, though he had never been certain if he had actually won that argument, or if Eden had let him win, since he had been due. Whatever the case, Cameron Morgan, the resident jockey of Saber Hall, had been mounted on the victorious Arabian during each event.

The experimental breeds of cattle Sebastian had brought with him from England were showing great promise as beef and dairy stock. Eden had suggested—as only Eden could—that Pembrook Plantation be given first choice of the bull calves to improve its herd.

Sebastian smiled wryly as he stared down at the three-story brick mansion that had been refurbished according to Eden's specifications. Wide bay windows had been installed in every room. The attic that Eden had converted into a library was surrounded on the south and east with enough glass to pass as a lighthouse tower. But then, Sebastian reminded himself, guardian angels simply could not have their lofty view obstructed . . .

The crack of a rifle shattered the peaceful silence of the warm spring afternoon. The young mare Sebastian was riding shifted uneasily beneath him. The sleek white Arabian colt was to be a surprise gift for Eden. Sebastian had left most of the training to Cameron Morgan, and the mare had been stabled at nearby Mount Vernon to prevent Eden from seeing her unexpected gift.

Another shot exploded behind the great house, and the colt danced nervously. "Easy, girl," Sebastian cooed.

"Sounds like trouble, sir," Cameron Morgan murmured.

The young jockey, who had accompanied Sebastian to Mount Vernon to fetch the mare, reined up beside him. Together, both men squinted into the sunlight to see the great hulking figure, and a petite female, striding toward a tree. Sebastian frowned. He had a pretty good idea what had been going on during his absence.

"It looks as if my wife persuaded Tully to give her the shooting lessons I have purposely avoided."

The freckle-faced young man grinned broadly. "She does have that big brute eating out of her hand, doesn't she?"

Sebastian slanted the jockey a teasing glance. "This, while she feeds you from the other hand, Cameron. Don't think I haven't seen my wife trotting off on the Arabian stallion you have saddled for her."

Cameron squirmed awkwardly. "Well, she—"

Sebastian flung up a hand in a deterring gesture. "Don't bother with lame excuses. I'm sure Eden convinced you that preventing her from riding that spirited stud was an unreasonable command that had originally come from her overprotective husband. And perhaps this gift of a gentle mare will return her tyrannical husband to her good graces."

Cameron stared consideringly at the colt. "The mare, I believe, sir, will be much easier to handle than the stallion. But your lovely wife is another matter." He grinned encouragingly. "But I believe you are just the man who can handle that spirited female you married. In fact, the stable boys have placed bets—" Cameron shut his mouth so fast that he nearly snipped off the tip of his tongue.

Sebastian watched Cameron's face turn pink beneath his generous smattering of freckles. "Wagers on what? Who really rules the roost at Saber Hall?" When Cameron's face turned a darker shade of pink, Sebastian grumbled under his breath. "I thought so."

"If it's any consolation, sir, I didn't hesitate to bet on you!" he enthused.

"Did you indeed?"

The blast of a discharging rifle prompted Sebastian to trot the mare toward the scene of the conspiracy that was taking place. As far as Sebastian was concerned, Eden had no need to learn to fire the Kentucky rifle, because she was not going bird hunting during the spring festivities she had planned for her family's first official visit to Saber Hall. Sebastian would not be talked out of his decision, and that, by damn, was that!

"My goodness!" Tully hooted as he stared, disbelieving, at the holes in the target he had nailed to the tree. "Bull's-eye. Three of them! I have never seen such incredible beginner's luck."

It was hardly beginner's luck, Eden mused silently. She had coerced one of the new fieldhands, who had served in her father's militia, to instruct her in the art of weapons each time Tully and Sebastian left the plantation.

She had lured Tully outside this morning, as soon as Sebastian left on his mysterious jaunt to Mount Vernon, to prove to the bulky hulk of a man that she could handle a rifle well enough to join in the scheduled hunt. With Tully to recommend her skills with weapons, Eden was certain Sebastian would reverse his ridiculous decision and let her join in the activity *she* had organized.

Besides, Eden thought to herself, participating in this hunt was very important to her. It would be the first—and last—time she could enjoy rigorous outdoor activities for several months to come.

"So, do you think I am accomplished enough with a rifle to join in the hunt?" Eden questioned Tully.

"With that kind of accuracy?" Tully replied, still staring at the triple bull's-eyes. "M'lady, I always thought his lordship and I were good, but—"

"Well, well, how nice to return home to find a conspiracy forming behind my back."

The deep baritone voice caused Eden's hands to freeze on the rifle.

Tully's back went rigid, and he swallowed visibly.

Muted footsteps thudded on the carpet of spring grass. Eden lowered the rifle barrel, pivoted, and then blessed her stern-looking husband with a smile that rivaled the brilliance of the sun.

"Sebastian, I'm so glad that you're back. Tully said my marksmanship is excellent."

"So I heard," Sebastian said gruffly.

Tully said nothing. He took a sudden, avid interest in the birds that were fluttering around on the tree limbs above him.

"And being the hostess of my family's first official visit to Saber Hall, it only follows that, given my adeptness with a rifle, I should be included in the hunt, don't you think?"

"No, I don't think so." Sebastian's formidable expression invited no argument. That, as usual, didn't faze Eden.

"Knowing how much I love being outdoors, I can't imagine that you would want to deprive me of the pleasure of adventure."

Tully cleared his throat, then turned to stare at the air over Sebastian's head. "Excuse me, yer lordship, I just remembered something I need to do."

Sebastian swallowed a smile when the gargantuan hulk of a coward took himself off in a flaming rush.

"Knowing what a reasonable, tolerant husband you are," Eden continued, still smiling cheerily, "I know you want to retract your decision, having witnessed the evidence of my marksmanship."

Sebastian frowned somberly. "Do not argue with me, Eden. Hunting was designed for men."

Eden elevated her rifle barrel. "Women have been excluded from it far too much, in my opinion. And I advise you not to argue with my loaded rifle. It could be bad for your health."

Sapphire eyes twinkled up at him with spirited mischief. Yet, Sebastian held his ground. "No." The single word was definite and uncompromising.

"Sebastian, please. One of the things I have always admired about you is your unerring ability of self-defense. What if I should ever meet with highwaymen during my jaunts around the countryside? Consider how my skills with weapons could ease your concern for my welfare. Don't you fret when I return a few minutes later than you have anticipated?"

"Certainly, but—"

"And wouldn't you rest easier knowing that, if trouble arose, I was capable of protecting myself?"

"Probably, but—"

"Don't you realize that I want you to admire me as much as I admire you?" She propped the rifle against the tree and then floated toward him in a swirl of bright blue muslin. "Sebastian, I am sorry to report that I have begun to outgrow my interest in livestock. There is this restlessness within me that is demanding change."

Sebastian winced. There was that cursed word again. Eden could outgrow her need for everything else, but God help him if she ever outgrew her interest in him. He couldn't bear that—not now, not after he had discovered all the wonders of paradise. Anything else would be pure and simple hell!

Petal-soft lips whispered over his mouth. Her luscious body melted into his masculine contours. Sebastian felt himself boiling down to the consistency of hasty pudding.

"Your lordship, I really do need a new direction for the next few months. And I promise, come fall, I will have outgrown my penchant for target practice and hunting."

That wasn't all Eden would be outgrowing, come fall, but she wasn't ready to make the announcement yet.

When her breasts brushed against Sebastian's chest, and her knee insinuated itself between his thighs, Sebastian's iron will wavered. Eden had the uncanny knack of tearing down every point in a debate, leaving him to wonder if his decrees were unreasonable.

"Please, Sebastian," she whispered as her arms glided over the lapels of his jacket to loop over his shoulders. "I promise I will be cautious the day of the hunt. And with a guardian angel watching over me—"

His eyes rounded. "A guardian angel? What guardian angel?"

"Why, you, of course." She smiled up at him, her eyes mirroring the intensity of her affection for him. "With such a competent protector riding at my side, how can you deny me this one small request?"

"How indeed?" A reluctant smile quirked his lips as he gathered Eden close to his heart.

Eden cuddled in his enveloping arms, her cheek resting against his chest. "To deny me would be admitting that you don't consider yourself competent in protecting me, wouldn't it?''

"Would it?" Sebastian inhaled the fresh, clean fragrance of her chestnut-colored hair and felt another layer of his defenses melting away.

"Absolutely. Can you imagine the blemish on your reputation if the gossipmongers in the area got wind of the information that you didn't include me in the hunt, because you didn't feel you were capable of defending me properly? So you see, your lordship, the only way to save face is for you to invite me to come along. Any other decision would ultimately make you look foolish and inadequate, don't you think?"

"And we couldn't have that, could we?"

"No, certainly not!" Eden insisted. "And I will fulfill my obligation of joining the hunt, thereby proving that I consider you to be the perfect protector."

"Thank you, sweetheart. I'm deeply touched by your consideration and your faith in me."

"You're welcome. I want everyone to know how much I honor, respect, and trust you."

Sebastian sighed in defeat. He had been maneuvered by powers of reverse persuasion. But he still intended to have his consolation for losing this latest debate with Eden and learning that the servants and grooms at Saber Hall had wagered against him.

Clasping Eden's hand, Sebastian escorted her toward the honey-locust hedge that surrounded the garden.

"Where are we going?" Eden questioned. "I thought I made it clear that I have lost interest in pruning vines and planting bulbs."

"Yes, but the ornamental Saber shrub needs your attention," he said as he propelled her toward the secluded gazebo.

"Oh, that ornamental Saber shrub." She chortled as

she came eagerly into his arms. "Now that is a different matter entirely. I have a great interest in that."

"Actually, it's a horse of a different color," Sebastian murmured as he ambled behind the gazebo to lead the colt from the bushes. "For you, Eden. Every legendary angel should have her own white horse to fly around on."

Eden stared at the magnificent animal. "Oh, Sebastian, she's beautiful!" She leaped into Sebastian's arms to shower him with grateful kisses. "Have I told you lately how much I love you?"

"Not since early this morning." His lips feathered over her collarbone, then brushed over the gaping bodice of her gown to savor the taste and texture of her creamy flesh.

When he carried her into the gazebo and pressed her back to the wall, Eden curled her legs around his hips and moved sensuously against him. "Your lordship?" she whispered.

"Yes, angel eyes?"

"Just how many ways are there to do this?"

A rakish grin pursed his lips as his flicking tongue drew her surrendering moan. "One hundred and one . . ."

"I love you with all my heart and soul, Sebastian," she murmured as she felt the hard evidence of his desire consume her. "Some things will never change—"

As rapture engulfed Sebastian, he made a solemn vow to spend a lifetime inventing ways to intrigue his wife. Eden kept him striving to explore new dimensions of passion that communicated his all-encompassing love for her.

"Your lordship?" Eden murmured much later. "There is something I want to tell you. I had planned to wait, but perhaps now is the time. I have a gift for you, too."

"What is it, Eden?" Sebastian drew Eden with him to the hammock that rocked gently in the breeze.

Eden lounged in the hammock, nestled contentedly in Sebastian's sinewy arms. "I want you to know that I believe you are the perfect husband, and, come fall, I know you are going to make an exceptional father."

"Dear God!" Sebastian jerked up his head, his gaze narrowing accusingly on Eden. "You played me unfair. You talked me into letting you hunt and shoot before springing the news on me." Sebastian sat up so quickly that he nearly catapulted them both—stark-bone naked—from the hammock. "Confound it, Eden!"

"You don't want our child, Sebastian?" She looked hurt, disappointed—at least that was the impression she was striving for.

"Of course I want our child. That is not the point."

Eden drew him back down with her on the hammock. "I am ever so glad to hear that." Her lush body glided seductively against his. "Now, how many ways did you say there were to do this?"

Sebastian gazed down into her lovely, radiant face and sparkling blue eyes. Right there and then he decided he might as well wager against himself in the betting pool in the stables. He could no more deny this bewitching angel her whims than he could fly to the moon. Eden had given him her trust, her unwavering devotion, and soon a child—the personification of his undying affection for her.

"I love you, angel eyes," he whispered, his voice crackling with a maelstrom of emotion.

When he shifted sideways, drawing her against him, she smiled impishly. "Is this one hundred and two?"

Sebastian returned her grin, and then he came to her, giving all of himself to a love that he knew would last throughout eternity. "And wait, my love, until you see one hundred and three . . ."

In the depths of his silver-gray eyes, Eden saw the sweet promise of every tomorrow to come. Wholeheartedly, she gave herself up to Sebastian and set sail in the magical seas of his encircling arms . . .

ROMANCE FROM FERN MICHAELS

DEAR EMILY   (0-8217-4952-8, $5.99)

WISH LIST   (0-8217-5228-6, $6.99)

AND IN HARDCOVER:

VEGAS RICH   (1-57566-057-1, $25.00)